Journey to an Earth that has been destroyed and reshaped into an alien world where magic is real, demons walk the face of the planet, dimensional *Rifts* lead to countless other worlds, and humankind struggles to survive.

An world where magic and technology collides. A place where the human and the inhuman clash in war and game of cunning.

Rifts Earth — at the threshold of an infinite Megaverse®, yet locked in chaos. Follow the story of but a handful of such warriors in their own struggles to do more than survive.

Book Two: Deception's Web sees Lieutenant Merrick and his unit return to civilization, but are haunted by their experiences in the wild. Peace and relaxation are shattered when one of their own is court-martialed, and the team becomes entangled in a web of deception.

Book Three: Treacherous Awakenings is the final part of Adam Chilson's **Rifts®** trilogy. Treachery revealed, questions answered, war and revenge bring this story to an end.

The **Rifts®** novels are based on the popular **Rifts®** role-playing game and sourcebooks.

Treacherous Awakenings ™ is the third book in a trilogy,based on the Rifts® Role-Playing Game series.

Warning!
Violence and the Supernatural

The fictional Worlds of Rifts® are violent, deadly and filled with supernatural monsters. Other dimensional beings often referred to as "demons," torment, stalk and prey on humans. Other alien life forms, monsters, gods and demigods, as well as magic, insanity, and war are all elements in this book.

Some parents may find the violence, magic and supernatural elements of the novels and games inappropriate for young readers/players. We suggest parental discretion.

Please note that none of us at Palladium Books® condone or encourage the occult, the practice of magic, the use of drugs, or violence.

Please Note: Strong Language and Violence may be inappropriate for readers under the age of 17.

Other Palladium Products

Send 50 cents for Palladium Books' 40 page catalog of role-playing game books, T-shirts, and other items.

Palladium Books Inc.

12455 Universal Dr. Dept. N

Taylor, MI 48180

Or visit our Web Site: **www.palladiumbooks.com**

Rifts® Treacherous Awakenings™

The Third in a Trilogy

Adam Chilson

Rifts® Trilogy
Book One: Sonic Boom™
Book Two: Deception's Web™
Book Three: Treacherous Awakening's™

Base on the worlds, characters, text, game rules, concepts and Megaverse® of the **Rifts®** Role-Playing Game series created by **Kevin Siembieda**.

Palladium Books® Inc.
www.palladiumbooks.com

Published by :
Palladium Books® Inc.,
12455 Universal Drive,
Taylor, MI 48180

First Printing — January, 2000

Printed in the United States of America.
ISBN 157457-036-9
Palladium Cat. No. 301

For Palladium Books
Keep Role Playing!

Special thanks to

My wife, Dawn, for showing me all the editing mistakes I made in the past three books.

And to all of you whose good advice I probably didn't listen to.

Chapter 1

Crackling bolts of energy jumped from Torrak's claws down the edges of the crimson sacrificial dagger. The body in the pentagram shuddered one last time and wheezed it's last. The undulating heart slowed, with each beat losing life force energy into the summoning ritual. At last the heart stilled, the throb of power through the pentagram lines mimicking its living pulse. Torrak stepped back, feeling the beat of his own heart match the incessant throbbing surge of power at the nexus. The victim's body shuddered once more as the last life force was ripped away into the swirling blue cloud of energy.

Yellow eyes gleamed in Torrak's demonic skull, power sweeping over him in a rush of blue and white sparks. His pulse quickened, echoing the rhythm of the ley line. Energy discharges ran across the mage's fine scaled skin and arced between the curved horns of his head. Life force absorbed, Torrak was powerful enough to complete the summoning ritual.

"Zarr Kale Meza Zarrakon!" The first phrase of the lengthy incantation was begun. Torrak chanted in gradual crescendo at the crackling pillar of power swirling at the nexus center. With each arcane phrase the pillar grew more turbulent until its brilliant white core split wide in a fury of sparks and thundering discharges. The fabric of dimensions tore with a deafening roar, a Rift coalescing between worlds never meant to merge.

Hot wind blew through the open portal, smoke and ash catching up in flurries about Torrak's billowing cape and sash. Through the Rift came the agonizing wails of tortured souls denied the privilege of death. Dark reddish-grey clouds rained burning ash upon a landscape of cracked earth and boiling pits of slime. The pervading stench of smouldering flesh wafted through the doorway, its scent like fine perfume intoxicating the mad dimensional shifter. Torrak's teeth gleamed in a widening grin. The moment of struggle was upon him.

"Larvathas Demonican Tyllith Kale Torrak!" The Gromek waved his hands over the corpse of his sacrifice while he chanted, the flesh of the body starting to quiver and squirm. Tiny holes formed in the rapidly decaying flesh as thousands of maggots ate their way to the surface. Torrak concluded the spell as the last bits of rotten flesh were devoured by the scavenging swarm.

Inexorably drawn by forces of magic, the creature stepping through the Rift glared hatefully at the summoning mortal with its set of three stalk-like eyes. The ground shuddered for each of its three trunk-sized legs striking soil of a foreign dimension. Torrak stared up at the monster with awe and amazement, a creature of such power now at his beck and call.

Saliva dripped in giant globs from the Magot's gaping maw, rows of cracked teeth aching to pulverize the bones of the foolish Shifter. All three eyes twisted downward to better view the horned mage. This puny mortal would pay dearly for wrenching it from its home dimension, it was only a matter of time.

Torrak's gleaming yellow eyes glared back defiantly. Not one iota of rebellion would be accepted from the demon, now his slave. Forces of will collided, throwing the surrounding flow of energy into chaos. Mystic energy spat bolts of lightning from miniature storms and the crackling frame of the Rift. What remained of the Magot's hold on its home disappeared with the closing portal. Spinning wheels of magic current shot away from the nexus center and the pounding flow of energy resumed its age-old course unimpeded. The Magot's huge bulk slumped and eyes hung low in defeat. Torrak was now its undisputed master.

"Hear me, slave, and obey without question," Torrak growled at the enormous beast. "I have one simple task for you to perform, and then you may return to your home."

Shifting from one massive leg to the other the Magot reluctantly bellowed its consent. The magic binding it to this foreign place and alien being was too strong to break. Its master held up a black helmet with a skull-like faceplate, thrusting the death helm at one of the giant eyes.

"This is the face of your enemy. Look and remember."

The Magot stared at the death mask, and the single red eyepiece remaining in the right socket stared back. Behind the missing left eyepiece was the empty space normally occupied by a human skull, and a scent of death only the Magot could taste.

"Follow the ley line west until the moon has set on the horizon, then go north to the camp of humans wearing this symbol. Destroy them without hesitation or mercy, not one is permitted to live. When you have slain the last of these humans and trampled their machines into the ground, then you may return to your home. Fail in your mission and I will condemn your very essence to oblivion!" Torrak waved a spiked mace in menacing gestures, adding weight to his demands. The creature slunk back, sensing the power radiating from the runic weapon and feeling its will reaching out for the life force around it.

"Now Go! Do not fail!"

Tree limbs snapped like match sticks and fell to be trampled by massive tri-toed feet as the Magot lumbered away on its mission. Torrak watched it go, feeling the strain of his intense focus take its toll on his physical body. But then there was nothing like the rush he got from a summoning. A satisfied smile spread from horn to horn. He was certain nothing would save his Coalition enemies now.

"SAM 15 to SAM 117B. How's it lookin' down there, buddy" Darren Corley radioed his partner on patrol five miles away.

"Pretty quiet, man."

"Dude, how many time I gotta tell you. Don't use the 'Q' word, you'll jinx it."

"Nothing since the moon went down. I'm still picking up quite a few living things, nothing big though." Steve viewed the forest from 300 feet up, his airborne flying exoskeleton cruising a casual 150 mph. Thermo-optical imaging turned much of the landscape shades of purple and black, bits of red and orange representing warm blooded creatures standing out against the cool background. So far all Steve had seen were packs of deer, the occasional carnivore, and thousands of nocturnal rodents. Nothing to pose even the slightest threat to the Coalition encampment several miles away.

"Keep your perimeter at 5 miles and swing south by the ley line again."

"Again?" Steve whined. "I checked it half an hour ago."

"Relay through Skull 41 if you run across anything. SAM 15 out." Darren signed off and goosed the two rear booster jets of his SAMAS power armor to clear the rise of a small hilltop. Night patrol was generally a boring task Private Darren Corley avoided to the point of insubordination, but when a hot-shot Captain ordered, Darren did his best to at least give the impression of obedience. After that he pretty much did whatever he could get away with. Rank meant very little to Darren anymore, it was combat experience that marked who would live and who would die. Having a couple of shiny bars wouldn't keep some slobbering monster from tearing you limb from limb. No amount of training could fully prepare someone for the horrors that waited outside the safety of fortified cities and heavily guarded borders. At one time Darren would have scoffed at the possibility of death, but now at the age of 18 and with many grisly battles behind him, Darren had learned a degree of respect for his enemies.

"SAM 117B to SAM 15, do you read me?" Steve's garbled voice came over the radio comm link.

"Use the relay, 117, you're pushing transmission range."

"SAM 117B to SAM 15, copy?"

"C'mon, Steve, get with it," Darren muttered and banked into a turn. The lower right maneuver jet flared up and the winged exoskeleton swung to the left. Short black wings whistled in the cold night air then leveled out when the turn was complete. Darren shoved the engines to the max and felt himself propelled up to 300 mph. The rush of acceleration never got boring.

"SAM 117B to SAM 15. Do you copy?" Steve's transmission was received much clearer as Darren closed the distance between them.

"15 here, what's up."

"There's this thing running down there."

"Okay, what kind of 'Thing' are talking about?"

"It's big, about 20 feet tall I think. It's haulin' like a sunnava gun. Got its thermo 'bout a mile from the line. Want I should shoot it?" Steve asked hopefully.

"Hold up, dude, wait 'till I get there." Darren was feeling the familiar pulse of adrenaline in his veins and the lure of action. Past experiences tempered the shoot first, ask questions later syndrome for the moment.

"It's a monster, man. That means we kill it, right?"

"This ain't border patrol, dude, we don't waste ammo on things that might not bother us. Not this far from a reload depot, man."

"That's not what Captain Pritchett said."

"Forget Pritchett. He's been runnin' D-Bee control in border towns for too long. Technically we're under Lieutenant Merrick's command, and he doesn't want us shootin' every non-human thing we see. Chill man, I'll be there in a sec."

In the distance Darren could see the eerie blue glow of a ley line running to the horizon. Over a hundred feet tall, the surging power rode over hills and through valleys, bound to the planet by some mysterious force. It didn't surprise Darren to discover a monster in the vicinity of the ley line, for many supernatural creatures and Dimensional Beings seemed drawn to the surging energy. The most infamous of all were practitioners of arcane arts that intentionally brought supernatural monsters into the world to do their bidding. Other creatures had the power to enter and leave a dimensions at whim, something that made them all the more dangerous and unpredictable. This was mankind's Earth, human's world, and the Coalition States Darren served sought to purge the land of these inhuman invaders and re-establish Earth as the domain of man.

"It looks like it's heading toward camp." Steve circled around the running monster. "Do I shoot yet?"

"Nuh-uh. Not yet." Darren slowed to get a better view of the tri-legged monstrosity galloping through the dense forest below. Three eyes bobbed on three tentacles above an enormous mouth. The thick bulk was covered in a mottled flesh, visible patches of decay showing black on infrared optics.

A voice back in Darren's head warned of danger, but it was a voice from the past predicting the future. What little belief Darren held in psychic clairvoyance was amplified by the appearance of this strange creature. Having been warned of this beast by someone who'd never been outside an arcology's armored walls gathered support for the psychic version. Darren had shunned psychic foreboding once before, and it had cost him the love of his life. The same mistake wouldn't be made twice.

"SAM 15 to Skull 41, come back." Darren radioed the Coalition base camp.

"We gonna shoot it?" Steve readied his rail gun.

"Dude, watch it, yer gettin' pretty close. You don't know what it can do. Lemme check in first. Policy, man." Darren caught himself sounding like an over-cautious officer, the kind he really hated.

"It doesn't got any weapons. It don't even got arms."

"None you can see. Chill out. SAM 15 to Skull 41, come in, please."

"They aren't gonna answer, I tried calling earlier and didn't get nothin'." Steve circled closer to the monster.

"SAM 15 to Skull 41! Mike, Lisa?"

"Sir, just thought you might wanna know about this ugly monster with really big teeth that's headed for you two."

"Is this your idea of a joke, Private?"

"No-way, sir, there's this nasty looking three legged thing makin' tracks for base camp. I'm pacing it at 35 mph, pretty straight line north. 'Bout twenty feet tall, kinda hard to tell cuz it's smashing a lot everything around it. Doesn't look like anything I've ever seen, but I've got a really bad feeling about it." Darren wasn't about to broadcast his belief in psychics over Coalition air waves. Statements like that would land him in front of a firing squad in short order. The Coalition didn't take kindly to psychic aberrations and mutations of the pure human.

"How long until it reaches base camp at its current speed?"

"I dunno. A few minutes, I guess. Yer the one with the education, dude. You figure it out."

"How far away are you?"

"Like 4 miles. 3.89 on the HUD."

"That gives us about 6 minutes. Have you established hostile intent?"

"Hold on a sec. 117's goin' in closer to see what it does. Maybe we can just scare it off."

Steve's SAMAS dropped to within 90 feet of the monster and swung around in its path, rail gun at the ready.

"It stopped!" Steve aired triumphantly while hovering in the Magot's path. The creature surveyed the strange humanoid exoskeleton with each of it's eyes. The SAMAS stared back with its death mask helm and glowing red eyes. The Magot's quarry had been found.

"So much for it being docile. It's charging SAM 117." Darren relayed the monster's bellow and attack. Steve let loose a burst of forty metal slugs from his C-40 rail gun and jetted up out of harms way.

"Darren! I just put forty slugs into it and it didn't even cringe!"

"You catch that, sir?"

"Affirmative, SAM 15, try to control it's movement and keep it away from base camp."

"You got it, dude." Darren flipped off the weapon safeties and leveled the rail gun muzzle at the target. "Let's kick some monster tail."

Both exoskeletons circled the running beast once before diving into their attacks. Darren noted with some satisfaction a trickle of blood running from a gash ripped into the monsters hide from his rail gun. If it could bleed it could die.

"This sucker's tough!" Steve commented, voice shaking slightly from fear and excitement. "I've nailed it four times and it's just gettin' mad."

"Take your time and make every shot count. Try and hit the same spot every time. Sometimes these these kinds of things can take a load to bring down." Darren placed the laser targeting dot over the oozing gash and pulled the trigger. Metal slugs left the C-40's barrel in rapid succession, each with enough force to punch a hole through dozens of human bodies and keep going. The burst of forty carved a deeper notch in the creature's body. It stopped on its course to deal with the two flying things harassing it.

"Back off a little bit. We got its attention. Maybe it'll reconsider where it's goin'. Try and herd it." Darren banked and came around for another run on the same side. Two eyes followed Darren's movements, the third fixing on the other exoskeleton. Without warning a yellow beam of light streaked from the open eye and bathed the black power armor in an eerie glow. SAM 117B crashed into the forest, leaving a swath of broken branches and fallen limbs.

"What the ...?! Steve? Steve, do you read me?"

8

Darren watched the other two eyes swing his direction.

Chapter 2

Darren veered sharply to the left as two yellow beams streaked past his right wing. The creature started off again in the direction of the Coalition camp, ignoring the sting of forty slugs impacting its body.

"SAM 117, come in. You okay, buddy?" Darren hovered above his partner's stationary power suit. Judging by the way it lay twisted around fallen limbs and branches, Steve was unconscious at best. "SAM 15 to Skull 41."

"Go ahead."

"Better wake everybody up and get suited for a fight. SAM 117B is down and that thing is one tough bad boy. It's got some kind of eye beam or something. Personally I'd rather not find out what it does."

"Already on alert. I'll call up 117's medical readout, you keep blasting away at the hostile, but keep your distance." Mike breathed deeply and made his decision. "Were going to 2nd stage alert. Skull 41 out."

"15 out."

"Lisa, oh, you're already on it." Mike turned to find the communications officer seated at her console. Display screens lit up with charts and data, one in particular causing her to sigh deeply.

"SAM 117B?" Mike knew the answer.

"No life signs. None at all." Lisa looked over at him with sad blue eyes. "It's like he's not even in the power suit, but the SAM's still sealed."

"Maybe he got out and re-sealed it before we could call it up. Better suit up, Lisa. Sorry." Mike looked her over fondly. Lisa read sincerity in his steel blue eyes, but the situation still ticked her off.

"Some other time." She tossed her long blond hair to the side. Their relationship was awkward to begin with, and the strain of duty was testing its limits. Mike kissed her lightly on the lips, then flipped a yellow switch above the Skull Walker's command console. Wrist computers and headsets throughout the camp emitted a series of high pitched tones, signaling a new threat level and ending many soldier's slumber. Mike slowly began the drudgery of donning uniform and body armor.

Lieutenant Greg Merrick rubbed his hands together to keep them from stiffening in the cold morning air. Already the camp was bustling with activity in preparation for a horrific battle. Picking out his own men among the infantry troops was simple enough, they were the only ones who seemed to know what to do. Greg hated joint operations, especially with a back-seat captain and inexperienced troops mingling with his special ops unit. Every man in his unit, with exception to the rookie pilot of SAM 117B, was a combat veteran handpicked for the mission. Having to relinquish command to Captain Pritchett seemed unfair to the men who trusted Greg's judgment and experience. So long as the Captain didn't unnecessarily endanger his men, the chain of command would be observed. Lieutenant Merrick's respect for order had many times taken second place to his respect for human life.

Robot vehicles moved into defensive positions, whining hydraulics and the thud of armored feet sounding above the chatter of troops. Greg cursed the Captain's inexperience in field operations as the camp lit up from spotlights of several mechanized units. At least his crew manning Skull Walker 41 had the sense not to make themselves an easy target. Greg looked up at the giant skull resting on a six legged base and signaled it to move into position. Like a giant spider, the 30 foot tall robot crawled to the south end of the encampment and scanned the rolling hillside with powerful infrared searchlights set into the skull's eye sockets. Two huge rail cannons protruded from either side of the skull, each capable of driving metal slugs through an armored target miles away. Many a creature had been returned to its maker on the receiving end of the those guns.

"Sir, SAM 312 is warmed up and ready to go." A red haired technical officer jogged up, helmet in hand and wearing loosely clamped environmental armor. The harsh lights made him look older and more rugged than he really was.

"Thanks." Greg slapped 2nd Lieutenant Brian Adams on his armor-plated shoulder and strode briskly toward a cluster of robot and power armor pilots suiting up in their SAMAS exoskeletons. Thrusters and maneuver jets thrummed softly on standby, waiting to propel the light power suits into the air. Coalition SAMAS made up the backbone of the armored military forces. The fast, lethal units could fill in for infantry, and tanks, and provide air-ground support. Very few industrial cities could stand up to a well-armed squad of SAMAS leading the charge for a mechanical strike force.

The exoskeleton carried a lightweight rail gun, with laser targeting link to the pilot's heads-up display and multi-optic systems. A feed belt connected the C-40 rail gun to the power armor's nuclear power pack and rear mounted ammunition drum. Electrically charged rails accelerated metal slugs to supersonic velocities by electromagnetic force. Fired in rapid succession, a burst of kinetic steel could rip a 20th century tank in half in the blink of an eye. If the C-40 rail gun wasn't enough to bring down the SAM's target, then a pair of self-propelled mini-missiles attached to each forearm could be brought into play. Standing just over 8 feet tall, the Coalition's power armor was one of the smallest and deadliest in the known world.

Climbing into the open power armor, Greg made sure each limb was in its appropriate location before speaking the 8-digit operator's code. The chest slowly moved back and locked in place, padded clamps gently closing around Greg's arms and legs. Last, the front half of the unit's head swung over and locked down. Greg made a fist with each armored hand to insure a close fit, then shook his head from side to side to work out the folds in the head and neck padding. The heads up display showed all systems in perfect working order and ammunition count full. It was time for action.

"Lieutenant Merrick to SAM 15, over."

"SAM 15 here. I hope all that light I see coming over the next rise means everybody's ready to blow this thing. to hell." Darren's voice came over the radio far too loud. Greg readjusted the volume to spare his ears further assault.

"What's your '20?"

"Uh, section G-17, no, G-18, hell if I can remember Pritchett's codes. South of camp following this three-legged, three-eyed, ugly cuss."

"How far?"

"'Bout a mile and a half, just coming up on the ridge. I've been able to slow it down some, but this bad boy took everything I could throw at it and it's still moving. I'm outta ammo 'cept for a pair of scorchers in my CM-2. Want me to launch them and head back?"

"No. Stay on the hostile and don't lose track of it. I'll trade places with you in a moment."

"Better hurry, man, this sucker's bleedin' but it ain't dyin'."

"Lieutenant Merrick to Captain Pritchett."

"Pritchett here, what can I do for you, Lieutenant?" The Captain's cheerful voice seemed incongruous in the combat situation.

"If I may make a suggestion, Sir, it might be wise to assign the Sky Cycles and a pair of SAMAS to make a roving patrol of our flank and rear. The monster could be a diversionary tactic for another hostile force."

"It's probably just another monster, Lieutenant, but if you think you can do without the added firepower then I'll assign the Sky Cycles to guard duty."

"Thank you, sir."

Securing the C-40 in his right hand, Greg lifted off and extended the shoulder mounted wings. Rear thrusters fired up and within seconds Greg was skimming tree tops in Darren's direction. Not wanting one of Pritchett's overzealous grunts to mistake him for a target, Greg activated the wingtip running lights. Normally he considered use of the flashing red strobes an ideal method of informing the enemy of his location, but on the other hand, friendly fire could be even more deadly.

The landscape took on an alien appearance under illumination of the SAMAS' chest infrared spotlight. Less than 2,000 feet from the hilltop was an ugly creature running with an uneven gait. Circling above it were a pair of blinking red lights. Greg smiled. Apparently Darren had no desire to be shot either.

"Mornin' Lieutenant! It's all yours."

"I see it. Go ahead and use your mini-missiles and then head back for reload. Better give the firing lanes a wide berth."

"You don't gotta tell me twice. I'm outta here." Darren's SAMAS veered away, then slowed for a pause in mid-air. Left forearm extended, Darren aligned the laser targeting dot on the monster's running form. Two flaming trails sped from the launcher. Plasma warheads detonated an instant before striking the creature's back. It and the forest around it disappeared in an expanding ball of white hot flame. The Magot's eyelids shut over each eye as plasma washed its body, scorching flesh and dematerializing portions of its back. Darren rotated then streaked away from the burning patch of forest.

Closing to 300 feet, Greg was amazed to find the Magot still on a course with the Coalition encampment. Most creatures, no matter how stupid, tended to avoid places and things that caused pain. What could be driving it to keep moving in the same direction after Darren had emptied a full ammo drum into it? In another minute it would be in the kill zone of heavier robot armament. Greg selected a targeting transmission frequency so units in the encampment could call up his sensor feed, then put a burst into it to make sure the sights were accurate. As it topped the rise, Greg seriously doubted it would last another minute.

Fingers twitched above triggers in anticipation. Troops took their places behind a small earthen berm surrounding the camp. Behind them a row of four robot vehicles prepared to pulverize anything that moved. Rocket teams, soldiers, and turret gunners waited for the command to fire.

"Quit wavin' that thing around. There's nothin' out there yet," Nim remarked, annoyed at being awakened in the middle of the night. Even Partial Conversion Cyborgs needed beauty sleep.

"I've been kinda wantin' to test out this CV-212." Bill caressed his new laser assault rifle. Shooting targets wasn't the same thing as real action. "S'posed to be better than a C-12."

"Not better, just rigged to beat that laser resistant armor," Nim corrected. "The only difference is it's got some variable frequency beam, or something like that. I'll take my C-14 'Firebreather' any day over that prototype thing."

"Awlright boys, better git ready for some down and dirty action. Mount bayonets!" Cowboy plopped down with his fire squad and started attaching a high frequency bayonet to the end of his bulky plasma rifle. Armor clad soldiers from Pritchett's unit observed the veteran troops with curiosity. Some looked at their own weapons and polished black armor, comparing them to the dirty black and green armor and battle worn hardware of Merrick's special ops unit. All were armed to the teeth with an assortment of firepower not even sanctioned by military. Private Ben Gerald finally spoke up.

"Hey, man, since when did they start issuing Vibro-bayonets?"

"That's 'Corporal' to you, son." Cowboy rose to his full height and looked down at the outspoken soldier.

"Sorry."

"No problem." Cowboy shot a smile at his fire team and locked down his helmet face piece.

"So what's with the bayonets?" Ben continued. "I've never even seen guns with mounts for 'em." He pointed to the metal protrusion on Cowboy's rifle where a bi-pod mount should have been.

"Had 'em specially modified for us after our last tour. Pretty cool, eh?"

"Why? If something gets close enough to stab, why not just shoot it?"

"Obviously he's never been eye to eye with a Brodkil demon, right before it smashes your skull in with its fist," Bill put in.

"Hopefully nothin' ever gits that close, but if it does, sometimes keeping it away from you is all you can do," Cowboy advised.

"Besides, who says you can't do both? Stab it and shoot it." Nim added.

"Yeah, but—"

"Fire in the hole!" the Abolisher robot warned over its loudspeaker. Three sets of twin 144 mm auto-cannons rose to bombard the creature, now on its final run toward the camp. The Abolisher's crown of weaponry covered a full circle of fire, and the giant robot could rotate at the torso to assault a single target with all six auto-cannons. Troops along the camp's edge flinched even before the first shells were fired.

"What an idiot!" Nim commented. "Telling the enemy we're gonna fire over the loudspeaker. That's what the radio's fore!" he shouted to the 30 foot humanoid tank.

The report from the auto-cannons echoed from hillside to hillside, jarred half awake soldiers to full alertness. Cowboy and his squad barely responded to the wake up call. Cybernetic sound filters implanted in their ears muffled detrimental noise and prevented acoustic shock waves from damaging ear drums. The follow-up explosion erupted from the hillside two seconds later.

"It knows now,." Cowboy remarked, watching the Magot's hideous maw get slammed into the ground with explosive impact. Backing the scope magnification down a few notches, Cowboy waited until the range finder gave him the green light on effective range for his C-27.

With a low growl, the Abolisher's upper body rotated to bring the next pair of cannons to bear. The sensor turret atop its head counter-rotated to maintain a visual targeting lock of the running monster. To the Abolisher's left two Skull Walkers opened up with rail cannons. Another pair of 144 mm shells arced toward the target.

"Sir! Did you see that!?" the pilot of Skull Walker 191 exclaimed in amazement. Shells cratered the earth and threw trees skyward where the monster had been an instant before. It leapt nimbly out of the line of fire and came crashing down 40 feet closer than it was before. Captain Pritchett leaned foreword with a calm amusement and watched multiple views of the Magot on the Skull Walker's main view screen.

"It's learning." Changing tactics to avoid being hit. He rubbed his unshaven jaw thoughtfully with a bionic hand.

"It's getting closer, sir, and we're not having much luck hitting it. There's not much to lock onto." the gunner's voice had a strained tone to it. The pilot's compartment hummed with low vibrations as the twin rail cannons flung metal slugs at the approaching monster.

"Advise Enforcer 920 to move up and lock four CMS-16s on the target. Give all rocket teams the clearance to fire at will."

"Yes sir." The communications officer relayed the orders.

William Pritchett leaned back in his seat and put both bionic hands behind his head. Despite the relaxed demeanor, his heart was beating faster than he'd ever admit. Border patrols were much different. He could just call in fire from nearby firebases or patrolling aircraft. Somehow it never occurred to him that this thing might actually make it into his camp. After a forced yawn and the creature still not dead, Pritchett gave the order to fire.

Four missiles left the UAR-1 Enforcer's launch system and streaked toward a patch of burning forest half a mile away. Flames shot from behind troop rocket launchers and mini-missiles traced invisible infrared beams through the air. For a moment the hail of fire from the robots and flying exoskeletons was absent, a split second of calm before missiles converged and plasma warheads expanded away in spheres of white hot energy.

Smoke, flame, and faintly glowing earth were visible when the plasma fires sputtered out.

"We got it!" the gunner exclaimed triumphantly.

"Do you see a body?" Pritchett pointed to the view screens.

"After that? What body?"

"There should at least be body parts, but I see nothing."

"SAM 916 and 475 are reporting no sign of the monster. Dead or alive," the communications officer translated the chatter over communication channels.

"Put SAM 916 on rotating patrol and tell Sergio to return to base camp."

"Yes sir."

"Pritchett to Lieutenant Merrick, over," the Captain spoke into the short range radio built into his left bionic arm.

"Merrick."

"Have you been monitoring communications?"

"Affirmative."

"Is this type of thing common?" Have you ever encountered a creature like this before?"

"Not anything that could take that kind of punishment and live." Greg was surprised at being asked. "Run a full sweep with infrared, ultraviolet, and thermo. Sometimes you can pick up things invisible to normal optics and the naked eye. Look for anything our of the ordinary, even inanimate objects and bizarre looking animals in the area."

"I'll keep that in mind. Thank you, Lieutenant."

"Maybe it just disappears when it dies," the gunner offered.

"Maybe. Maybe it doesn't. Whatever it was it took a full ammo drum from an ace SAMAS pilot who doesn't miss, and at least a few volleys from our guns. Do you think we should all go back to sleep and just hope it might be dead?"

"No, sir."

"Neither do I. If by some chance it gets past the perimeter micro-wave fence without tripping an alarm, what it could do to this camp I don't want to find out."

Suited up in black composite armor, Lisa Andrews sifted through the continuous comm chatter coming over her headset. Dave leaned back in the pilot's seat and rested his head against the padded rests. Neither bothered to strap in even though the pilot's compartment was tilted back slightly with the angle of the skull-like body and rail can-nons fixed to each side. Dave's eyes began to close with returning sleep, but Lisa slapped his armor plated chest with knuckle spikes.

"Stay awake, Dave, we haven't been ordered to stand down."

"Three-thirty in the morning," Dave muttered, smoothing out his sandy brown hair. "Can't these things ever wait until everyone is awake before pulling this crap? I was having a good dream."

"Let me guess. Bars, cold beer, women —"

"Don't rub it in." Dave grinned faintly.

"One of these days some woman's going to cure you of that, you know."

"Never happen. Only thing gonna keep me from partyin' is a cof-fin an' six feet of earth, and that's assuming I don't got a shovel."

"Do all RPA's have this insatiable urge to live life on the wild side?"

"Yeah, mostly. Ever meet a robot or power armor pilot who did-n't?"

"Now that you mention it, no."

"It's kinda like a commandment or something, ya know, like those Pre-Rifts cults. A big fraternity, ya know? Thou shalt party."

Red lights flashed and a warning tone indicated a breach in the microwave fence.

"Oh man, that's close!" Dave lowered the cannon angle and a huge eye filled the view screen. Lisa practically fell out of her seat.

"Reduce magnification!" she ordered, reaching for the sensor controls herself.

"How the did it get this close!?" Dave centered the targeting dot on the center eye. 80 metal slugs from each cannon splattered bits of watery tissue from the Magot's last good eye.

"Oh my god, that thing's forty feet from camp!" Lisa interpreted the flashing targeting displays. An actual view of the Magot took the place of the mangled eye.

"Fire at will!" Captain Pritchett's order blared over communication channels. Forest disappeared in a swath 80 feet wide and hundreds of feet behind the dying monster. Red laser beams and fiery plasma poured into it while a hail of metal slugs rained mercilessly. Smoke and flame rose in a billowing cloud that washed back over the berm with searing intensity.

"Cease fire! Cease fire!" the captain yelled. Slowly the torrent stopped, several troops getting in a few last shots for good measure. Dave viewed the burning haze on the view screen, not sure whether to laugh or be upset. It would take the rest of the night to put out the fires created by the deadly barrage. A charred, mangled heap lay just 50 feet from the row of soldiers along the berm. Already a few brave troops approached the smoldering mound of flesh. It was fairly evident the beast wasn't getting back up, but Cowboy and his squad continued sporadic firing before hacking it up with high frequency swords and bayonets. Pritchett's men stared on stupidly.

"Oh my God." Lisa called up SAM 117B's medical readout.

"You checked that already. Is he alive?" Dave asked.

"He shouldn't be." She blinked and pointed to the human form on the screen, and the rapidly dropping vital statistics. The injury chart showed profuse bleeding from all major joints. A single tone emanated, finalizing Steve's death. Below the row of body functions a blinking "Deceased" signaled what should have been almost instantaneous.

"Skull 41 to Merrick. Confirmed termination of hostile. One casualty. Private Steve Wilson."

Chapter 3

Hot steam mingled with smoke from dying fires in the blackened clearing south of the Coalition camp. Morning sunlight would reveal the plume of white smoke to anyone within miles. Greg was thankful they were almost finished extinguishing the last few hot spots. For the first time during the trek he was grateful to have the slow, clumsy APC at his disposal. An attachment on the front end turned the armored vehicle into a relatively effective bulldozer, something that had prevented the forest fires from spreading too quickly for other measures to be implemented. Still, Greg thought to himself, the armored personnel carrier was better suited for urban combat than traversing the wastelands and was probably going to be more trouble than it was worth.

Clouds of hissing steam billowed from the last visible flames of a burning stump. Greg lost count of how many trips the pair of Sky Cycles had made to the nearby river to haul huge buckets of water from cables attached to the crafts' undercarriage. Greg intentionally neglected to inform Captain Pritchett about the supply of fire retardant grenades and equipment stashed in his own unit's vehicles. It would take longer to put out the forest blaze with a bulldozer and Sky Cycles, but if a fire got started in their camp he wanted the option of quick response.

"Want me to get another load?" the pilot of the hovering craft asked over the comm.

"That's probably good enough. Take a break, then assist Sergeant Winters with ground clean-up."

"Yes sir," the pilot responded, grateful for the chance to rest. Hover jets kicked up ash and whipped smoke into a fury as the small, one man fighter descended to the ground. Landing gear deployed and the Sky Cycle's weight came to rest on three sets of wheels. The engine whine slowed and the pilot hopped to the ground from the open, motorcycle-like cockpit.

"Don't forget we're moving out at 09:00."

"I've got recon duty, sir, I haven't forgotten." The pilot leaned against the foreword laser turret and detached the face plate of his helmet. Greg couldn't help notice the pilot was no more than 17 or 18 years old. For one of Pritchett's unit the RPA wasn't half bad. It occurred to him that he didn't even know the pilot's name. Somewhere in the back of Greg's mind something told him this man would never be going home.

"Adams to Merrick, over."

"Merrick. You done with my SAM yet?" Greg looked back to camp to see the person calling him on the radio. His unit's technical officer had borrowed the power armor to replace the heavy ammunition drum on Darren's exoskeleton.

"All done. What do you want me to do with 117B?"

"It's cleaned out?"

"Almost, sir." Brian paused, thinking of the fractured, bloody pulp he'd found inside it. "Who's going to pilot it? Private Peterson has Mike's SAM until he gets back from recon, and PFC Brown is the only other person checked out to fly it, except she's on the CR-1 rocket team. I need to know who's flying it before I change the access code. Voice recognition."

"You're going to run 117."

"Me? Can't you get someone else to do it?" Brian argued. "Who's going to drive my rover?"

"Cowboy can take your hover. I want you in the SAM. Time to earn those bars, Lieutenant."

"Yes, sir."

Brian Adams had received his commission to 2nd Lieutenant under mysterious circumstances. Not that Greg thought the educated officer inferior, but front-line combat was an experience he felt every officer should have, academy graduate or not. Greg often used himself as the model, having come up through the ranks from an enlisted private and seen more than his share of action before transferring to the officer's corp. That history earned him a respect greater than the design of his armor and emblems of his uniform. The Coalition States offered the opportunity of power to those ambitious enough to grasp it. Locked in a constant struggle to preserve humanity, the chance to rise through the ranks came at the expense of the Coalition's enemies. Monsters and creatures from the Rifts posed a continual threat to the millions of people living within Coalition borders. Magic users, aliens, Dimensional Beings, psychics, and mutants were the declared foes of humanity and had to be eliminated for mankind to survive. At times Greg found himself at odds with the edicts laid down by the military government he served, but he'd seen more than his share of atrocities committed by practitioners of magic and the inhuman. The cause to respond with violence was strong.

Greg started walking back to camp, removing the face plate of his own helmet to let the cold morning air sharpen his wits. His shoulder length brown hair fell out and blew in the breeze unrestricted. Full environmental armor could be a lifesaver, but it limited mobility, dulled the senses, and often became troublesome to wear. Going into battle without it was unthinkable, although it wasn't likely to stop anything more powerful than a single laser blast or flying shrapnel. Greg thought of it as a second chance suit, in case he zigged when he should have zagged. Anything that could save the life of a soldier once made each troop as good as two, in the eyes of the military. The heavy infantry version of the armor suit was one of the best in the known world. Naturally his unit would have nothing to do with the lighter versions, and had gotten approval to modify the standard skeletal motif in favor of more practical use. While heavier and more clumsy, the armor added an edge that could make the difference between life and death, victory and defeat.

Calm pervaded where chaos reigned hours earlier. Very few personnel were visible, either resting or assigned to fire duty. Greg could hear Brian cursing some stubborn mechanical device to the fires of eternal hell, but decided to leave him alone with his frustration. The robots standing in a group cast long shadows in the early morning sun. Pritchett, Greg cursed. Clustering the armor units like that. No matter which robot a missile hit, the others would suffer collateral damage. He looked up at the sky, grateful for the near perfect weather and good visibility. Hopefully his patrolling units would detect an enemy first.

"Wow, man, beautiful morning." A voice just about launched Greg into the air with surprise. Lounging in the front seat of a hover rover with a cup of hot coffee was a wild haired man with long, orange dyed beard and psychedelic painted body armor.

"What the — how the hell — what are you doing here?!"

"Drinkin' coffee, man. Did you know you're all out of sugar?"

"I...." Greg's jaw dropped in complete disbelief.

"Hey, man, you all right?

"Delwin. Delwin Moon Beam." Greg stammered the name of the man he'd heard Darren talk about. Until now he had thought Darren was full of it.

"That's me, man."

"How the did you get past the microwave fence?!"

"Whoah, you have a microwave fence?"

"The one surrounding our camp. How did you get past it?"

"Oh, those little poles? I just climbed a tree, man, like with the birds and the squirrels, man. Thanks for the coffee. I woulda asked, but there's was like nobody around and I didn't think you'd mind. Want some? I made enough to share." Delwin pointed with his foot to the full pot on the dash.

"I don't want any coffee!"

"Hey man, no more caffeine for you." Delwin slid the pot farther away with his foot. "You got some serious negative waves for such a beautiful day. Be happy, man. Think of green grass, colorful flowers, pretty birds, and send out some positive waves for a change."

Greg stood speechless, devoid of any intelligible response worthy of the lunacy he was encountering. This man had bypassed all means of detection and infiltrated a Coalition encampment for the purpose of drinking a cup of coffee, and having a conversation about positive waves vs. negative waves. The peculiar line of logic blew Greg's mind.

"What are you doing here in West Virginia? You were last seen in Youngstown."

"Sight seein', man. Saw yer fire last night and thought I'd come over an' roast up some marshmallows, but I forgot the marshmallows. Bummer, man. Is Darren here?"

"Wait here. Don't go anywhere or do anything."

"No problem, man," said Delwin. "I'm cool."

Greg found Darren napping in the back of the other hover rover. Procedures called for an intruder alert, but Greg figured it was already too late for that. Besides, Darren had some explaining to do.

"Who did you say is here?" Darren looked at the lieutenant incredulously, black hair falling over sleep swollen green eyes.

"That Crazy, the one that helped us at Youngstown. The one you said pushed a Glitter Boy down a mineshaft. What's he doing in my camp?!"

"Don't ask me, dude, I don't have a clue. Ask him."

"He wants to talk to you. Find out what he wants and get him out of here before everyone wakes up or Captain Pritchett finds out, understand?"

"I didn't know what he was talking about half the time in Youngstown. How am I supposed to get rid of him?"

"I don't care. Tell him you saw a field of weed fifty miles that way." Greg pointed a random direction.

"Whatever, sir." Darren muttered, pulling himself out of the covered vehicle. No question of Delwin's presence anymore.

"Delwin?"

"You know it, baby."

"I never thought I'd see you again. How ya been, dude?" Darren shook hands with his odd acquaintance.

"Absolutely superb, man, like growin' with life and aligned with the cosmic waves of harmony. Am I sensing positive waves from you this bright morning?"

"Uh, something like that." said Darren. "Sure."

"Righteous, man. I'll be going now." Delwin abruptly announced.

"Uh, man, why did you come here in the first place?"

"To see if you were here. I'll see you later, man." Delwin started strapping on the jet pack sitting in the passenger seat next to him.

"Wait a second, dude," Darren never thought he'd be trying to get the crazy man to stay. "You didn't tell me how Van and the others are doing."

"Oh, they're fine, man. 'Bout twelve miles north. Goin' the same place as all youse."

"They're here?!"

"Yeah, man, I'll tell 'em I saw you. It might not be cool you should come by, though."

"Why?"

"Cyndiara, man. You know, you really broke her heart, man."

For a moment Delwin actually sounded lucid. Darren's heart dropped and became a pit in his stomach.

"Is she okay?"

"I don't know, man. Sometimes she outs these real downer vibes, but I cheer her up with my flute, man. You look bummed too, man, maybe I should cheer you up."

The moment of lucidity was gone. Before Darren could prevent disaster, Delwin's wooden flute was waking up the entire camp with a grating version of reveille.

"I get it! I'm happy! Cut it out, Delwin!" Darren grabbed the flute out of his hands and shoved it back in Delwin's purple belt pouch.

"I wasn't done, man."

"I think I saw some stuff growing down by this ley line south of here. Like fields of it, man."

Thruster wash nearly knocked Darren off his feet. Shouts of dismay followed Delwin's frenetic, low altitude course south through the camp. By the time weapons were ready, the man in psychedelic armor was gone. Darren looked at Greg and shrugged.

"Hey, I told him what you wanted me to say."

"Captain Pritchett to Lieutenant Merrick. What's going on out there?" Pritchett's voice inquired over the comm. Darren shrugged again and headed for his SAMAS before Greg could make him give an explanation. His patrol would take him out of sight and sometimes off radar. Darren planned on making an extended tour.

"There you have it." Sinclair Van De Graf shut down the Techno-Wizard modified view screen. "At least Delwin found out what you asked him to." He turned to a stunning red haired woman sitting in the ATV next to him.

"I don't know what to do now, Van." Cyndiara stared at the blank screen. Moments earlier they'd viewed Delwin's meeting with Darren by a combination of magic and technology. The image had been somewhat distorted coming through Delwin's eyes, but was still traumatic for Cyndiara. Just seeing her former love was enough to make tears well up in her bright green eyes.

"Sorry about the glitch in the viewing. I'm not sure if that was a problem in my device or interference from Delwin's brain implants, or maybe all that stuff he smokes." Van looked at his newest creation with pride. "It seems to work, though."

"What am I going to do? What if Darren finds us, or we run into him on the way to Liberty? What am I going to say?"

"I wouldn't worry about it until it happens. Sooner or later the two of you will get the chance to work things out." Van leaned back and regarded Cyndiara thoughtfully. Her long, curly red hair fell past the middle of her back, and the green, skin tight body suit she wore revealed a figure of nearly perfect proportions. It never ceased to amaze Van how prejudice and fear could drive a man to forsake a woman he obviously loved. Van couldn't imagine why Darren would abandon her simply because she'd been born with psychic pyrokinetic abilities. The Coalition mentality, who could understand it?

Darren was Van's only friend in the Coalition military, a friendship quite unusual in the present day world. For nearly a century the Coalition States had waged war on practitioners of magic and what they considered mutations of humanity. Thousands had been slaughtered in the name of self defense and preservation of human kind. Many killed were nothing more than peaceful beings whose inhuman ancestors became trapped on this strange planet called Earth. Others, unfortunately, like the evil Federation of Magic, gave the Coalition a very firm basis for their prejudice and fear of the unknown. Somewhere in the middle of constant strife the two men had found common ground.

"I know, I'm getting emotional again." She noticed him staring at her with his intense, dark eyes. "I promised I wouldn't, but I never expected to see him again."

"I can still take you back to Youngstown on my Sky Cycle if you want."

"No. I've ridden one of those things before and I don't want to do it again. They're dangerous." Cyndiara used a lame excuse.

"Suit yourself. You're the one driving the Mountaineer, we'll leave when you're ready." Van patted her on the shoulder and climbed out the full sized door in the side of the giant all terrain vehicle.

A blast of cold wind snapped his dark hair into his eyes and chilled his skin through the black, long sleeved sweatshirt he wore. He stepped back inside long enough to retrieve his modified composite body armor. Being courteous, he left Cyndiara with the privacy of her grief.

Outside in the small camp Van began suiting up, ignoring the questioning gaze from his companions. If they really wanted to know what Delwin had found out, they could ask Cyndiara, or attempt to decode Delwin's own version when he returned. A large, armor-plated Gigante sat cross-legged by the comparatively tiny camp fire while Sir Renfield and a small woman huddled together for warmth. Somehow Van didn't think Anja looked very comfortable pressed against the knight's cyber-armor.

"What you see on little magic box?" the giant finally asked. Targo and Van were childhood buddies, though as a child Targo was still bigger than most adult humans.

"It worked pretty good for a first test of the prototype, but I think I can improve the viewing range and clarity." Van strapped on the lower torso and leg sections of his armor. Targo's brow crinkled as he pondered the answer.

"You see Darren on box?"

"Darren? Of course, but it was kind of fuzzy and stretched."

"What he say?"

"He told Delwin there was a field of stuff down south of the ley line."

"Oh brother," Sir Renfield mumbled.

"Is Cyndiara okay?" Anja asked.

"Who knows? Better to just leave her alone for awhile."

"Maybe." Anja stepped around the giant and walked to the ATV's door, her waist length, rust colored hair blowing to one side in the wind. Van didn't argue with her or try to stop the Mystic from going inside. Anja possessed an empathic and understanding nature like no other Van had ever met. If anybody could find the right words to say to the heartbroken Cyndiara, it was the gentle Mystic.

Van turned back to finish donning his armor and noticed the Cyber-Knight's unfriendly gaze. Competition for Anja's affections, even unintentional as they were for Van, had created a schism between the knight and Techno-Wizard right from the start. Sir David Renfield was too honorable to openly display his anger at Van's selfish motivations, and Van had reached the point where it just wasn't fun to antagonize the Cyber-Knight any more. The tense standoff had finally run its course and become a grudging tolerance. Traveling alone in the wilderness of North America was extremely dangerous, and for the sake of safety they would tolerate each other until they reached the small town of Liberty in the Pre-Rifts state of Maryland.

"You better cover that thing before a Coalition patrol comes by." Sir Renfield pointed to Van's repainted Coalition make Sky Cycle. "You might have to explain where you stole it from."

"I did not steal that Sky Cycle, I traded a hover cycle for it."

"Some trade. You traded a stolen Coalition hover cycle for it."

"Yeah, but I didn't steal the hover cycle either. I found it."

"Believe what you want to, it was still dishonest and that thing is going to get all of us in trouble if they find it."

"The black market sells them up at Northern Gun and at just about every other industrialized city, so it's not like I'm the only one around with a stolen Sky Cycle. Besides, who says they're going to catch me?"

"I'm not worried about you, it's the rest of us they'll come after when you run away." Sir Renfield bit his lip and stopped himself from making another slighting remark.

"Are you two chickens pecking at each other again?" a weathered looking wilderness scout walked up to the fire, energy rifle across his shoulders. "Why don't you just duke it out and quit squabbling."

"Morning Kahn Na Tai, glad you see you too." Van greeted the irritable scout by his Simvan name. How Mr. Kent acquired the adopted name from a cannibalistic D-Bee tribe Van didn't know. According to Anja, the name meant "Iron Will" in Simvan, although she herself wouldn't comment on how he got the name. All Van knew was the man had more scars than a platoon of combat veterans.

"Did you find a route for us?" Sir Renfield inquired.

"About as clear as you will find in this country. There's a good place to cross the river up ahead, and then we follow an old highway northeast up into the mountains. Day and half of travel, if we get started soon. I don't want to cross the Potomac when it starts raining."

Both Van and Renfield looked at the clear sky, but decided not to contradict the scout.

"What are the chances of running into the Coalition convoy on the way?" Van asked, a little wary himself about getting into an argument over his prized acquisition.

"Good chance. I'm not sure if we should go ahead of them or behind them. We can make better time if we pass them and keep moving at a steady pace, on the other hand they're clearing the old highway of overgrowth as they go along, so our ride would be much easier if we travel behind them. Your call."

"I could have been at Liberty days ago, but I'd hate to leave you guys defenseless," Van offered his opinion.

"It's not as though we can't handle trouble without you, Van." Sir Renfield glanced over at a large, infantry style power armor next to Van's Sky Cycle. "Feel free to go ahead any time you want."

"Wouldn't dream of it. I'm shocked you would ever think I would desert my friends. I say we move quick and get to Liberty before the Coalition does, just in case they stir up trouble on their way. I don't want to be caught in the wake."

"For once I agree. That lieutenant we worked with at Youngstown, the one with the long hair, he didn't seem half bad, for a Coalition officer that is. I don't think he's running the show this time."

"Whoever they have in command is a moron," Mr. Kent scoffed.

"Yeah. Him make too much noise and make mess of trees. Him moron!" Targo broke the intensity of the discussion with his enthusiastic agreement.

"Well let's hope the Coalition is all we have to worry about. They should leave us alone, especially this far away from C.S. territory. My main concern is the Federation of Magic. We're not out of what they call their territory, and so far we've seen and heard too little from them. That's got me worried," Van advised. The Coalition considered all magic practitioners to be part of the Federation, when in actuality most wanted nothing to do with the evil cult. Federation members were a few very powerful sorcerers, but they commanded legions of creatures from demonic dimensions and ruled the inhabitants of the wastelands with an iron fist. A run-in with a Federation lord could often be disastrous.

"So what are we standing around for. Why are we just sitting here? Let's move." Mr. Kent urged.

"Women."

"What?"

"Women." Van jerked his head at the ATV.

"Oh."

Glowing yellow eyes focused on the line of Coalition vehicles tracing the remnants of a 300-year-old highway through the wilderness. For hours the vulture had observed the mighty military force breaking camp and resuming its trek east. Torrak's familiar rustled it's black feathers and hooked its curved beak into the rotten meat of a dead animal, intent on finishing its meal before taking flight back to its master. Torrak would not be pleased that his enemies were on the move in his direction again.

Spiraling slowly into the small village, Darren noticed the complete absence of inhabitants. Situated on the banks of the river his unit intended to cross earned the village a scouting party. Either the village was abandoned or the villagers were terrified of his flying SAMAS. Sometimes Darren forgot was the death motif and skull-like of his power armor intended for intimidation to begin with. Signs of habitation were everywhere so Darren concluded it was his own presence causing the illusion of vacancy. He toyed with the idea of landing and trying to convince the people that the Coalition was their friend, but the words of peace wouldn't go far coming from the skull-like head of a 8 foot tall, rail gun wielding power armor.

"Merrick to SAM 15, over."

"SAM 15 here."

"What's the village look like?"

"Pretty bare. I seriously doubt it's much of a threat, if at all. Everyone's hiding. Wait, someone just ducked behind a building."

"Don't start any trouble, Darren."

"I'm not." Darren swung lower and hovered around the corner of the log cabin. An ugly humanoid creature with lumpy brown skin and three oversized eyes stood in front of a small child of similar appearance. Both cowered back, the adult attempting to shield the child with its body. Darren felt foolish and somewhat of a bully for scaring them so badly.

"Sir, it's just some D-Bees. I don't see any weapons. Probably a whole village of these ugly turds. Not much of threat."

"Captain Pritchett wants you back on rear guard. Oh, damn. They got the APC stuck again."

"Dang, that didn't take long," Darren remarked. Four times in as many hours the elongated, eight wheeled APC managed to get itself stuck in ditches and small gulleys, and each time had to be helped out of its predicament by the 18 foot tall Enforcer and Lumbering Abolisher robot. The vehicle wasn't suited for the terrain it was expected to traverse, something Greg had brought up several times well before the mission began. Captain Pritchett liked the APC.

"SAM 15, Alpha frequency, preset plus 12."

"Gotcha." Darren turned his radio to a preset scrambled channel reserved for communications just within Merrick's unit. "You reading me?"

"Loud and clear."

"Why the channel switch, sir, gonna call Pritchett some more names?"

"Something fishy is going on. Pritchett just told me to assign Sharp to long range scout in the south and is pulling back all our people and replacing them with his own men."

"Is there some hostile force coming up behind us?"

"Nothing so far. I don't like it, whatever he's up to."

"Its probably nothing sir, sir. You don't have nothin' to worry 'bout." Darren joked.

"Just the same, stay on a five mile radius and be ready to respond quickly. Switch back to preset. Merrick out."

"15 out."

Climbing to three hundred feet, Darren made a bee-line for the river bank where the lead units were gathering to cross. SAM 612 of

Pritchett's forces flew toward him from the opposite direction, intentionally taking a collision course.

"Sergio, you jerk, come get some," Darren breathed over the radio, not changing course. At the last instant the other SAMAS veered right, just missing a wing to wing collision by millimeters. Darren fought to keep the engines from stalling as he entered the backwash of the other exoskeleton.

"Any time you're not busy," Sergio's cutting remark followed.

"You've been fighting helpless nomads too long. You wouldn't last two seconds against a real opponent."

"Ooooh, hotshot ace gettin' his feathers ruffled?"

The unfriendly banter ended, but Darren felt himself move one step closer to a real confrontation. Sergio was one of Pritchett's "Yes Men," and crossing him was like crossing the captain. Sooner or later Darren believed it would come down to more than just an exchange of words.

Chapter 4

Cries of anguish followed the four men being dragged from their homes and beaten senseless by animated corpses. Women and children cried in fear for their own lives and those of their family members. Brodkil demons looted food stores while a hideous locust demon directed animated dead in the capture of new bodies to be made into zombie warriors. Observing from the back of his horse, Lord Credo was pleased by the chaos created by his minions. Bringing terror to the pitiful lives of these peasants brought excitement to his otherwise dreary life.

As a Federation Lord, he cared little for the matter of his fellow Lords and their petty squabbling. The only one he kept in regular contact with was a crusty hermit by the name of Anyon. The Federation considered Lord Anyon a classless outcast among themselves, but feared his power even more now that he'd slain Lord Valdor in a titanic wizard's duel. Lord Credo found it heartening how little Anyon cared for conquest, the pursuit of magic his first obsession. They traded spells from time to time, but never their most prized and powerful incantations. Credo felt something akin to the reclusive Anyon. and was content with the power he held over the small villages and nomadic tribes that inhabited upper West Virginia.

This was the largest and most enjoyable of the villages in his self proclaimed domain, located near the ruins of the Pre-Rifts city of Fairmont. The town's former protector, a Mystic of many years experience, had his tongue removed by one of Credo's Lasae demons. Now the defenseless town was subject to his every whim.

Humans were such an inferior species compared to the mentally and physically superior Elven race, Credo contended. Always wasting their pitifully short lives on mundane pursuits rather than attempting to achieve greater feats of the imagination. Looking around at the dirty farmers and frontier people mingling with D-Bees to survive only strengthened his belief in superiority. Proof positive was the iron grip he held over them, completely unbreakable by any means they could devise. And they had tried, and of course the punishment was worse every time.

Something struck his horse's neck and fell to the ground. The animal jerked its head back more out of surprise than pain. A fair haired woman raised another stone, hoping for better aim at the man she hated.

"Seize her."

"Stinking corpses of former villagers ambled foreword and grabbed the thrashing woman before she could hurl the stone.

"Bring her to me."

Controlled as puppets by the demon in Credo's charge, the animated dead dragged the woman to stand beside the horse she'd mistakenly struck. Launching itself from Credo's shoulder, a small insect-like demon came down on her shoulder, digging sharp claws into her flesh. With a lightning flash slash, it cut a tiny wound in her cheek. A thin line of blood formed at the slice as the Lasae prepared to gouge out her right eye.

"Trix!" Credo shouted angrily, dark eyes flashing. The tiny demon's head snapped back around with a guilty expression on its insect face. "No. You may not injure her, Trix."

Two small antenae drooped in disappointment. Credo patted his shoulder, and with astounding agility the eight inch demon returned to it's perch to play with Credo's thick, straight black hair.

"You bastard." May seethed, hatred burning in her eyes. Credo was amused by her foolish bravery.

"You would be the wife of one of my new slaves. Why test my patience? You wish to take his place?"

"You can't do this! Let my husband go!" May shouted, trying to break free of decaying hands.

"I am doing it. Obviously you are mistaken."

"You can't do this! It isn't right!"

"It most certainly is right, or someone would stop me. I am more powerful than you, than any of you, therefore I can do what I want with you and everyone in this village. Why is this so hard for you to understand?"

"It's just not right! Let him go, you can't do this!" May started sobbing.

"Why? Why can't I?" Credo asked with a puzzled look. Normally such an outburst would have resulted in the slow torture and eventual death of the offender, but this woman showed a wisp of intelligence and possessed an aristocratic beauty so often lacking in women of the frontier. Credo was intrigued, though he would think nothing of letting Trix dismember her slowly should he lose interest.

"How can you be so cruel? How can you treat other living, feeling beings like this? It's not right. You have to stop." She pulled herself together and held his gaze with teary eyed hatred.

"Why should I? There's nothing to stop me, and that gives me the right to do as I wish. If you possessed such power as mine, then perhaps you would understand that rules and moral concerns don't apply unless they can be enforced by a society. Obviously this is not the case here, for I am far superior to any of you and not subject to the rules you use to govern yourselves. Don't you understand? What is right and wrong has always been determined by those who hold power, and I have decided it right to take these men for my personal army. If I decide you should die, then it is right because I say it is. Accept this and perhaps I will be kinder to your village in the future."

"I have children! Who will take care of them?"

"I'm not going to kill you, that would be counterproductive. You must live to bear more children, to continue your race. It would do me no good if I had no stock from which to select my slaves, now would it?"

"You're sick. You're deranged."

"On the contrary, I'm here, and you're there. This is called long range planning. So many death cults are self defeating. Death without meaning. Your death would have little meaning, but the death of these four men means that your children may live a little longer. These men's transformation into undead form allows many of you to live on and not suffer prolonged, agonizing deaths at the hands of my minions. You see, of course, how this is mutually beneficial."

"Someday you will pay for this, I swear it."

"Somehow I doubt that very much. I serve Annubis, lord of the dead, and my existence does his glory. Should the unfortunate occur, my salvation is secure in the services I have rendered him. You, on the other hand, will simply die and turn back to dust, assuming you are so lucky. I believe I have the better of the two plans."

"If I die, at least my soul is mine and not sold to anyone!"

Credo stroked his smooth chin thoughtfully, pondering her insult.

"You've laid out an interesting challenge, one I don't intend to pass up. In three days the moon will be full and I will perform the ritual that will forever remove any vestige of life that remains in the man you care for. A fate worse than death, so to speak, for he will exist forever as something not quite alive and not quite dead."

"You monster."

"I offer you one chance to save your husband from this fate, should you decide to accept, of course."

"What? Anything!" Hope appeared on her face, much to Credo's inner glee.

"You must make a pact with Annubis and agree to serve him, through me of course, in any means he desires. For the rest of your life."

Her look of hope turned to defeat. Credo's heart leapt with triumph. If she agreed to the terms, he would then force her to assist him in performing the long, extremely painful torture of her husband before the ritual completed and turned her husband into a zombie anyway.

"I, I..." her voice trailed off.

"No need to decide right away. You have three days to choose the fate of your husband, and yourself. I give you my word he will not be harmed, severely, until then. How much do you love him? You do love him, don't you? Do you really hold life so dearly as you claim? You know how to contact me if you decide to save him. Your silence in three days will also be an answer, but then you already know the consequences of that." Credo smiled. "Release her, I don't think she will be so foolish again, will you?'

"N-, No." She stammered, brushing strips of rotten flesh off her released wrists and arms.

"Just in case you start considering a more militant option, several of my minions will remain in your village, to preserve the peace, of course. Do as they ask. Brodkil can get cranky if they don't get their way."

Credo signaled the select minions to stay and turned his horse to leave.

"Three days, my dear, three days."

Morning found the town of Liberty more active than usual. Exchange of power always carried with it the possibility of war breaking out in the streets. Armor clad mercenaries walked the streets in groups of four or five, clearing routes for vehicles and convoys. Storekeepers locked up their shops and hid inside with weapons to defend themselves from looters. Amid the hectic activity children played about, enjoying the heightened level of excitement.

Disguised as a Wilderness Scout, Lieutenant Sorenson made his way through town on a hover cycle as though he'd done it a hundred times before. Hours of studying aerial photographs and intelligence reports allowed him to appear as though he knew exactly where he was going. Nobody stopped to question him or ask that he turn over his heavy energy rifle as per the posted town ordinance. Normally a law enforcement officer would have the newcomer either leave his heavy weapons in his vehicle or have them locked up in the police station until ready to leave. A person carrying enough firepower to level a building with a few blasts wasn't very well trusted within city limits. From experience, however, he knew most frontier people were reluctant to give up their weapons, even for short visits to civilized areas. It would seem suspicious if he complied too readily. Looking around, Mike saw that many citizens wore sidearms as freely as coats and hats. Today, however, there were no official police or town defenders. There was some transition of power going on — that Mike knew — but he needed to learn more.

Outside Watkins' General Store, Mike parked the battered looking hover cycle next to an assortment of other all terrain vehicles. The general store was a three story building with wood paneling over high density, armor plated walls. Twelve foot tall double doors led into a large room filled with tobacco smoke and other foreign scents. Quite a bit warmer than outside, the room was heated by a wood burning stove in the corner. Mike got a few looks from the assortment of patrons gossiping at the counter and around the room. A few stares went to the particle beam rifle across his back, but no one moved to question its presence. Most were armed as well or better.

"What can I get you, friend?" the large man behind the counter asked cheerfully. One of his eyes bulged out suspiciously like a cybernetic implant and judging by the bulk of his right arm, it too was a mechanical replacement. This must be Watkins, Mike concluded, noting with some amusement the owner's Coalition make C-18 side-arm and poorly concealed C-12 stashed behind the counter. Intelligence reported this man had ties to several black market smuggling operations, and the stolen weaponry definitely supported the theory. For the time being Mike would let it slide. He wasn't here to track down illegal gunrunners, he was assessing the potential threat the town posed to the Coalition and determining if it would be safe to house his troops when they arrived. If there was any gossip to be heard and attitude to evaluate, it would be here and in nearby saloons.

Captain Pritchett's unit was to establish a Coalition presence in the area, and hopefully make good relations with the local human population. Strategically the town could be very important for the preservation of Eastern North America, with rumored threats of invasion coming from the risen continent of Atlantis. Having an unofficial outpost in the region would give advance warning of invasion long before it reached Coalition borders.

Greg Merrick's special ops unit was theoretically supposed to keep Pritchett from getting into trouble by covertly removing threats to his operation. Mike knew better, for a secret agenda existed above and beyond the establishment of a remote listening post. Finding and eliminating some of the Coalition's most wanted enemies was what really motivated the approval for such a dangerous assignment. Orders Mike had received just prior to embarking implied the plots went much deeper than crushing a few measly rebels and their leaders. The exchange of power taking place in Liberty could jeopardize both agendas.

"Batteries that fit this," Mike responded gruffly to Watkins and thrust a pair of night vision goggles onto the worn counter top.

"What brand and how many?"

"Whatever comes in one of those green and white packages."

"Comin' right up." Watkins seemed accustomed to uneducated sorts, like most of the rugged, bearded patrons in his establishment.

"And a couple mini-missiles. Scorchers if ya got 'em," Mike added, observing the locked display of weapons for sale at the other end of the store."

"I got 'em. What kind of igniter?"

"The squiggly kind with the three wires that fit in the back. I hadda use my last pair on a demon deer comin' out from Kingsdale. That guys gonna cost me five big ones." Mike spat a wad of tobacco into the copper pot near the counter. He detested tobacco, but had learned the art of chewing and spitting while on a mission in the northern wilderness of Minnesota. Any mountain man with a brain knew you had to chew tobacco to be a man. Mike couldn't wait to get the yellow and brown dye off his teeth and get rid of his dirty disguise once the charade was over.

"You're from Kingsdale?" a short, squat D-Bee with three oversized eyes asked in perfect American. Mike hid a smile at having his bait taken so easily.

"Not to begin with, just passin' through. World a hurt gonna start up there with the Coalition, that's what I say." Mike leaned against the counter and started unwrapping another pungent wad of tobacco.

"Quite a trip from Missouri territory. Made it myself a couple times." A well armed mercenary spoke up from his place by the wood burning stove. "Served in the Kingsdale army for four years. You ever make it down to Arrons Fairground?"

"Was there three days ago. Grabbed me an extra clip for the P7. Pretty cheap, too." Mike patted the stock of his rifle. The Headhunter appeared satisfied with the bearded scout's authenticity and continued smoking a large, hand rolled cigar. The emblem on the Headhunter's body armor matched that of several Mike had seen on vehicles and troops on the way into town. A triangular badge with a skeletal hand gripping a bolt of lightning. In silver lettering at the base were the words "First Strike". The silver bar on the mercenary's armor indicated some type of paramilitary rank. Mike pressed ahead with his information gathering.

"What's all the fuss about outside? Somebody spot a Splugorth slaver?"

"Zenjori and his 'Army of the New Order' are gettin' their butts kicked outta town, that's what," the mercenary answered.

"Good riddance," a tall creature slobbered in agreement.

"I'm surprised they're leaving so peacefully. I expected more trouble." Watkins placed a package of "Super Cells" next to Mike's goggles.

"Yeah, they're just scared we'll kick their tails, that's all." The mercenary blew a ring of smoke in contempt for the former town defenders.

"Still, I'm surprised Zenjori took responsibility for the crimes his men were accused of committing. He even assured us they would be disciplined and he would turn over military responsibility to your band, Aken," the three eyed D-Bee argued.

"Don't get me wrong, I wasn't keen about takin' on the Army of the New Order here in town, but Zenjori knew he'd lose, that's why he backed off." Aken blew another smoke ring.

"It will all be over and they'll be gone in a few hours. Then it's back to business as usual." Watkins and Aken shared a look that didn't take a genius to figure out.

"Those guys won't twist anyone's arms here in Liberty again, not if we can help it," Aken boasted as the store doors swung slowly open. The shadow of a giant four-armed cyborg fell over Mike and the store owner. Two red eyes inset in a vaguely skull-like metal head scanned the room with intimidation. Not a sound followed Drake's unannounced presence. Aken made no move for a weapon, instead calmly whispering into his headset and readjusting the ear piece.

Zenjori Suka's second in command stood in the doorway and stared at the member of the rival mercenary company. Fear didn't control the Headhunter, but he was obviously distressed by the 9 foot Full Conversion Cyborg. Backup was on the way, but if Drake decided anybody in the room should die, there would be little even an armored squad could do to stop him. Nobody wanted to mess with an ex-Coalition combat cyborg, especially one with a price on his head.

"How would you like me to remove your bionic arm for you. No charge," Drake rumbled threateningly at Aken.

"C'mon, Drake, you know better than to start trouble. Not now," Watkins urged. Hydraulics whined and the floor creaked with each step the cyborg took towards the counter. Mike found himself standing next to one of the top targets on his list, a former combat cyborg gone bad. Mike had no intention of revealing his identity.

Drake slapped a universal credit card down on the counter, making the entire wooden frame and metal reinforcement shudder from the impact.

"I want to buy all the mini-missiles, explosives, and ordnance you have."

"Sorry, Drake, all I've got is a dozen frags and a pair of A.P.'s. If you want anything else yer gonna hafta go —"

"Don't lie to me. If you lie to me it will make me mad." Drake leaned closer, metal eyebrows meeting in a menacing scowl. "I want all of your stock, even the stuff in your vault."

"This man has already purchased most of my stock." Watkins motioned to Mike and gave him an almost pleading look.

"Tough. You can refund his money. I'll give you 25% more than he was paying." Drake glared at Mike, a growling sound coming from his closed metal jaw. No wonder the bounty on this renegade was almost a million credits, Mike thought.

"What can I say?" Watkins shrugged at Mike. "Credits are credits."

"The rest of you drooling idiots listen up." Drake commanded attention. "As much as I hate this sniveling little town, it's only fair I give you warning. Our spies have confirmed a large Coalition army is headed this way, and their lead forces should be here in one or two days."

"So what?" Aken countered.

"This lead group will try and win your trust, all the while plotting against you and waiting for the main army to arrive. They might even try bringing in small groups at a time so you won't notice, until there's so many that not even the mighty 'First Strike' can do anything about it. Then you will obey Coalition laws and be under Coalition rule. Everybody in this room who isn't 100% human will be taken out and slaughtered, along with all their family and friends. Those of you that manage to escape will be hunted down like animals and killed while you sleep, and those aiding your escape will be executed without trial. I know. I was once one of them. What they will do to this town is nothing compared to a few rowdy soldiers from the Army of the New Order. When your women and children start disappearing and the dead start piling up, then you will know I was right."

Silence followed until clanking metal feet sounded outside the store as two power armor units arrived to ensure the peace.

"That's a load of stuff and you know it, Drake," Aken spoke up, braver now.

"Wait and see," Drake replied in a crisp metallic tone.

"The Coalition are a bunch of bigoted fools, but even they aren't stupid enough to pull anything out here where they can't have an armored battalion at their beck and call. They don't make any offensive unless they're sure they'll win, and you know it. If the Coalition wants to send a force out here, fine, let them, just so they don't start nothin' Maybe they'll even kick some D-Bee tail, no offense meant to those present here, of course." Aken grinned at the unhappy lot of Dimensional Beings around the room.

"Just remember that when your friends start dying off," Drake warned, waving a metal fist back and forth.

Mike waited patiently for the transaction to take place, curious to see how well-armed his opponents were going to be. Nearly a million credits and an ATV changed hands. Mike was worried. He spent some more time gabbing in the store before leaving, not wanting to attract suspicion. After a tour of saloons and bars, Mike decided to remain in Liberty until Pritchett safely arrived. Political unrest could shift the balance of power as quickly as a gun, and Mike needed to be certain that the powers to be weren't going to be aimed at the Coalition convoy.

"All vehicles and personnel are accounted for, Suka San," Drake reported to the short Asian man who commanded the mercenary army.

"Same goes here." A bald, Partial Conversion Cyborg sauntered up, heavy plasma cannon draped over his broad shoulders. Zenjori Suka looked at his two commanders and nodded, then turned to acknowledge his least trusted sub-commander, a winged humanoid with a horned head and glowing yellow eyes.

"Torrak, where were the Coalition forces last you knew?" Zenjori spoke with a smooth, controlled, yet demading voice. Torrak's hatred of humans was no secret, and the rebel leader had made it clear more than once who held the power and who did not.

"My familiar hasn't reported their condition after last night's attack, but I believe they have survived and are one or two days away." Torrak's guttural voice hurt the well trained ear.

"Timing couldn't be much more ideal. Since my former benefactor in the Coalition has ignored my warnings, we will use this opportunity to keep the Coalition out of this region for some time to come."

"I hope you have some kinda plan, Suka San, cuz now we're on a lake in Feb without a paddle." Kruno swung the heavy rifle down and rested the barrel over one metal arm. Zenjori shifted his weight, beginning to be irked by the commander of "Carnivore" squad.

"I always have a plan."

"Of course. I still don't know why we hadda leave. We coulda taken First Strike with only suffering 80% losses and 60% loss of gear. Maybe even better cuz Donnovan wouldn't commit his unit to a full scale offensive with civilians around."

"Very good, Kruno, I see you're thinking with your plasma rifle again," Zenjori snapped, then changed to a more understanding tone. "You're a good commander, Kruno, I don't doubt your abilities in a fight, but it was your men that put us in this situation to begin with. I was discreet in my dealings with potential troublemakers in town, while your men brutally murdered five people and took liberties with their wives. If we had stayed and resisted the townspeople in replacing us with First Strike, it would have been a bloodbath. When it was over, whatever was left couldn't stand up to a platoon of Coalition foot troops, much less a combined mechanized and infantry assault. So, in the interest of self preservation I decided we'd follow a more intelligent course of action. Rather than engage in full scale combat, which likely we would lose, we pull out gracefully. When the Coalition arrives, that is when we begin our offensive. Not a frontal assault, like I'm sure Drake would suggest, but surgical strikes made to look like Coalition or First Strike actions. We polarize sides and feed fears until First Strike and the Coalition fight each other or one side leaves. The weakened survivor will be loathed by the general populace of Liberty thanks to some well laid plans and carefully executed maneuvers. Liberty will beg us to return, and our terms will be much more demanding this time. Patience will pay off in the end. In the meantime, we entrench and gather strength. The Coalition is too far out for reinforcements, where as we can always recruit a steady supply of warriors who detest the Coalition."

"Sorry, Suka San, I wasn't tryin' ta knock ya. Sounds like a hellaciously good plan to me." Kruno kicked the barrel and swung the rifle back to his shoulders.

"In a few moments we will know if we have other powerful allies to assist us." Zenjori looked to the man materializing at the edge of a ley line 150 feet away. Colnae wore ornate blue, green, and gold trimmed clothing that fit his slender form perfectly. A well trimmed goatee and impeccable grooming made the Line Walker appear more like a playboy than a practitioner of magic attuned to the surging lines of power encircling the globe. By the look on Colnae's face as he approached, Zenjori concluded the meeting with Colnae's Federation Lord hadn't gone well.

"Colnae, my companion, what news do you bring from Valdor's castle?"

"Valdor is dead." The mage's features hardened even more. "He was killed in a wizards' duel with Lord Anyon, and the help he promised died with him," he confessed bitterly.

"Is there nobody else in the Federation you can turn to?"

"Nobody of consequence, even if I wasn't considered 'ronin'." Colnae spat the words out. "Valdor left his apprentice Chalra in command before he perished, and she now controls his army and domain. She won't help us. She's not even a Federation Lord!"

"Perhaps she would be willing to help us strike a blow at the Coalition," Zenjori offered.

"I was treated very rudely by Chalra's warrior witch, Sahara, and told that if I ever set foot in her castle or nexus I would die, very unpleasantly. Chalra refused me audience and left orders that none of her minions should aid or in any way protect us. The mighty Federation of Magic won't lift a finger against her because she has the favor of powerful allies in Atlantis. There will be no aid from the Federation of magic, none officially anyway. Sorry, Suka San." Colnae apologized bitterly.

Zenjori closed his eyes momentarily, quickly readjusting his plans to exclude aid from North America's most powerful allegiance of wizards. At last he turned back to Torrak. The Gromek's mouth was twisted into a smug, self-satisfied grin.

"I assume you have the ability to summon and control legions from other dimensions, being the powerful Torrak of the Gromek, do you not?"

"If I did, I wouldn't be here with you." Torrak ground sharp teeth together. "I am capable of controlling a number of creatures, but too many will sap my strength and leave me vulnerable to more rebellious minions. A few powerful creatures under my control are better than legions. What do you wish me to do?"

"Legions would suit us well, but if you can summon up a few creatures as shock troops to throw into Coalition lines, the confusion might allow us opportunity to strike them hard."

"If I wish to. It would require time."

"Time we have plenty of. Begin at once, Colnae will remain with you to keep you aware of activities along the ley line while you prepare. You are familiar with our primary fallback point, we will be setting our base camp there."

"What, exactly, do you want me to summon?" Torrak tried to test Zenjori's arcane lore in front of his men. Zenjori just smiled.

"Be creative," he smiled warmly. "Whatever things you summon will be at your beck and call, so have fun. The real enjoyment begins when you turn them loose on our mutual enemies, the Coalition."

Crashing timber grabbed Kro-Mar's attention as he flapped lazily in a Southward direction. Keen ears picked up the sound of a falling tree somewhere nearby, and since Kro-Mar had nothing better to do, he decided to investigate. Rows of black spikes whistled in the wind as the Great Horned Dragon glided above the tree tops.

Several suitcase-sized pouches hung from numerous straps on his green scaled body, their contents a variety of junk he'd collected in the past few months. A CD vid player, a Techno-Wizard modified mini-missile, two hundred feet of parachute cord, a collection of compact disks, and other trinkets Kro-Mar intended to play with once he reached his lair in southern Virginia.

His little exploration trip was memorably horrific, and rated the worst in 34 years. Maybe in six or seven months he would set off on another adventure, a much better one to be certain. Life in general was full of excitement for the young hatchling.

Finding a small valley where humans were working steadily on constructing large log cabins, Kro-Mar circled four or five times, all the while waiting for one of them to look up and scream. It was so amusing to watch them scurry to their fragile little shelters, as though the wood enclosures could actually stop a mighty dragon like himself from reaching them. It was even more fun when he would rattle their homes and set fire to various objects in their little villages, as if he couldn't just mash them inside their homes without half trying. This was all very much like a child stirring up an anthill just to see what would happen. After his recent experiences with humans, he knew some of them had a nasty sting. Kro-Mar exercised a little caution before engaging in one of his favorite tactics — shadow passing.

This game could be played in several different ways, the shortest version was to pass his shadow over a group of humans and then slowly angle back in their direction just when their terror started turning to relief. The newest revision employed the use of simple invisibility magic and could be drawn out so long as he had power to maintain the invocation. Pass the shadow, then turn invisible, wait awhile, then pass the shadow and turn invisible again. Great fun, especially when the people on the ground got nervous and called others out to confirm the strange phenomenon. Appearing on the ground in their midst had fantastic results.

Opting for the short version, Kro-Mar started his terror run by swooping low past a group of humans dragging a log from the woods. Oddly enough they didn't seem to notice. Perhaps it was because they were so involved in their work, Kro-Mar reasoned, and came around for a closer pass. Evidently these particular humans were dumber than they looked. How could they possibly fail to notice a 50 foot long dragon with nearly a hundred foot wingspan pass just forty feet above them? None of the workers appeared to have noticed his presence. This was puzzling.

Landing between the row of four cabins and eight humans dragging the log, Kro-Mar ensured the terror would begin. Instead the slowing humans came to a stop, running into Kro-Mar's giant clawed fist. Eight glassy-eyed stares looked up at the fearsome dragon. Kro-Mar gave his most terrible roar. Unblinking eyes continued to stare up at him.

Leaning back on his long thrashing tail, Kro-Mar was perplexed at the freak behavior of these human peasants. Didn't they understand the equation? He was a powerful dragon and they were frail humans. They were supposed to be scared!

Reasoning they just needed more direct persuasion, Kro-Mar flicked a giant finger at the closest human, not hard enough to kill but with enough force to knock the peasant off his feet. Apparently unhurt, the human simply got up and waited patiently for Kro-Mar to get out of the way.

"Give me your valuables and I might spare your miserable lives," Kro-Mar rumbled. They looked around at each other with puzzled expressions then returned to their blank stares.

"Give me your valuables or I'll eat all of you!" He threatened. More exchanges of incomprehension and mindless stares.

These couldn't possibly be normal humans, Kro-Mar determined. Maybe this was a lobotomy colony or an inbreeding farm. No, Kro-Mar ran over more plausible alternatives. It had to be the work of magic. Focusing closely on the body of the person he'd just thumped, Kro-Mar could see a faint amber glow he wasn't familiar with. A few mumbled words expanded his vision to see a spectrum of magic and other psychic emanations. Very much to his surprise, the auras of the humans around him gave contradictory testimony. The usual spark of life found in humans was completely gone, replaced with a fluctuating amber glow. All of them were dead, yet brought brought back to a pseudo-existence by some type of magic. Kro-Mar laughed, feeling relieved that his macho dragonly image wasn't failing. These were nothing more than zombies.

Curiosity took over, and Kro-Mar suddenly felt the urge to see exactly what a zombie was all about. Did they feel pain? Did a zombie come back to "life" after it was destroyed? Did zombies taste good? How far could a zombie be thrown? Testing one of his theories,

Kro-Mar snatched the closest undead and chucked it as far as he could. The zombie wailed as it flew headlong through tree branches and bounced off tree trunks. Sure enough, when its flight ended and it stopped tumbling, the zombie got up no worse for wear. This was going to be fun, thought Kro-Mar.

Soon the air was filled with the sounds of flying zombies, their cries of protest simply making the new game all the more fun. Kro-Mar giggled as a zombie from the construction crew lumbered over with a dull ax. Giggling like a badly tuned diesel truck, Kro-Mar raised a giant foot and smashed the zombie into the soft topsoil. Lifting his foot slightly, Kro-Mar peeked underneath and found to his delight a new arrangement of body parts. The engine idled louder.

Craning his neck around his wing, Kro-Mar breathed a streak of flame at the closest log cabin. The partially constructed cabin disintegrated instantly. Terrified zombies fled the blaze only to be torched by Kro-Mar's flame breath. Finally, Kro-Mar thought, he'd found something zombies were afraid of.

Quickly growing bored of flaming the fleeing undead, Kro-Mar snatched up a tree trunk and began swinging it like a golf club .

"Fore!" He shouted as a zombie sailed for the "green" on a nearby rise. Great fun. Semi-mobile golf balls. Leaping from zombie to zombie, Kro-Mar practiced his long drive, failing to notice Lord Credo and his demons arrive at the charred remains of the log cabin.

"Stop this!" Credo shouted in perfect Dragonese. Kro-Mar froze mid-swing, head snapping around with a guilty look much like a child caught launching bottle rockets into the neighbor's chicken coop. Turning around, Kro-Mar trudged back to the man on horseback and his demon troops. No mere Elf was going to tell the magnificent Kro-Mar what to do.

"How dare you interrupt me!" He roared, coming to a stop forty feet from the mage. Brodkil demons readied their weapons but made no move to attack. Kro-Mar started wondering what he'd gotten into.

"Look what you've done. It's going to take days to get back on schedule. You must compensate me for my loss," Credo demanded.

"Be quiet or I'll eat you!" Kro-Mar threatened.

"I'm so scared." Credo responded sarcastically.

"You should never have invoked my ire! I am the most powerful dragon you will ever meet, foolish mortal!" Kro-Mar paused for effect. "I am the great Kramer!"

As soon as he said the words, Kro-Mar felt incredibly foolish. A stupid human once mispronounced his name, and now in his moment of glory, Kro-Mar repeated the mistake. How could that happen? Several Brodkil snickered, others laughed audibly. The corners of Credo's mouth switched upward with a devious smile.

"The great Kramer, did you say?" Credo rubbed his chin. "Sounds vaguely familiar."

"Kramer the magnificent!" Kro-Mar dug himself in deeper. His slip of the tongue made him look incredibly stupid, but he couldn't back down now.

"Ohhh, Kramer the Magnificent! Destroyer of log cabins and bane of the zombies," Credo taunted with false sincerity.

"And don't you ever forget it! I can and do as I please. Teach me how to make these zombies and I might spare your miserable life."

"Foolish hatchling, I grow tired of your games." Credo's expression turned deadly serious.

"You've been warned! Don't make me do bad things to you!"

"Apparently you have no inkling of who you are dealing with. Hand over four of your teeth and I might consider allowing you to continue your existence a while longer."

"If you want four of my teeth, come and get them yourself." Kro-Mar felt magic energy pulse through his veins in preparation for combat. There was no way an Elven mage and a dozen demons could be a match for his command of magic and fierce temper. They just didn't realize it yet.

Credo smiled and slowly dismounted.

"I thought you'd never ask. Seize him!"

Brodkil released battle cries and leapt forward without fear. Before they reached Kro-Mar he was gone, leaping ten feet behind Credo. Kro-Mar loved it when a plan came together, even when it was something he came up with on the spur of the moment. But wait, the Elven mage was still speaking, turning slowly to direct the complex spell. Bracing for impact, Kro-Mar quickly recited an incantation, invisible barriers forming a field around him. The flow of words from Credo ceased and Kro-Mar felt a a strange sense of being affected by the spell, but not sure how or what to fight off. No matter. The mage would be dead shortly.

Resorting to cave man tactics, Kro-Mar swung the tree trunk he still held like giant club. Kro-Mar struck himself in the foot, splintering his weapon and eliciting a cry of surprise. Credo just smiled, aggravating the dragon further.

The words to Kro-Mar's spell flowed out in rapid stream, but suddenly the last phrase didn't come out right, results fizzling in a pop of expended magic energy. Generally worried, Kro-Mar frantically tried to remember the correct invocation, but his mind kept stumbling over itself in the process.

Brodkil swarmed over him, dropping his magic barrier in seconds with their mix of hand-held and energy weapons. Thrashing about at them, Kro-Mar only succeeded in tripping on his own tail, ramming a charcoal timber up his nose from a burnt cabin. Sneezing fire, he choked on the cloud of smoke and dust that followed. Something was terribly wrong.

As his thick scales gave way to wounds, Kro-Mar realized it was time to make his departure. He could always come back for revenge later. Envisioning a place he'd seen two miles away, he attempted to teleport there. Nothing happened. Again he tried, but his natural abilities seemed unresponsive. Now there really was something wrong.

High frequency blades penetrated muscle and tendon, and sections of green scales disappeared in clouds of vaporized molecules. Anger took over and Brodkil sailed away as Kro-Mar went berserk. Credo backed away, more afraid of being hit by a flying 9 foot tall demon than any attack the dragon could intentionally muster. When the red haze cleared, Kro-Mar stood in a circle of hesitant demons waiting to attack him again. Escape was the only recourse left to the humiliated dragon.

Gracefully leaping over the line of advancing demons, Kro-Mar tripped on the closest one and slammed into the earth. This was not a pleasant experience. One minute he was master of the universe and the next, a bungling clod with mashed potatoes for brains. The stinging pain resumed.

Thrashing his way free again, the hatchling dragon took flight on tattered wing and bleeding body. Ion blasts followed his ascent, but Kro-Mar couldn't recall the words of his protective spells. Flapping as hard as his tired wings could go, he fled the scene of his disgrace until a small hill blocked the line of fire. Safe from the weapon fire, Kro-Mar made a flawless Albatross landing.

Kro-Mar spat more foliage from his mouth and tried to correct his spread-eagle position at the end of a long furrow. Suddenly the words to his spells were crystal clear. This was not one of Kro-Mar's better days.

Chapter 5

Blood drenched the soil outside the burning huts. Bodies lay in place where they died trying to escape the endless onslaught from Coalition weapons. Sergio dropped lower and kicked a fleeing D-Bee with the foot of his SAMAS. Brains splashed over the black finish and misted the air behind him.

Slowing to a complete stop, the Coalition RPA touched down and targeted a mob of D-Bee peasants that escaped the foot troops' advance. Selecting single round discharge on his rail gun, Sergio ripped holes through the running peasants with each metal projectile. There was no need to waste ammunition on a village of unarmed D-Bees. They were relatively easy to exterminate.

"Merrick to Pritchett, over," Greg called the mission commander over the comm. The lines of smoke rising from the distant village could only mean one thing. Greg feared the worst.

"Pritchett, go ahead Lieutenant."

"We're finished crossing the river, sir, and I'd like to know what's going on up ahead, sir."

"Nothing we can't handle without you, Lieutenant," Pritchett responded in friendly tones. "Some of my men were fired on when they made contact with that village of D-Bees your man checked out. Don't worry, it's being taken care of."

"I was under the impression the village wasn't hostile."

"I was too, like your man first indicated, but unfortunately my men came under attack when they went to confirm. You never can trust D-Bees, always with some sinister intentions, even when they don't appear to. Safest to take the offensive first. We don't have to worry about this village attacking us again."

"Sir!" Darren's voice sounded over the comm. "They're slaughtering defenseless people!"

"As you were, Private Corley," Pritchett responded angrily. "They're not people, and they brought it on themselves. Maintain your current patrol until ordered to do otherwise."

Darren choked back the "up yours, sir" and simply disobeyed orders. Flying low to the treetops, he throttled up to 300 mph and aimed his exoskeleton for the lines of smoke. He didn't care if it was just another mass of D-Bees being slaughtered, it wouldn't be the first time he'd been around such actions. This time, however, it just didn't seem right, plus he had a pretty good idea who made up the story of being fired on, too.

The sight that met his eyes was sickening. Four Coalition soldiers and a Psi-Stalker casually walked through the burning village shooting everything that moved, sometimes only maiming then moving on. Those fleeing for their lives were being cut down in rows by SAM 612.

"SAM 15, you are in violation of a direct order! Back off or suffer the consequences," Pritchett ordered from the safety of his skull walker. Darren refused to respond, instead cutting velocity and tackling Sergio's SAMAS from behind.

"You're dead! You're dead!"

The wrestling match carried both SAMAS through the wall of a home. Fighting his way free of falling beams, Sergio slammed SAM 15 in the chest with his C-40. The barrel of Darren's rail gun knocked SAM 612 back down, tip pressing against Sergio's faceplate.

"Back off or I'll cut you down." Sergio snarled.

"Go ahead, pull the trigger." Darren shifted his weight to pin Sergio's free arm to the ground. "All yer gonna do is scratch my SAM, I'll blast your brains out the back of your skull."

"Sir, Captain Pritchett! I'm being attacked by SAM 15," Sergio called his commander.

"SAM 15, you are relieved of duty! Return immediately and surrender your SAMAS!"

"Darren. Cool it," Greg instructed. "Get back on your patrol. Right now."

"Yes, sir," Darren acknowledged the chain of command and pulled his weapon from Sergio's face. SAM 612 slid on its maneuver jets while Darren gave it a swift kick in the groin before leaving the scene of slaughter.

"Merrick to Captain Pritchett. Perhaps it would be better to discuss this incident off the air."

"Lieutenant Merrick. I'm holding you responsible for the actions of yours."

"Of course, sir, as you are responsible for the actions of your, men."

"What's that supposed to mean, Lieutenant?" Pritchett refused to take the matter off the air.

"I'll discuss it with you in person, not over the radio."

"Fine," Pritchett responded after a long pause. "Agreed. Come aboard Skull 191 immediately. You have some things to explain.

Dropping through the top hatch of Skull Walker 191, Greg discovered the Captain calmly shining the chrome on his dress armor. Greg's SAMAS waited outside on the ground.

"Leave us," Pritchett ordered the robot's crew, and didn't speak another word until they were gone.

"Captain," Greg acknowledged the higher ranking officer.

"Your SAM 15 is way out of line, Lieutenant, but that's only a symptom, not the seat of the problem."

"SAM 15 was out of line, yes, but respectfully, sir, SAM 612 and Beta Fire Squad are jeopardizing our mission by engaging in unprovoked attacks on unidentified parties."

"They were fired on."

"They didn't even need to go to the village, it was already scouted out and deemed to be of no threat to our present course. By assaulting a non-military target, your men jeopardize our mission objectives of establishing pro-Coalition sentiment in the surrounding area. Not only that, but your men risk incurring retaliation by our enemies. Sir." Greg put it as diplomatically as he could.

"I'll decide how I go about my mission objectives, not you, Lieutenant. I've been very patient with you and your unit, up until now. Your discipline is almost non-existent, and your actions and attitude are questionable. I realize your men have seen some deep field action, but that doesn't excuse them from the rules of conduct. We are on a mission to establish a Coalition presence, and part of that is projecting an image uniform with Coalition standards. By the time we reach Liberty you will have your unit cleaned up and be sure their weapons and armor pass inspection. You will remove all non-Coalition armament, and make sure they only display Coalition armor and equipment. And you need a haircut, Lieutenant."

"Sir, I'm the one who issued those weapons to my men, and there's a good reason for all of them. Don't forget, our presence here is also to eliminate threats to your objectives. In battles with magic users we discovered kinetic and explosive weaponry more reliable and effective, therefore the issue of imported Triax made projection firearms."

"We're not running an advertisement campaign for Triax."

"And my unit was never sent out here to parade around making friends, Sir. We are here to fight, not dress up. Low profile. If you want I can call up our specified duties and—"

"I know what the computer says, Lieutenant," Pritchett responded irritably.

"We fight, you take the credit. We clean up, you do the show."

"Very well, then I would appreciate you not ever questioning how I choose to display the Coalition image. The village suppression is justified under the terms of my orders."

"Put it in your report, sir, I'll put my interpretation in mine," Greg flashed back with determination in his grey eyes. For a moment Captain Pritchett felt intimidated. He'd heard stories before. No backing down.

"Private Corley is relieved of duty until we reach Liberty, at which time he will be placed under arrest until a field court-martial can be conducted."

"Respectfully, sir, if you press that issue, I will fight you on it as far and hard as it takes."

"Are you threatening me, Lieutenant?"

"Of course not, sir. We're out here in the field a very long way from Coalition territory. I have a very well-trained and experienced unit capable of taking on a force well over three times its own size. My men protect their own, as I do. You figure it out, sir." Greg stared back and steeped his fingers. The captain appeared on the verge of losing his temper, but after what seemed like minutes his composure softened.

"Reports of this incident will, as you pointed out, be filed and radioed to HQ. I expect your report will include the disciplinary actions brought against Private Corley."

"Of course. There will be disciplinary actions, as I feel appropriate."

"I have friends in the Coalition military, Lieutenant, friends who have power over many things. You are dismissed. Have your unit take point. If there's anything out there to fight, your well-trained unit should be the first into combat."

"I'm glad we've reached an understanding, sir."

"Situations change, Lieutenant, much faster than you can possibly realize."

Ominous dark clouds brought dusk faster than expected. Troops cleared firing lanes around the man-made clearing atop a small bluff in preparation for the night. Lisa Anderson sat at her communications console in Skull 41 hoping to receive some word from Lieutenant Sorenson. Finding a defendable site had been left up to Pritchett's 1st Lieutenant, Parker Goldstein. The mountainous terrain and dense foliage meant an enemy stronghold could be over the next hill or hidden nearby and nothing but an up-close foot patrol would find it. At Greg's insistence, certain additional precautions were being taken to ensure the camp was impenetrable and the coffee well guarded.

"Coming in," Brian Adams announced from the open top hatch.

"Oh, hi Brian. What do you need?" Lisa felt a little uncomfortable with Brian in such close quarters. For a time he'd been overtly infatuated with her, and when she started dating Mike Sorenson he'd become very cold and distant. The red haired officer dropped down beside her.

"Cowboy discharged an entire canister on that stupid worm thing last night. I just need to stick the canister in the charging unit." He squirmed to one side and slotted the energy canister in the nuclear powered charger. On his way back out he hesitated as if he had something else to say. Finally he edged back inside and sat in the pilot's seat.

"Everything running good?"

"Like new." Lisa spoke without looking at him. She hated the hurt look she'd seen in his eyes the last time they'd talked. "Dave's been complaining about the balance being off, probably because you installed that CR-6 missile launcher on the back. Don't worry about it, it's just Dave being Dave."

"I told him it would handle differently, but he said he wanted the extra firepower."

"You did a good job with it. I couldn't even tell a difference in the ride."

They sat, the awkwardness growing with each passing moment.

"Have you heard anything from Sorenson yet?"

"Just one transmission that it was clear for us to go ahead as planned."

"Oh." Brian fidgeted with the fuse box under the pilot's control panel.

"Hey, this is new." Lisa sat up straight and readjusted her headset.

"What?"

"Somebody is hailing us on UF-12. There's a man asking for Lieutenant Merrick by name." Lisa got a puzzled look on her face.

"Find out who he is."

"This is Coalition advance recon unit Edward 5. Who am I responding to?" Lisa's blue eyes narrowed when she received the reply.

"What's going on?"

"He says his name is Sir Renfield and he's requesting permission to approach our camp and speak to Lieutenant Merrick or the current commander. How did he know Lieutenant Merrick was here?"

"No way!" Brian spoke in disbelief. "That's the Cyber-Knight from Youngstown! You remember, the one that convinced the lieutenant to use my idea about the ore transport."

"I remember you didn't like him very much."

"I didn't trust him, there's a difference. He had those magic users with him. How do I talk to him?" Brian started pushing buttons on Lisa's console. She slapped his hands away and activated the compartment audio system.

"Sir Renfield, this is Lieutenant Adams. We met at Youngstown. What do you need?"

"How are you Lieutenant Adams? It's nice to hear from you. Are you the commander of your expedition?" The strong voice sounded sincere.

"No, but I can relay your request to the chain of command if you tell me what this is about." Brian was already pushing the rules, better not push any farther.

"I'll cut to the chase then. A village north of you is being terrorized by the Federation of Magic. I have with me an individual from that village who is requesting Coalition intervention to free her and her village. She is human, as is most of her village," Sir Renfield added.

"Stay on this frequency, I'll contact my C.O. and relay your message. Lieutenant Adams out."

"Thank you, Lieutenant."

"Gotta fly. Keep monitoring and keep me updated on Charlie pre-set plus 4," Brian ordered and started back out the hatch.

"Yes sir!" Lisa emphasized the sir and saluted.

"What's that supposed to mean?" Brian gave her a puzzled look.

"For a second there you actually sounded like an officer." She winked.

"What do you know, I actually did." Brian grinned. "How did that happen?" He left the Skull Walker much happier than when he entered.

Captain Pritchett's hand slammed itself flat against the surface of the small meeting table. May jerked slightly, startled by the commander's sudden action. The bright lamp above their heads illuminated the meeting in harsh contrast of light and dark. Coalition officers stood watching the meeting between the captain and the peasant, wondering why the Cyber-Knight behind the fair-haired woman even thought the Coalition would seriously consider taking action this far from C.S. territory. Pritchett brushed away the dead insect beneath his hand and glanced up at the mercury lamp with annoyance.

"Damned bugs can't tell the difference between a light and the moon."

"Please, sir," May continued. "I know my village isn't near Coalition lands and we don't have resources to offer in return, but we are suffering at the hands of your enemies, the Federation of Magic. If you could just kill one man and destroy his small following, it would save so many lives." She leaned forward and reached for the captain's hand. Pritchett casually withdrew his hand and engaged in an old habit of "cracking" his knuckles, though his bionic hands hardly responded as his flesh and bone once did. The red gash on her cheek was no doubt from ill treatment at the hands of some murderous fiend, he thought, and it really was too bad he couldn't risk his men and equipment to help her. The village was just too far away from the Coalition and not close enough to Liberty to be of strategic value. It was a horrid shame that humans were suffering, but he wasn't prepared to take on the Federation of Magic, even a small portion of the evil guild. It was just too risky. At last he placed both hands on the table and gave his final answer.

"I'm sincerely sorry, May, that your village has fallen victim to the inhuman treatment of the Federation. Were it closer to Coalition borders I can assure you that kind of treatment would never happen. Unfortunately it would only be worse for you if we were to come in, guns blazing. Even if we managed to destroy this evil Credo fellow and his demons, there would be others from the Federation that would come and kill all of you once we were gone. We wouldn't be helping you by aiding you right now, we could be condemning your village to a fate worse than you already have. I hope you understand, we can't risk our lives in your dispute with the Federation of Magic, and thereby ensure your death and ours. Life is too precious for that. I'm sorry." Captain Pritchett shook his head sincerely.

"What if we're willing to take our chances? It can't get much worse for us," May protested.

"I'm sorry, but Coalition aid would only escalate an already treacherous situation. Perhaps, in a few weeks, we could hire a mercenary company to defend you or sell you arms. Perhaps you could convince this noble Cyber-Knight to raise an army on your behalf?" Pritchett waved his hand at Sir Renfield.

"I have already pledged my support."

"See there, all is not lost," Pritchett smiled wide and pushed his folding chair back to stand. "I hope things turn out well for you."

"You're not going to help her village?" Sir Renfield asked pointedly.

"I would think a Cyber-Knight would understand," Pritchett shot back. "I thought you were supposed to protect the innocent, not endanger them."

Sir Renfield let the response on the tip of his tongue pass unsaid. It would only make a tense situation worse.

"Come, May, You've done what you could and it's a long way back to your home."

Fighting back tears of disappointment, May rose and held her head high. The looks she received from many Coalition personnel told her not all agreed with their commander's judgement, but there wasn't any indication they were willing to defy him. They all knew the Cyber-Knight's pledge was genuine, but one Knight and a handful of warriors couldn't stand up to a Lord of the Federation.

Riding on her horse beside Sir Renfield's Samson power armor, May finally broke down and cried.

Delwin's wooden flute provided a musical background for the sounds of war preparation. Targo heaved on his giant ammo and power backpack, repeatedly checking the laser targeting on his rail gun against the HUD protruding from the side of his helmet. Sir Renfield and Mr. Kent went over last minute checks of a weapon arsenal laid out on a thick cloth. The discordant music seemed to aggravate the level of pre-battle excitement.

"Delwin, please stop doing that!" Renfield demanded through clenched teeth.

"Always with the negative waves," Delwin stopped to shake his head sadly. "Always with the-"

"Please, anything but the positive-negative wave stuff. Please!" Sir Renfield pleaded.

The sharp overtones resumed.

Stepping from the Mountaineer in full battle regalia Cyndiara was a sight to behold. Curls of bright red hair fell down the back of her polished plate and chain-style armor. Under her arm she carried an ornately decorated helm. From her shoulder she unslung a menacing projectile rifle and placed it next to the other weapons for final inspection.

"So what did he say?" Mr Kent grunted without looking up from his ion rifle.

"Van said, and I quote, 'If they want to die they can do it just fine without me.'" Cyndiara spoke haughtily.

"Van not help?" Targo asked incredulously.

"Van think we die!" Delwin screamed, barely startling the group. "Van think we die! Die, die, die! Ahhh! Help! Aunti Em, Aunti Em, Van think we die!" he shouted from a tree limb. Nobody paid the bizarre outbursts much attention any more. After weeks in his company, nothing he said or did came as a shock anymore.

"I think I'm going to have a little discussion with Van." Sir Renfield set his jaw and straightened his broad shoulders. A small hand fell on his arm. Anja looked up at him with a pleading look.

"Maybe I should talk to him."

"No, he'd only say something rude just to hurt you. This is a task for me." He gently removed her hand and stomped into the ATV with intent to verbally rip Van apart. The Techno-Wizard sat engrossed in some new modification to a Coalition make C-14.

"What's this I hear about you staying behind?" Sir Renfield chose the blunt approach.

Van never looked up.

"Sounds like you have a pretty good grasp of the situation."

"You're willing to stand by and do nothing while innocent people suffer?"

"Willingness has nothing to do with it. Suffering happens." Van's head snapped up and anger burned in his dark eyes. "As a matter of fact, I've seen more suffering than you may ever witness. It wasn't willingness that made me walk away. It was the simple fact that nothing I could do was going to make one bit of difference in the end. If I quested for every hopeless cause I could find I would be dead, and the cause would still be hopeless and people would still suffer."

"Sometimes you have to try anyway."

"Jeez, David, do you have any idea what you're getting yourself into?" Van's posture softened. "You're outnumbered better than 5 to one by creatures that could kill you all by themselves, there's an army of dead things waiting for the command to rip you limb from limb, and not to mention a Federation Lord who could take all of us on his worst day!"

"I'm not afraid, are you?" Sir Renfield shot back.

"Yeah! Even if by some freak chance you win, all you've done is just tick off the Federation. Does that sound like something smart to you!?"

"It doesn't matter because some things have to be done regardless of the consequences. If everyone had your attitude where would this world be? Overrun by evil and darkness. You can't just hope somebody else will do the right thing. Somebody has to make a stand, but I can see you're too interested in yourself to care." David snapped and headed for the hatch.

"Don't do this, David. I've seen far worse than what this one Federation Lord is capable of. If I really hated you I'd tell you to go ahead with this attack."

"Good-bye, Van." Renfield stepped outside and shut the hatch behind him. He wondered if the crowd gathered outside could see how flushed his face was.

"Told you." Cyndiara walked away and sat next to the campfire.

"Let me talk to him." Anja pressed past.

"He's just going to make you cry." David tried to stop her.

"Not this time." She gave the knight a smile and pried open the heavy door. Climbing into an open seat beside Van she intently watched the progress of his modifications.

"Now I suppose you're going to try and talk me into committing suicide with the rest of you." Van slid a metal casing into place over the grenade tube.

"No," she responded sweetly. "What's this thing do?" She pointed to the altered weapon.

"It's supposed to teleport a grenade to its target directly, that means I can shoot something without actually having to be watching it or be in direct line of sight."

"Oh."

She observed him place a thick coil of wire over the opening where the grenade was supposed to come out. His long sleeved shirt caught on the edge of the trigger guard and pulled away from his wrist, revealing the edge of a brightly colored tattoo she'd never noticed before. Van pulled the sleeve up self consciously.

"Did you need something?" He asked.

"Not really. I just wanted to say good-bye, after all I might never see you again." She looked into his eyes with a sad expression.

"Well, you don't have to go either, you know."

"Yes, I do, but there's nothing in it for you so I understand why you don't want to come." She took his hand and gripped it gently. A flash of heat between them surprised both. Van felt himself losing will power and couldn't help noticing Anja's flushed cheeks when she pulled her hand away. Eyes met, communication going beyond the realms of conscious thought. Deep in the recesses of Van's mind a little voice called him a sucker, but the battle was already lost.

"When are you leaving?" He asked, pretending to return his attention to the weapon modifications.

"Tonight sometime. Kahn Na Thai says we should finish it tonight before the full moon."

"I have lots of work still, but I suppose I could fly out there on the cycle to check on you a little later on."

"That would be very thoughtful, you wouldn't have to stay if you didn't want to." She smiled happily.

Van cursed himself for allowing her to manipulate him.

"It won't take me long to catch up on the Sky Cycle. Go ahead without me."

"Okay! Thank you so much, Van, I knew we could count on you."

"Yeah, sure," he replied, somewhat confused as to why he'd agreed so easily. It was a lost cause, yet one way or another he was going to wind up in a battle against all odds. It sure would have been nice to know why.

Rumblings of discontent could be felt everywhere Greg Merrick went in the Coalition camp. Having been left in charge while Captain Pritchett led a night reconnaissance of a city ruins, Greg had the task of maintaining order. As much as he'd protested the commander's night excursion, Greg was relieved to have the Captain and his cronies out of his hair for a few hours.

Half a dozen soldiers playing cards suddenly grew silent at his presence, but it was the group of his own men near Skull 41 that had Greg's attention. Darren's 'conniving' tone carried over Cowboy's 'let's kick some tail' support. It didn't take a rocket scientist to figure out they were up to something. All eyes turned away and guilty looks replaced enthusiastic ones when Greg made his approach.

"Oh, hi Lieutenant." Cowboy shifted the weight of his plasma cannon from shoulder to shoulder nervously.

"Hi, Lieutenant." Darren acted as though he knew the officer was there all along. "Me and Dave are gonna patrol the perimeter, just to make sure none of them D-Bees out there sneak up on the camp tonight."

"Like hell you are." Greg crossed his arms.

"Sir?"

"Don't 'Sir' me, Darren. I'm not an idiot."

"Okay, so we might accidentally come across some demons being controlled by this magic user. These things happen all the time, ya know."

"Uh huh," Greg responded with a sarcastic nod. "And I suppose the rest of you were planning to go on patrol, too?"

"Well, ya know, sir, we do need some practice, ya know, in night maneuvers," Cowboy offered.

"I was going to make sure they received some proper anti-magic drills." The deep booming voice of Sergeant Winters came from the rover parked to Greg's left. Greg squinted, trying to make out the sergeant major in the dark.

"You're in on this too, Jerry? I can't believe this."

"The men could use some practice. They're gettin' lazy." Jerry Winters came closer followed by the the CR-1 rocket team and more troops.

"I see. Practice maneuvers, huh?" Greg sounded skeptical.

"Yes sir!" Darren spoke up. "The sergeant major thinks we're all gettin' rusty and there's only one way to fix that."

"Practice, sir." Brian stepped from behind Darren.

"You too? Is there anybody here who doesn't want to get court-martialled?"

"Technically, sir, Captain Pritchett never ordered us not to engage in covert night operations," Lisa added.

"And if those operations, sorry, practice operations were to discover a legitimate threat then we'd have to take the necessary actions," Brian continued.

"Alright, everybody just shut up for a second." Greg looked at each face of the soldiers under his command. "This would have to be on a volunteer basis only."

"We're all willing, sir." Lisa spoke for the group.

"Yeah, any chance to kick some D-Bee tail, 'specially if they're messin' with humans."

"There's only one way I can approve this, 'practice maneuver.' I'm in command of it."

"Sir?"

"Quit 'sirring' me, Darren, you hear me."

"We better get movin' then." Winters awaited orders.

"Load heavy, we may be forced into a siege situation, simulated, of course," Greg ordered and the unit scattered to comply.

"I didn't think you'd do it, dude." Darren slapped Greg's arm.

"That's sir, Darren."

"Well make up your mind!" Darren grinned and ran for his SAMAS.

"Lieutenant Merrick?" A female voice came from behind.

"Yes?" He turned to see Corporal Lexington accompanied by over a dozen members of Pritchett's unit.

"Are you planning on going to the aid of that village?"

"Of course not, Corporal, just some simple practice maneuvers. If we should happen to encounter hostile forces while on these maneuvers then naturally we would defend ourselves."

"We want to come, sir."

Greg's knee-jerk reaction was to say no, but the determination in Corrinne Lexington's voice convinced him of her sincerity. Without intending to stare, Greg noticed the thin, jagged white scars running across the corporal's otherwise very attractive face. He understood her conviction.

"You pilot Enforcer 790, correct?"

"Yes sir. This is my co-pilot, Private Jameson. We'll be bringing the UAR-1 with us."

"Your captain might not approve."

"Some of us don't always agree with the captain, sir." She spoke solemnly, followed by nods from others adding support. Their unity wavered when Pritchett's first lieutenant made his way to the front.

"What are you doing, Lieutenant Merrick?" the buzz-cut officer demanded.

"Night practice maneuvers."

"Sure you are ..."

"Do you have a problem with that? If so we can find a nice quiet place to discuss it," Greg threatened.

"I'll inform Captain Pritchett, you know."

"That's up to you, I'm leaving the camp in your charge while I'm gone."

"My charge?" Lieutenant Goldstein responded, amazed at being offered the responsibility.

"Why not? Just because the captain doesn't trust your abilities doesn't mean I don't. I'm sure you're up to the task," Greg lied.

"That's not the problem, the problem is you're disobeying Captain Pritchett's orders!"

"No I'm not. The captain never said I couldn't conduct practice maneuvers."

"Hey, it's your backside, not mine. I'm going to make a note in the records that I strongly object to your actions."

"Fine, you do what you have to do."

"If you will excuse me, I have a radio call to make." The squat officer made a bee-line for the Abolisher. Greg quickly radioed his Skull Walker.

"Merrick to Skull 41."

"Uh, yes sir?" Lisa responded.

"Test all long range frequencies right now. It would be a shame if all long range frequencies were jammed, right now. The test might also erase records of recent transmissions."

"Yes sir, conducting a test right now." Lisa caught the drift, observing Lieutenant Goldstein on the main screen.

"And send a message on UF-12 to Sir Renfield and company. Tell him to hold off his attack until we get there."

Chapter 6

Five more invisible targeting dots joined the fourteen already painting the Brodkil demon's chest. The demon munched on a leg of lamb, oblivious to the danger to its existence.

"Squad 4 in position," Cowboy's voice played over the Skull Walker's comm.

"Stand by squad 4," Lisa advised. "How's it look, Sharp?"

"Sharp here. All clear so far. It doesn't know we're here," the sniper observed from a treetop a mile away. Visible from his position were four small fire squads hidden just outside the corner of the village. Standing by itself, guarding the main entrance through the flimsy barricade, was the nine foot tall demon.

"Hold back on the heavy firepower unless the demon survives the first attack. On my command." Greg aimed his C-40 rail gun at the Brodkil's head but didn't shoot. "Fire."

Fifteen laser beams converged on the Brodkil's upper body. Half of the demon's body disappeared instantly, and what remained fell in a smoldering mass of body parts.

"One demon down," Greg reported. "Winters, move to position B. Skull 41 and Enforcer 790 advance north and secure your positions. SAMs follow pre-designated flight plans," Greg coordinated the next stage of attack. With the sentry down, his unit could secure the village and prepare for the counter-attack.

"Merrick to Renfield." Greg switched to the universal frequency to converse with the leader of his unconventional allies.

"This is Renfield."

"Sentry down, clean and clear. Better tell that woman to have the inhabitants find whatever cover they can, preferably below ground level."

"Word is already being spread, but I'm glad you thought of it."

"Remember, your task is to ensure the safety of the villagers, we'll do most of the heavy fighting. You're there in case something gets past us."

"Understood. We'll stand by to assist you if you require help containing the counter-attack."

"Roger that. Merrick out."

"Renfield standing by."

Moving on foot to avoid creating additional noise, Greg took his SAMAS into the open and awaited the call from his spotters that would soak the ground with demons blood.

Towering above the squat log cabins, the Skull Walker and Enforcer made their way as quietly as multi-ton robots could go. They weren't going to sneak up on anything short of a hibernating buffalo, and the chances of that were slim. Any sentries or guards left in the confines of the village would know soon enough there were dangerous intruders present. That was exactly what Greg had counted on.

"Heads up. Two Brodkil three o'clock," Lisa warned of the two nine foot heat signatures moving to intercept.

"Where? I don't see them." Corrinne searched the open spaces with the Enforcer's sensor turret and found nothing.

"Cut your I.R. and switch to thermo. Brodkil can fool your optics sometimes. Look out, two more at your 11."

"I see them now."

"Skull 41 to Merrick. We flushed them. We are under attack by four Brodkil, correction, five Brodkil. Request assistance."

"We're on the way Skull 41. Merrick out."

"Take the three at 11, we'll get the other two," Lisa instructed as the skull-like body rotated to bring the rail cannons in line with the running demons.

"Affirmative."

"Stay on it." Dave fingered the trigger and watched one running heat form get knocked off it's feet by twin bursts from the Skull Walker's rail canons. The second one ducked low and sprinted beneath the cannon's arc of fire just as both ripped a twenty foot long furrow in the dirty street.

"I got him." Lisa's HUD lit up and the laser turret below the skull's chin swivelled around to blast the demon beneath the robot.

Startled at being hit at such close range, the demon lashed out angrily but only caught air. Twin laser blasts burned craters next to the first pair in its chest.

"Other one's up. Hold on," Dave advised, brushing aside a house with the spider-like legs. Too close for twin convergence, Dave centered one rail cannon on the injured demon and cut it in two with a stream of metal slugs. Hearing the sound of claws on metal he set about trampling the other demon.

Enforcer 790 charged forward into an open area and brought its shoulder-mounted rail cannon down at the trio of demons. Metal left the barrel to carve its way across a demon's face. Dropping its bulky rifle, the Brodkil covered its bleeding face in agony.

"Got 'im!" Private Jameson announced enthusiastically, promptly repeating the treatment of the next before it could fire its forearm mounted ion blaster.

"Just keep blasting them until they stop moving," Corrinne instructed, calmly clothes-lining the third demon as it ran at the Skull Walker. Reaching down with the Enforcer's giant hands, she grabbed it tightly around the neck and between the legs. Lifting the squealing demon above the robot's head, the Enforcer brought it forcefully downward and snapped the Brodkil's spine over the robot's upcoming knee. Corrinne casually tossed the screaming demon aside.

"Damn! Missed it!" Jameson tried to compensate for her movements.

"Get ready to fire," Corrinne advised, grabbing the next one by the throat and lifting its head in front of the rail gun's barrel. "Fire."

Demon brains and demon skull splashed the black finish of the Enforcer's fist. Corrinne let the headless demon slip to the ground and finish its convulsions.

"The other one's running away."

"No it's not," she responded, calmly getting a running start before flattening the wounded demon with a leap kick. The earth shuddered under the weight of the giant robot, stunning the demon so thoroughly it could hardly keep the giant hands from grasping its head and torso. Corrinne twisted the head around several times before tossing the lifeless body to the ground.

"Behind you 790!" Darren's warning came over the radio. More Brodkil joined the battle.

Skull 41 had its demon pinned beneath its pair of forelegs and was laser frying what was left when another Brodkil leaped up its side. The Enforcer took on its new opponent with a vengeance, but Skull 41 had a more difficult problem. Climbing atop the giant robot, the Brodkil began trying to pry open the top hatch.

"Not so fast, ugly." Lisa switched to the top rear laser turret normally used against aircraft and swung it around to face the demon a few feet away. Even thermo-optics showed the look of surprise on the demon's face when twin laser beams blew most of its arm off.

"Chill on the blaster, babe, I got your rider," Darren advised and kicked the Demon's side as he went by at 70 mph. "Down boy!"

More house timbers splintered beneath spider legs as Dave backed away from the now grounded demon. It must have known what was coming next. Eighty slugs tore the earth where it had been a moment before.

From the sides rail guns spit kinetic steel, throwing the demon to the ground with the impact. Greg advanced quickly, slamming it back down with a second set of bursts from fifteen feet away.

"Now Brian!" Greg shouted.

Brian rushed the demon and rammed the point of his rail gun into the monster's hide, but more importantly, a barbed dart with it.

"Hold your fire!" Greg shouted over the radio, waiting to see if the Brodkil's better judgement took over. Wounded and severely overmatched it backed away slowly, then ran squealing even as the last blood of its comrades reached the ground.

"Hold your fire, 790."

"It's going to get away!" Corrinne protested.

"Exactly what I want it to do. It's wearing a radio transmitter that's going to show us exactly where the Federation Lord is hiding. Trenton, your lead is on the move." Greg signalled his full conversion cyborg waiting at the edge of the village.

"Acknowledged, sir. I'm tracking it now." Trenton's finely tuned sensor systems located the retreating demon. Keeping his distance the heavily armored man and machine gave pursuit.

"Dang, Corrinne," Darren commented at the bodies around the Enforcer. "I take back all those mean things I said about you coming along. Please, accept my apologies!"

"Forget it. Buy me dinner when we get to Liberty and we'll call it even."

"Deal."

"Continue on to your designated positions. The Wild Cards can take care of any problems inside the village perimeter. Merrick to Winters, you dug in?"

"No! What the hell did ya expect from me, a miracle?"

"Better get off your butt and get dirty, too, things might be happening faster than we expected."

"We'll be ready for those D-Bees, you can count on it."

"That what I like to hear, Jerry, because with any luck we'll be steering them right into your lap."

Through layers of foliage, Trenton watched the gathering forces with increasing apprehension. Rank after rank of skeletal warriors lined up behind demons and zombies. Although it appeared most of the heavy hitters had already been destroyed, two apprentice wizards and the remaining forces would be enough to test his unit's mettle. Trenton observed the preparations, waiting for the dreaded Federation Lord with pointed ears to make his appearance.

Lacking a heart to pump adrenaline through his non-existent veins, Trenton's nervousness gradually became agitation. More machine than man, he couldn't release the tension in a way normally suited for a flesh and blood man. Agitation progressed to aggression, forcing Trenton to fight the urge for immediate combat. The call had been made, his unit made aware of the exact number and composition of the enemy. Once the forces left for the counter-attack, the moment of release would come, and who or whatever remained at the Lord's compound would have to face the fury of a Full Conversion Cyborg unchained.

Credo silenced the ravings of his wounded Brodkil. Visions of the future had foreseen a great danger to all he'd established, but Coalition interference wasn't part of the premonition and was the last thing Credo expected. The presence of ground based robot vehicles two miles from his home could only mean they were part of a larger force. No commander in his right mind would launch an attack against a Federation Lord with only half a dozen mecha.

Without a doubt the village had summoned their help, and Credo had a pretty good notion who in particular was going to suffer the worst for the folly. He'd make sure the rest of the village found out the consequences of rebellion by acts of severity randomly administered to all. First, however, he would rid himself of a dangerously close threat.

Distinctive outlines of tall robot vehicles could be seen against the night sky above the squadid log cabins of the village. No question of the Coalition's trespass on his domain. Credo snarled orders to his trusted demon allies and loyal apprentices. A frontal assault on the pair of robots guarding the north entrance would be futile, and engaging the armored exoskeletons at the east and south would bring the others quickly to their aid. A battle in the open would rip his forces to shreds. It seemed an obvious trap to sneak in from the dense forest to the west, too obvious in fact. Did the Coalition commander just assume he was an idiot? From the forest line outside the village barricade, Credo contemplated strategy for his small army.

Returning from its scouting mission, Trix leaped to Credo's shoulder and chattered noisily in the mage's ear.

"Speak slower, Trix, you stutter when you get excited."

The wildly animated oration slowed its rapid pace.

"A third exoskeleton and four troops lay in ambush, you say?"

The tiny demon's head bobbed up and down furiously.

"My opponent has spread his forces too thin and is not prepared to deal with me. It would have been nice to have had time for better plans, but fortunately the battle can be fought here and not closer to home. One by one these intruders will fall, too weak apart and too late to stand united."

Credo turned in the saddle to give specific orders to his minions.

"Bashir, you will proceed immediately to the southern entrance and waylay any Coalition forces there. Kill them quickly," Credo instructed a large, black demon who looked back with a mocking grin. Specific instructions were laid out to the Jinn demon. From Credo's experience the powerful demons had a way of twisting their mortal masters' words into something unintended. Bashir left in an apparent pleasant mood, the orders of his master not too far from his own personal desires.

"Yazell, move carefully to the south and around the village. Wait until Bashir has the Coalition forces occupied, then make your advance quickly into the village itself."

"Yes, my Lord," the Demon Locust growled spitefully, humming its wings in disrespect. Such disgrace for a greater demon was almost unbearable, but Credo's magic held it to unwilling servitude.

"Move through the village leaving nothing but dead in your wake, choosing from the fallen to supplement your forces as needed. This will serve to divide our enemy's force even more and teach these loathsome peasants their place. Now go."

Yazell thrummed his wings louder but followed orders. Animated corpses left in ranks to follow their puppet master's demands.

"Carreb, my apprentice, you will take all but a fraction of my force and carefully approach that silly little ambush. When close enough you will spring the trap on them and overwhelm their meager defenses. Trix and five zombies will signal your attack by a distraction created in the village not far behind their western front."

"May Annubis aid and protect you, my Lord," Carreb wheezed through the amphibious flaps of his frog-like face.

"Our god will be pleased at the glory we bring him this day. Death will pave the way to salvation."

"Oww! God, git yer elbow out of my face plate!" Cowboy whispered harshly.

"Move your head!" Bill practically yelled back.

"For the last time, shut up down there!" Sergeant Winters' metal-shod foot came down on somebody's head. Walking the length of the covered trench, Jerry Winters did his best to keep the ambush from becoming public knowledge. Three other soldiers hid in poorly assembled clumps of shrubbery scanning pre-made firing lanes with passive nightvision scopes. Periodically sticking an exoskeleton appendage up in the air for all to see, Brian added a touch of ineptitude to what appeared to be an idiot's ambush. Buried in loose branches, Private Peterson watched from a rooftop for trouble on the move.

"Holy moly, Sergeant Major, I must be seein' thirty of 'em tryin' ta sneak up on us," Joel Peterson whispered into his helmet radio.

"That's it? Those guys better have sent more than that or I'm gonna be real disappointed."

"Uh, I wouldn't worry, Sarge, there's like three times as many on thermo than I got with starlight."

"That's more like it."

Screams from the village began rising up in a chorus.

"Stay down 'till I give the word." Winters growled. "How close, Peterson?"

"Twenty yards."

"Sarge, I can see 'em too!" A soldier in the bushes shifted position.

"Hold yer fire 'till I say so." Winters casually shifted his C-27 to one hand and slipped a disposable rocket flare into his free hand. He hated being the bait.

"South end is under attack," Peterson relayed from the roof.

"I don't care. Where are they now?"

"Fifteen meters, movin' faster now."

"Steady, nobody shoot 'till I say."

Wild inhuman war cries erupted from the thick woods as demons, monsters and zombies charged the enemy. Winters raised his right hand and fired a brilliant magnesium flare high into the night sky.

"Now! Fire!"

Dirt covered branches burst upward as Coalition troops popped out of their covered foxholes. Illuminated by the descending flare were hoards of demonic fiends craving human flesh. A war cry of equal fury arose from both battle hardened veteran and green recruit alike. The floodgates of firepower opened wide and devastating waves swept over the advancing army like a river undammed. First and second advancing lines were vaporized in an instant, giving the third and fourth a second or two longer to live. Those that didn't kiss the ground were vaporized in clouds of ash and steam, allowing more energy beams to slice through to the commanding demons.

"Peterson, now!" Winters yelled.

Peterson hit the remote detonator and the forest floor seemed to leap upward, anti-personnel mines blasting cowering fiends and demon commanders to oblivion. In the span of 30 seconds Credo's glorious army was reduced to wafting mist and powdered charcoal.

"Watch your left flank!" Peterson shouted.

Two wolf-headed demons had sidestepped the barrage and now howled their attack, battle axes raised high.

"Whooopie!" A flash of psychedelic color flew by one of the demons and relieved the being of its ax. Twenty or so weapons burned down the weaponless creature before it even knew Delwin had disarmed it.

Landing directly in front of the other twelve foot demon, Delwin fended it off with the ridiculously oversized battle ax.

"Halt! Who goes there!? What's the password!?"

"Roaharrh!"

"That's not it!" Delwin shouted, jabbing the creature in the armored chest plate. "Try again!"

"Hey! You! Hippy! Get out of the way!" Brian shouted.

"Get that crazy sunnava gun outta the way!" Winters screamed, trying to avoid torching the crazy man with his plasma cannon.

With a mighty windup good, the Alu demon sent Delwin's ax spinning into the side of a building.

"Your powers grow weak, old one," Delwin spoke in a low, deep voice. "You cannot defeat me now."

Whipping out an imaginary saber, Delwin rapidly waved the "blade" back and forth, all the while making stupid "whawing" sound effects. Baffled, the demon stepped back.

More strange sounds and menacing thrusts pushed the demon another step back.

"Hey! fool , get the outta the way!"

At last the demon risked whatever the crazy man could do to it and swung the ax to cleave the human in two. Nimbly sidestepping the blade, Delwin pranced up the ax shaft to stand face to face with the Alu demon.

"No more beer for you! I'm gonna give you the noogie from hell!" Delwin furiously made good his threat, giving the demon a noogie like it had never experienced before in its life. Rage overtook it like wildfire and Delwin was forced to back-flip to the ground to avoid becoming a demon biscuit. In a flash Delwin's high frequency saber was ripped from its sheath and brought to the ready.

"Hey, man." Delwin bent down to inspect the demon's clawed foot. "I hope you didn't tip your pedicurist."

Without another word Delwin swiftly chopped off the demon's big toe.

The demon backhanded Delwin into a clump of fallen trees.

"Fire!"

Burning bits of armor and hairy flesh exploded in all directions.

"About time!" Winters stood and slotted a new energy canister in his smoking weapon.

Deafening thunder accompanied a blinding flash as lightning struck a soldier in the head. The charge flowed down the armor to the ground but knocked down the stunned occupant nonetheless. Walking through the smoking remains of his command came a tall, frog-headed mage in mismatched armor and discolored robes. Barely audible words left its mouth flaps as Carreb wheezed another spell.

"Kill it," Winters ordered.

Laser and plasma weapons fired with repeated accuracy at the shuffling figure to no effect. Plasma dissipated harmlessly and laser beams simply ended their course.

"Magic user!" Cowboy, along with half a dozen others tore their TX-5 projectile weapons from chest holsters and let the air ring with the sound of weapon reports. Legs, arms, and other body parts railed away from the tight cluster of explosions.

Cowboy pumped the slide, a spent casing hitting the ground still smoking. "Foreign weapon actually worked!"

"Guess it always goes to prove one thing...." Bill went up for a high-five.

"Only good D-Bee's a dead D-Bee!" the chorus followed.

Bones shattered and dislocated limbs flew in every direction in Targo's path. Seeing the animated dead murdering the villagers made something snap inside the giant. Wading through mobs of stinking corpses, Targo lashed out with a violence frightening to behold.

Zombies lashed out with clubs and swords only to be flung aside like rag dolls. Animated dead were smashed by giant fists and kicked aside without a second thought. Trailing behind Targo's swath Sir Renfield tried to bring the giant's seldom seen temper under control while others fended off waves of undead.

Flames erupted with searing intensity and formed a blazing wall before Cyndiara. Eyes glowing like white hot embers, Cyndiara's body burst into flame, burning the decaying hands off would-be attackers. Slowly she stalked blackened earth, moving the wall of fire before her like a shield. Nothing in its path survived more than an instant, the flame consuming all and leaving nothing but barren ground behind it. Those spared the inferno quickly found themselves in the giant's tender grasp.

Thrumming wings above the scene of carnage kept Yazell out of harms way for the moment, the Demon Locust simply enjoying the havoc he'd created. Now that most of his cannon fodder was gone, it was time to get down to business and destroy the small group defending the villagers, starting with the maniac giant.

Lightning arced from the sky and fell on Targo with deafening report. Electrical discharges sparked across his armor and connected with anything grounded nearby, the brunt of the charge passing through Targo's body on its way to earth. Ripples of power spread away from the giant's feet in hectic tendrils, leaving charred fissures in the smoking ground. Targo looked skyward, slightly dazed from the incredible discharge of electricity. The rampage ended.

Residual current ran across Targo's thick armor plating and knocked out the targeting display over his right eye. Targo lifted his rail gun and fired repeatedly without benefit of targeting systems. Slugs cut the sky to the right and left of the flying demon, coming just close enough to make it continually readjust its position. A second rail gun opened alongside the first, Sir Renfield standing shoulder to shoulder with Targo in his infantry style power armor suit.

Slowly but surely the demon's near indestructible hide was penetrated by a continual bombardment of steel.

Smashing the skull of an aimlessly wandering skeleton, Mr. Kent felt the presence of a new danger. Whirling around he saw Anja blow a zombie to bits with an explosive tipped arrow, then look around herself with a similar premonition. Both possessed a psionic trait that often warned of danger not yet evident. Something other than the dwindling undead and flying Demon Locust threatened their lives. Without warning, Anja selected a wire wrapped arrow from her quiver and pulled it back with the crystal tip aimed at Mr. Kent's head. Just as the scout felt razor sharp claws begin tearing at the flexible neck armor, Anja loosed the Techno-Wizard modified arrow. Lightning shot from her compound bow in the blink of an eye and removed an eight inch demon from Mr. Kent's left shoulder.

Trix screamed a high-pitched wail as he flew through the air from the shock. The demon struck wooden beams and bounced to the ground. Confused and disoriented, it looked up to see two scouts and two Mystics rushing toward it in a blurry haze. It bared rows of razor sharp teeth to warn them off, but leaped aside to avoid being hit by however many scouts and Mystics were actually shooting at it. Back and forth it leaped, once attacking a blurry image that really wasn't there. At last he knew which woman with the bow was the real one.

Leaping over ten feet, Trix aimed his barbed body for Anja's open face. Something smacked him first, before he could strike. Trix slid off the magic barrier surrounding her, one more thing to ruin his day.

Anja tried one more time to snatch the nimble demon, frustration taking hold instead as Trix scurried at an easier victim. Anja thought fast. Selecting a spell from her small repertoire, she concentrated for a moment and recited a mantra. Reaching one open hand toward the tiny demon she grabbed hold with telekinetic tendrils. The startled demon scolded her with incoherent chatter as it was lifted off the ground and flung helplessly from wall to wall of the village cabins.

A pillar of fire rose up beside Anja.

"Put it in the flames," Cyndiara instructed, her body still engulfed in fire. Trix's tiny body was whipped around to face the ten foot psionic blaze. Terror gripped the Lasae demon. Six hundred tiny fires reflected in every segment of its compound eyes. Trix entered the inferno with a pitiful scream, antennae and spines burning in seconds. Blood boiled and flesh turned to steam, practically exploding the demon's exoskeleton with a distinct pop. Cyndiara smiled with an equally distinct satisfaction.

Another stroke of lightning brought Targo to his knees but the giant refused to go down all the way. Muscles tightened involuntarily and with a rigid grip he again raised the rail gun against the greater demon. Sir Renfield renewed his assault with vigor, the realization of exactly what he faced starting to sink in. Very few mages could control a powerful demon, much less a greater one. This Credo commanded many, and the battle hadn't yet reached the Federation Lord.

Out of the darkness a mini-missile aligned itself with the hovering demon. Instants before impact, glowing lines shot from tiny holes in the rocket's tip. Magic cords enveloped the demon's elongated body and humming wings to make it prisoner of a magical net. The lines tightened, ending the flap of wings and bringing Yazell crashing to the ground.

"Best keep your distance from it," Van advised from his airborne Sky Cycle. In seconds the demon would be free of its bonds, but by then Van planned to put it in a world of hurt. Arming five mini-missiles in each side-mounted launcher, Van loosed a flaming volley of destruction. Yazell screamed even as the armor piercing warheads bore down on it. Ten explosions sounded as one, tearing the wings from Yazell's body, cutting deep into flesh and bone. The ground shuddered beneath it as Yazell's gasps for air fell on deaf ears.

Even Sir Renfield rushed forward with the others to blast the fallen demon while it was still stunned. Rules of fair play and honor set aside for the moment, he fired burst after burst into the creature before it could recover enough to kill any of them.

"Thank you Van!" Anja expressed her joyous appreciation.

"All in a day's work. Hold the fort until I get back, Darren's got big trouble with a Jinn at the south end. Good luck!" Van waved back at the Mystic and spun his Sky Cycle south.

Falling stone caught the edge of Darren's rear thrusters and nearly brought him crashing down with it. A cabin splintered under the weight of a multi-ton stone wall, allowing it to smash its occupants. Bashir laughed and magically erected another wall in Darren's flight path. Demolition detail was so much fun.

Standing fifteen feet taller than the upright log barricade, Bashir gnashed rows of crooked teeth and rubbed gritty black hands together in anticipation of destruction. Flying toward him was another human war machine; just one more mechanism to convert to useless rubble. Bashir's crazed eyes followed the Sky Cycle, waiting for it to come within range of a powerful invocation. Technically Credo had told him not to delay, but then again it hadn't been specified how much time constituted a delay. Bashir enjoyed circumventing Credo's wishes almost as much as the combat.

Van throttled down and dove the Sky Cycle. When the forward targeting display had the demon's head centered, he triggered the second of four specially modified mini-missiles attached to the sides of the cycle. A split second later glowing tendrils shot around the demon's head and upper body. Roaring in frustration, fought against the bonds as Darren came back around for another pass. Forty slugs burst from the rail gun and ripped a line up Bashir's back. The demon vanished, glowing white bonds falling in a heap.

"That's gotta be you, Van, nobody else I know would paint their craft bright red," Darren broadcast on UF-12.

Van hovered slowly to the ground and hopped off the Sky Cycle without powering it down. SAM 15 landed twenty feet away.

"Greetings. Didn't think I'd be running into you in a place like this." Van waved cheerfully, feeling a bit self-conscious about the stolen C-14 rifle and Coalition Sky Cycle.

"Me either. Nice wings." Darren pointed the rail gun at the glowing strands on the ground. "What the hell did you do to that thing? I only shot it once. Something doesn't seem right."

"It's a Jinn, and you're right, it shouldn't have died that quick."

"How perceptive of you." The demon reappeared ten feet behind them.

"Oh man!" Darren raised his weapon to fire but something was dragging him back, metal feet cutting furrows in the earth. Pieces of metal, pots, pans, and iron objects all around converged on a super-magnetized point twenty feet behind Darren. One hundred ninety pounds of ferrous steel in the C-40's ammunition drum pulled the light exoskeleton inexorably to the magic magnet. In the last ten feet Darren's SAMAS completely left the ground and slammed into the other junk attached to the magnetized stone wall.

Looking back at his Sky Cycle, Van watched it rock dangerously to one side on its landing gear then tip and roll. With a sickening collision it smashed into Darren's immobilized exoskeleton and remained pinned by the magic magnet.

Van breathed a thank you to the designers of his composite body armor. Constructed primarily from molecularly bonded ceramics and synthetic webbing, his Triax make Explorer body armor wasn't drawn to Bashir's elemental spell. What few ferrous items he carried were insufficient to pull him to the wall.

On instinct Van channeled energy from his body into special micro-circuitry he'd built into his armor. Techno-Wizards emphasized a joining of technology and magic, often combining spells with modified devices to create inexplicable marvels. To date, the Van De Graf Invulnerability Field Generator mark 3 was untested in combat. Van spun around to put it to the challenge.

"Little human," Bashir rumbled. "Little stone human." The demon began a new incantation.

Killing a Jinn was next to impossible, or so Van's Shifter friends at the guild had told him. Beating it at its own game of subterfuge and deceit wasn't likely either. A plan formed in the spur of the moment and Van fumbled for one of his devices.

Van suddenly felt a strange tightening of his body as magic worked its way through his defenses. Putting every force of will into fighting the Jinn's spell, he clenched and unclenched his fist as proof of defiance. Bashir paused, wondering why his petrification spell had failed. No matter. If his magic couldn't penetrate the glowing red barrier around the human, then he would simply trap the mage until his magic faded away.

Pulling the small, spiked cylinder from its belt pouch, Van twisted the top and a row of thirty lights came on, one between each pair of small spikes. Receiving a sudden flash of insight, warning of danger Van looked over his shoulder to find a forty foot wall of stone tipping over on him. Van dove for the base of a tree stump ten feet away but the wall caught him first. Out of his hands the device flew and Van was slammed to the ground, partially pinned by tons of stone. The stump saved the device from being smashed, but Van's legs and torso were imbedded in soft earth trapping him in a prone position. Just out of reach was his modified C-14 rifle. Crackling energy ran over a portion of his armor as the V-IFG mark 3 malfunctioned. The barrier began to decay with every passing second. Atop the stone slab Bashir danced a victory dance, contemplating which of his two prisoners was going to die first.

"Ah man," Van struggled against the odds. "I hate it when this happens."

Chapter 7

Palm circuitry glowed in Van's outstretched hand as Mystic current flowed through and was converted to telekinetic force. Taking hold of the rifle with an invisible telekinetic grasp, Van pulled the weapon to his hand. The force field around his lower body weakened further.

In almost complete darkness beneath the slab Van looked at the modified weapon and hoped his alterations would work. His thumb switched the C-14 function from the upper laser to the lower grenade launcher. Along the length of the launch tube were coils of wire protected by molded fiberglass and the end of the barrel itself was covered in a bizarre mix of homing circuitry. Van cycled a modified grenade and visualized the Jinn atop the stone slab. A small red light turned green and an audible tone told him the device had a fix on his target. A hammer drove a pin into the primer followed by a focused, expanding explosion. The grenade entered the enclosed barrel with enough force to blast through the blocking circuits. Instead the barrel circuitry hummed briefly, charged by magic currents coursing through the coils. For one instant Van's teleport device altered two points in space, bringing them together for the small projectile.

From apparently out of nowhere, the grenade struck Bashir in the head, and stuck there.

Inside the grenade casing, a series of Mystic batteries drew force to the tip. Spreading over the surface of Bashir's body was an invisible coat of magically created adhesive. Bashir soon discovered the effect.

Grabbing hold of the tiny grenade, Bashir found his fingers adhered to his head. Moving his feet was impossible as they were securely bonded to the stone slab. Hearing the sounds of battle go badly and not wanting to be caught in this helpless position, Bashir did the first thing that came to mind. He negated the stone wall and dropped to the ground. Bashir's feet stuck with equal impediment.

Free for the moment, Van rolled away from Bashir's claws and snatched up the device he'd dropped by the tree stump. Bashir was cursing madly as Van sprung a long spike from the end of the cylinder and stuck it into the top of the stump. Van was startled when the Jinn's frustrated roar became a laugh.

Bashir's body dematerialized into a gaseous white cloud of mist, the spent adhesive grenade falling through his immaterial body to the ground. Moving within four feet of the Techno-Wizard Bashir rematerialized in all his physical glory. Having a few tricks to play on mortals always came in handy.

Pressing a metallic button at end of the cylinder, Van channeled Mystic energy from his body into the device. Powerful waves radiated from the cylinder and met Bashir's brain like an incoming freight train. Try as he would to fight the debilitating effects of the generated trance waves, Bashir felt control slipping away to whatever spell assaulted his body. Willpower gone and intelligent thought eradicated, Bashir stood motionless awaiting the command of his temporary master.

"Nod your head if you understand what I'm saying," Van instructed, telepathically probing the Jinn's mind for any trace of deception. In a trance Bashir nodded. The demon stood helpless as Van reached over with a pronged device and pulled away the last bit of psychic energy from Bashir's body, preventing him from weaving further magic should he break free of the trance spell.

"Your race is cursed to do the bidding of any who render you vital aid or make you captive. Is that true?"

The Jinn nodded reluctantly.

"Then I have three wishes for you to accomplish. One, you will sever any ties now and in the future with the Federation of Magic and any of its members and minions and never in your lifetime meddle in the affairs of the Federation of Magic and its dealings with mortals. Two, you will return without retribution to your dimension of origin the instant I tell you to. Third, never again in your infinite lifetime will you enter this world or aid any others in entering this world or by any way or means allow another by inaction to enter this dimension for any purpose whatsoever. That is all, now leave!"

Bashir's mind raced for parameters to skirt and gain quick revenge on the mortal before him but the curse restrained his action and bound him to follow the horrible tasks assigned him. With one last roar the black skinned demon was banished to a life of hell forever.

The cacophony of clanging metal pots and pans as they hit the ground let Van know Bashir's spell was broken. Stone walls vanished and Darren pushed himself away from the pile of junk converged around him. Van retrieved his equipment and with Darren's help, turned the Sky Cycle right-side up.

"It's really gone this time, right?" Darren asked hopefully. "No *Night of the Living Dead* re-run?"

"No, it's not dead, but gone for good. I guarantee he's gonna be the laughing stock of the Jinn community for the next four or five million years." Van held up the spent cylinder proudly. "I wasn't even sure if it would work. Tried something I never worked with before. Gotta make more of these babies!"

"Dang, it's good havin' you back, man, even with all your screwball magic.!" Darren almost knocked Van off his feet with a friendly pat on the back.

"I hate to admit it, but it's good getting back in the action again."

"Mucho stuff has happened, like you wouldn't believe. After all this is over, we gotta kick back some brewskies and swap stories."

"Works for me. What next?" Van reached into his Sky Cycle's left air intake and removed an iron skillet. Cries from the rubble around them and sounds of battle elsewhere in the village brought the reunion to a halt.

"Dude, you still got that weird little V-med thing that makes sounds and heals people?"

"Yes, but I need to conserve my energy in case we run into this arch mage character."

"Let's go waste 'im. I'll cover ya, you do the magic."

"Good idea, before he summons up that Jinn's big brother. I'll call Anja on the radio and let her know there's injured over here."

Darren blew the dust out of the SAMAS thrusters with a short burst of flame.

"Ready when you are."

"Let's kick some Federation tail."

Two silhouttes on horseback filled Sharp's AQ-3 targeting display. The one on the left appeared tall and slender while the one on the right was a bit more pudgy. To the Coalition spotter's delight, neither appeared to be wearing armor. Without taking his eyes off the pair, Sharp turned light amplification to maximum and a grainy image showed the two riders in stages of greenish light. Sharp smiled when the computer enhancement kicked in and their features came into focus. By all information, the one with the long ears was the main target of the whole operation. Credo, the Federation Lord.

"Sharp to Skull 41," he whispered over the radio.

"This is Skull 41. What do you have?" Lisa sounded bored.

"One, possibly two magic users approximately half a mile from your position. One of them looks like the Easter Bunny."

"Roger that. Keep him in your sights while I get orders."

"Holding," Sharp muttered, wondering which idiot code-named the targets. It sounded like a Darren.

"You still there?"

"Yes."

"Merrick says waste 'em both and move in to cover the mage's compound. Trenton's having some problems."

"Copy that. Sharp over and out."

Breathing slowly and deeply while he concentrated on the targets, Sharp blocked out the surrounding world. The range finder placed the Federation Lord at 2987 feet. Not taking any chances, Sharp selected the high power laser on his JA-11 sniper rifle just in case the magic user had light armor plate beneath his outer cloak. Sharp switched the weapon to audio control and prepared to issue the death command.

"Zollan, I think it's time we were going," Credo gave the order to retreat in the form of an opinion.

"Yes, my Lord, we can defend ourselves much easier at home than here," the pudgy human apprentice agreed.

"Strange that it would be the Coalition." Credo commented, turning his horse for home.

"Of course when they leave the village, it will be ours again, my Master. Your zombies will rise again and then we will exact revenge for the villagers' treachery.

"No, for some reason I don't think so. The future I have foreseen is one much different than you imagine, my, apprentice." Credo emphasized the word apprentice just to see Zollan's teeth grind. It was amusing to see how far he could push a pupil before they finally snapped.

A laser beam collided with Credo's body and dissipated over his heavy cloak.

"Now this is something I didn't foresee." Credo spoke with curiosity in his voice. "The cloak appears to be worth the gold I paid, wouldn't you say, Zollan?"

Zollan's clipped scream was followed by his cauterized upper body landing in between his two feet. Zollan's face bore a look of utter surprise for the moment it took his brain to die.

"It appears fate has other plans for your soul, Zollan. I was not the only one aware of your rebellion." Credo calmly pulled the hood up over his thick dark hair. "Pity, I would have enjoyed watching you die much more slowly. Shame you can't avenge your death, and I doubt the sniper will allow me the honor."

Another laser beam answered against Credo's shoulder.

As if it were a leisurely ride in the park, Credo spurred the horse to a gentle canter and amused himself by predicting where and when the next laser beam would strike.

"If you want me you're going to have to try much harder than that," Credo addressed the unseen sniper. "My life is not yours to take.

Treetops bent in a wake behind the two low flying craft. Both were primed for action, and to wait for the ground forces to arrive might cost them the edge. No time was wasted upon their arrival at Credo's well built fortification.

Flames were already rising up from inside the log walls when Van's Sky Cycle spat two mini-missiles from side launchers and tore down a wider hole in the outer wall. Concussions of sound accompanied splintering wood from a swath already being cut by the Full Conversion Cyborg inside the perimeter. Darren's rail gun cut down preoccupied sentries one by one as the two flew into the heart of the fort. Disorganized troops fled to the central wood and stone structure for sanctuary but soon discovered the walls provided little deterrent against laser beams and kinetic steel.

Rising temporarily to command a small pocket of resistance, a Brodkil demon took the charge, followed by Ghouls and Hell Hounds. From the smoking path of carnage an irate Full Conversion Cyborg met the challenge. The charge ended abruptly as it began when the only one left standing was the blistered Brodkil demon. Trenton's left forearm launcher flared up in a cloud of smoke as three mini-missiles left in rapid succession. Fear gripped the Brodkil an instant before its body was torn in half by three consecutive detonations.

"Way to go Trenton!" Darren congratulated the Cyborg.

"I got tired of waiting. The mage hasn't come back yet," Trenton advised the hovering SAMAS.

"Then let's make sure there's nothing left for him to come back to."

"Darren, you should have been an officer," Trenton joked, finishing a barb-tailed creature with a powerful discharge from his right forearm cannon.

"Naw, you know how much I hate being responsible." Darren returned the battlefield banter, ignoring a group of fleeing Annubis cult members.

"What the hell is that?!" Trenton pointed his C-27 back at the smoking hole in the fort's wall. Plunging out of the darkness was a huge, winged demon in ornate dragonscale armor. In its giant gauntlets was a rail gun no doubt removed from the grasp of some mechanical victim of the past. Behind it came a hoard of demonic troops and the handful of zombies remaining in Credo's army. Left in command while Credo was absent, Kroatis had mistakenly led a force on patrol around the fort, leaving the enemy an opening for attack. Kroatis dared not fail his master now. Letting out a roaring battle cry the Baal Rog demon charged the nearest enemy.

"Shit," Trenton exclaimed unemotionally and emptied the C-27's canister.

The Baal Rog disappeared inside a cloud of expanding explosions from Van's remaining mini-missile payload. Smoke swirled around the hovering Sky Cycle as it passed overhead, clearing the view of a very upset demon examining the remnants of its favorite weapon. Kroatis screamed with rage at the damage to his ornate armor and trophy weapon. Whirling about, the demon watched the red Sky Cycle land beyond the far wall, but a new problem prevented immediate revenge.

A high pitched wind up and discharge from the Cyborg's particle beam tore away scales and burned flesh. In the demon's right hand a long fiery whip formed, and in his left a brilliant ball of flame. For the moment his troops could occupy the other humans, but the Full Conversion Cyborg was his alone to destroy. Eyes glowing red with fury, Kroatis spread his wings and leaped high, whip leaving a fiery trail behind it as it sang a path to Trenton's mechanical body.

Watching from the tree line, Credo chuckled at the scene before him as if it was all just a show for his entertainment. Three against thirty didn't seem like fair odds, but his antagonists seemed to hold their own quite well. If they knew what awaited them once they reached his laboratory, they would flee for their lives while they still had time. Credo had been careful to leave his prisoners in the deep underground bunker beneath his fort. Their lives would supply him with the life force needed to destroy any that stood in his way of escape. He'd considered making a stand from the beginning, but such things were futile and needlessly costly. Better to run and fight again another day than die heroically but uselessly. Credo was bored of the squabbling Federation of Magic anyway, and his visions of the future suggested the disorganized guild would destroy itself in the end. It was time to move onto bigger and better things.

"Goodbye, old friend." Credo patted his mount's neck affectionately. "You've served me better than the most powerful demons of hell."

Invoking protective magic Credo urged the horse to a gallop and rode directly into the scene of mayhem.

Darren lost count of how many creatures he'd cut down with his rail gun. The magazine count in his HUD registered 48% so he chose his targets carefully and fired with precision. Hovering out of harm's way he did his best to ensure a fair fight between demon and cyborg.

Coalition reinforcements were on the way from the village, but lots could happen in a short time.

Riding into the foray was a cloaked man on a horse. Darren might not have taken notice except for the cheers suddenly coming from the dwindling monsters below. To the north, Van was pointing at the rider and shouting, all the while hacking through demons with a sword and hand-held telekinetic shotgun. The man on horseback had to be the next to die.

Swinging the C-40 in a wide arc, Darren pulled the trigger and sprayed 40 slugs at the visibly vulnerable mage. Metal slugs ripped through flesh and shattered bone with little velocity lost. The horse screamed, thrashing its head back and knocking Credo to the ground. Its legs entwined to bring the dying beast to the ground. It shuddered and convulsed in the blood-soaked earth around it. Getting up slowly Credo gave his dying steed a look of pity then strode confidently down the open corridor of protection provided by his loyal troops. Supersonic metal cut through beasts and glanced off his invisible armor, ricocheting in every direction. Thrown to the ground by the impact, Credo whispered the words to a complex spell and vanished before the eyes of the beholders. Once more he rose and calmly walked toward his sanctuary.

Slicing through a Ghoul's upper body, Van dodged a storm of swinging clubs to reach the mage. Magically enhanced optics in his helmet enabled him to see what the arch mage believed was invisible. The Flyssa's blade carved a notch in a Grave Ghoul's neck, giving Van the chance he needed to be clear of attackers. Nimbly rushing forward, Van shoved his modified TX-5 against Credo's magic barrier and blasted the Federation Lord to the ground with telekinetic buckshot.

Unexpectedly Credo's movements changed from slow and methodic to quick and erratic. Leaping up with the grace of an Elf, Credo sidestepped Van's second blast and sprinted for an opening in the wall.

"Darren! Cover me!" Van shouted and plunged in after him.

"Ahh." Darren smashed a pursuing Ghoul and followed Van inside.

In the blood soaked courtyard, the first Coalition units to arrive opened fire.

Once past the smoke and fallen timbers Van found a wide corridor with concrete floor and incandescent bulbs strung along the high ceiling by extension cords. Scuffling boots and contorted speech could be heard from the end of the hallway. Darren's SAMAS crashed through a fallen support and skidded to a halt next to the Techno-Wizard.

"Do you see 'im?" Darren's whisper blared over the SAM's voice amplifier.

A door at the end of hall slammed shut before either could get off a shot at the misshapen creature closing it. A bolt fell into place on the other side.

"Sweet dreams." Darren read the heat signature through the wooden door and discharged a single slug from his rail gun. Wood splintered and a dark spot appeared in the warm target on the other side. The D-Bee's body slumped to the floor.

"Stay close, we don't know what else is in here," Van advised and jogged to the door. One slice of the blade severed the door's lock and bolt. It swung open on its own under the weight of the body still gripping the handle on the other side.

Van searched the next room for signs of danger, but there was nobody inside the lavish bedroom. Adjusting a knob on the side of his helmet, the room came to life with a vibrant array of auras. Nothing in the room was alive, but many objects radiated in tones of magic, including a large circle beneath a thick oriental rug.

"Do you see him?" Darren asked again.

"No, but there's something weird going on with the wall behind the bed." Van stalked the room, weapon ready. "Don't step on that rug. There's something under it and I don't know what it does."

"That wall's warmer than the others," Darren observed the slightly brighter hue of the wall on his thermo-imaging optics.

"Easy. There's still danger here, I can feel it."

"Maybe he didn't come in here."

"Where else could he go? I was right behind him. I'm sure I heard talking from in here, too."

"I've got something on sound amplifiers. Quiet a sec." Darren adjusted the audio pick-up and tuned out the sound of battle outside.

"What's being said?" Van asked impatiently.

"I'm not sure. It's in another language or something. Two voices, one's a woman and the other's some dude. It's loudest near that wall, but sounds like it's coming down a hollow tube."

"There's probably a room on the other side. That means there's some kind of mechanism to open it." Van yanked all four bed posts but nothing happened.

"There's always the Darren Corley patented Precision Barrier Removal System." Darren imitated Van's voice.

"Oh, what's that?"

"This."

Getting a running start Darren slammed the exoskeleton through the wall.

"That works." Van casually stepped through the wide opening.

"Damn, another empty room."

"There's a trap door." Van pointed to an obvious brass ring not completely covered by a thick rug.

"So there is."

Darren stomped twice and disappeared through the newly created hole. Van could hear him crash through supports all the way down.

"Okay, so that was stupid," Darren muttered to himself, breaking more remnants of what used to be a ladder as he moved into the circular concrete tube at the bottom. A single light twenty feet down the horizontal shaft showed a slight downward cant farther on. Cautiously Darren stepped into the concrete tube, hearing his footsteps echo all the way down it. The sounds of receding footsteps returned from the tunnel.

"Van!" Darren shouted over the amplifier.

"Right here." Van stood next to the 8 foot SAMAS.

"Oh, sorry, I didn't see you there. How did you get down here?"

"The only thing you didn't break was the rope and pulley system above the trap door."

"There's somebody up ahead."

"I'll go first, just don't shoot through me to hit the bad guys."

"How boring."

"You got anything on thermo?"

"There's some kind of conduit running beneath us that's warmer than the concrete, but nothing up ahead. U.V. shows some stains on the floor, but it doesn't look fresh."

The two crept forward, armored feet dashing the possibility of stealth. Another light bulb showed the tunnel beginning to level out.

"You hear that?" Darren asked.

"No." Van strained to listen.

More exoskeleton sounds. A muffled scream echoed up the tunnel. Neither man required communication to synchronize movement, and with fluid precision flowed down the hall towards the sound. The fetid stench of death permeated the last stretch of poorly lit tunnel. Bursting out the other end, Van rolled behind a stone pillar, a blazing ball of fire searing past to blacken the walls behind him.

Advancing a bit more quickly, Darren took what cover he could behind a pillar on the opposite side of the temple, rear thrusters scratching the wall behind him. Howls from a triad of creatures brought Darren's rail gun around the pillar in response. Stumbling across the open temple floor were three linen wrapped corpses, and below an ornate throne were the bodies of newly slain humans. Seated on the throne was a man with the head of a hyena, adorned with an Egyptian headdress and wielding a curved staff.

Credo rose in his full battle regalia, delusions of godhood possessing his thoughts and actions. How dare these unbelievers desecrate his temple before he could raise hellfire to consume it in honor of Annubis.

Van made a break for the throne but was flung to the far wall with a rush of wind from Credo's fingertips. Dodging from pillar to pillar, Van renewed his approach more carefully. Grabbing a torch from its iron grating, he set a mummy screaming in terror as its body burned away in layers. For an instant Van locked gazes with the human effigy of Annubis, and then the battle was begun.

Using the pillar as a shield, Van empowered the back-up modifications of his armor and primed his powerful hand-held weapon.

Stone shattered behind him as flames poured past his armor ineffectually. Spinning around, Van fired through the opening in the pillar. Bolts of telekinetic force struck Credo's magic barrier and threw him back over the throne. A quick glance over his shoulder showed him the last mummy being ripped limb from limb by Darren's exoskeleton. Time to finish the Federation Lord for good.

The temple was suddenly plunged into darkness so thick not a ray of light from the flickering torches could pierce it. Incoherent verses of a powerful spell were being invoked from somewhere in the darkness, mingled with the loud, heavy steps of an armored exoskeleton. Darren stepped into the center of the temple and looked from side to side at the clearly defined heat signatures around him. He knew the speaking mage had to be stopped before the spell was completed, but he was invisible to thermo-imaging optics in the ornate battle suit. Switching to infrared, Darren activated the SAMAS spotlight and I.R. filters. A narrow beam of vision cleared in the thick magic darkness. Back and forth the beam sliced through blackness until it discovered the chanting mage reaching the climax of his spell. Reflexes took over, and Darren was amazed to see his own left arm come up and fire without conscious effort. The mini-missile trail was a mere flash in the darkness as it shot the 20 feet to detonation. Pillars shattered and the throne melted away as plasma expanded with violent coercion. The force of the enclosed explosion threw Van to the temple floor and struck every object with conflicting impact. Credo's magic barriers surrendered to the onslaught, his body slammed through the far wall and affectations burned away instantly. Unable to withstand the blast, Credo's magic staff turned to ash.

"Ooooh, that's gotta hurt!"

Light poured in through sections of the smashed wall, streams through smoke accenting Credo's position. Air rushed in to feed dying fires, making swirling patterns in the streaks of light. Darkness ceased, revealing the mauled temple and melted bodies. Darren wasted no time mourning the dead and moved to deal with the living. The smoking armor suit was running down the short concrete hall, with Darren's exoskeleton closing the distance fast. Around the corner Credo ran, for once in his life beginning to fear his adversaries. He needed more lives to squelch and life force to absorb, but the entrance to his dungeon seemed so far away. Rapid speech saved his life with a simple invocation. Credo never paused to witness the Coalition SAMAS collide with he glowing blue wall of force. Slamming the thick door behind him Credo threw the bolt to lock his enemies out of the dungeon for one more moment.

"Damn!" Darren cursed, slamming into the magical wall. "I'm getting sick of this magic!"

"Shoot it!" Van yelled, coming up from behind with a slight limp. "It's not that strong."

"Get back around the corner. This is gonna ricochet." Darren took two steps back and loosed a stream of metal slugs. Rounds hit the barrier and left tiny white marks in the glowing field. Two more bursts scattered mushroomed slugs across the stained floor but annihilated any vestige of the energy field.

"Big surprise. It's locked." Van ran to the front and yanked the metal chain on the door.

"Not to worry, master key coming through."

Darren took the door off its hinges without half trying. Tossing it aside, he moved cautiously into a large chamber illuminated by incandescent lamps suspended from a high ceiling. The walls were lined with makeshift cages and cells, and the stench of human waste was almost overpowering. Various torture devices occupied the center of the chamber and beyond it a shimmering wall of force blocked a tall arched hallway. Whimpers and cries from dozens of prisoners mingled with screams of those in the chamber's center. Credo was nowhere in sight.

"He's not here!" Van covered his mouth in reflex, allowing similar systems in his armor to activate and purify the air. "He's gotta be down that hall."

"Good god —" Darren continued his tirade, unable to express his horror at the center of the room. Above the dying was a suspended cross, a beautiful woman unmercifully crucified upon it. Blood dripped in pools from the two others on either side of her. Both men stood in momentary shock.

"Anja, this is Van, do you read me?" Van tried to contact Anja over the radio but only got static in return.

"We gotta get them down." Darren grabbed the base of the center cross and gently ripped the chains from pulleys attached to the ceiling. Lowering it carefully to the floor, he moved on to the other two. Van went to assist him.

Something clicked in Van's brain as he watched Darren's attempt to free the tortured. All was not as it seemed, although he couldn't say exactly what. Danger lurked so close he could feel its icy fingers brush his flesh and make his skin crawl beneath the armor. He looked around the chamber for any sign of danger, but all he saw was death and suffering of innocents. Darren had gently set the last of the three crosses on the floor and was carefully pulling the metal spikes from the bodies of the injured. Van's heart froze when Darren reached the center cross and pulled away a spike from the woman's wrist. Thick greenish blood oozed up from the open wound and trailed away on the spike.

Adjusting his optics to view the aura of the unfortunate maiden Van choked out for Darren to stop. Waves of red and black emanated from the woman's evil core, an evil so extreme it defied human comprehension. Only once had Van viewed such an aura, and that was the closest he'd ever come to losing his life. Darren pulled the second spike from the woman's arm.

"Darren! No! Kill it!" Van screamed, adjusting the choke on his weapon for concentrated fire.

"Kill what?"

"Her! The demon! It's a demon you idiot! A succubus!"

"Huh? A suc u what?" Darren looked back down at the ravishing redhead to find her shifting into a horrific black scaled creature. "Oh, man." he murmured.

Timbers splintered with no effort as the demon freed itself of the ruse. One shove sent Darren's exoskeleton sliding across the floor. Too numbed to respond, Darren just stared, eyes wild and mouth open in shock. The lizard-like demon hissed and turned on the Techno-Wizard.

Van's TX-5 breathed and green blood splattered the crucified victim on the left. The Succubus jerked with the telekinetic impact, its eyes glazed with pain and anger. Leaping fifteen feet in a single bound, it twisted in mid-air to avoid Van's second blast, coming down just inches from the gun's barrel. Powerful claws raked across magic shielding, sending Van's TX-5 flying into a crowded cell.

Reaching for his back-up weapon, Van was knocked to the floor by a blow to the chest. As the demon's claws raised for another blow, Van brushed across a secret panel on his forearm and pressed through to skin. The Flyssa was back in his hand and plunging its tip through scale and gristle. Reeling with surprise at its recent injury, the demon pulled itself away, leaving the tip of Van's sword coated in thick blood.

Slipping past the blade faster than Van imagined possible, the demon took hold of his arm and swung him against the bars of a cell. As metal fatigued and bent, Van tryed not to lose consciousness. An instant later the bars gave way behind him as the demon's other fist struck with deadly force.

Frightened prisoners dragged themselves to the corners, having seen what the demon had done to the others. One lone man scrambled for Van's weapon. May's husband pulled the trigger on Van's TX-5 but the modified weapon refused to respond without a psychic link.

Wrenching a bar from the cage, the demon wielded it as a club and thrashed its way inside the cell after Van. Repeatedly it swung the metal bar against Van's invisible Mystic armor until the make-shift club was bent to uselessness. Van's feeble struggle to regain his footing met with a blow to the helmet from the demon's clawed foot.

Green blood splattered Van's magic barrier and then ran down the sides of his body in streaks. Recovering from the shock of what he'd just seen, Darren bored a hole through the demon's back with a close range burst of metal. Shrieking horribly, the demon spun around clutching its gaping wound. Van's gun was handed back to him and he brought the sights in line with the demon's scarred head.

Centering the barrel on the demon's chest, Darren blew its heart out a six inch hole in its back. The head snapped foreword, caught by a concentrated blast from behind, brains raining down in a grayish-green mist. It wobbled then crumpled in a widening pool of green ooze.

"You okay, buddy?" Darren bent the bars wider.

"I'm okay." Van heard himself say.

"Hey you,." Darren addressed the one man standing apart from the other prisoners. "Where did that magic sorcerer dude with the long ears go?"

"Through there." May's husband uttered through swollen, blood-caked lips. He read something out of a notebook and that magic wall appeared."

"Do what you can to help the others. We're going after him." Van patted the man lightly on the shoulder and then moved to the shimmering wall with Darren.

The high arched hall had strange inscriptions carved into the stone walls, and the floor was comprised of cracked stone slabs. A feeling of dread grew stronger with every step they took toward the shimmering wall of energy. The fear was unlike anything either had experienced before. Each time they gazed upon the shimmering wall, it seemed as though untold horrors awaited them past its depths. In his studies, Van had heard stories of powerful magic barriers that could make the bravest soul flee in terror and the stout of heart falter. Darren stopped less than ten feet from the wall, metallic hands visibly shaking.

"There's something really bad in there, I know it!"

"It's not real. There's nothing real in there to harm you. You must believe that or you won't get through it."

"I, I just know if I go in there I'll die."

"You won't die, it's not capable of even hurting you." Van secretly hoped he was correct.

Darren took another faltering step.

"I can't believe this. I can't even get near it!"

"Don't worry about it. Stay here and help everyone get out in case something really nasty is actually back there."

"I can't make myself go near it."

"It's magic Darren! It's not your fault!"

Darren took two steps back.

"Right, it's magic. It's making me do this. I'm sorry, I can't make it through." The exoskeleton's hand clenched into a thumbs-up. "Good luck."

"Hey, it's me, remember? What could happen?" Van grinned momentarily then plunged into the shimmering barrier.

Chapter 8

Springing from the hidden recesses of Van's mind came horrors he never wished to acknowledge. Undead versions of loved ones hacked at him with bloody cleavers and sucked the blood from him like vampires. Fighting off the swirling mist of visions, Van stepped through the other side into an open corridor dimly lit by some unseen source. Again his heart leapt to his throat and caused icy fingers of adrenaline to shoot their spiked nails through his chest.

Lining the walls were rank after rank of Sunaj Assassins in black armor and demonic helms. At the end of the hall was a horrible tentacled beast with a single inhuman eye at the center of its undulating mass. Uttering a single arcane phrase, the creature ordered Van to join them or die.

"Wait!" Van yelled, but the first rank was already upon him. Without thinking Van fired the TX-5 and swung madly with his sword. The blade sliced a horn from one end and cut through the faceplate of another. Blows rained down on him in a torrent but Van refused to give in. With a single mighty thrust he caught the fangs of a Sunaj helmet and ripped it from the Assassin's head.

Thick black hair fell down over the Assassin's shoulders and dark eyes stared back with chilling malice. Choking in shock, Van stepped back from the handsome figure smiling at him with a evil grin. His attacker's face was his own!

"No, no this is an illusion. It's not real."

"Of course it's real, and now you must die so I can live," the Sunaj Van sneered, identical sword appearing in his hand. The other Assassins backed away to give them room.

"No! I know who you are, and it will never be me. You can't kill me because you don't exist and never will!"

"I do exist. Fight me! Your very existence depends on it!"

"No!" Van stuck the tip of his blade in the stone floor and holstered his weapon.

"You're a coward! You've always been the coward. Fight me!" The darker Van menaced him, black cloak flapping out behind him as he raised the sword to strike.

"You're not real. You can't harm me."

"Ahhhh!" The Sunaj swung the blade in a falling arc, then vanished.

The hall was vacant, without a trace of the evil beings that had been there before. Van slowly pulled his blade from the floor and looked at the blast marks his weapon had made in the wall near the shimmering barrier. Had it all been an apparition? He shook his head and tried to clear away the lingering images.

At the end of the hall was another wooden door. A renewed strength came over him and he broke into a run.

Blasting the lock from the door, Van kicked it aside and burst into the large laboratory. Bent over a metal filing cabinet was the Federation Lord. Credo's head snapped up and for a moment Van could see fear in his eyes. Devoid of armor and with his hands full of documents, Credo was at the mercy end of Van's telekinetic weapon.

"Move, speak, or even breathe and I'll blast you where you stand." Van slowly walked closer, watching the mage above three tiny dots on his weapon. He held his blade in his left hand, casually swinging it back and forth as he walked.

"If you kill me, you will lose out on the opportunity for power beyond your wildest dreams." Credo spoke smoothly.

"Anything you have I can take when you're dead."

"Anything except the knowledge I possess."

"I don't need to know how to torture and maim the innocent, or kill without remorse. You have nothing I want."

"Look over there and tell me what you see." Credo jerked his head at a section of open floor in the sorcerer's lab.

Van's gaze never wavered.

"That's a pretty lame play for a powerful Lord of the Federation. You're going to have to do better than that." Van pointed the blood-stained blade at Credo's left eye, trying to decide if he should kill the mage outright or keep him alive long enough for the villagers to exact revenge.

"And what can I do in a split second? You would be foolish not to look."

Van's eyes shifted then did an extended double take. Arranged on the floor were a series of circles, all with arcane symbols and a variety of components. The blade lowered momentarily.

Van's recent studies concentrated on wards and symbols. The same studies touched on ancient circle magic like the ones he saw here, and had seen his parents create when he was a child.

"Where did you find those?"

"They are mine. They possess power beyond your wildest imagination, and they are yours for one simple request."

"I don't need to learn your Necromantic rituals!"

"Not all would offend your sensitivity, but all are worth the price. If you don't value their power, then why don't you kill me?"

Van looked back at the circles and knew the secrets were lost to all but a few who would never share the knowledge. He stared at the mage who understood the circle's powers. The Elf stared back with a smirk that Van could have killed him for alone. The blade never moved.

"That's not all I can offer you, of course. There are spells I've translated from scrolls obtained from my Demon Locust. Spells of complexity and power meant only for the most powerful of demons and arch mages to master. They, too, are yours."

"Where?"

"Over there, on the computer." Credo looked at the small lap top at its docking station on the table. Van gave the Elf a look of disbelief.

"Right. I believe that. On the computer."

"It's a new world with newer inventions. You of all people should understand and appreciate the use of technology over archaic tomes that rot and turn to dust with age." The Elf's grin was more annoying than before.

"Budge and you die," Van growled, backing to the work table. The computer was already on, and Van reached out to it with his mind in a way only a Techno-Wizard could. Communicating with the device, Van requested and accessed file after file until the screen displayed a menu of incantations and other magic manifestations.

"If you allow me one request, I will give you the access codes."

"I don't need your access codes. I already know what you have on here."

"It will take time for you to learn such complex spells, of course, but I'm certain that if you've gotten this far then you're hardly an idiot." Credo grinned.

Van wanted to smoke him where he stood, but was restrained by the possibility of acquiring such powerful magic knowledge. It could take a lifetime to accumulate the knowledge contained in this lab, and it could all be his if he wanted it. Striding back to the mage, he stuck the blade an inch from his face.

"What treachery are you hiding from me?"

"None, of course."

"I warn you, if you are hiding something I'll kill you without thinking twice."

"You're the one who must decide between petty vengeance or a lifetime of wealth, knowledge, and glory. It would take you several lifetimes in fact, if you were to search out what I can give you right now." Credo's eyes focused on the writing engraved in the magic blade. His eyes grew wider. "Oh, my apologies, I never realized you were one of them."

"A lifetime's a long time."

"I think you will find that all it means is we will cross paths again, though on which path that will be, is up to you."

"What are you talking about?"

"I thought you...." Credo's voice trailed off and his eyes glazed for an instant of deep thought. "You do know, of course, don't you?"

"Know what?"

"If I were beaten by a mere human that would be too great a disgrace, but to have one of your kind defeat me is almost understandable. An honor."

"What are you babbling about?" Van hoped the Elf didn't know for sure what he'd suspected all his life.

"We are allies, you and I."

"Like hell we are."

"You are Aehriman, and I am Federation."

"I'll cut out your tongue and shove it down your throat!" Van's blood boiled.

"Surely you know. You must know."

"Not everyone is part of that evil! I should kill you for saying it out loud!"

"You're young, and in time, when you become more powerful you may change your mind." Credo spoke solemnly.

"Never! I will never be part of what my clan has started."

"Just the same, our paths will cross again someday." Credo slowly reached over and lifted a small wooden box from the top of the filing cabinet. Van made no move to stop him.

With eyes fixed on Van's blade, Credo carefully backed into the center of a large circle.

"Watch and listen carefully to my words. Someday this power will be yours, and then we will both serve the same masters."

Credo gently lifted a pair of Faerie wings from the box and set them in a small brass brazier at the center of the circle. Muttering a simple incantation brought flames to life in the brazier, consuming the Faerie wings in a flash of light. Credo raised his voice and shouted a phrase to unlock the physical bonds of space and link to another place far away. The last of the flames sparkled in the brazier.

"Acba yin Lo-kum yin Cherubot-kyn!"

The circle glowed brilliant white and a swirling vortex of colors swept over Credo's body. The colors dimmed and the circle faded to its dull luster. Credo was gone.

Letting his guard relax Van looked around the laboratory and then back to the shimmering barrier still sealing off the outside world. For the time being he would indulge himself in exploring his newfound wealth.

First light became the dawn of freedom for May's village. In shallow graves rested those who had died in the bloodshed of nightfall, but their lives were mourned amid awakening joy. Survivors piled remnants of Credo's army onto huge bonfires, and at Anja's direction, the heads of zombies were severed and buried apart from their bodies to prevent regeneration. Sir Renfield and Mr. Kent instructed villagers in the use of weapons captured from Credo's army, should it be necessary for them to defend themselves from other threats in the future. From the ashes of the still burning village a new one was being reborn.

Greg Merrick leaned against his parked SAMAS and watched his unit accept the heartfelt gratitude of men, women, and children. Cowboy had a human child on his lap, no doubt extolling heroics of days gone by and D-Bees slain. Sergeant Winters shared a food ration with a malnourished teenager, all the while maintaining his gruff facade. In the distance he could make out the Enforcer digging a line of graves for the piles of headless zombies being collected by Coalition troops and joyous villagers. Greg didn't feel the cold morning breeze biting his exposed skin for the warmth he felt inside. This was one of the reasons he joined the Coalition military. To help free humanity from the dark clutches of evil practitioners of magic and cruel dimensional beings. Although the deed would undoubtably foster positive attitudes towards the Coalition States, public relations were the least of Greg's motivations. To have so successfully struck a blow for humanity and freed a village of an evil tyrant was enough to be content.

"Good morning, Lieutenant Merrick." Sir Renfield wearily came to stand beside the Coalition officer. The knight's cape was tattered and his armor splattered with dried blood, but a calm look of satisfaction emanated from his face.

"Morning. Are you going to be okay out here by yourselves? We have to leave soon."

"We'll manage. I'm afraid we won't be staying very long either, but I think they can handle things on their own from now on."

Both men watched in silence at the joyful reunion of May's husband and family.

"Any word on the Federation Lord?" Greg asked after a long pause.

"As far as I know he managed to escape, at least that's what Sinclair Van De Graf told me. We didn't move fast enough to kill or capture him I'm afraid."

"Let's hope he doesn't return when we're gone."

"He's been soundly defeated and disgraced in the eyes of the Federation. If he has any sense he'll go far away and stay there."

"Just the same, I'd feel much better if I had a body to put in the fires." Greg spoke without looking at the Cyber-Knight.

"With good fortune one day you will. Well, I guess until we happen to join forces again, good-bye and thank you for all you've done." Sir Renfield straightened up to leave. "We couldn't have done it without you."

He extended an armor-plated hand to Greg. Greg looked at it with indifference, contemplating the ramifications of shaking hands with an undeclared enemy of the Coalition States. At last he grasped the Cyber-Knight's hand without reservation in a firm handshake.

"It's been good fighting on the same side, David, I hope it always stays that way."

Both men turned at Anja's tentative approach.

"Um, I wanted to thank you, Lieutenant, for taking such risks to help us. May told me what you had to do to come here. I know it couldn't have been easy."

"The hard part is yet to come." Greg half smiled, thinking of how angry Captain Pritchett sounded on the radio half an hour earlier.

"David, have you seen Van?" Anja asked quietly.

"Last I saw him he was in the makeshift hospital we set up for the wounded. Something's kind of fishy about that story he told me about Credo. He wouldn't tell me much."

"I'll talk to him. You two stay here and talk man stuff." She smiled and walked away, poorly concealing a devious smile. Maybe she wasn't the smartest person in the world but that didn't mean she wasn't aware of the changes taking place in the two men's minds.

Greg caught Renfield staring at Anja's behind as she skipped away. When the knight realized he'd been caught he tried to think of something pious to say, but the smile growing on Greg's face was infectious.

"Yep." Greg nodded conspiritoraly.

"Yep." Sir Renfield cracked a smile in agreement.

Arriving at the tarp covered hospital area, Anja could hardly believe her own eyes. Where half hour before fifty pallets bore the injured and dying, now all were devoid of any beings whatsoever. No broken, bleeding bodies met her eyes, instead a lone figure sat leaning up against the wooden center pole. As she quietly moved closer, Van opened tired eyes and smiled faintly. Anja looked at the empty, blood stained mats and back to the Techno-Wizard.

"You?"

Van nodded. Anja sat beside him and held her bow across her lap.

"You okay?"

"Just very, very tired. That's all."

"There were so many. How did you heal them all?"

"It's a long story, but mostly I cheated." Van held up a small, whirring device with flashing lights.

"Your salt shaker thing?" Anja joked, and Van smiled thinly.

"Yeah, my salt shaker thing." He put the V-MED back in a pouch with a host of other weird looking devices. Anja's liquid aqua eyes were on him and he could feel the gentle empathic probes searching his surface thoughts, but he was too tired to block her out. Lying would get him nowhere, so Van broke down and gave her the truth, or at least enough to cover what he didn't want her to know. She reached out and touched his hand.

"Van, you don't need to feel guilty about the sorcerer escaping. You were the only one of us with any chance of stopping him, and you did all you could. Nobody can ask you to do more than that. We're all very proud of what you did, nobody else could have done it."

Great, Van thought to himself, now he was feeling more guilty than before. Gazing into her eyes he suddenly realized how open and honest she was with everybody, and how much she deserved somebody who could do the same. Something he could never do. He was a fool to have ever considered romantic interests.

"That's not true." she whispered.

Van mentally chastised himself. *Too tired to think straight. Better quit while your ahead.*

"I wish I could tell you everything, Anja, I really wish I could, but there's just no way. My life is complicated." He stood and released her hand.

"I'm not asking for all that," she whispered.

"What you deserve, what you need, I can't give you. What I want isn't fair to you either. I'd better go check on my cycle." Van fumbled for any excuse that would get him away from her. Secretly though, he itched to delve deeper into what he'd uncovered in Credo's laboratory.

"Will you think about it, for me?"

Turning back, Van was again transfixed by her pureness of heart and possessing beauty. Forces tore at him from many directions, but at last love, reluctantly gave way to his obsession for knowledge.

"I'll think about it." he muttered and strode away with a stiff gait. No matter how hard he tried it always wound up the same. This time, however, the stakes were a great deal higher.

Darren circled the body of the last fleeing Brodkil to fall, just to be sure it wasn't playing dead. Splattered innards reassured him the demon was finished, and the weary RPA headed back to the village where his unit was gathering for the return trip. Most of the fires started throughout the village had either burned themselves out or were extinguished by morning. Now visible under the lightly clouded sky, the plumes of white smoke rose in less than a dozen places.

"Merrick to SAM 15. What's your 20?"

"On my way back from your north-east. I'm gonna make one last sweep of the north side and then I'll be there."

"Make it fast, we're on our way out right now. I've got Brian on point for now, so I'll need you to switch with him in case we run into any trouble."

"I'm down to 28% on my slug drum. Maybe Brian could use the extra practice," Darren suggested.

"Where's your extra drum?"

"Back at camp."

"Why?"

"C'mon Lieutenant, y'know I hate slingin' a spare drum. All that extra weight is a pain in the rear. It cuts down my mobility."

"Just the same, I want you on point as soon as you're finished with your sweep. I'll take your 28% over Brian's 90%, if you know what I mean. If we really need, to I'll swap my spare for yours."

"That's more stylin'. SAM 15 out." Darren pulled a sharp U-turn and headed back for the real reason of his delay.

Bright red hair caught early morning sunlight, making Cyndiara stand out against the drab log cabins. She covered her eyes as Darren's SAMAS touched down several meters away. Darren felt a sigh of relief to see she was alone. She watched him with mournful eyes as he exited the exoskeleton and slowly came to stand a few feet away.

"I didn't think you were going to stop." she spoke, green eyes searching his. "I thought you were just going to leave again."

"C'mon, babe, I wasn't going to leave without seeing you first." Darren moved a step closer but got no warming response. "It's good to see you again." He looked away, feeling awkward.

"I never thought I would see you again." Tears welled up in her eyes.

"Me either. It, it really stinks, but I have to go. My unit's waiting for me." Darren almost wished he hadn't stopped at all. The pain of seeing her again was too much.

"You're still going to Liberty?"

"How did, where did you hear that?"

"Delwin."

"Huh? Ohhh. Delwin." Darren thought back to the odd meeting 24 hours earlier.

"Yeah, Delwin." Cyndiara's features broke into a thin smile.

"Well it was good seeing you again. I really have to go." Darren tried to escape the awkward pause.

"Will I see you at Liberty?"

"You're going to Liberty?

"Yes." she made uncomfortable eye contact.

"Well, yeah, then I guess so. If I make it, anyway. Yeah, I'll see you at Liberty." Darren backed away nodding, then walked forward and gave her a stiff hug. It wasn't returned.

Without another word Darren turned around and jogged to the open SAMAS. There were lots of things he needed to think about before they met again.

Warned ahead of time by Sharp as to the reception waiting at base camp, Lieutenant Merrick halted the returning convoy to converse in private with Sergeant Winters. The two stood just out of earshot, but both knew anyone in a mech would secretly be listening in. Birds chirped happily in the trees as the men tried to plan a way out of armageddon.

"Well ya know whatever goes down, I'll back ya." Winters spoke confidently, more for the benefit of those listening than Greg's.

"Like I said, we have several options here. One, we just return and pretend we didn't circumvent direct orders, taking our chances Pritchett won't attempt a field court-martial."

"And then there's always the stuff we gotta hack when we get back to C-town."

"I'm not concerned with that. My guess is a tribunal will give us medals when they find out how we took down a Federation Lord and saved a human village without losing a single man. No, Pritchett knows that too, that's why he has to deal with us by himself to save face in front of his troops."

"Forget 'im," was Winters advice.

"Don't think I haven't thought of other options too." Greg leaned closer and talked quietly. " Sharp's in position. A clean kill.

"Well let's do it then. Sharp's sly, he can git clear."

"But that leaves Goldstein in command, and that spineless sissy will do whatever Pritchett's goon squad wants."

"Have Sharp waste him too."

"As much as I'd like to, I'm afraid that might spark the same kind of direct confrontation we're trying to avoid. Unfortunately we may be past the point of solving this without violence. If it comes to that are you ready to go all the way?"

"All the way."

"Let's do it. My way first, but if something happens to me, you know what you have to do."

Chapter 9

Dust and small pebbles pelted the mud-caked legs of the Enforcer as Sergeant Winters brought the hover rover to a stop before a line of troops in the Coalition camp. Every remaining soldier and piece of equipment appeared to be ready to move on to the next destination, but Winters knew from their positions it was more to prevent any of the returning forces from escaping. There was no other reason for having every hatch and turret manned, or every troop in a state of combat readiness. If a stand-off degenerated into a confrontation, it would be anyone's guess who made it out alive.

Captain Pritchett stood beneath his command Skull Walker accompanied by what Greg often referred to as the "goon squad." Two Full Conversion Cyborgs and half a dozen other members of Pritchett's unit stood by to obey any order given by their commander. While most on both sides would hesitate to fire on their own, Winters doubted the goon squad would have such reservations.

"Cowboy, Bill," Winters growled in a low voice. No other order was needed for the men in the rover to move into action. Bill casually stood and leaned on the rover's swivel mount rail gun while Cowboy and his fire squad sauntered over to where Greg was exiting his SAMAS. Winters nodded to Brian and the technical officer strolled up beside the captain's APC and leaned his SAMAS against the side hatch, forcing Lieutenant Goldstein back inside. The Skull Walkers faced off at fifty feet, and the Abolisher's cannons twitched slightly lower to cover the smaller Enforcer inching up on it. Both sides knew the Enforcer was the wild card, capable of tipping the odds on whatever side Corrinne chose. If she got close enough to any of the larger robots, it would be relatively simple to take them out hand to hand.

Forty yards back in the forest Sharp aligned his sights on the poorly concealed sniper on the opposite side of camp. All of this was way too much like all the old western vids he'd watched in underground theaters back in Chi-Town. The air was electric with tension and Sharp couldn't help but whistle a select tone from his favorite western of all time.

"Dang, Merrick's has guts," Darren mused to himself as he watched Greg calmly stride across no-mans-land toward the Captain. "No armor, no weapon, just guts."

Falling in step behind the lieutenant were Cowboy, Nim, and six others to help even the odds. In a fair fight against the two opposing cyborgs, they didn't stand a chance, but Cowboy and Nim held weapons in one hand and a shaped charge behind their backs with the other. A fusion block detonating on the back of a cyborg's head generally removed it from the picture for good. Dealing with the others would be a piece of cake by comparison.

"If it flies, duck an' we'll cover ya back to yer SAM." Cowboy whispered.

"Hopefully that won't be necessary," Greg replied.

For some reason he wasn't scared, or even apprehensive. Here was a potentially lethal situation and yet he was without a twinge of fear. That worried Greg more than anything else, and he wondered how in control of his tongue he really was. It wasn't just his life he was gambling with. Coming to a stop just feet from the captain, Greg calmly looked over the welcoming party with a disinterested gaze.

"Morning, Captain, we're back from maneuvers and ready to move out as soon as you are."

"I hope you have a very good explanation for your actions."

"I beg your pardon, sir?"

"I don't want to hear some story about night maneuvers and training. You disobeyed a direct order, Lieutenant." Captain Pritchett's jaw set hard and his face grew redder.

"What order would that be, sir? Specifically."

"You knowingly and willfully countermanded my order not to aid that village!"

"And at what time did you order me not to engage in training maneuvers? Sir?" Greg felt a strange sense of glee riding in where politically minded caution should have been. He knew the right things to say and how to say them, but that wasn't how it was coming out. He'd been out in the field too long, Greg concluded, and was enjoying this confrontation too much. Pritchett's face twisted in anger, then smoothed over to a putty-like smile that poorly masked his rage.

"Very well, Lieutenant, as of twenty minutes ago I reported this incident to the head of Chi-Town Espionage Division, Colonel Lyboc, and I've been given the authority to relieve you of duty, permanently. Lieutenant Goldstein will assume command of your unit," Pritchett announced matter-of-factly, looking to the APC where his first lieutenant should have been.

Lieutenant Goldstein tried to worm past Brian's SAMAS but the exoskeleton kept shifting its weight from side to side, daring him to take the chance of being crushed. The career minded officer wasn't stupid. He wanted nothing to do with Greg's special ops unit, and had told the captain so repeatedly. Something told him he'd wind up getting fragged by friendly fire in the very first battle. Finally he climbed through a top hatch and hesitantly approached the showdown. Greg's keen senses read a different truth in Goldstein's eyes.

"You're a liar, sir." Greg turned back to Pritchett.

"I'm, what?" Pritchett blinked, never losing the putty smile.

"You never called H.Q., and you never talked to Lyboc."

"Are you calling me a liar?" Pritchett's hands shook with rage.

"Yes, I'm calling you a liar. Lyboc's a lying, backstabber, but I'm out here doing his dirty laundry, and he's sure not going to jeopardize his mission because of you. Respectfully speaking, of course. Sir."

"You can believe what you want, Lieutenant, I'm still relieving you of duty on my own authority." Pritchett practically shook with barely controlled fury. He'd all but admitted his deception to the men under his command.

"I don't think so, sir." Greg heard himself speak, almost tauntingly.

"Restrain the lieutenant."

Everything happened at once. The sound of weapons being readied and shuffling of feet came from all sides, and within seconds almost every gun in camp was facing another gun. Two cyborgs on either side of Pritchett stood like statues in mid-step, each with a fusion block latched to the backs of their heads and finger hovering above the detonator button. The Abolisher found itself precariously balanced on the Enforcer's hip, just seconds from being thrown down and pinned. Those troops that might have backed Pritchett before glanced at each other trying to make up their minds.

Greg smiled broadly at Captain Pritchett without once looking around at the stand-off, the stakes raised to new levels.

"Now what, Captain?"

"Sergio." Pritchett ordered the SAMAS forward, and drew his own weapon to level at Merrick's head.

Sergio took his time moving forward, hoping to see fear in the lieutenant's eyes. Instead the world spun crazily and the back of his head slammed against the inside of his helmet so hard it made stars fly. Through galaxies and nebulas Sergio made out the very large end of Darren's rail gun pointed directly at his left eye piece.

"Give me an excuse," Darren breathed, holding the other exoskeleton down with an armored foot. "Please, give me any excuse to waste you."

Greg shrugged his shoulders.

"This isn't what I wanted, how about you?"

"Don't forget I could blast you where you stand!" Pritchett flipped the safety off his laser sidearm.

"Not a groovy plan there, Captain." Darren pointed his left forearm mini-missile launcher at the mission commander, never allowing the rail gun to waver from its deadly mark.

Pritchett looked at the loaded mini-missile tubes, then back at Merrick. The explosion would kill the lieutenant instantly, but Pritchett knew he wouldn't be around to see it. A breeze blew cold sweat from his forehead, and he glanced slowly around him at the tinder box waiting to explode. The putty smile returned, and he placed his sidearm back in its holster.

"Perhaps this isn't the best time to resolve the issue."

"I didn't think so either." Greg smiled back.

"I will of course file a lengthy, detailed report of this incident. You will be court-martialled without a doubt."

"Not likely. You see my own report will go something like this. While conducting a nighttime training maneuver, our exercises brought us close to a small village, very much like the one encountered earlier that day by the river, except inhabited by humans. We came under fire from hostile forces camped around this village, and upon investigation discovered them to be monsters controlled by a Federation Lord. Acting in the interest of self preservation and the policies of the Coalition States, I ordered a retaliatory strike which not only destroyed many inhuman creatures but killed a Lord of the Federation of Magic. The human village in question was freed of these monsters' tyranny. Through the skill and bravery of both my own men and Captain Pritchett's, not one of our brave soldiers was lost." Greg paused, letting his words sink in. "Do I need to add the part where you tried to arrest me for destroying enemies of the Coalition?"

Pritchett stood silent for what seemed like forever.

"Include what you like." Pritchett never lost the smile. "But then I would be forced to include the part where your men assaulted my unit and directly threatened me with death." Pritchett glanced over at Darren's mini-missile launcher.

"Maybe it would be better if we all just forgot the whole thing happened. Long day, strain of the battle with the creature the other night, no doubt made all of us a little edgy, wouldn't you say?" Greg found the words he should have started with.

"I would have to agree, officially of course."

"Of course."

The two exchanged fake smiles. Greg looked around him, feeling strongly elated.

"Darren, you may stop directly threatening Captain Pritchett with death."

"Yes sir. What about him?" Darren jabbed the prone SAMAS with the tip of his rail gun barrel.

"Him too."

Darren stepped off Sergio's SAMAS, signalling a lowering of weapons and relax of posture. Corrinne returned the Abolisher to its upright position. Sergio jerked to his feet, enraged but under control. Cowboy and Nim stepped away from the cyborgs, holding the fusion blocks in plain view in a taunting manner.

"We're leaving now. Have your unit assume point, maybe they could use some daytime exercises as well." Pritchett smiled again, feeling a bit uneasy now that the Enforcer's crew had shown their true colors.

"Wouldn't have it any other way." Greg grinned. "Sergeant!"

"Yes sir!" Winters barked.

"Move out."

"And that's why I'm seeking gainful employment with your mercenary company," Credo finished his long winded interview with Zenjori Suka, leader of the Army of the New Order. Finding the notorious mercenary group had been child's play compared to getting hired by them. Most of the members were distrustful of Elves, for which Credo could think of many reasons that were well founded. However Zenjori had been amazingly courteous and charismatic, and had listened to his story with an almost aristocratic air Credo that appreciated.

"It seems we both have suffered injustice at the hands of the Coalition. You've heard correctly, we do pay very well, especially for someone of your obvious talents," Zenjori replied smoothly, cocking his head in Torrak's direction. "But you see we already have a proficient mage. What do you have to offer that my Gromek Shifter does not?"

"I wouldn't dream of slighting your Gromek Mage." Credo accented 'your' and was pleased with the Gromek's scowl. "I'm sure for a Gromek his powers are astonishing. What I can offer you is not a few simple spells known by any passing wizard, but the command of demon legions summoned forth and controlled by my magic. I'm certain that working together with Torrax I can provide you with an edge the Coalition will not be prepared for."

"My name is Torrak, and I will not work with Elven garbage."

"You will do as I say as long as I am paying you," Zenjori snapped, feeling a growing dislike for both. The Elf at least seemed intelligent and educated, but also a possible threat.

"My apologies, Torrak, I assumed you would have welcomed the opportunity to gain some greater spell knowledge. Forgive me for my short sightedness." Credo bowed graciously, and his heart skipped a beat when he first saw the mace. Suspended from Torrak's belt was a black, spike-headed mace that radiated a magic aura like Credo had never seen in all his 250 years. The mace at Torrak's side was a greater rune weapon, and Credo suddenly realized where his destiny was taking him.

"Give me a moment to speak with my associates." Zenjori bowed politely and motioned Colnae to his side. "What do you think?"

"He's telling the truth, but not all of it."

"I agree. Notec, your assessment please," Zenjori asked the wispy haired advisor.

"He has ulterior motives, for sure, but he does genuinely loathe the Coalition and could be a powerful ally."

"There's something familiar about him, but I can't quite put my finger on it." Colnae stroked his gotee thoughtfully. "I have it. I saw him at a wizards' convention several years ago. I know who he is. This man is not who he claims to be. He's a powerful member of the Federation. His name is Credo, not Syrrig, and from what I've heard he is one of the more learned, and treacherous Federation Lords."

Zenjori observed the slim Elven Wizard, trying to determine if it was worth the risk to hire him.

"Are you certain?"

"Yes."

"Why would he be here, with us?"

"To spy, perhaps, but a Federation Lord wouldn't do it himself, he'd send others in his place. Maybe his story about being attacked by the Coalition is more true than we first believed. On the other hand, what if this is the Federation's way of sending us help without officially supporting us."

"Keep an eye on him. I'm going to hire him for a three month trial period, that should be long enough to deal with the Coalition forces. Don't let on that we know who he is. Play along with it for now."

Zenjori smoothly moved back into the negotiations, giving Torrak a disappointed glare.

"These are my terms, Syrrig. You sign on for a three month trial period, for which you will be paid 1,000 credits a week. You will be re-evaluated in one month's time, and if you've proven your credentials your pay will be adjusted appropriately. Your starting pay may seem low for your standards, Syrrig, but it's the best you can do without proven loyalty and ability."

"I understand, Zenjori, and have no prideful obstacles to overcome. To paraphrase a wise adversary of mine, pride leads the way to destruction, and arrogance hastens your demise. I accept your terms."

"Very good. Colnae will draw up the contract and Drake will issue you armor and your choice of weapon."

"And then I'd like to get better acquainted with your Gromek shifter." Credo smiled at the sullen mage. "Come, friend Torrak, I'm certain I have many wonderful things to teach you."

Anger rumbled deep in Torrak's chest, building to a barely controlled rage. The only race he hated more than humans was Elven kind. Visions of the elf dying in his grasp were interrupted by a low, soft voice invading his thoughts.

"What's the matter, is a little abuse too much to endure for the prospect of greater power?" the runic weapon asked his thoughts.

"Be still, Mind Crusher. I decide what is too much," Torrak barked harshly, loud enough for those around him to hear.

"Very well, my master. Your will is my command," the weapon cooed to Torrak's mind.

Torrak's yellow eyes fixed on Credo's back, mentally ripping him apart limb from limb. He would learn what he could, then find a slow painful death for the Elf to endure.

At his side Mind Crusher chuckled softly in two minds instead of one. The fun was just beginning.

Scrolls, charms, and magic paraphernalia lay in disorganized piles around Sinclair Van De Graf. Having completely lost track of time many hours earlier he delved deeper and deeper into the secrets of phrase and circle before him. To accumulate such a wealth of knowledge could take a human a lifetime, but here it all was for the taking. Van thumbed through the descriptions of powerful circles, committing every bit to memory for later analysis. It might take years to learn the secrets unfolding before him, and many decades to master them completely, but time was of little concern. Van had more than most.

His interest went beyond curiosity, and found its root deep in his soul. As a child he'd watched his father perform arcane rituals in circles such as these, accomplishing feats of magic beyond comprehension with a few simple words. The rewards contained in their secrets weren't some ethereal concept or dream, but tangible power waiting to be used. The prospect of things to come enthralled him, bringing unattainable desires within his grasp.

Many of the rituals described in detail were of a nature so disgusting that Van cringed at the thought of anyone performing them. Sacrificing all manner of living things, ripping a beating heart from a dragon, grinding bones into dust and mingling them with a burning tongue severed from some hapless mage, and everywhere there was blood. Blood in circles, blood on the altar, and blood flowing from his own veins to seal the circle's power. At first it all seemed too abhorrent to consider, but the hunger for power edged away reservations and rationalized brutal action for just rewards. The end always seemed to justify the means.

There was a soft patter of feet in the adjoining hall outside Credo's laboratory. Van reacted on reflex, aiming his TX-5 at the noise.

"It's just me." Anja smiled, eyes fixed on Van, not the gun.

"Sorry." Van shamefully holstered the gun.

Anja padded forward and looked around the lab. Strange odors and unfamiliar scents assaulted her senses and wrinkled her nose involuntarily in disgust.

"It doesn't smell very good in here."

"I didn't notice."

"Well, I'm all done up there, and I thought I'd come down here and see what you were up to." Anja dropped her bow and quiver to the floor and sat down right beside Van. She leaned over the book in Van's lap, letting her long, rust-colored hair fall across Van's arm.

"I didn't think you were interested in such things." Van moved his arm self-consciously.

"What does it say? I can't read."

"It's a passage describing the flow of magic energy from the dying serpent into the circle nexus." Van turned the page and showed Anja a graphic, hand sketched picture.

"That's disgusting."

"That's what I thought too. Actually I thought I might show this stuff to the guild master at Lazlo. He might know a way to convert this to what we call 'clean magic'. It's the latest trend, coming from some other dimension, a parallel Earth, I think. Clean magic works manifestations without the use of crutches like ingredients and rituals. Most of the magic taught up there is going that way."

"I use clean magic," Anja announced, shutting the book and placing it on the floor. "I wish most people were as thoughtful as you are." She leaned against him.

"Well a lot of this stuff here is, well, never mind." Van felt guilty all over again. "Is everybody ready to leave?"

"They already did. A long time ago."

"They did? How come you're still here?"

"Cuz I told David to go on without me and I'd get a ride with you when you were done." Anja looked up hopefully and Van averted his gaze.

"Guess that doesn't leave me much choice."

"Nope." she grinned.

"I wasn't planning on leaving just yet."

"That's okay. I'll wait."

Van let out a frustrated sigh. Anja was up to something again, Van was sure of it. What could he do? Did she know how easily she could manipulate him, or was it something she just did without half trying? Her sweet, naive nature was blasting his selfish excuses to smithereens.

"I suppose I could study most of this later. Want to help me carry it up to the Cycle?"

"You're keeping this stuff?" Anja looked around wide eyed.

"Just long enough for me to memorize it."

"Why? This is evil."

"No it's not, magic is only evil if it's used for evil."

"Magic comes from the soul, and if the soul is corrupt, so is the magic." Anja moved to sit cross-legged in front of him. "Remember, we talked about this before?"

"Kind of, but not exactly." Images of their discussion on good, evil, and magic played back in Van's mind. She'd looked so forlorn in gossamer white fabric and holding his coat around herself for warmth. Her hair still retained a wildness to it much as it had then, and her liquid aqua eyes still held him enthralled whenever he dared gaze into them. A pain in his chest reminded him of the disapointment he'd felt when he discovered what Anja really meant by pure. Somehow he couldn't separate it from his view of her.

"I'm sorry," she whispered.

"Please, stop doing that, okay?" Van stood up feeling all the more stupid for leaving his thoughts open to her once again. "Look, if I want to study these circles and learn new spells, I'll do it my own way, not like this Federation Lord."

"But what of the cost?"

"Huh?"

"What value do you put on your own life, your own peace of mind?" The anger in her voice arrested Van's attention. She stood to her full 5'2'' with determination.

"What are you talking about? These are spells. Value of my life?"

"When you start down the path these books will lead you, you start destroying your own standards and morals. It might not happen now, it may not even happen for years, but gradually you'll lose sight of what is right and get dragged down to the same evil as the man you got them from. It corrupts a little at a time, each bit of power eating away at your humanity. I don't want that to happen to you."

Van stared at her, his jaw dropping in astonishment. This was the last kind of response he'd expected from the typically soft spoken Mystic.

"I won't lose sight of my values," he stammered.

"Do you even know what your values are now? What do you value? Power? Wealth? Belongings? These are shallow things without true reward."

"I have other values."

"I'm not going to judge you or your values, Van, that's not my place. I place a value on my own magic, a very high one, so I understand how important it is to you. My pureness is my highest value, my virginity the key to the powers within me, the powers I use to help others. You need to ask yourself how important all this stuff really is to you. Is it worth giving up your friends, loved ones, and maybe even your soul?" Anja waited for Van's dark eyes to meet her gaze. At last he raised his eyes and gave her a smile.

"I suppose happiness is a value, isn't it?"

"A very important one. True happiness, lasting happiness."

"They say money can't buy happiness, but it does come at a price." Van looked longingly at the stacks of material he hadn't finished reading.

"I'm not asking you to give up these things, not if they're that important to you. I just want you to really, really consider what you're doing." Anja spoke so quietly Van could barely hear her.

"That I can do. Honestly and sincerely." He reached over and placed a hand on her armored shoulder. She smiled and pressed a warm cheek against his hand.

"Thank you."

"No, thank you. I just remembered something somebody said to me earlier today, and I have every intention of proving him wrong. Grab your helmet, it gets windy riding on the back of a Sky Cycle."

Lisa released her body harness and squirmed impatiently at her communications console inside Skull 41. Seven hours trapped in the confines of the robot's pilots compartment was pushing her to the limit. She'd spent most of the night and day before in it too. Enough was enough. If they were moving it wouldn't be so bad, but waiting for the Captain to finish negotiations made time drag on longer than usual.

"You better put that back on," Dave advised, pointing to the loose harness straps.

"Why? Nobody's going to start a fight." Lisa pushed the seat back and stretched her legs. Just the same she glanced at the main view screen to make sure none of the mercenaries were aiming weapons at the halted Coalition convoy. Members of the mercenary company "First Strike" had met them just outside Liberty and requested a meeting with Captain Pritchett to discuss the Coalition's conduct in the primarily D-Bee populated town. After a few tense moments of political posturing, Captain Pritchett convinced the mercenary defenders that the Coalition was simply visiting and wouldn't cause any trouble for the town's non-human population. All that was left was the setting of ground rules regarding weapons and armor in the town proper. 45 minutes later Lisa didn't care anymore, she just wanted out of the Skull Walker.

"Can't wait to grab a shower and jump in bed with Lieutenant Studly?" Dave teased.

"Oh be quiet. I just hope Pritchett lets the NCO's stay someplace nice."

"Point me to the nearest bar and I won't care where we stay."

"Who do you think you're kidding? Point you to the nearest cat-house is more like it."

"Hey, that'll solve both problems." Dave grinned.

"Skull 41, this is Captain Pritchett, do you copy?" The officer's voice blared over the internal speakers. Dave winced and Lisa scrambled to put her headset back on. Dave mouthed words at her she was glad she couldn't hear.

"This is Skull 41, go ahead."

"Is there a problem with your communications, Corporal?"

"No sir, I was running a frequency scan while we waited, were you trying to reach me?" Lisa lied.

"Not a problem. Listen carefully. You are to move your mechanized unit to a location designated by the town officials and secure it along side Skull 191. There will be four shifts, six hours each, guarding our mechanized units. You and your pilot will assume 1st shift and be relieved at 2400 hours. Sergeant Winters will inform you about duty stations and help you work out a definite patrol route. Is there any problem with this?"

"No sir, no problem," Lisa drawled, flipping off her main console.

"Good. Pritchett out."

Lisa threw her headset at the console.

"Follow Skull 191," she passed the order on to Dave.

"Big chief tick off little squaw?" Dave matched her pout, crossing his arms in mock defiance.

"You can be really annoying sometimes, Dave."

"Sorry, but that's just me. No, really, what's up?" Dave returned to all seriousness.

"That jerk knows we've been up over 36 hours and so he puts us on first guard shift until 2400. I hate this."

"That butthead." Dave shook his head. "Of all the nerve." He continued to mock her.

"Drive Dave, and don't step on the mercenary's hover rover, please."

"Oh man." Dave swerved and barely avoided a politically unwise maneuver.

"You need sleep. Bad."

"What I need is a cold brew in one hand and a babe in the other. I suppose one out of two isn't bad." Dave reached for her behind.

"Dave!" Lisa spat through clenched teeth. Both of them had been in the Skull Walker way too long.

"Aw, yer no fun." Dave swiveled back to the robot's console in order to avoid smashing the posted 'no weapons' sign.

"Try me when I've had a few drinks," Lisa kidded to ease the tension. She was just happy to be moving again, even if Dave was swerving like he'd already had a couple too many.

"Ahh, I can hear the blond mating call." Dave cocked his head as if listening intently., then threw his head back and slumped to one side. "Ohhhmmagod, I'mmmm sooo drrunk."

Lisa belted him in the jaw.

Chapter 10

Darren never thought a stiff styrene pad could feel so good. By the time his patrol ended just about any place even remotely flat was calling him to come lay down. Now that his body reached a horizontal resting place, his mind crammed sleep through conscious thought to immediate dreamland.

Weird plant-like things crawled to reach him from someplace below, their spiked fingers mutating and growing in writhing ferocity. Darren wasn't sure what they were exactly, but a gut feeling told him they were bad.

He opened his eyes and looked at his wrist computer. A half an hour had passed in the blink of an eye. Darren shut his eyes.

They were back, groping for him as he passed overhead, long tendrils, twisted and deformed. The tendril plant things transformed into hideous shag carpet things, then mutated again so the carpet grew back into the plant-like things reaching out to grab him.

This was really weird, Darren's conscious mind observed, but was too tired to wrestle REM over reality.

They were closer now, stabbing and twisting, all around him. Sharp spines and pointy leaves swirled around with increasing madness until they all converged at once. Vines and branches grabbed his body and wrapped themselves around him, shaking him and shouting his name.

And shouting? Darren's conscious mind tried to make sense out of the bizarre sensory assault.

Opening his eyes, Darren found Cowboy desperately trying to restrain him.

"What the hell are you doing?" Darren asked, bewildered.

"What the hell am I doing?! I tap you on the chest to wake you up and you go berserk! You okay, buddy?" Cowboy stood up, hitting his head on the top bunk. "Owww."

"I was having the strangest dream." Darren looked at the time. Another 15 minutes had gone by since he last checked.

"Musta been one nightmare."

"Uh, yeah. What did you wake me up for?"

"There's somebody outside wants to see ya. That red haired broad you brought back from Youngstown."

"You won't narc, will you?" Darren asked the larger soldier.

"I don't narc on my pals, man. You know that."

"Thanks dude."

"Better make sure Sharky don't see ya, though. That guys been creepin' 'round these cabins tryin' ta sniff out psyches. I told 'im I'd kick his backside if caught him snoopin' 'round our cabin, so keep an eye for the freak in the bushes. Just yell if ya see 'im and me an' the boys'll come out and beat him to a pulp."

"Thanks Cowboy." Darren started opening the door, then paused. "Cowboy?"

A cold blast of air gave Darren a taste of what awaited him outside. Flurries of snow whipped around his bare feet and ripped through the fabric of his uniform. Four hours before the sky was almost clear, but now it was so dark one couldn't see the stars. The snow was just a teaser for an icy sludge that hit moments later. Darren's body shivered involuntarily. Running across freezing ground, he leapt clumsily onto the partially completed board walk that connected most of the rental cabins. Cyndiara stood just a few feet away beneath a section of the completed awning, her expression a blend of amusement and sympathy.

Darren limped over to her, rain soaking his hair and uniform.

"I think I got a splinter in my foot." he stated.

"That's just what I traveled a thousand miles to hear," she nodded.

"It hurts."

"That's too bad."

"You could be more sympathetic."

"But then I might have you follow me half way across the continent."

Both stared deeply into each other's eyes, searching for some reassurance they were both out in the unforgiving weather for the same reasons. Cyndiara looked up at Darren's handsome features and tired eyes, then reached out a small hand to touch his cheek. Cyndiara was suddenly in his arms, held close and tight against his chest. Darren could feel her warmth through her heavy coat and clothing. He welcomed her embrace, unafraid and unashamed. Tears formed in his eyes and he wept for the first time since the night he'd left her weeping in the rain a month earlier.

"How could I have been such an idiot," he spoke into her damp red hair. "I am so sorry for what I did to you."

"I know."

"I want you back so bad, Cyndiara. I promise it will be different." He gently pulled away so he could see her eyes. She was crying.

"Will things really be different?" she asked softly.

"I promise."

"I, I want to believe you, Darren, but...." she bit her lip, heart wrenching in agony to believe him.

"I know I hurt you, Cyndiara, and I wouldn't blame you if you torched me to ash right now. But please believe me when I tell you I love you more than anything else. I don't care if you're a Burster, I don't care if you're Psychic, I wouldn't even care if you were a magic user. There isn't anything I will let come between us, not again, not anything! Even if you never want to see me again, I want you to know I will always love you, to the day I die. And I will forever ask forgiveness for what I did." Darren knelt on the cold wooden slats and clasped her hands in front of him.

In the dim light Cyndiara could make out the scar on his right hand, the scar that symbolized everything they had in common and reminded her of everything they did not. Choking in emotional agony, Cyndiara wrapped her coat around Darren and pulled his head to her chest.

"I do forgive you, Darren, I forgive you."

For many long minutes they held the embrace, letting cold rain wash away the pain they both shared. Cyndiara became aware of Darren's increasing shivers and generated an aura of heat to still his shaking.

"Stay with me tonight."

"Where?"

"My hotel. I rented the master suite." She smiled coquettishly. "It's not like I didn't have the money."

"Okay." Darren needed no other persuasion.

"Put your boots on. You wouldn't want to get another sliver."

The two left the cover of the awning and sprinted for the nearest shelter down the street.

From the shadows a slinking figure giggled fiendishly to itself. Captain Pritchett would certainly hear of such blatant treason, Sharky would be sure of it. Then he would kill the both of them.

Torrak glowered spitefully at his Elven teacher. The entire lesson had been filled with double-edged comments and belittling mannerisms, all of which the Elf pretended were accidents and slips of the tongue. What made the ordeal unbearable was the audience observing from the opposite bank of the creek. More than once he'd seen the reflective power armor suit almost double over with its pilot's laughter. Every time the Glitter Boy moved into patches of sunlight, the rays would catch its mirrored surface and reflect light right in Torrak's eyes. Torrak was sure the human pilot was doing it on purpose just to annoy him. More than once the Gromek Shifter desired to pry the pilot from his near indestructible power suit and drown him in the freezing water of the creek.

"One more time, Torrak, just to make sure you understand the precise movement required for the spell," Syrrig/Credo prodded, enjoying the humiliation Torrak was experiencing.

"I don't understand why it is necessary for me to do these, these obscene movements with my right hand."

"I suppose I can explain it to you one more time, we still have an hour or two before noon. As I've told you before, the original spell called for the yanking of some six appendages, not one. I managed to convert the spell to just one, but it requires doing it six times as long. Unless you can metamorphosize into a creature with six such appendages, you must follow the hand movements exactly or the spell won't work," Credo lied. So far he'd made the Gromek do every detestable motion and body movement he could think of for a spell that required only three distinct phrases to form and focus magic energies. He hadn't had this much fun in a long time.

"How do these movements make me swim like a fish?" Torrak growled, looking at the swollen, muddy creek with trepidation.

"I never managed to translate why it was necessary, more than likely a spell of aquatic origin. What's important is that you believe they are necessary. One cannot cast magic without belief, that is a basic requirement I'm sure you're already aware of, TorrAK. If a mage believes it necessary for him to wear the same pair of underwear every day in order to cast magic, then without that smelly pair of undergarments it is impossible for him to successfully invoke a spell. All that training and focus of energy he's learned is useless without belief. So, unless you believe those motions are a necessary part of focusing and channeling your mystic energy for the desired result, it won't work and you'll be wet and miserable all over again."

"I understand the fish gestures." Torrak demonstrated by making a fish face and flapping his wings and arms like fins. "But there's no reason for a sexual reference in this spell." He went through the series of movements exactly as Credo had instructed.

Sunlight struck Torrak in the eye as the Glitter Boy doubled over with laugher again. The troops on the opposite bank were practically in tears.

"Well it's time you put your abilities to the test." Credo glanced across the creek and winked. "Now, concentrate on darting through the water like a fish, and when you have completed the movements once more and recited the incantation, just dive on in."

As best he could, Torrak concentrated on swimming like a fish, but the hip thrusts and hand movements just didn't fit in and the constant display of light from the opposite bank broke his concentration the instant before he jumped. Plunging into the icy cold water, Torrak choked on vegetation and spit mud from his mouth. Floundering in the shallow water, Torrak felt rage overtake him. In a desperate lunge at Credo, Torrak slipped and planted his horns in the steep muddy bank instead.

Credo never laughed. Torrak raised his muddy face to see the elder wizard gazing down with smug sympathy.

"That's a good start, TorrAK, but as they say, practice makes perfect."

Cracking open the Glitter Boy's armored pilot's compartment, Kreg Rencroft pulled himself free and dropped to the ground, still chuckling to himself at the magic lesson he witnessed earlier. Looking skyward at the dark thunder clouds in the distance, he stepped back to close the Pre-Rifts manufactured exoskeleton against a sudden storm burst.

Striding across the small mercenary base, Kreg stepped in a puddle and muddied his spotless armor suit.

"Damnit." He tried to wipe the mud from his boot, only succeeding in smearing it further. If there was anything he detested it was getting dirty. He didn't mind charging into the thick of battle or facing down a robot vehicle many times the size of his Glitter Boy, just so long as none of the blood and gore actually touched his impeccable appearance and attire. His obsession with cleanliness carried over to the maintenance of his power armor as well. The dense molecularly-bonded chrome armor had to be polished to mirror perfection and every battle mark in its surface repaid tenfold. It had almost gotten to the point were he didn't want to take the ten foot power armor into combat for fear of damaging it, but Kreg knew that eventually the inevitable would occur. Very few power armor units carried the firepower of a Glitter Boy, with its electromagnetic mass driver the winner in any slugfest. Instead of firing a burst of metal slugs in rapid succession, the Glitter Boy's "Boom Gun" accelerated 200 slugs in a fall-away casing that would impact a target long before the sound of the sonic boom ever reached the unfortunate victim. Each time the cannon split the air, a localized sonic boom would follow the projectile cluster in a V-shaped wave to the target. With the mass and velocity of the projectile cluster, the boom gun could often strike and kill a target with only one shot, long before the enemy was in a position to return fire. That was how Kreg liked to keep his battles. Very rarely did his recipient of kinetic steel ever shoot back.

Hopping from dry spot to dry spot, he made his way to the command vehicle where most of the company leaders awaited his arrival.

"Kreg, catch." A man wearing a drug injection harness threw a helmet at Kreg's head.

"Crap, J.J., watch it." Kreg fumbled with the helmet.

The augmented "Juicer" was Kreg's best friend, but always seemed to forget about the comparatively slow reflexes of everyone else around him. Kreg turned the bronze colored helmet over in his hands, noting its light weight and lack of any environmental features. Glancing up he saw the rest of the command staff watching him.

"What do you make of that, Kreg?" Zenjori asked.

"It wouldn't fit me, that's for sure." He examined it closer. "Looks like some alien design. Definitely humanoid, though."

"Look through the eye shield."

"Are these polarized?" Kreg tried to see through the dark eye shields, but no light passed through. "Where'd you find this?"

"J.J. found it near a wrecked robot of some kind. Must have been a fierce battle, trees burned away and blast craters all around. The rain destroyed any tracks, and the only thing J.J. could find intact was that helmet buried under a tree limb." Zenjori pointed to the helmet and motioned for Colnae to continue the explanation.

"That helmet belongs to a race of Warrior Women. Blind Warrior Women."

"I feel like I'm the only one who doesn't know what's going on here." Kreg looked around.

"My Federation Lord once told me about these Warrior Women and where they come from. They're minions of supernatural creatures from Atlantis, and their presence means other powerful creatures are here also."

"Is this good, or bad?" Kreg tossed the helmet back to J.J., somewhat miffed at being the last to be informed.

"It's definitely not good, I can tell you that for sure. Typically, if that helmet really is from one of these Warrior Women, they don't travel alone. Four to six warriors accompany what I've heard called a Slaver's Barge. A creature with many tentacles and incredible powers controls them. From what little I've heard, these things should be destroyed at all costs. Since you usually operate away from the main group, we thought you should be aware of the possible threat."

"How will I knew when I see one of these Warrior Women, or Slaver Barge thing?"

"You will know, Kreg, there's not many things you could mistake it for. As for the women, be on the look out for similar styled helmets," Zenjori advised. "Shoot first, don't think about."

"That's it?"

"No. Early this morning a Coalition SAMAS bearing the number 312 flew within one mile of where you were stationed. What's more it flew past your position undetected. Why?" Zenjori asked nicely, without a shred of malice in his voice.

"It must have been running silent, without active radar or targeting, I guess. It's pretty hard to spot a SAM in the rain when it's only running on passive systems. That's really unusual, they don't usually do that. Who spotted it?"

"I did." Drake rumbled, pointing to his multi-optic eyes. "Thermo."

"Point is, Kreg, I'm not mad at you. I just want you to be aware that the Coalition forces in Liberty aren't as stupid as others we've encountered. They've been in Liberty two days and seem to get along with the D-Bee population better than we expected. What's more, each day their patrols come closer and closer to our position and nobody here has gotten a shot off at them. As far we know, the SAMAS that was here this morning has reported back for reinforcements. I'm sending a few men back into town in disguise to gather some information and keep us updated on the Coalition's movements. We may even be able to stir up some trouble. Drake has a few things prepared to make certain the Coalition runs into some sticky racial relations with the local populace. In the meantime, please be more observant. J.J. will be your eyes and ears. I want the two of you stationed on blind "C" just in case they try a sneak attack from the north."

"The Coalition make a sneak attack?"

"Assassin's rule #3, mate. Always watch your back."

"Just one question." Kreg hated being belittled, even if it was his own fault. "Drake, if you spotted the SAM on thermo, how did you read its number?" He asked suspiciously.

"Because it stopped, landed, and came up on foot to mark your position with this." Drake lifted a tiny remote targeting device from one of his leg compartments.

Kreg stared in disbelief.

"Thirty feet, Kreg. Don't let it happen again."

Three o'clock in the afternoon found Greg Merrick awake and restless. Six hours of sleep wasn't enough, but laying awake was all he could accomplish. His discoveries earlier kept playing back in his troubled mind. More disconcerting was his own atypical behavior. He hadn't needed to get anywhere near the Glitter Boy to mark its location, and yet something kept driving him to keep pushing the edge, just to see what he could get away with. That wasn't like him at all. A full recon of the rebel camp could be performed by more qualified personnel. Finally, unable to get battle plans and confusing thoughts out of his head, Greg took a cold shower and went in search of Lieutenant Sorrenson.

Signs of development were everywhere. Ditch diggers laid giant sewer pipes and construction crews raised buildings for the influx of migrants. Greg was amazed at how well humans and D-Bees worked together in building the town. He'd heard none of the usual racial slurs or division of labor he'd grown accustomed to in the Burbs outside Chi-Town. It was like another world where all the rules he knew didn't apply. It was all so different from the oppressive, dirty atmosphere where he'd grown up in the shadow of a giant fortress city. A feeling of hope and comradery pervaded in a town that could never happen within Coalition borders.

"I must be cracking up," Greg thought out loud. "I need to finish doing what I came here for before I lose it completely."

Muddy footprints converged on the "Match Head Saloon". Greg couldn't resist swinging the double doors like he'd seen in a Pre-Rifts western vid. The effect wasn't all he hoped for. A heavy reinforced oak door at the end of the entryway provided more substantial protection from the weather. Standing at the entrance was a mercenary from First Strike, fully armed and ready for trouble in case the saloon's name inspired more than a "friendly" brawl. Nodding politely to the guard, Greg swung open the heavy door.

"Quite a crowd for this time of day, wouldn't you say?" Greg commented.

"It's always like this," The mercenary half shouted over the bedlam coming from inside.

It seemed like half the occupants were wearing a Coalition uniform. At one end Greg could see Donnovan, the First Strike commander having a heated conversation with a pair of mercenaries. Everywhere there were bottles in front of inebriated patrons, most of which wore gray and black with a C.S. insignia. Mixed in were D-Bees and others quite obviously not Coalition.

"And I thought I had a problem with discipline," Greg murmured to himself, squishing his way through to where Captain Pritchett sat along the bar.

"Morning Lieutenant. Up earlier than I expected." The captain gestured to an open stool. "Let me buy you a drink."

"Don't mind if I do. Thanks, sir."

"One for him and one for me," the captain signaled the owner and bartender. The four-armed cyborg nodded cheerfully to Greg and with the speed and accuracy only a professional could perform, placed a mug of ale in front of both, wiped off the foam, and washed the bar with a rag all at the same time. Greg stared at the amber liquid and then at the empty mugs all along the bar.

"Have you seen Lieutenant Sorenson?" he asked without touching his ale.

"Not since yesterday. Find anything interesting on your patrol?"

"That falls under the specific objectives of my unit, sir, unless you want to risk your men fighting my battles."

"Just answer this. Does your new objective pose a threat to my mission?"

"More than likely, no."

"Then keep your little secrets if you want to."

"I'll do that." Greg swallowed a gulp of ale. Pritchett smiled at the expression on Greg's face. "Too much hops." He stared at the bitter drink. Across the room Greg caught the stare of a mercenary, but the man looked away abruptly. "Who are those two Headhunters talking to Donnovan?"

"I don't know. They came in about half an hour ago," the Captain replied without looking. "They friends of yours?"

"No. I've seen them before, but I can't think where." Greg raised his mug for another swig and slammed it back down. "I know where. That one with the cybernetic eye and black bionic arm. I saw him on the bounty board down the street." Greg reached for his gun but then remembered he wasn't permitted to carry heavy weaponry within town limits.

"What's the matter with you, Lieutenant? We aren't here for bounty hunting."

"I don't like the way he keeps looking over here," Greg commented, then took another big swig of the ale. No doubt about it, he considered, he really was losing control. Greg smiled to himself, inwardly contemplating how much longer it would take before he snapped completely.

Loud laughter from a nearby table arrested Greg's attention. Four soldiers from Pritchett's unit slapped each other on the back while they retold war stories.

"No way, man, I saw you miss that D-Bee from four feet, man."

"Hey! I cut it in half just like that!" The other soldier spilled his drink while making a slashing gesture with his mug.

"No, no, I saw you, too, man. Four feet. Four feet!"

"I musta' blasted fifty of 'em and they still kept runnin' from Sergio like he was the angel of death or something! Like they could run away!" another soldier added.

"Four feet. You missed at four feet!"

"Man, shut up, I got it on the second shot."

"Man, you missed it at four feet, not just once, either!"

"Shut up"

"A whole village of ugly three-eyed D-Bees and you miss the one four feet away from you!" the soldiers continued teasing.

"Blew his eyes in three directions!"

Another round of cheers and high fives over the table followed. Before Greg could tell them to keep it down, their table was tipped to the floor. A very angry, three eyed D-Bee with lumpy skin wielded a large ion blaster at the group of suddenly silent soldiers.

"Uh oh,. Trouble." Greg moved back from the line of fire.

"That was my family!" The D-Bee roared and spit.

The entire room silenced itself.

"Cool it, Wade. Hand over the blaster," the mercenary by the door requested , facing down the barrel of his rifle.

"Stay out of this, Aken. They didn't kill your whole family." Wade responded in almost controlled tones. The safety slid off his ion blaster.

"Hey, man, we didn't know it was your family. Sorry," one of the soldiers offered.

"Yeah, I mean, us 'Dead Boys' can't tell one D-Bee from another, ya know?" A nervous laugh followed the lame excuse.

"You go to my home village, slaughter my family, friends, and relatives, and all you can say is 'I'm sorry'?" Wade asked in perfect American.

"Drop it now, Wade," the mercenary commander requested firmly from the other end of the saloon.

"I'll drop it, Donnovan, just after I shoot the human that killed my family."

"It was him!" One soldier pointed to the other.

"Well, you know, us D-Bees can't tell one human from another." Wade aimed the barrel at the accuser's head. "I guess I'll have to kill all of you, starting with you."

Wade jerked and inhaled a short gasp. Something hot and sticky ran down his chest. Looking down Wade saw the sharp point of a double edged high frequency blade. A lispy whisper came from behind.

"I killedth your family."

The blade jerked upwards, slicing bone and skull until it was free.Wade's brains spilled from his split skull as his body fell to the floor.

Aken stared at Wade's lifeless corpse and the spreading pool of body liquids.

"Thory abouth the meth. I will be happy to clean ith up." The bald Coalition Psi-Stalker smiled, revealing a long pair of implanted teeth.

"Good work, Sharky," Captain Pritchett commended him.

The room remained silent. Greg edged closer to the mercenary with the bounty.

"Aken. Place this Psi-Stalker under arrest on the charge of murder," Donnovan instructed calmly.

"That was self defense. That thing was going to kill my men and who knows who else," Pritchett objected.

"That's what it looked like to me, but I still have to follow procedure."

"You will do no such thing. Everyone here was a witness in defense of that action. It wasn't murder and you know it."

"Just the same, I follow the rules. Your Psi-Stalker will probably be free by tonight. We can bring him before the justice of the peace in a matter of hours. I don't make the rules, Captain, I just enforce them like I'm paid to," Donnovan explained. His left mechanical eye panned back and forth audibly in the silence. Looking from face to face he examined the men in the room. A few had heard of Donnovan in mercenary circles. He had a reputation for being thorough, honest, and fair with his allies and completely unmerciful to his enemies. His mercenary company "First Strike" made no excuses for jobs they'd failed, for the number of successes compensated more than full. It was clear to everyone in the room who held the upper hand in Liberty. Clear to everyone except Captain Pritchett.

"Nobody is getting arrested for acting in self defense," Pritchett snarled and Aken stopped. Two gun barrels aimed at him from a pair of Coalition cyborgs. Captain Pritchett flexed his bionic arm and a small laser rod popped up from its concealed housing. "Leave, Sharky."

Greg slid behind the wanted mercenary.

Weapons came out from under tables and from behind the bar. Off duty First Strike personnel apparently didn't abide by town weapon ordinances. Donnovan calmly walked to the bar, stepping around the pool of blood that spread over the floor. Nobody moved. Nobody breathed. Donnovan sat at the bar.

"Give me a scotch, Henry, on the rocks."

The bartender poured a full glass and ducked back behind the bar.

"Tell your men to back off," Pritchett ordered in a monotone.

"You know, from where I'm sitting I can't see all those illegal weapons you and your Cyborgs are carrying. In fact, by the time I finish my scotch and turn around, I might have forgotten I ever saw them. Look around, Captain, this isn't the Coalition States."

Donnovan took down a third of the scotch. "I would think you wouldn't want to do anything that might jeopardize your, shall I say, fragile position?" Donnovan took the scotch down another third. "It would be a shame if something happened to you and the surviving members of your unit were forced to go all the way back to the C.S. without you." Donnovan swirled the ice around in his drink.

Sharky gulped, his beady black eyes losing count of how many guns were aimed at his bald head.

High pitched servos on Pritchett's arm returned the weapon to its secret housing.

Donnovan finished his drink.

Weapons slid back into hiding, both Coalition Cyborgs stepping back from Aken.

Donnovan spun slowly around on the bar stool.

"I don't see anything stopping you from arresting this man, do you Aken?"

"No sir." Aken nodded to Donnovan and slipped out of a pair handcuffs from a belt pouch. Sharky surrendered his blade without a whimper of protest and was cuffed in front of dozens of Coalition troops. Arriving to take him to the Liberty jail, a pair of mercenaries half dragged him through the bloody mess on the way out.

Greg stepped up to the wanted mercenary and slammed his head into a supporting beam. The man wheezed and slumped to the floor loudly.

"Take that."

"I don't believe you just did that, Lieutenant." Pritchett stared with dropped jaw.

Nobody moved to interfere. Greg smiled, feeling much better about the world. The mercenary's partner started pulling a weapon to defend his companion, but the sudden drift of muzzles in his direction discouraged him.

"Better leave, Trench." Donnovan advised.

"I was just on my way out. We'll contact you later with the drop site."

"You do that."

Trench hastily shuffled out and the saloon started coming back to life again. Whispers gradually became a multitude of story versions retelling the recent events.

"Never a dull moment at the Match Head, aye, Henry?" Donnovan reached over the bar and rapped the bartender on the back. Henry stood up, thankful a more severe tragedy had been averted.

"The scotch is on the house."

"Thanks."

Greg heaved the mercenary onto his shoulders and started making his way from the saloon, avoiding the mess on the floor.

"What do you think you're doing, Lieutenant?" Pritchett grabbed Greg's arm.

"Making a few quick credits. Any objections, sir?"

"Yes. You're not a bounty hunter, you're a lieutenant in the Coalition military."

Greg shrugged. The mercenary twitched, and Greg dropped him to the floor, snatching his arm and twisting him into a full nelson. Donnovan shook his head and laughed.

"You got guts just walking up to someone you don't know and bashing their skull against a wood beam. It's a long way to Kingsdale, Lieutenant."

"You're wanted in Kingsdale?" Greg asked his prisoner incredulously.

"Read the wanted poster, dipstick."

"What are you doing all the way out here?"

"I'm wanted in Kingsdale, that's why I'm here." the mercenary explained in sing-song. "Are you going to let me go or take me all the way back to Missouri."

"What did you do?"

"I wasted a D-Bee."

"And?"

"And so this D-Bee was rich and I took its money. Guess its family was rich, too, and put out a contract on me. What did you think those posters were? Anything else you want to know? My favorite color? How about —"

"Shut up."

"You may as well let him go, Lieutenant. I was doing business with him before you introduced his head to that support over there." Donnovan leaned back against the bar and waited.

"I'll let you go if you answer a few questions." Greg lessened the pressure.

"Orange, and —"

"How about you tell me who you're currently working for. That C-18 in your belt tells me you have some connections I ought to know about. Where'd you get it?"

"It's not mine, man, they gave it to me to use."

"Who?"

"Man, I can't tell that."

"If you don't, I'll pay someone to take you back to Kingsdale."

"If I tell you, you gotta let me go."

"I could just bash your head around some more."

"Man, not here. I can't talk to you here."

"Why not?"

"Because."

Greg started moving for the closest beam.

"He's working for someone who you might know, Lieutenant," Donnovan volunteered. He could stop the Coalition officer if he really wanted to, but something about the lieutenant's style amused the mercenary commander.

"Okay, outside it is then." Greg guided the mercenary out the door and down the street behind the saloon, releasing him only when the C-18 was aimed at its previous owner.

"Listen. I'm a professional, just like you, we just get paid by someone different is all."

"We aren't anything alike." Greg flipped off the safety.

"Man, I don't care about you or who I work for either, but if I tell you they'll track me down and kill me."

"If you don't, I'll kill you. In fact, maybe I'll just blow your body in half and send the pieces in for the bounty." Greg's gray eyes danced crazily. Something inside him almost believed he'd do it.

"Okay. The bounty is 50,000 credits. I can pay you that much and ten thousand more to let me go."

"Where does a worthless thug like you get 60,000 credits?"

"I, I just got it, working." The mercenary carefully extracted a card from his coat pocket and extended to Greg.

"Who are you working for?"

"Look, man, if I tell you then I've gotta split 'cuz they'll kill me when they find out."

"You're starting to tick me off, and lately I've been feeling really violent, understand?" Greg snatched the card away and shoved it in his pocket.

"I was hired by a mercenary group. Army of the New Order. All they wanted me to do was —"

Greg grabbed the Headhunter's bionic arm and cut it in two with the C-18 laser pistol. Hydraulic fluid splattered the man's terror stricken face as the crazed Coalition officer clobbered him repeatedly with his own arm. Greg stepped back and pointed the severed arm down at the cowering mercenary.

"You're going to tell me everything you know, and then you're going to make up things I want to hear because I'm going to ask you questions you don't know the answers to, just to see how good you lie. And every time I don't believe one of your lies I'm going to re-move another piece of your body, and not just the fake parts, the parts that hurt and bleed and make you scream. Then, when I'm done, I'll mail whatever's left of you back to Kingsdale. In pieces. So you'd better give me some really good reasons to let you live, otherwise you've got nothing to live for. Now, tell me everything you know about Zenjori Suka and the Army of the New Order."

"Right on schedule. Trench never fails," Drake commented as the mercenary trudged up the steep embankment.

"Where's Micky?" Kruno inquired about Trench's absent partner. Both squad commanders hopped down from their hover rover to question Trench.

"Some hot shot lieutenant at the Match Head just walked up to Micky and bashed his head against a wooden beam. I didn't stick around to see what happened after that." Trench breathed heavily from his recent exertion and leaned against the rover.

Drake and Kruno exchanged worried looks. Drake worked his mechanical jaw in an irritated fashion.

"Did you place all the targeting devices?"

"All the ones I had, yes, but I think Micky still had most of his sewn into his jacket. I wasn't about to try an' bust him free, not with Donnovan and a room full of Dead Boys."

"How many did you place?"

"Five, on my way out of town. I got number four aimed right at the Coalition APC. Stupid fools left the radar on, and I just locked on the frequency." Trench smiled proudly.

"Kruno, hand me #1."

"Here you go." The Partial Conversion Headhunter lifted a large, disposable missile launcher from the back of the rover and handed it to Drake. Effortlessly lifting it to his shoulder and steadying it with three arms, Drake disarmed the safety catches.

"Lock me."

"Got me one active target locked on." Kruno linked the missile's targeting computer to one of the remotes Trench had placed while in town. "Yer hot."

Drake walked away from the rover and went down on one knee.

"Better stand farther away than that, Trench, unless you want to lose your face." Drake waved the Headhunter away with his free arm. Tiny spikes on Drake's knees and toes dug into the earth as he planted himself firmly. The Cyborg's metallic hand closed around the upper grip and slowly pressed the trigger mechanism.

White smoke and flame erupted behind the launcher, completely obscuring the nine foot cyborg from view as the missile left the platform. The roar of the missile faded into the distance, leaving only the sounds of startled birds. Drake tossed the smoking launcher aside and counted the seconds in his HUD. Smoke twirled around his feet in weaving mists above moist earth. The cyborg stood, raising a hand and counting down the seconds on his fingers. Two seconds before zero the sound of a distant explosion reached their ears.

"Give me #6 and switch it to #4's targeting beacon."

"Gonna give 'em the heavy, eh?" Kruno chuckled and tossed the cyborg another missile.

"This warhead should be enough to penetrate a Mark 5's pilot compartment, wouldn't you say, Trench?" Drake asked as cheerfully as Trench had ever heard the cyborg sound before.

"Uh, yeah. Radar dish is right over the pilot compartment."

"We got a signal. Good work, Trench." Kruno beamed.

"Lock me."

"You're locked. Missile's hot." Kruno flipped switches on a brief-case sized portable computer with wires running to a plug in the missile launch platform. "How do you want yer Dead Boys cooked? Regular or extra crispy?"

The roar of the missile launcher answered Kruno's question. Drake didn't wait for the returning missile report and tossed the spent launcher by the first one before returning to the rover.

"Give me a frag and lock it on #7."

"One whomper comin' up." Kruno heaved another missile from the stack in the rover and set it in the cyborg's arms.

"How many Coalition troops did you say were in the Match Head?" Drake asked Trench with a hint of smoke trailing off cold metal lips. The scorch marks on his black armor still smoldered, making him look more demon than machine.

"Musta been at least twenty, not including their captain, a couple cyborgs, and an officer or two. Donnovan was in there too, why?'

"Kruno, activate beacons 6 through 10 and lock me."

"But those were on Micky," Kruno objected.

"You always claimed one of your Headhunters was worth 4 Coalition troops, Kruno, looks like Micky's worth more than that." Drake smiled as only a cyborg could smile, metal eyebrows meeting in the center of his forehead.

"Yer a cold, son of a gun, Drake." Kruno shook his head, then grinned. "What can I say, my men are better than yours."

"I'll concede that only if you get your entire squad of Headhunters to walk into town with fusion blocks and homing beacons strapped down the front of their pants."

"You care to place a small wager on Micky?"

Both squad commander laughed, Trench shifting his weight uneasily. More explosions sounded in the distance, the second missile reaching its target and sound returning.

"No more APC." Drake stated.

"Beacons 6 through 10 activated and locked. Yer hot."

"Thank you."

"Just go someplace other than the rover to launch that thing."

"I told you, man, they're gonna missile the town!" Micky insisted after the second explosion sounded on the far side of Liberty.

"Where's the next one?" Merrick yelled, still pointing the C-18 at his captive. The improvised interrogation was almost over when the explosions interrupted.

"I don't know. They didn't tell me. Look, man I told you everything I know. Please, ya gotta let me get out of here before more missiles come in. You can tell Donnovan everything. Either get it over with or let me leave."

"Get out of here." Greg waved the pistol down a back alley.

Micky scrambled to his feet and edged nervously away.

"Beat it, before I change my mind and decide to shoot you anyway." Greg figured it was a mistake to let the Headhunter go, but he'd already gotten much valuable information and had other things to worry about.

"Thanks, man, yer cool." Micky bolted down the alley, holding one hand over the leaking end of his bionic arm. For a moment Greg felt like laughing at his own stupidity for not searching the mercenary before letting him go, but then again the information was probably enough. Checking the safety on the C-18, Greg then crammed it into the pocket of his uniform and started out toward the black pillar of smoke rising above the town.

He wasn't sure what happened first; the deafening roar of an incoming missile or the explosive shockwave that knocked him to the ground. The alley Micky had just run down was now greatly widened, the smoking debris and general devastation leaving no question to Micky's demise.

Head throbbing and body numb, Greg pulled himself to his feet and staggered over to observe the missile strike. The crater was a good ninety feet from where he'd been standing, and only the presence of several buildings and a heavy metal boiler had prevented missile fragments from ripping his body to shreds.

Breaking into an uneven run that jarred his senses with every step, Greg made his way to the black pillar of smoke. He counted three more explosions from other parts of town by the time he reached the second missile's destination. Coalition troops were everywhere, including Captain Pritchett who dolefully watched his Mark 5 Armored Personnel Carrier burn.

Most of the 33 foot long vehicle was unscathed except for the seared paint and soot covered exterior. Bright metal fires blazed away at the frayed armor shards where the forward pilot's compartment once had been. Soldiers in full environmental armor tried in vain to extinguish the inferno with fire retardant foam, but only succeeded in keeping the fire isolated to the front section. Captain Pritchett and several other soldiers stared in bewilderment as Lieutenant Merrick started to laugh.

"Who bought it?" Greg asked between cackles.

"Lieutenant Goldstein." the Captain responded hesitantly. Greg's shredded clothing and wild hair showed he'd been near an explosion, no doubt the cause for his shell shocked behavior, Pritchett thought.

"Let me guess. You had him in there monitoring communications and active radar."

"Yes, why?"

Greg laughed even harder, convincing some bystanders that he was completely off his nut.

"The missile tracked in on the APC's radar tower," Greg stammered, tears forming from hysterical laughter.

"Lieutenant, do you know who did this?" Captain Pritchett inquired angrily.

"Yes, as a matter of fact I do. The Army of the New Order. For all we know it might have been Coalition ordnance and hardware, like this C-18 I pulled off that Headhunter." Greg tried to be serious.

"I have a few questions for that man."

"Me too, sir," he laughed, trying to keep a straight face. "But I don't think he's going to answer any of them. No more than twenty seconds after I released him he wandered right into the center of this really big explosion, sir." He laughed harder.

"What do you mean, probably Coalition ordnance and hardware, Lieutenant?" Pritchett's patience was nearing its limits.

"This C-18 I pulled off him will probably match up with the serial numbers of equipment stolen in a raid on an outpost near Cedar Lake." Greg wrestled his cackles under control. "I'd have to check with Lieutenant Sorenson to find exactly what was taken, but a good bet is the Army of the New Order made off with a few disposable launch platforms."

"Could have been Wellingtons," one of Pritchett's NCO's offered.

"Could have been something an Operator jury-rigged on the back of a hover rover for all we know," Greg chuckled. "Doesn't make much difference to Lieutenant Goldstein."

"Lieutenant Merrick, do you know where this Army of the New Order is located." Pritchett ground his teeth together in suppressed frustration.

"I do now. Why?"

"Because this attack cannot go unanswered. Tomorrow morning I'm going to lead a full scale assault and make sure they never attack my unit ever again."

Van sighed and ran his hands over the sharp metal edges and warped armor plating on his Sky Cycle's air intake. Finding another dense metal shard deep in the cycle's intake turbine, he took hold of it with a pair of vice grips and yanked the foreign object free. Dropping it into a pile of fifty slugs just like it, the Techno-Wizard resumed the search for metal slugs.

"Two days out and I get blasted by some mechanical chick on a robot monster. Way to go, Van." He talked out loud to himself. "Funny, it sure seemed like a good idea to go looking for the rail gun, guess you didn't think someone else would already have it. Smart one, Van." Part of the reason for his trip to the east was to search for a powerful new rail gun that had surfaced on the frontier, but nobody knew the exact origin. Only a handful had ever surfaced up in Lazlo, and Van thought he'd try and track one of the compact, self contained weapons for himself. "Real smart."

"What happened to your cycle?" Anja's question startled him so badly he dropped the vice grips down the intake. Van turned around slowly, trying not to show his irritation. The rented shed had only one entrance, and he'd forgotten to shut it. Anja stood a few feet away and watched him with a puzzled expression.

"Did I come at a bad time?"

"No, I just didn't hear you come in. How long have you been standing there"

"Just long enough to hear you talking about some mechanical beastie. What happened to your leg?" she glanced down at the shredded armor and caked blood on his lower left leg. Smooth, uninjured skin could be seen through holes in the armor.

"Some of the metal shards went clear through the intake and caught me in the leg. I was pretty lucky the armor stopped most of it, my magic isn't strong enough to heal a severed leg."

"Who shot you?" Anja sat on the ground and started arranging the pile of metal slugs into the shape of a horse.

"This woman riding what looked to be some kind of monster. The whole reason I came to Liberty in the first place was to check out some cool alien weaponry and artifacts some friends of mine at Lazlo told me about. Of course they didn't say anything about those weapons actually being used by someone, but I should have guessed. I'm flying along east of here, and I see this woman riding a monster, so I land nearby to talk to her and she tells me to leave the area or she'll kill me." Van sat on the floor across the pile from Anja.

"And then she shot at you?"

"Not quite. I get a little closer, I'm curious, you understand. This woman's has these like antenna things sticking out of her head or helmet, and what looks like all this cybernetic stuff. I know she's not a slaver or anything, so I figure I'll get closer and check her out. Well, as it turns out, her mount is this weird kind of animal cyborg or robot, and I want to know exactly what it is. I flip over to my special optics and see that it's not alive at all, but completely mechanical. She starts yelling at me to get away and when I look at her aura, I find she'd nothing but a robot too, just with fake hair and some skin grafts. I start backing off and she fires these laser beams from her hands at me. Thankfully I'd powered up my mystic shields and made it back to my cycle before she figured out it wasn't hurting me. Then, as I'm lifting off, she pulls out this huge gun that must have been at least as tall as I am, and holds it with one hand. I just have enough time to activate the shielding on my cycle when she blasts me from fifty feet away. All I can figure is her gun is some type of powerful, flechette style rail gun, because the next thing I know my engine is eating armor fragments and my leg feels like someone just hacked it off with a chain saw. I mean, Jeez, one shot and wham! My cycle shield is gone, my personal shield is gone, and these metal shards are ripping through armor like it's not even there. Needless to say I got away from there as fast as I could and used the V-MED before I bled to death. And get this, as I'm leaving, I see three more coming out of the woods, looking exactly like the one I was talking to. Tomorrow I'm going to see If I can sneak up on one of them and can get a better look at the stuff they have, maybe even borrow some of their gear, just to check it out. How was your day?"

"Van, you would not believe what happened here while you were gone. It's all over town. You didn't hear?"

"No, I just talked to one of the First Strike mercs when I flew in and came straight here."

"Well," Anja wound up for her story. "Remember Zenjori Suka and his cutthroats?"

"Like I could forget what they did to Youngstown."

"Today they shot a whole bunch of missiles into town and tried to hit Coalition soldiers. They tried to make it look like First Strike did it, but they didn't fool anybody. A lot of people got hurt, but mostly Coalition soldiers. A missile hit one of the cabins they were in, but the walls had some armor built in and they weren't killed. One missile hit that eight wheeled thing and killed one of their officers, though. Tomorrow I hear they're going to retaliate. Do you think we should help?"

"I can't believe that guy was stupid enough to attack the Coalition again. They probably would have left him alone. I think the Coalition can handle it. At least he's not holding civilians hostage this time. They can do their worst and not mess up too bad."

"Cyndiara made Darren promise to try and capture Zenjori Suka so she could kill him herself for what he did."

"There's a time for revenge, and of all people, Cyndiara deserves whatever she can get. If I thought the Coalition wouldn't shoot at me, I might help. Jeez, I better get working or I'll never finish before tomorrow morning." Van hopped up and stared at the damaged Sky Cycle.

"I miss my horse." Anja looked at the mechanical contraption.

"They've got stables here, you know."

"I know. That's where I spent most of today. There's this really pretty chestnut mare with a really sweet temperament. They say she isn't for sale," Anja pouted, then brightened. "Oh, Van, I almost forgot why I wanted to talk to you." She jumped to her feet. "What are you doing tonight?"

"Fixing Sherylinn."

"You named your Sky Cycle Sherylinn?"

"Why not? She really came through for me today. She deserves to have a name."

"Sherylinn's a good name." Anja patted the cycle's mini-missile launcher as if it were a living thing.

"I don't know where I'm going to scrounge up the parts I need to do the modifications I really need."

"Well if you get hungry, I made a really big dinner because I though Darren and Cyndiara were coming, but they're mad at each other right now so they're not coming. Want to have dinner with me?"

"Sure. Jeez, I don't think I've eaten since this morning. I forgot."

"How can you forget about food?"

"Just thinking about other things, I guess."

"Well Sherylinn isn't hungry so she can wait. Come on." Anja grabbed his hand and led him out of the shed.

By the time Van had showered and changed into a black silk shirt and soft black pants, his appetite screamed for appeasement. He barely knocked on her hotel room door and it was open. It wasn't the aroma of roasted turkey or freshly baked bread that demanded his attention, though.

"You like it?" Anja asked, twirling around once in the slim, white satin dress. Van had wondered what she'd kept in the heavy suitcase he'd hauled up to her room when they arrived in town, and now he felt it was worth it.

"Yeah, uh, you look, exquisite. It's perfect, Anja. If I'd have known you wanted formal attire I wouldn't have come dressed like this."

"You could always wear the dress David bought me," she joked.

"I don't look good in that shade of blue."

"Come in, I'm almost done setting the table. I called Cyndiara's suite again, but there wasn't any answer so I don't think she or Darren are coming." Anja finished laying out the silverware on a white tablecloth. Van closed the door behind him and sauntered over to the table. Anja murmured something softly and the two candles sparkled to life.

"Get the lights?"

"Sure." Van flicked off the tacky hotel room lamp and sat opposite the Mystic. He looked around, amazed at how well she'd made the room actually seem like home. For a moment neither spoke, Anja's gaze transfixed by the way the candle's flickering light gave Van's dark eyes an almost luminous quality.

"This all looks very good, Anja. I don't think I can eat it all."

"That's okay. I can always put whatever's left in the refrigerator for later."

Again the awkward silence and mysterious ambiance prevailed. Van could feel her gentle telepathic touch and Anja's questioning thoughts, but for some reason it didn't bother him as much as it used to. They ate in silence, mutual thoughts and emotions slowly mingling freely for the first time. When they were done eating the silence continued. Walls and barriers that could take years to overcome fell aside for greater understanding. When the candles burned low in the brass holders, both drifted to the soft rug before the fireplace. The soft brush of a hand and slow gentle embrace sent thrills of warmth and excitement thorough Anja's body. She surrendered to his arms and let his hands caress the smooth white satin of her dress.

The black silk of his shirt slid back from his wrist to reveal a small tattoo of a heart impaled by a wooden stake. An aura of magic radiated around it.

Gone was the feeling of warmth and tenderness, horror invading Anja's emotions in strengthening tides. Snatching his other wrist she slid the sleeve away to reveal a tattoo of a sword, a powerful aura of magic energy surrounding it. Pulling herself away in fear, Anja crawled to the edge of the rug. Her body shuddered as the full realization sank in.

"No." She shook her head, tears forming in her eyes and running down her cheeks.

Van hadn't moved, or even looked up at her. Instead he sat with head bowed and hands clasped in his lap, no longer trying to conceal the marks. Anja had sometimes wondered why he often wore long sleeved shirts even inside where it was warm, and she remembered several occasions when he'd hidden the tattoo's aura by wearing bizarre circuits around his wrists. Now she knew why.

"I would have told you. Eventually."

"Told me what, Van, that you're a member of the Federation of Magic?"

Van's head snapped up, frightening Anja all the more. He held up both wrists for her to view.

"Is that what you think these mean? You think I'm part of the Federation?"

"I've been told there were tattooed warriors serving the Federation of Magic. Assassins, with tattoos like those. Evil ones who kill without mercy."

"But that isn't why I have these. You don't really think I'm a member of the most nefarious Legion of Wizards on the planet, do you?"

Anja shook her head, knowing his words were true. Van's eyes took a distant look, and his expression was sad.

"I wouldn't doubt for a moment that many of my clan are very much a part of the Federation. Perhaps it's them you've heard about."

"What, Van? Who are you really?"

"Do you want to know?" Van asked quietly, a sadness in his voice.

Anja moved closer.

"Yes, I want to know."

"I'm not very proud of my heritage, Anja, and if you really knew why you wouldn't blame me for hiding it."

"I don't blame you, I just want you to be open and honest with me." Anja's heart ached at the mental agony Van was going through.

"I am a descendant of an ancient race that once inhabited a continent called Atlantis. By their own folly, my ancestors caused the near destruction of my race and sent the continent of Atlantis into the watery grave of another dimension. Those that escaped did so by scattering throughout the Megaverse, to far off places and unexplored dimensions. What was once a great civilization fell into separate clans, all blaming the others for the city's fall. I am a member of the strongest Atlantean clan, but I claim no part in the evil they are doing now that Atlantis has returned to Earth. They've made pacts with demons and evil creatures so powerful it bends the imagination, and what they've done to fulfill their side of these pacts I shudder to conceive."

Van's voice wavered, but he never broke his gaze.

"What does all this mean?" Anja stammered, overwhelmed by the truth

"That's up to you, Anja. I can tell you that when the truth of what my clan has done is discovered, it will shame my race and end with them all being hunted down and destroyed by the other remaining Atlanteans. I can't stop what's been started, but I don't have to be a part of it. I am human, Anja, but I will live for hundreds of years after you are gone."

"I don't care what your clan's done, all I care about is you. I don't care if you live longer than me, it's the time we share that counts." Anja grasped the few things of value that really mattered to her, tears still flowing.

"I will live beyond your years, and endure the pain of your parting for the rest of my lifetime. But for as long as we have, I could love you."

Anja sniffled and wiped tears from her cheeks. Deep down, past all the words and things she didn't understand, she knew his heart really meant it.

"You would love me even though I will grow old and you won't?"

"Yes. I can promise there will be dark times in our lives, but we would live through them together. I can accept you as you are, and respect you for what you believe to be true, Anja. You've shown me how much else there is to experience. That's something I value, enough to commit my life to to. To you."

"Are you asking me to be your wife?" Anja's heart beat faster and faster, pulse quickening and hands trembling. Van looked at the dwindling fire, struggling with a self serving nature that warned him his life would never be the same. He was at a crucial turning point. Life would never be easy, and if it was it probably meant he was going the wrong way. If he made a vow he would honor and keep it, not for religious pretenses or spiritual beliefs, but for his own soul.

"Yes, I guess I am. Marriage as an institution I don't really believe in, but what it stands for, I do. To call you wife means I will never leave you, in sickness or health, good times or bad. It means we'll always work things out, no matter how difficult, and we'll always stay together until death forces us apart. Yes, Anja, I'm asking you to be my wife." Van turned away from the fire and looked into her misty eyes.

Anja's eyes trembled when she spoke.

"Yes." she smiled and tears flowed again. "In sickness or health, rich or poor, good times or bad, until death we do part. I love you, Van." She moved closer and Van pulled her to him.

Her body burned with fire against his body when he gently lifted her chin and kissed her on the lips for the very first time.

Chapter 11

Steam ascended from the heated jet pack on Sharp's back as he entered the commander's cabin upon returning from an early morning reconnaissance. Forgetting to salute his superiors, the Coalition scout set his modified JA-11 sniper rifle on the center table and lifted his helmet faceplate to give his report. The officers in the briefing waited patiently. Captain Pritchett calmly reached out and moved the rifle off the corner of his map, noting the non-standard weapon and bulky, fabricated mounting for the oddly shaped targeting system.

"Is something wrong with your C-10, Corporal?"

"C-10, sir? I don't use a C-10 rifle anymore," Sharp responded, not expecting the question or intending to be rude.

"I can see that. Your armor I can understand, but what's wrong with using standard Coalition armament?"

"I get twice the range with the Pre-Rifts rifle, plus C-10's are always going on the fritz. This baby is tough for being almost three hundred years old." Sharp patted the rifle fondly.

"Well then, what did you and your fabulous rifle discover this morning?"

"Visibility's down to about 1200 feet, and getting worse with the way it's misting out there. They must know we're coming because they moved south-east in battle formations. There's a valley I think we can catch them in if we move fast and don't blow our position."

"How many?" Lieutenant Merrick asked from beside the wood-burning furnace.

"I counted about a dozen vehicles and another 60 troops, mostly D-Bees. It looks like they aren't too well armed, but man for man they outnumber us."

"Mechanized?" Pritchett inquired.

"NG-Multibot, 4 Samson P.A.'s, Titan Combat, and a V-10 with some type of rail gun, I couldn't quite make out the exact type."

"Air power?"

"Nothing actually in the air when I was over there, but I could hear thrusters every now and then. Sounded like SAM's. Lieutenant Sorenson was creeping on the second formation, and he reported half a dozen more vehicles and ten to twenty cyborgs escorting an Ultimax."

"Looks like Zenjori has some teeth this time," Brian commented.

"Only a few sharp ones." Pritchett smiled cheerfully.

"What else, Sharp?" Greg sauntered over to the table.

"That's all Sorenson and I saw, sir."

"Aren't we forgetting the Glitter Boy? And I know he's got more than a few cyborgs and worthless D-Bee troops to throw at us."

"How do you know?" Pritchett asked suspiciously.

"Because I've been in their camp. I saw the tents and vehicles."

Pritchett looked skeptical.

"I've seen them, almost touched them. Plus, I've been talking to some mercs in First Strike, and they told me the Army of the New Order had over 20 cyborgs, several dozen Headhunters, and at least two Sky Kings. Sharp, you said there's a valley that looks good for an attack?"

"Yeah. They were in two formations at either end. We just swing the SAM's from one end, move our armor from the other, put infantry on the ride line, and we've got them squashed," Sharp gave his assessment.

"We've been up against Zenjori more than a few times, and I think this is just what he wants us to think. It's a trap."

"Really, what makes you so sure, Lieutenant?" Pritchett placed both bionic palms on the table.

"This Suka knows his only chance is to beat us in a full scale confrontation, and even then it's quite possible he'll lose. This he knows. He's not going to split his force and and let us isolate and eliminate each group, one by one. Anybody knows that a force on the ridge line could keep both formations from backing each other up. He's not going to take that chance."

"Why wouldn't he split his forces? He did it after Youngstown and we'd have had him if it hadn't been for-"

"Shut up, Brian," Sergeant Winters warned the red haired officer, disregarding rank.

"Right, Brian, he did split his forces at Youngstown and we almost beat him. He won't make the same mistake again." Greg leaned forward, his long hair falling around an unshaven face. "Don't you see? Read the history of this rebel leader and you'll know him. He doesn't care if he loses half his army if it draws us into a trap!" Greg slapped his fist on the table for emphasis.

"What makes you so sure?" Pritchett asked coldly.

"Because he thinks he knows exactly what we'll do, and up until now he's been right! That attack yesterday wasn't some petty attempt to destroy us, he wanted us out there, where he can take us out without facing First Strike. He thought he'd get us fighting First Strike, but he's gotta know that didn't work out, that's why he moved right into the patrol route we've been maintaining. He wants us to know exactly where he is. He's sick, and probably thinks we're the entire reason all of his plans here in Liberty fell apart. Sick, but not stupid, deranged, but still tricky. That doesn't mean we have to step right into his trap."

"I think you're overestimating this Zenjori character, Lieutenant." Pritchett looked haughtily around the room. "But you've brought up some interesting points that I'll consider. He wants a fight, we'll give him one."

"Okay, here's what I suggest. You and your unit advance and take on the first, maybe second formation from one end of the valley. It's not going to be easy, but I think your unit can handle a stand up fight. Sooner or later Zenjori will have to spring his trap or at least give up his plan to keep from losing. When he shows his hand, that's when my unit strikes him with everything we've got and doesn't let up until we've got every last one of them."

Everyone waited in silence for the captain's approval.

"That has got to be the most feeble attempt yet, Lieutenant."

"Sir?"

"Send the captain charging in as bait in a trap, and then stand back and wait for these rebels to do your dirty work. Come now, that wasn't even sneaky."

"Well, respectfully begging your pardon, sir, but a second ago you weren't even sure it was a trap. If I'm wrong you've got nothing to worry about."

"Fine, why doesn't your unit move in first, and we'll stand by to attack."

"Quite respectfully, sir, you haven't been real zealous about charging into battle."

"If I make it an order, you will follow it." Pritchett worked his jaw in irritated fashion. This officer was definitely on the edge of a court-martial.

"Up yours, sir."

Sergeant Winter's low rumbling laugh sounded from across the room.

"Do you have something to add, Sergeant Major?" Pritchett scowled.

"No sir. Nothing you'd care ta hear."

"This is what's going to happen, and I won't make it an order unless I have to." Pritchett reigned in his anger. "Rather than split our forces, we'll move together as several separate squads, engaging the enemy by designated fire teams. A unified force should be able to isolate and destroy one rebel position at a time. If, and when an ambush takes place, we break off and counterattack the ambushing force by designated squads. Just in case there are rebels dug in along the sides of the valley, I'll send my Dog Packs along the ridge lines to give us advance warning."

"What about a contingency plan? Sending everyone into a trap is a dangerous risk." Greg leaned forward over the table, gray eyes smoldering.

"Granted, there are many variables in any combat situation. If it becomes necessary, we will regroup and then counter-attack. My Abolisher and Sky Cycles will stay back and provide cover fire, protecting our retreat if it becomes necessary."

"Not good enough."

"Well it's going to have to be good enough! I'm warning you, Lieutenant. You're behavior is dangerously irrational, and if you continue crossing me —"

"You'll what? Threaten me some more?" Greg shot back defiantly.

Winters smiled to himself. For a moment, Captain Pritchett appeared intimidated by the younger officer. But the aura of command returned. Nobody was going to take that away from him.

"We don't have time for your belligerent behavior and lack of respect, Lieutenant. You're setting a very poor example here." Pritchett breathed slow and heavy, trying to maintain a level of calm. "The assault goes as planned, so please cooperate without further outbursts. Your fire teams will take point, within range of our armor units for cover. If your squads are as good as you say, they shouldn't have any trouble flushing out and eliminating a few D-bee and Headhunter squads. As enemy armor exposes itself, your troops will take cover and let our mechanized converge and destroy. My infantry will back up your fire squads and provide close fire support for our mechanized units. Choose your teams, lieutenant, and report when you're ready to move out. That part is an order, Lieutenant."

"Quite respectfully sir, If I feel my men are needlessly endangered, I will pull them out, with or without your permission." Greg leaned closer. Pritchett took a step back. "Sergeant Major!"

"Yes, sir?" Winters stepped up.

"We have orders to follow." Greg broke eye contact with Pritchett and stalked to the door followed by the broad shouldered NCO. Winters grinned and slapped Greg on the back.

"I knew you'd come around."

Soldiers of fortune stood beneath the rain-soaked trees and waited for the miserable weather to let up. A number of bear-like warriors complained endlessly about the conditions they were expected to fight in, but quickly silenced their grumblings when Kruno flew slowly by in his hover craft. The Army of the New Order paid well, and most of the hired guns would rather endure a few hardships than wind up with a blaster at the back of their skulls. One binding trait other than common greed kept them together and loyal to the mercenary army. All of them hated the Coalition.

Crashing through a low hanging branch, Kruno's hovercraft made a right angle turn and flew over the ridge away from the gathered forces. Curses from the hatch gunner brought a smile to the mercenary captain's lips, and he swerved at the next low flying clump of branches he saw.

"Watch it!" Trench shouted down into the pilot's compartment.

"A little water and a few leaves ain't gonna hurt the rail gun, Trench!"

"Screw the rail gun! I'm talkin' about me!"

"Hey Trench, reach over and pull the twigs out of the sensor turret. I can't see where I'm going." Kruno lied.

The odd-shaped hover craft was actually the upper half of a Norther Gun manufacture Multi-Bot. Kruno never understood why the strange looking robot never achieved much popularity. It was built tough enough to survive heavy combat plus the upper half of the robot could detach and operate independantly as a hover craft. Once re-attached, it served as the robot's command center and pilot's compartment.

"Kruno! You're doing that on purpose!" Trench complained.

Kruno winked at his co-pilot and swerved again.

"Kruno!"

"Hehehehe."

"Holy mother of D-Bees!" His co-pilot pointed to the view screen.

Six giant, winged Gargoyles stood to one side of the second mechanized force, Torrak and Credo proudly displaying their summoned warriors. The fifteen-foot demons glared with hateful eyes at the sub-creatures around them, but were bound by magic not to harm them. Zenjori flagged down Kruno's hover craft and watched with satisfaction as the mercenary captain stared in disbelief at the giant demons.

"Casters musta been busy last night," Kruno shrugged finally and hopped down from the hatch.

"What are you doing back here, Kruno? Why aren't you with your squad?" Zenjori inquired. Standing a few inches taller in his Triax make exoskeleton, the mercenary leader still had to look up at the Partial Conversion Headhunter.

"It's yer orders, Suka San." Kruno addressed Zenjori with respect, not understanding the racial indescrepancy he and everybody else took for granted. "They stink like rotten apples in a barrel of rum in summer."

"Do they?"

"You want me to march right down the center of the valley and stop when I reach the mouth. That's suicide if the Coalition attacks while Drake's 'Sledge Hammer' squad is sittin' on their tails back here."

"We went over this before, Kruno. Carnivore squad advances down the valley and holds position while Sledge Hammer slips across the valley and up to position on the ridge," Zenjori explained patiently. "The Coalition will be expecting a trap, that's why our third force will pretend to be the ambushing party to cover Sledge Hammer's position."

"And if Drake's screwing around when I get attacked, it's me takin' it. How do I know I won't be left under fire?"

"You have my word of honor."

Kruno caught himself before he mentioned what he thought of Zenjori's honor.

"And how long do I stump-sit at the valley mouth?"

"As long as it takes the Coalition to get there. My spy in Liberty informs me that the Coalition has mobilized its entire force and is currently en route. If it makes you feel better, I'll have our demonic squad over there move to draw fire as soon as Sledge Hammer is in position."

"I know what my boyz is capable of, and they ain't gonna handle no frontal attack from no Coalition force of that size. I ain't got the manpower or the firepower."

"That's why Drake and the demons will assist you once the battle is under way. First the Demons, then Sledge Hammer from the Coalition's flank," Zenjori explained in an exasperated tone of voice. "Now move into position before the Coalition gets near. Now, Kruno."

"Okay, boss," Kruno acquiesced cheerfully and climbed back into the hover craft. Heading back the same way he came, Kruno thought about exactly how much he trusted his life to Zenjori.

"Forget Zenjori!"

"Uh, Kruno, it might not be smart to disobey orders," Trench advised, having locked down the rail gun and closed the hatch.

"Like he's gonna back me up in time. This is what we're gonna do. I want a fall back position dug in and fire lanes cleared 'zactly where the squad is now."

"But Zenjori told us to advance to the valley mouth."

"And we will. Juss some of us ain't gonna move. We'll take on the Dead Boys and then fall back to our varmit holes and hold out there, droppin' mines in the C.S. path. If we can fight 'em to a stand-still we can hit them before they hit us."

"But what if we don't get backed up?"

"Then we hold out to the last man, and make them Dead Boys pay for every step they take."

Vegetation stirred slightly two hundred feet from the Bear Man mercenaries. None of them noticed. Rain soaked twigs and leaves bent silently under armor clad feet, bringing Cowboy and his five man fire team into perfect position to slaughter the unsuspecting warriors.

"Fireteam Alpha to Beta," Cowboy whispered over his helmet radio.

"This is Beta," Trenton's voice came back over the comm.

"I've got six hostiles. Back me. We're taking them."

"Roger."

Cowboy motioned to his team and assigned each of them a target with a series of hand signals. Infrared laser beams found vulnerable sections on the Bear Men's armor and marked the location for destruction.

"Fire."

Leaves and wet branches exploded behind the dismembered bodies of all six mercenaries, laser beams and plasma bolts passing through unoccupied space between body parts.

Popping out of their concealment thirty feet to the left of the Bear Men's remains, a second squad of mercenaries took aim at the stand of trees Cowboy's squad fired from.

Laser beams fell in rapid succession and plasma eradicated armor and living matter alike. The next rebel squad disappeared into the smoking craters left in the hillside without getting off a single shot.

"Thanks, Trenton."

"No problem."

"Fireteam Alpha to Fireteam Beta, you're clear."

"Copy," Sergeant Winters responded and moved the largest fire team up the hillside.

"Sharp to Charlie. Watch your nine o'clock, there's four or five rabbits moving back up the valley." Sharp observed the battle from the opposite ridge

"Where? I can't see a damn thing. Too many trees." Winters halted his squad and crouched, trying to get a glimpse of the enemy.

"They can't be more than fifty feet from you."

"I can hear them." Winters waved his squad into concealment.

"D-Bees mostly, and they must be able to hear you too. A cat-like thing stopped them. They're running back for the creek."

"This is Alpha, we'll take 'em. Cover us Beta." Cowboy leapt down the muddy embankment and ran across a stretch of open ground towards the creek. His fire team moved in behind him with equal enthusiasm, making use of trees and bushes to conceal their movements.

"You got 'em, Cowboy," Sharp called in.

"Where?!" Cowboy practically yelled over the radio, dropping lower behind the gnarled roots of tree. "It's too dense down here."

"They're right there!" Sharp whispered back urgently, watching the other squad cautiously try and outflank Winters position. "Twenty feet, coming right to you!"

Cowboy stood and swung around the tree trunk to face an equally startled cat-like D-Bee carrying a bulky laser rifle.

In the same movement Cowboy thrust the C-27's bayonet through the cat's open faceplate and swung the dead D-Bee in the line of fire with its four companions. Cowboy's armor was splattered with boiled blood as he sighted down the cat's helmet and erased the D-Bee's head to dispatch a human rebel coming up behind.

"Get down!" Nim shouted and fired four grenades from his C-14 at the remaining partially armored rebels.

Armor fragments and body parts flew away from the tremendous explosion. The blast echoed up the valley, announcing the battle's official beginning.

Tossing the shredded corpse of the cat off his body, Cowboy wiped blood smears from his helmet's eye pieces and took a moment to admire the smoking, three inch wide hole bored through the tree trunk four inches from where his head had been.

"Yeah!"

Kruno tilted his head and listened to the sounds of battle roll past. Once again locked in place and part of the large robot, the hover craft now served as command central for the firepower at his disposal.

"We just lost our point group." Trench relayed from the communications console.

"How many'd we get?"

"Armin says none." Trench listened to the rebel spotter. "But then he's having trouble tracking enemy movements."

"These Dead Boys is gettin' better. How far now?"

"Little over half a mile. Armin's got a spot on the Skull Walker at about 4,000 feet."

"They're runnin' silent then cuz I'm not pickin' up active radar."

"Armin's got the Skull pegged, preparing missiles to fire." Trench reached over and raised the V-shaped launchers into position.

"Not yet. Only one Skull Walker?" Kruno shifted in his seat to make sure Trench didn't blow the robot's position.

"Armin, it's only one Skull Walker?" Trench asked on the scrambled frequency. "Armin. Armin, do you copy?"

Kruno began to laugh, slamming his mechanical fist down on the leg lock.

"Radio Zenjori and tell him to send in J.J. If I don't gots a spotter, I'm gonna make sure they ain't gots one neither."

Sharp switched the AQ-3 targeting system to full magnification, making sure the enemy sniper wasn't just playing dead. The computer-enhanced image came up crystal clear a moment later and settled the question. Most of Armin's skull was missing, helmet and all. A twinge of sadness mingled with exuberance, Sharp always felt a rush when he made a perfect shot, but taking life wasn't something he reveled in. There was no time for contemplation. The Coalition scout set about to locate another target.

The AQ-3 beeped at him in his helmet. Sharp dropped from the tree just as a laser beam cut the canopy in half. A quick burst of thrust from the jet pack set him safely on the moist forest floor. It had taken some time for Sharp to figure out the complex systems of the Pre-Rifts AQ-3 targeting system. The first time he'd switched on the SCMS he'd knocked out six passive night scopes and a thermo-imager, all of which were attached to weapons of his buddies. Brian Adams had tried to explain in irate terms that SCMS stood for Sensor Counter Measure Systems, and that there was a reason he'd left that particular function off the menu. Whenever the SCMS picked up an active targeting beam, it traced it back to the source and counter-attacked with an intense laser beam directed at the optics. Brian tried to explain the difference between passive and active SCMS, and promptly wired the AQ-3 to operate only on passive scan and passive response. Now it merely watched for active optical scans and targeting beams, only giving audible warnings when a targeting beam came within close proximity to the targeting system. Brian did his best to wire in most of the AQ-3's functions to Sharp's helmet Heads Up Display and JA-11 sniper rifle. Sharp could only imagine what it must have been like to have a fully operational and integrated weapon and targeting system the way it was intended.

Calling up a tactical overview on the AQ-3, Sharp moved along the edge of the ridge to where the computer told him the infrared targeting beam originated.

Another warning sounded in Sharp's helmet.

Jumping over a rotten log, Sharp narrowly avoided another high power laser beam. This time the tactical display wasn't needed. Up in a tree forty feet away, J.J. fired through the log and blasted earth between Sharp's legs.

No longer concerned with long range accuracy, Sharp switched the JA-11 to ion blaster and cut the forest down in the enemy sniper's general direction.

Leaping from the falling tree, the drug-enhanced reflexes of the sniper reacted instantaneously upon impact with the ground. Rolling out of the fall without loss of balance, J.J. launched his body between ion beams and tackled the startled Coalition soldier.

Down the slick blanket of fallen leaves the two tumbled until a tree trunk stopped their descent. As if his every move was in slow motion, Sharp tried to push the "Juicer" away with the JA-11. J.J. flung it away from both of them, his own rifle lost someplace in the tumble.

Before Sharp could react, the assassin in plate armor had a high frequency saber aimed at his head. Rolling as far as he could under the juicer's weight, Sharp watched the blade slice clear through a tree trunk inches away. As the tree began to tilt, Sharp grabbed hold of the Juicer's chestplate and let the warrior's chemically augmented strength pull both of them out of the way. There was a moment of imbalance and the downward tumbling resumed, saber winding up imbedded two feet into the ground.

Sharp's jet pack jammed between two saplings and brought them both to a halt. J.J. lost his grip and slid farther, grabbing onto a root and swinging his body around the base of a tree. Wedged in place on his back like a flipped turtle, Sharp acted out of desperation, drawing both C-18 laser pistols and leaning back to deforest J.J.'s place of refuge. Dodging falling branches and all but a few laser blasts, J.J. scrambled out of the smoking pile of limbs to hear something bounce off his armor and disappear into the foliage.

"Dodge that." Sharp taunted, and engaged his jet pack.

Something in J.J.'s head reminded him of Assassin's Rule #2: Get out while the getting's good. While probably never meant for this situation, the rule seemed to apply. Throwing himself headlong down the slope J.J. was hit with a shock wave and flung against a tree at terminal velocity. The lights went out and the bio-chip attached to J.J.'s drug injection harness kicked his body into a regenerative trance, oblivious to the raining limbs and debris.

Skidding to a clumsy stop, Sharp whirled to watch his handiwork. Cybernetic sound filters cut in and he watched the fusion block explode in near silence. As the ground shock wave rattled him inside his armor, the world of sound returned at relatively safe decibles. Sharp cheered the descending forest and rising pillar of smoke, certain his nemesis was at last no more.

Looking out over the valley through the battle forged clearing, Sharp had little time to celebrate.

"Oh man!"

Metal slugs tore a trail thorough earth as four Samson power armor units unleashed their firepower. A jet-assisted leap into visual concealment saved Sharp from almost certain shredding. Running for the resting place of his rifle, he listened to the hail of metal rip its way through the forest behind him.

Coming to a large rock set in the hillside, Sergeant Winters was pleased to discover the unobstructed view of the valley. The treetops came just ten feet above the top of the rock, giving his fire team the advantage of height and concealment. Already his CR-1 rocket team was taking up position behind some foliage on top of the boulder, covered by eight soldiers with a devastating array of weaponry.

Down in the valley, Alpha and Beta teams were dispatching groups of rebels caught in a wedge-shaped crossfire when Sharp's fusion block detonated a thousand feet away.

"Sir, Sharp's under fire by four NG-X9's." The CR-1 operator pointed to the infantry Power Armor Units.

"You think I can't hear 'im screamin' on the comm, Rachel? What's the range?"

"1,400 feet," she spoke into the multi-optics scope attached to the bulky rocket launcher.

"I guess we'll hafta mess them up an' see if it don't flush some rebel armor into our mechanized. Everyone take a bead on that dirty, gray painted guy down there." Winters laid flat on the rock and checked the distance himself.

"They're all dirty gray in this mist, Sarge. Screwin' up the targeting beams, too."

"Watcha got in that thing?"

"CR-1? A scorcher, Sarge."

"Take it out and slap an AP."

"You got it." Rachel ported the launcher for her partner to switch the mini-missile load. "Now what?"

"Pick one of them, I don't care which one. Listen up Charlie, when Rachel marks it, everyone fire a tight burst to take it down, then git yer cans off this rock and find some cover."

"So long, baby," Rachel breathed and let the mini-missile fly.

Retractable fins popped out and kept the rocket on course to its detonation. The warhead's cone collapsed on impact the same instant a shaped charge fired through the Samson's shoulder armor plating and destroyed the supporting mechanical workings. The rebel power armor staggered back in the localized explosion.

"Drop it." Winters called down the death sentence.

Misplaced laser beams and off course plasma vaporized the forest in a circle of destruction around the target. For every blast that missed, three more broke molecular bonds and burned through armor. The Samson flailed to the side and threw up its arms in a defensive posture. Arms slagged away and the body withered like a plant in full sun. The pilot's scream was cut short as plasma and molten slag pierced the power armor on its way out the back.

"Back!" Winters barked and slid down the rock to the hillside. Half of the rock fragmented with hundreds of metal slugs tearing through and out the other side. Soldiers dove away from the hail of rail gun fire, armor stopping rock shards from maiming flesh and bone. As quickly as the rail gun fire started, it ceased, leaving the stench of metal and stone dust to wash down on huddled troops.

"They stopped firing," Rachel observed, sliding a rocket from her own pack into the still smoking launcher.

Sergeant Winters lay on his back and slotted a new energy canister in his C-27. The mist shifted and the air swirled in a peculiar fashion above them. Loose stones tumbled down from the boulder's shattered heart. Perched just fifteen feet away, a Gargoyle flapped its wings slowly and roared menacingly.

"Oh hell," Rachel whispered on dry lips. "What is that?"

Sergeant Winters shrugged.

"Kill it."

Those not gripped with terror at the nearness of the hideous monster fired madly with everything they had. Fully automatic weapons fire burned hundreds of holes through the Gargoyle's twisting body. Entering it's body through a missing section of chest, Rachel's mini-missile detonated. Spine and wings sailed away from the sudden outburst. Through the reddish mist, Rachel could see daylight through the creature's heart.

Kruno tossed his coonskin cap on the pilot's console and secured his padded helmet in place, covering his bald head. If the battle continued the way it was going, he might end up crawling from his robot's dismembered body to engage the enemy on foot. He wasn't about to let that happen without giving as good as he got, but the Coalition armor still hadn't showed its hand. Something wasn't right. His monster back-up wasn't doing what it was supposed to, either.

"Sarvo wants to know where you want him and the Samsons," Trench relayed from the radio. "Linden's X9's totally wasted and spillin' radiation from its pack."

"Tell him to fall back and git snug between us and the Titan. We're in for the last stand."

"Repeat, Sledge Hammer squad is under attack by Coalition SAMAS, do you copy Carnivore?" Drake's low synthesized voice came over the speakers.

"I read you. We're gettin' munched down here. Where my back up?"

"We've been found out. A pair of SAMAS are slowing us down, with two more covering them from someplace on the other ridge. We're taking heavy fire. Just hold on until we isolate them and break through to you."

"So much for an ambush," Kruno muttered. "Them Dead Boys musta known all along." He signaled Trench to cut transmissions.

"What now, Kruno?" Trench looked worried.

"Punch up short range waves, I've got a feeling we're sitting ducks in a swimming pool full of mashed potatoes right now."

"There's four flyin' things goin' down the valley and two Sky Cycles commin' up fast. Computer won't gimmi a recognition on them four!"

"Rotate the torso and lock the missile launchers."

"But the other four!" Trench targeted the nearest airborne blip.

"Those are Gargoyles brainless! Right now those things is the only thing keepin' them Dead Boys' ground forces from waltzing over and punching our cards but good!"

Darren tripped and fell, splattering mud all over the black finish of his SAMAS. Explosions shook the ground and sent fiery balls into the sky where he'd been standing a moment earlier. Fifty yards away, Drake's cyborg squad continued the advance.

"SAM 15, fall down the ridge then skirt south to lead them into Pritchett's armor." Greg advised, having disregarded the captain's orders the moment they arrived at the valley. His troops didn't have to know the difference. He crouched in a gully not far away, waiting for the hail of fire to lessen enough for him to move again. "Let them think they're driving us back."

"Let them think they're driving us back? They are driving us back!"

"What's going on up there, 117, you're supposed to be covering SAM 15?"

"But I'm getting shot at by an Ultimax!" Brian whined. In a fair fight his SAMAS didn't stand a chance against the X-1000 Ultimax power armor unit. Everyone knew that.

"Sorenson! What's your excuse!?" Greg moved down the gully and popped up to knock a light exoskeleton off its feet with a burst of metal. Three more Terrain Hopper exoskeletons bounced in to fill its place.

"This is 419. I'm busy. Two X-10 Predators." Sorenson evaded the two heavier flying exoskeletons, just barely escaping a constant barrage of laser fire. What the two Triax make units lacked in speed and maneuverability, they made up for in firepower and heavy armor.

"Stay back!" Darren slid his C-40 through a gap in tree roots and fired on the nearest armored cyborg. Metal struck armor and warped it in a line from waist to shoulder. The cyborg staggered back, then continued undaunted. Somehow in the confusion of battle, teamwork had been flushed down the toilet in favor of a free-for-all, and all Darren wanted was to get away with most of his power armor still intact.

Captain Pritchett rubbed his armored hands together with glee. The advance group had done far better than he'd anticipated, but now they were in trouble and it was up to him to charge in guns blazing and save the day. The enemy ambush was exposed, making the rest of the battle the kind of stand-up fight he'd trained for. Although he hated to admit it, Pritchett had to hand it to Merrick's unconventional approach. It was going to make the victory all the more resounding for his mechanized advance.

He'd never seen a Gargoyle before, but from the chatter on the comm, Merrick's ground troops were having some trouble finishing off the last one. Pritchett hoped they didn't kill it before he had a chance to see it in action.

"Red, Gray, and Yellow squads advance with pattern Delta."

"On our way!" Two hover rovers full of infantry followed the lead squad of six on armored hover cycles.

"Silver squad advance in wedge formation, attack pattern Indigo."

Trees crashed and were smashed under foot as Pritchett's Skull Walker rose off the ground on its six legs and moved forward. Enforcer 790 got up off its knees, and brushed aside tree branches blocking the sensor turret. The Abolisher mirrored the Enforcer, lumbering through the forest while making no attempt to silence its advance. The two power armor members of Silver squad lifted off the ground to hover just above the treetops. None had turned on active targeting systems, so their presence was not yet discovered.

"Skull 41 has radar lock on one of the Gargoyles." Corporal Lexington's finger flipped open the missile launch system. Advancing ahead of the main group, Merrick's Skull Walker was the only armor unit using active targeting, fire linked to the other mechanized units.

"Fire at will, Corporal." Pritchett leaned close to the view screen to watch for missile trails speeding away from the Enforcer.

Caught in the vicious plasma explosions, the flying creature's wings were melted to bone. Trailing smoke from burnt skin, the Gargoyle crashed into the forest thirty feet from the smoldering body of another of its kind. Lisa and Dave rushed the Skull Walker closer, homing in on the heat signature. Firing through hundreds of feet of forest, Dave unchained the rail gun's firepower and shredded the fallen Gargoyle before it could get back to its feet.

The path up the valley was open to advance. Alpha and Beta fire teams had managed to bring down the Gargoyles and handful of other monstrous defenders, but not before a Gargoyle had landed amid the troops and ripped a grunt's arm off with a single slash. Fireteam Charlie held back, administering first aid to the fallen while Alpha and Beta dug in to ambush the advancing cyborgs on the ridge.

Skull 41 entered the clearing through the path it had made in the forest, approaching the dead Gargoyles with caution. One of the creatures suddenly rolled over and grasped the Skull Walker's foreleg in desperate rage. Dave dropped the rail guns to fire at point blank. Part of the creature's skull disappeared, but the faltering grip on the leg didn't let up. Dave dragged the stubborn creature twenty feet before freeing the Skull Walker of the Gargoyle's death grip.

Two more Gargoyles appeared on radar, leaping up from the forest and flying overhead, intent on vengeance. The beasts' eyes fixed on the wedge of advancing robots.

Fear flashed through Captain Pritchett's mind, an emotion he seldom allowed himself to feel. The creatures diving at his robots believed they could win. Could they? Even if not, the monstrous creatures were willing to throw themselves at him in a futile attempt to maim. That in itself was frightening.

"Shoot it!"

Robots assaulted the valley with the roar of rail gun fire and percussion of rapid fire auto-cannons. The Abolisher scored a direct hit, followed by hundreds of slugs from SAMAS and mecha. The creatures screamed and dropped amidst the robots, wings shredded and bodies oozing blood. Without losing a step the Enforcer pounced on one downed monster and slammed its spiked knee into the Gargoyle's spine. Wrapping giant hands around the Gargoyle's neck, Corrinne began slowly relocating the monster's head.

The other Gargoyle stumbled to its feet, Pritchett's Skull Walker rotating on its base to catch it in the gut with a single rail gun burst. The Gargoyle lunged forward, ducking another burst and bracing itself to flip the spider-like mecha on its back. Lifted up on two of six legs, the Skull Walker's crew desperately tried to keep the robot from being flipped.

Corrinne dispatched the prone Gargoyle, then leaned down on one hand and rotated the Enforcer's body to bring the rail gun's line of fire under the larger Skull Walker. Switching to the rail gun's independent targeting she centered the targeting, dot on the Gargoyle's knee. It roared victoriously as the Skull Walker's weight began to shift over its two grounded legs. The cry of victory turned to pain, eighty slugs breaking bone and ripping muscle. The monster's legs buckled under the robot's immense weight. All six legs sunk into earth and Captain Pritchett's Skull Walker crawled away at top speed.

Screaming inhuman curses, the Gargoyle struggled to get at the Enforcer. In one fluid motion, Corrinne took the Gargoyle's wrists and rolled back, launching the creature to the feet of the Abolisher. Claws raked a gash in the black finish of the larger robot, but the Abolisher simply reached down with oversized hands and took hold of the wounded Gargoyle's skull. In a clumsy, but effective tactic, the Abolisher held the struggling demon between its armored legs and twisted the head until the neck stopped popping. The Gargoyle's world went dark.

The Abolisher tossed aside the mangled beast as if it had been nothing more than a trifling annoyance. Captain Pritchett breathed a sigh of relief but seethed with anger inside. He'd shown fear in front of his robot's crew.

"Silver squad, maintain wedge formation and continue the advance."

Chatter on the comm marked more rebel troops and armor biting the dust at Merrick's direction. Pritchett was feeling more stress. It would be unbearable if fewer than twenty of Merrick's troops managed to clear the path up the valley without any assistance. Not much else was keeping them from doing just that. At the very least Pritchett figured he could hold back just enough to let Merrick's unit suffer the wrath of the ambush they'd uncovered, then move in at the last minute to save the day.

"Sir, Merrick is calling for assistance," Pritchett's communications officer practically yelled inside the small compartment. "He says there's no way four SAM's can hold off the second assault group. He's leading them in our direction but can't slow them down any more."

"He shouldn't have taken action without advising me in the first place. Tell him he'll have to wait until I finish the rebel group holed up in the valley first. Then we'll hit the second force with everything we've got."

"Beta squad just took down another X-9, sir," Pritchett's gunner commented on the cheers over the comm.

"Where are Red, Gray, and Yellow squads? And someone tell me why Skull 41 is advancing past point? Do we have a lock on anything yet?!"

"No, sir, Skull 41 and Alpha and Beta squads keep taking out everything first. Should we go active, sir?"

"Do it. Full sensors, everything," Pritchett ordered.

Radar and full active targeting came alive.

"We're loud, sir."

"Now, maybe we'll have some action." Pritchett leaned forward, expecting to find new targets to destroy.

A warning tone sounded instead.

"Someone's locked in on us, sir," the communications officer seconded the tone.

Two seconds later the Skull Walker shuddered and veered to one side. System displays flashed warnings in bright red and multiple damage control systems lit up with data. The sonic boom caught up with the projectiles an instant later.

"Hit! Came from three o'clock! I got a return targeting beam!"

"Return fire!" Pritchett practically climbed into the gunner's seat with anticipation.

The Skull-like body rotated, tilting upward to aim the pair of giant rail cannons. The Abolisher rippled wild, demolishing a stretch of forest in a series of detonations. Through the haze of smoke an infrared targeting beam swung to the center of the Skull Walker's right eye.

Two hundred slugs left the Glitter Boy's mass driver and crossed two thousand feet in a fraction of a second. Eye and spotlight shattered as one, giving little resistance to immense kinetic force. Projectiles pried through secondary armor and cut through the chicken plate, view screens and displays joining the inward rush of shrapnel. Sparks blazed from the right console and flooded the compartment with smoke and debris. The Skull Walker staggered backwards like a drunken spider. Auto purge systems struggled to exhale smoke and extinguish fires, bathing the pilot's compartment in an eerie red glow.

"Get us out of here!" Pritchett shouted, seizing the shoulder of the pilot and shaking. The shoulder plate came off in his hand and the mutilated body fell apart to reveal dozens of holes through the back of the pilot's seat.

"Full retreat! All units fall back to designated locations! Full retreat!"

For the first time in his life, Captain Pritchett felt real panic trying to control him. It wasn't the first time in his career his life had been endangered, but he'd never been forced to combat one of the most lethal combat units ever built. Years of horror stories and combat vids of Glitter Boy battle aftermaths flashed through his mind in an instant. Tearing the remains of the pilot away from the mangled controls, Pritchett desperately tried to locate backup systems through the sparks and smoke.

"Full retreat, sir?!" The communications officer shouted for confirmation.

"Full retreat! It's a trap! Fall back to designated locations!"

Pritchett sat in the pilot's seat, mindless of the blood and gore. Locking the remaining leg clamp in place and throttling foreword on manual control, he turned the robot about face just as a third blast severed the right foreleg from the body.

"Merrick! Stop that Glitter Boy before it blows us all to hell! Somebody shoot that thing!"

"It's shut off active targeting, sir!" Corrinne backed the Enforcer into some trees and searched the hillside for some sign of the attacker.

"Full retreat! That's an order!"

"Retreat? He's gotta be nuts! We've almost got 'em!" Cowboy blasted the last Headhunter protecting the Multi-Bot's flank.

"I just confirmed it with Skull 41. Pritchett's callin' a full retreat," Trenton grumbled in disgust. His squad had only one Samson power armor keeping him from overrunning the enemy lines, and the remaining pair of robot vehicles were too occupied with the harassing Sky Cycles to engage in close combat. The combined firepower of Alpha and Beta could drop them both in a matter of seconds. Charlie team was keeping rebel reinforcements from reaching the front-lines, two rebel transports were on fire and a third damaged beyond repair. The few remaining Headhunters were too scattered and disorganized to provide effective resistance, and none of them wanted to die alone.

"Sharp to Winters, over."

"What do you want?" Winters growled, intent not to back his squad off without finishing the job.

"You better clear out while you can, Sarge, Captain Pritchett and all our mechanized are in full retreat, and our SAM's just lost the ridge. Pritchett's not behind you and there's a Glitter Boy watchin' your trail all the way out of the valley," Sharp warned.

"Sergeant Major! We are in full retreat to fall back positions. Follow orders!" Pritchett was returning to his usual imperious self.

"Forget your orders! Get back here and take out that Glitter Boy!" Winters shouted back.

"Sarge, you better go now," Sharp relayed. "Lieutenant Merrick and Darren are going to keep the Glitter Bow occupied so you and Pritchett's infantry can clear the valley."

"Jerr! Get back to the rovers! Double time!" Merrick ordered between sonic booms. "Sharp! See if you can keep their heads down!" Greg cursed himself for taking part in the joint operation to begin with. He'd known what would happen all along and still went against his better judgment.

Sharp picked a mercenary hidden in some shrubs, cutting a baseball-sized hole through the rebel's chest with his sniper rifle. He could see Beta squad meet up with Winters, trading off the wounded to Trenton's massive mechanical shoulders. Another remnant rebel popped out of a foxhole to pursue. Another laser blast vaporized the D-Bee's scaly head. Two more quick shots at the Titan, another to blow out the sensor turret on the Multi-Bot, and Sharp engaged his jet pack to escape the team of cyborgs just topping the rise behind him.

Kruno was never one to believe in godly deities or religion, but as the Coalition forces retreated on the verge of victory, he caught himself giving thanks to every human and D-Bee god he'd ever heard of.

"They're leaving!" Trench shouted at the one remaining sensor feed. "Do we go after them?"

"After them? With what? We gonna huck turnips at 'em?"

"I don't get it. They were winning, and then they retreat."

"Fate or intervention, my friend, I'll take it either way. Some of us is survivors cuz of ability, and others jus cuz of fate. We jus made 'em both today. Now we're gonna open up a whole can o' whoopass on them Dead Boys."

Kruno smiled happily, targeting the nearest Sky Cycle leaving the battle zone. He'd already wasted four missiles trying to shoot down the maneuverable fighters, but they kept flying so close, the warhead safeties wouldn't arm. Now that wasn't a problem. Selecting one of the two smart missiles left in the launchers, Kruno's finger danced over the fire button contemplating the effectiveness of firing without a positive lock, but in the end slammed the button with an armored fist.

The Sky Cycle's hazard display went haywire, suddenly registering three incoming warheads, all from different locations in the valley. In a desperate attempt to avoid all three the pilot banked sharply in a full circle and let the searching missiles pass him by. The lead missile banked and veered back around. Hoping to outrun its sharp turn, the pilot shoved the cycle to the max speed just feet above the treetops. The missile closed the gap at twice the cycle's speed, locked onto the heat of the craft's engines. Plasma erupted from the Sky Cycle's main thrusters and the top fin shot forward, removing the pilot from his seat. Thrown clear of the burning craft the pilot's speed was slowed to 400 mph through the pliant treetops before a great oak abruptly ended the velocity completely. Blazing fragments of the cycle blanketed the forest around the lifeless pilot.

Chapter 12

The one and only cybernetics facility in Liberty was overcrowded and understaffed. When Fransisco Alvarez escaped persecution within the Coalition States he never expected to see C.S. military officers waiting patiently in his office, or a wounded C.S. soldier on his operation table.

A month before when he'd opened the "Frontier Body Builder" cybernetics center the response had been incredible. Very few Cyber-Docs with full equipment existed beyond the borders of industrialized states. The two-story complex that served as both home and business suddenly became dwarfed by demand. There were more humans and D-Bees needing superior medical care and augmentation than he had time to handle. By the time he hired and trained added staff the demand grew even more. Turnaround on implants was so fast he'd not even had the time to see how much money he was making. All he knew for sure was his business was more successful than he'd ever dreamed possible. Now, with the Coalition present, Fransisco wondered how much longer it would last.

Replacing the wounded soldier's arm with a cybernetic one took about three hours, but it would be days before Fransisco would prescribe rehabilitative activity. One thing that still bothered him after years of practice were those individuals who willingly foresook their living bodies in favor of synthetic ones. Slight localized augmentation was understandable, and extreme physical injury definitely warranted conversion of man to machine in order to preserve life. The Coalition soldier had little choice in matter, he would just need time to adjust for a piece humanity lost forever.

Fransisco set aside his medical gear and checked the monitors one last time before leaving the operation room. Down the hall he could see two Coalition officers through the window of his office, and a nervous twitch felt the revolver at his side for comfort. He patted it reassuringly and walked in to discuss payment.

"Dr. Alvarez, success, I assume?" Pritchett stood and smiled, extending his hand in a gesture of friendship.

"Yes, but he won't be much good to you for awhile." Fransisco ignored the gesture and sat at his battered oak desk. Most of the furniture in his office was modernistic, making the dark stained wood seem incongruous.

"The Sergeant here is your patient's direct superior," Pritchett motioned to Trenton.

Fransisco turned his attention to the full conversion cyborg, noting that not even the head or face remained human flesh of appearance. Inset glowing red eyes stared back from a monstrous skull-like visage. No wonder so many primitive cultures associated the Coalition with death, Fransisco mused. Even Coalition borgs retained the frightening motif.

"How much of his body did you have to replace?" Trenton asked in a modulated human tone.

"Just the arm and shoulder. Many of the torn muscles and ligaments had to be replaced with bio-synthetics as the wound trauma was fairly severe. If you don't mind my asking, what happened to him?"

"We were attacked by a flock of giant creatures while on standard maneuvers. One of them managed to grab that man's arm and rip it off, armor and all." Pritchett relayed his version of what happened to fire team Charlie. Trenton looked over, eyebrow plates lowering in disapproval.

"Standard maneuvers, huh. Your man kept babbling over and over about finishing the New Order. That wouldn't happen to be the Army of the New Order, would it?" Fransisco slid his hand beneath the desk and checked to make sure his ion pistol was still in it's holder. A Cyber-Doc's profession was often a risky one.

"You've heard of the scoundrels then," Pritchett smiled.

"Zenjori told me you might come here, but I didn't believe him."

"If you know Zenjori, than you know he's a criminal and a coward." Trenton stood, towering over the desk. "He and his army are the reason I look like this today."

"Regardless of what you say about Zenjori and the Army of the New Order, I and many others wouldn't be here if it wasn't for him. I heard Zenjori had a problem with some of his undisciplined men, but overall he did much to help the people of this town and established Liberty as a safe haven. You're not going to be very popular around here if you try and kill him. The people of this town agreed to hire other mercenaries for protection, that's fine. You have no business hiding here in Liberty behind First Strike and then attacking Zenjori's army just to run back for protection again. Many of us don't want the Coalition here in Liberty at all."

"I'm sorry you feel that way, Doctor, I hope we can change your opinion of us. In time," Pritchett diplomatically tried to diffuse the tension.

Merrick's men were outraged at the retreat, and showing concern for the wounded would go a long way to diminish their anger and reduce chances of strife between the two Coalition forces. Dealing with an outspoken Cyber-Doc was child's play compared to explaining himself to furious combat veterans who already wanted to shuffle the chain of command.

"My services are for everyone, human, D-Bee, even Coalition troops, Captain," Fransisco stated disdainfully. "But my fees vary according to how much I like my clients."

"That's what an expense account's for," Pritchett joked, pulling out a black card with military logo etched into it. "I would be happy to pay whatever fee you feel appropriate, within reason of course."

"I'll be keeping him in a bed until tomorrow morning in case of complications. 15,000 now and 15,000 tomorrow morning when you come pick him up."

"That's a bit steep, don't you think?"

"Obviously you've never been in a downside body chop-shop, Captain."

"Can't say that I have." Pritchett handed the black card over.

Flipping the card deftly in one hand, Fransisco slotted it into the computer on his desk and turned it so the Coalition officer could see. A quick analysis showed the card was clean and Captain Pritchett authorized the transfer of funds to Fransisco's personal account.

"Just a word of advice, Captain." Fransisco returned the card to its owner. "Choose your enemies carefully."

"Thank you doctor, I will send someone tomorrow morning with the remainder of your payment. I sincerely hope that if we can't be friends, at least you and I won't be enemies. I'm not the monster you think of me."

"Explain that to the families of the D-Bees you mistreat, drive from their homes, and kill in cold blood. Good-bye, Captain."

Long after the two had left his office, Dr. Alvarez sat at his desk and tried to purge resurfaced memories from his years in Coalition Chi-town.

Flecks of gold sparkled deep within the brilliant diamond. Interwoven gold and silver bands of the ring came together where translucent obsidian formed the clasps holding the diamond in place. When light struck the multi-faceted gem just right it burst into a red star of unparralled magnificence. Deep within the diamond's core was a precious ruby fused like a glowing heart. Anja stared with breathless fascination as Van slipped the ring on her finger.

"I, I..." Anja searched for the words to say.

"Don't say anything. It's yours, to symbolize our bond. My mother and father made it long before I was born as a charm against the undead. I've been keeping it in one of my safes at Youngstown for a long time. I can't think of a better person to give it to than my wife. I hope that doesn't sound too sappy, I really mean it."

"It's not sappy, it's wonderful!" Anja hugged him with all her strength, joyous thoughts and emotions intermingling. Pushing away slightly, she gave him a saucy look. "I wondered where you were all morning."

"I would have been back earlier except a dragon tried to waylay me outside of town."

"Oh?"

"It was more comical than frightening. All I did was fly Sherilynn low to the trees, and it caught its tail in some oak branches and did a nose dive into a hillside. I almost felt sorry for it."

"I can't believe you flew all the way back to Youngstown just to get this ring for me."

"That only took part of the morning. Come, I've got another surprise for you."

Cold mist gathered in Anja's hair and made it cling to her face and body as they walked to a familiar location. Van felt a contentment he'd never experienced before to see her happy, carefree excitement. Even his passion for mystic knowledge seemed a hollow pursuit. There were so many things he'd been missing.

Anja's hand trembled with excitement the closer they came to "Martin's Stables and Future Blacksmith Shop." Van pretended to have a different destination in mind. She knew better, practically dragging him across the muddy street to the stable entrance.

"Hold your horses, no pun intended." Van grinned. "Close your eyes and at least make believe it's a surprise."

"Okay." Anja closed her eyes and let herself be led blindly through the stables. They stopped and she heard a familiar knicker.

"Surprise!"

"Tonisha!" Anja threw her arms around the mare's neck. "I told you I'd come back!"

"She's yours," Van grinned like a little kid. Anja hugged him tightly and brought down his head for a passionate kiss.

"Thank you."

"Spend some time with Tonisha, and when you're ready to pick out a saddle and gear come over to Martin's shop, I'll be there having a set of barding armor modified."

"Wait." Anja kissed him long and deep before releasing him. "Thank you."

Van was floating on air all the way out of the stables. Crossing the street, another presence brought him back to crisp reality. Sir Renfield leaned against the entrance to Martin's Future Blacksmith Shop, his often somber face harder than usual.

"Afternoon, David."

"You know I tried to buy that horse for her yesterday. They wouldn't sell it to me." The Cyber-Knight skipped unnecessary pleasantries.

"You don't know how to fix the CPU in a Northern Gun XCSS series robot horse." Van nodded to the metallic beast of burden outside the blacksmith shop. "I did Martin a favor."

The Cyber-Knight stared at the robot horse and shrugged.

"Strange that it would come down to something as trivial as that, isn't it?"

He doesn't know, Van realized.

"Depends on what you call trivial, David. She's a wonderful woman and I love her."

Sir Renfield's head snapped up to contest Van's claim, but the fire in his eyes gradually died.

"Do you respect her?"

"Yes."

Sir Renfield appeared unimpressed.

"I'm marrying her, David."

What was left of the smoldering fire in Sir Renfield's eyes changed to a watery sadness.

"That's a big step, Van. I want to wish you both the best, but I'm skeptical, you understand."

"I'll take whatever goodwill you feel like sharing. I don't blame you for being disappointed. I know I would be had things gone the other way."

"Be good to her, that's all I ask. I don't want to hold a grudge."

"Then don't." Van extended his hand. Sir Renfield looked at it. "We don't have to pals or anything," Van smirked.

"Good." David reached out with a strong armor-plated hand. "You really tick me off sometimes." The knight's solemn mask cracked a thin smile.

"Come on," Van moved into the shop entrance. "Help me pick out a good set of barding armor for Anja's horse. I may know all about machines, but I don't know jack when it comes to horses."

This was his greatest disguise ever. Kro-Mar looked at himself in the hotel bathroom mirror and admired his handiwork. Nobody would ever suspect he was actually a mighty Great Horned Dragon, not that he didn't look stunning as a human Pre-Rifts movie star. He'd spent hours trying to decide between Arnold Schwarzenegger and Mel Gibson, but finally opted for the wild and crazy character portrayed in the Pre-Rifts *Lethal Weapon and Mad Max* movies offered by the Black market and legal entertainment distributors. Those old action film were especially popular among mercs and soldiers. Kro-Mar pictured himself as the dashing, daring hero in disguise. The vid disks were an acquisition Kro-Mar was proud of, although the humiliation suffered in their attainment still bothered him during his mid-week naps. In fact there had been several mid-week naps lately, all replete with nightmares about Sky Cycles and badgers in heat. To make matters worse, the luck curse that stupid Elf had cast on him was making his waking life a living nightmare. Simple things like morphing and teleporting became unstable elements waiting to explode into more embarrassing situations. Twice that week he'd accidentally teleported into some ancient dragon's sleeping chamber — while the dragon was there. Kro-Mar shuddered, attempting to clear his mind of the unpleasant memories. Being a peach in a puree machine was not fun.

The continual trail of bad luck was with him as early as that very morning when on a whim he decided to chase a passing Sky Cycle, again. Not only did he fail to catch it, but failed miserably. Ferns tasted yucky.

When the last strand of hair was curled in place, Kro-Mar shook his head vigorously to give it the wild look. Although his natural metamorphic abilities were good, it would be centuries before he perfected them completely. Now it was a quick change of clothes and he was ready to play his joke on Liberty. Kro-Mar giggled when he realized he'd be teleporting right back to his rented hotel room when the joke was over. Maybe he'd have a chance to do the same joke twice. It was so much fun scaring humanoids.

Out on the street he smiled at humans and D-Bees he passed, testing his mimicry of the ancient actors voice and mannerisms. Kro-Mar could barely contain his glee, none of them knew a powerful being like himself was walking in their midst. All that remained was to find a suitable place in the presence of many people to morph back to his natural dragon form and frighten the unsuspecting mortals to near frenzy. Past experiences doing this sort of thing tempered the urge to scare the daylights out of the large mechanical beasties that often patrolled city streets. He needed someplace more enclosed, safe from attack but filled with beings to frighten out of their pitiful minds.

Drunken shouts and curses drew his attention to a large building across the street. Several humans wearing black and gray uniforms were beating another bald-headed man senseless. The largest of them, standing close to 6'7" wound up and knocked two long fangs from the bald man's mouth with a powerful punch. They all laughed heartily and pointed to the drooling figure laid out in the muddy street, then staggered back into the Match Head Saloon through a pair of hinged double doors. For an instant Kro-Mar could hear shouts and laughter coming from inside the saloon, undoubtably from countless more human soldiers blowing off steam like the few he'd just seen. Just the place to pull his little prank. Kro-Mar started across the street.

Wheels skidded in the mud as a multi-ton vehicle bore down on him. Kro-Mar stared for a moment, accepting the inevitable fate that would certainly befall him, as it had more times than he liked to remember. Somehow the transport vehicle swerved out of the way, brushing Kro-Mar with a gust of wind as it passed. Kro-Mar blinked, uncertain why he'd been spared the embarrassment of being run over, again. He stood in the street, still expecting some horribly bad luck to befall him. Nothing happened. Could it be his luck was actually changing?

He approached the hinged double doors, imitating scenes he'd seen in old west vids. The saloon door swung back and smacked him in the face. So much for luck. Kro-Mar barely withheld an angry urge to rip the doors off their hinges and make his own entrance through one of the walls. He could handle it. He was powerful enough not to destroy the building until after the prank. Carefully he pushed through the double doors and warily crept through the entryway, waiting for some new embarrassment to befall him. A mercenary by the main door politely let him inside the Match Head, a smug grin the only indication he'd seen Kro-Mar's encounter with the double doors. If and when Kro-Mar decided to eat anyone, the mercenary would be the first appetizer.

The Match Head was crowded — all the better — leaving only a few empty seats at the bar. Rows of uniformed soldiers were kicking back small glasses of liquid and downing mugs of ale. Having never had the sensation humans referred to as drunkenness, Kro-Mar sauntered up to the bar and took a stool in the midst of the enebriated patrons.

"Mel Gibson!"

Kro-Mar froze. He'd heard that voice before.

"Hey dudes, check it out! It's Mel Gibson!"

Soldiers along the bar and throughout the room stopped what they were doing and looked Kro-Mar's way. All of them.

"Uh. . . "

"Dude!" A human with black hair and green eyes led the crowd of soldiers to surround Kro-Mar. "It's you!. I thought you were computer generated"

"No way." says another of the soldiers. "He's dead. I mean the real guy lived before the Great Cataclysm. This must be his modern day look-a-like."

"Or maybe he's the real thing. Rifter through!"

"Wow, it could happen."

"Uh, yes?" Kro-Mar was in shock. How could this have happened? Of all the bars, in all the towns of North America, he'd picked the one with a human who could recognize his disguise.

"Man, how did ya get here?"

The soldiers ringleader pushed closer, alcohol heavy on his breath, he grabbed Kro-Mar's hand to shake it. The rest followed suit, slapping Kro-Mar on the back and fielding thousands of questions to his ancient movie star alter ego. Somebody pushed a beer in his hand.

"You got Rifted here, huh Mel?"

"What?"

"You know, the Rift that opened up and got you here! You remember, right!?"

"Uh, yes?" "But … um … it's all kinda fuzzy."

"I told you guys!" The ringleader got the approval of the crowd. Kor-Mar just grinned.

The Dragon wasn't the least bit sure what was going on, but the humans seemed to like his movie star alter ego. Drunk as skunks, they really thought he was the actor, from the vids. Perhaps it wasn't such a bad stroke of luck after all.

"Wow, where are you staying?"

"How long have ya been in town?" the big soldier Kro-Mar had seen outside asked, waiting eagerly for the reply.

"You gonna be 'round for awhile?" another soldier asked.

"Man, ya gotta tell us all about your adventures." The ringleader managed to get the crowd under control. "We've seen all your vids, even the ones on the ban list. We're like your biggest fans!"

"Um, yes. I was, Rifted." Kro-Mar downed the bitter beverage. It tasted yucky.

"That's so amazing! Get my buddy here another round!"

"A toast!" the big soldier boomed, enticing the rest to raise their mugs high.

"To Mel! Oh … we can call you 'Mel' can't we?" The metamorphed dragon grinned broadly saying, "sure you can, but my real friends call me Gibs."

"To Gibs!!"

Kro-Mar smiled, getting into the spirit of his fame. This was fun. Maybe his luck was really beginning to change.

Kro-Mar spilled ale down the front of his pants.

Devious plots and complex plans whirled around in Zenjori's head like a black maelstrom. The unexpected Coalition retreat had probably saved his mercenary army from certain destruction and now it was time for a bold maneuver that would ensure they never returned. He paced back and forth outside his camouflaged tent, tracking mud onto the ground tarp. Counter-attacks and assassinations could turn the citizens of Liberty against him further, but if the Coalition was blamed for senseless acts of brutality, it would make his own methods seem benevolent. There had to be a way to rid the territory of the Coalition and force Donnovan's mercenary army out of Liberty in one fatal blow.

"Colnae, come here a moment," Zenjori motioned to the most trusted of his magic practitioners. Colnae smoothed his white silk shirt and barked several orders to a blond woman washing his clothes. She cowered and obeyed, spilling water from the basin onto her tattered clothing.

"Yes, Suka San?" Colnae glanced back over his shoulder to make sure his brainwashed servant was doing what she was told. She'd been more or less an experiment to him, and her usefulness was nearing an end. She would be amusing to play with a while longer, and then Colnae anticipated finding a much more challenging subject.

"Colnae, are you capable of working metamorphic spells?"

"Why?" The Line Walker was all attention.

"Because it would be a shame if several well-known Coalition officers were to murder the family of some prominent D-Bee or council member in Liberty. It might even escalate into a full fledged confrontation between First Strike and the Coalition. Wouldn't that be terrible?"

"My, that would be unfortunate, especially if some officer were first seen harassing certain outspoken citizens about their anti-Coalition views. We wouldn't want to see that, would we?" Colnae stroked his goatee thoughtfully, playing along with the mercenary commander.

"Say, for instance, our good doctor Alvarez has his establishment burned to the ground by several Coalition soldiers in full armor and regalia?" Zenjori's dark eyes gleamed.

"Well all that would be very much in our favor, except I know no such magic."

"What about our friend from the Federation?"

"If he really is Credo, Federation Lord, then without a doubt he's capable of far more than you can imagine. Question is, will he cooperate?"

"I'm paying him, he'll do it. If not, Notec Depi will offer him some alternative forms of incentive."

"If you want my advice, Suka San, I would be careful in dealing with a Federation Lord, especially that Elf."

Zenjori regarded the younger man with a piercing gaze and disapproving expression. The mage wasn't challenging his authority but Zenjori disliked the inference. For a man who openly claimed political aspirations with the Federation of Magic, Colnae set a dangerous double standard.

"I'll consider your advice, my friend. Perhaps you should go speak with him and explain our intentions. We have two days to stoke the fires in Liberty before we meet First Strike for the arms sale. If I'm correct, Donnovan will try and keep the sale a secret, but he needs money too badly not to go through with it."

"I take it you plan on double-crossing, er, re-negotiating the terms of the sale?" Colnae grinned, and Zenjori patted him on the back in a fatherly gesture.

"Yes my son. As my wise teacher often told me during my many years of training, 'Truth and honor are like a wasp without a stinger. The wasp can fly, but he can not impart wisdom because he can be seen and heard by all because there is no tail.'"

Colnae's expression slowly changed to one of bewilderment.

"I don't get it."

"Neither did I, come to think of it, but I pretended to at the time. I think we'll have a little more fun at Torrak's expense. Next time he reports in, I'll pass on my master's sage advice and you pretend to understand completely."

"Do you have any idea what that's going to do to his reptilian intellect?"

"Yes," Zenjori smiled. "And we'll be enjoying every minute of it."

Angry shouts rose to pure pandemonium in Liberty's town hall. Threats and accusations grew intensely with each passing minute, threatening to spill over into a riot. In just one night there had been three fires and over a dozen crimes committed by the visiting Coalition troops. The accused stood in a row up on the crude wooden stage, among them Lieutenant Greg Merrick and 2nd Lieutenant Brian Adams. Armed policemen prevented the angry throng from dragging the six C.S. troops outside and hanging them from the nearest tree. Donnovan stood back and assessed the growing bedlam, toying with the idea of tossing a few flash grenades into the crowd. At last he drew his .44 automag and put six holes in the ceiling. Mayor Utherman gave him a dirty look, but the hall was silenced.

"Everyone just shut up! I'm sure you all have good reason for complaint, but either you start acting civilized or I'll cram each and everyone here into a jail cell." The mercenary leader stood and walked past a row of intimidated town leaders. Nobody messed with the golden rule: he who had the guns made the rules.

"They're gonna get away with it just 'cuz they're Coalition!" a woman shouted from the crown, and the uproar returned.

Donnovan pointed his gun at the woman. The crowd grew silent again.

"Nobody's getting away with anything, understand?" He waved the gun in a nodding motion. The crowd nodded along with the weapon. "Good."

"We had nothing to do with anything that happened last night. Most of us can prove that." Greg spoke in a low tone to the mercenary leader. Donnovan put his gun away and looked Greg in the eyes.

"I know. They don't."

"You're in charge, aren't you?"

"Rules are rules, Lieutenant. I must let them testify. Get it out in the open." Donnovan turned back to the crowd and signaled Fransisco Alvarez to come forward. "Which of these men tried to burn down your cyber-shop?"

"I didn't see their faces. They were wearing armor. Coalition armor." Fransisco glared at Brian Adams.

"I see."

"Hey, Fransisco, one of our men was in your place when all this came down. Why would we try and burn one of our own men?" Brian asked.

"Of course, it sure was convenient those two show up just in time, wasn't it!?" Fransisco pointed to the end of the stage where Darren stood with Cyndiara. "Set the fire, then let your Burster come save the day."

"That's stupid. We don't even like Bursters!" Brian contested, casting a nervous glance in Cyndiara's direction.

"Aken, who was on duty at the storage warehouse last night?" Donnovan asked, waving Fransisco back to the crowd.

"Matt and Mark. Nobody went in, nobody went out. Not one suit of armor is missing," Aken answered.

"See Fransisco, it had to be someone else," Brian shrugged.

"Naven, you said these officers attacked your wife and daughter?" Donnovan motioned to a tall, gangly D-Bee. The odd looking humanoid spoke through a translator device.

"I saw them with my two eyes. The long hair one in gray make funny sound and I make move to stop them. I can no shoot with gun."

"What kind of noise, Naven?"

"Say funny words over and over. Then he put knife to mate!"

One of the policemen shoved the D-Bee back from the stage.

"Lieutenant, how many Coalition troops use magic?"

"That's a ridiculous question, Donnovan." Greg shot back.

"The red-haired one! He's the one! I saw him kill councilman Tammit!" the woman shouted and pointed at Brian.

"Is that so?" Donnovan put his hands on his hips.

"Shot him in the back of the head, right in front of his wife and family!"

Many shouts of support and confirmation followed.

"You were supposed to protect us from fascist murderers like them! Do your job! Do your job!" Fransisco shouted, trying to get a chant started. Donnovan didn't have to finish drawing his gun before the chant faded away.

"And I've done my job. The red-haired one was at Gizmo's store all night repairing equipment, you want to contest that, speak with Gizmo and his crew. Those two over there never left their cabin until I sent for them this morning, and the Lieutenant here spent most of the night yelling at his C.O.!" Donnovan turned back to Greg. "Sorry, it's my job to keep an eye on you."

"But we saw them!" the woman screamed.

"I believe you. I believe you saw what someone wanted you to see, what I suspect Zenjori Suka and the Army of the New Order wanted you to see, to cause exactly the kind of problems we have here. Until I get some solid proof otherwise, these men are innocent and will not be harmed by the law, or vigilantes! You get that, Fransisco?"

"Oh, I get it all right. We just aren't paying you enough."

"Manta?"

"I'll get you solid proof, just you wait," the woman vowed.

"Naven?"

"I'll kill him!"

The gangly D-Bee got a rifle butt in the belly.

"Wrong answer, Naven. I think the rest of you get the picture. Now get out of here."

Grumbles and complaints accompanied compliance. Many hateful stares promised more than angry words would be flying around in the days to come. Donnovan didn't care. Tomorrow he was selling off his oldest armor units and tons of ordnance, and four or five days later it wouldn't matter what the townspeople thought of him. He'd honor his contract until a replacement for the town's defense could be found, or the current one expired, and then it was on to more profitable ventures in the mid-west and northern territories.

"Thanks, Donnovan." Brian shook his hand enthusiastically.

"Whatever."

"I guess I should thank you for snoopin' around." Greg put his hair back with a rubber band. The disheveled, unshaven look was becoming standard.

"You better watch yourself, Lieutenant. You might want to pick up a reliable equalizer just in case." Donnovan patted his .44.

"I'll do that."

"Oh, and tell your watchmen to wrap their gun barrels, just in case they were actually breaking the weapons laws. Moonlight glints off the blueing real bad."

"I'll pass that on."

Greg headed up stage for the rear exit.

"Lieutenant?" Donnovan called after him, not turning around.

"Yeah?"

"What are you doing in the C.S. military?"

Greg stopped, the quick mechanical response wrestling with the crumbling pillars of what he believed in.

"You know, I really couldn't tell you."

Torrak's yellow eyes glowed more brightly than before in anticipation of the lives he was about to take. His god had been gracious
enough to grant him a powerful spell through the link they shared,
and now he would sacrifice the two children in the demon's honor.
Both were mere street urchins Torrak had bagged during the twilight
hours and probably wouldn't be missed, not that he cared. Their
deaths would help fuel the powerful metamorphic spell he was about
to weave.

His Gromek blood burned with rage at the thought of the degrada-
tion he'd experienced the night before. He'd been subjected to
Credo's ritualistic magic in order to alter his form to that of a Coalition officer, then forced to wear a stolen human uniform. If that was-
n't enough, the Elf had tormented him further by "accidentaly"
turning Torrak into a human female with exaggerated anatomy. Most
of the comments made by Zenjori's gawking troops Torrak didn't
quite understand, but understood enough to make him nearly livid
with rage. All that behind him now, his god had seen fit to give in to
Torrak's impassioned begging.

"Mind Crusher. Foresee the future of my task," Torrak asked the
runic mace at his side.

"I see nothing," the soft whisper in his head replied.

"That is impossible. Do not fail me!"

"Your future is clouded. Troubled. That is all I see."

"You aren't as powerful as you used to be, Mind Crusher."

"My powers are eternal. Unlike yours."

"Be silent!" Torrak ordered in guttural syllables. Mind Crusher
hadn't been the same ever since the Elf arrived. For some unknown
reason the rune weapon had grown more silent and less helpful. The
night before it even failed to warn him of approaching danger and
Torrak had been forced to cast a fireball spell on a gun-wielding
D-Bee to save his own life, consequently killing the one best witness
to the crime he had committed. Zenjori was not at all pleased.

There would be no more failures.

Grasping each bound and gagged child in turn, Torrak clenched a
powerful clawed hand around each of his victims throats and crushed
their wind pipes. Lifeforce ebbed away with the rapid beat of the dy-

ing hearts. Torrak felt their life's energy surge over him in one last powerful wave. He dropped their lifeless husks and reveled in the high from the mystic energy.

"Martu Manus Esche Krum De Manus." Torrak closed his eyes and focused on the man he was to become. He felt his link to the unholy supernatural being he served grow stronger as the being completed the last phrases of the incantation. Clawed hands became smooth-skinned human hands, and sharp reptilian teeth became clean, white human teeth. Torrak's Gromek clothing fell about his body loosely. Grabbing a mirror from his duffel bag, Torrak compared his face with the one on the vid print. Greg Merrick stared back at him from the mirror. Humans were so disgusting.

Back in the uncomfortable gray and black uniform, Torrak tried in vain to make the red, black, and white armband stay in place, but the stubborn skull and lightning bolts logo kept slipping down his arm. Annoyed beyond his patience, he growled and tossed it in a crumpled wad by the corner stall. He didn't have time for such irritations. Gathering the rest of his things and stuffing them into his duffel, Torrak carefully placed Mind Crusher on top and zipped the bag closed.

Through the early dawn mist, Torrak crept towards the storage facility that housed the Coalition's most devastating armament. There would be far to many armed Coalition guards inside for even a powerful Gromek mage to handle alone, but that wasn't Torrak's main objective. Killing the outer guards from First Strike and making sure there were witnesses to the act would be sufficient to support Zenjori's plans for an arms sale between the two mercenary companies. By noon that day nobody would believe the word of a Coalition officer, especially Donnovan and his mercenary army.

Pulling a pair of dark sunglasses from his uniform pocket, Torrak concealed the one part of his appearance that could never be altered. As the owner and master of Mind Crusher he was forever cursed with his yellow glowing eyes, a curse even his vulture familiar was forced to share. Torrak enjoyed the fear his appearance invoked, the curse more a blessing in his eyes.

One of the outer mercenary guards halted his casual approach, but his objection was silenced with a stolen Coalition H.F. blade. Torrak left the blade still humming softly in the guard's neck as further proof. Now he had the mercenary's particle beam rifle. Everything was going just as planned. Torrak slung the rifle over the shoulder opposite his duffel and marched around the corner of a building to the largest storage structure in the complex.

The mist cleared away some and Torrak could see two mercenary guards drinking heavily and playing "stick the knife in that wood post over there" with large hunting knives. Both were clad in full environmental armor, but hardly prepared for an attack from a Coalition officer. As Torrak marched closer to the huge double doors, he felt a strange, sickening sensation wash over him. Something wasn't right. Both guards stopped their game and looked over at him.

"What do you want, Torrak?" one of them asked.

"Aren't you supposed to be someplace else? Those aren't your clothes," the other one pointed out.

Indeed, the clothes didn't fit well at all. In fact, they simply didn't fit a powerfully built Gromek in the least. Torrak looked down at his sharp claws sticking out the front of Coalition boots. The two guards were laughing at him now. Of all the possible complications to encounter, he'd never anticipated running into the only two men in Liberty who absolutely refused to believe in the existence of magic; Matt and Mark, the Rogers twins.

The pair looked like two nordic vikings, with long hair and massive stature. Renowned for their tolerance of alcohol and elaborate practical jokes, the identical twins were best known for their astute belief that magic and psychic abilities were, as they often put it, full of garbage. They'd come to rationalize D-Bees and monsters as science experiments gone wrong, genetic screw-ups undoubtably created by man. Their disbelief was so strong, it often disrupted the working of magic energies around them, in effect reinforcing their disbelief all the more. Even in the face of astounding proof, the two would eventually concede that whatever monster or demon they'd just killed must have been part of a drunken stupor, drug induced hallucinations or monstrous aliens from another world. To them, magic, psychics, and the supernatural didn't exist.

"Ahhrrg!" Torrak screamed in frustration, ripping off his sunglasses and throwing the rifle and duffel in separate directions. His cover was blown and his mission failed, but at least he'd have the satisfaction of calling down lightning on the two men who claimed magic didn't exist. Chanting his incantation loudly for any to hear, Torrak's frustration was elevated to new levels. Nothing happened. Matt and Mark were laughing harder, taunting him by repeating the exact same words and mimicking his hand movements.

"Espeaka en la enlesha, por favor?" Matt slurred.

"Did Zenjori send his big, bad, ugly, genetically altered mutant to make powerful big trouble?" Mark staggered, far too drunk to form intelligible sentences.

"Uh-oh, Mr. Lab Experiment looks mad. He's gonna magic us." Matt feigned fear.

"Both of you will die!" Torrak screamed, rushing to his duffel and yanking out the rune mace.

Matt and Mark watched and laughed, still mocking his "spell".

"Hmmf. I'm scared now. He's pointing a magic wand at us!" Mark teased, pretending to cower behind Matt.

"Blind!" Torrak commanded Mind Crusher.

Matt and Mark looked at each other and back to Torrak.

"Stun!" Torrak waved the mace at the brothers.

They laughed harder.

"Wait! He got me! I can't move my big toe!" Matt pointed to his feet.

"Oh-no! My little pinky's stuck!" Mark jested.

"Pain!" Torrak screeched at Mind Crusher.

The twins were rolling on the ground at the spectacle Torrak was making, not even recognizing the mental assaults they were fending off.

"Hey, we better shoot him with our special bullets." Mark winked at his brother and pulled a huge .45 from its holster, replacing the clip with another from his belt.

"Yeah, our special 'anti-mutant magic thing' bullets! Quick! before he magics us again!" Mark switched clips on an identical firearm.

Torrak started to worry.

"On the count of three." Matt chambered a round and aimed the gun at Torrak's horned head.

"On three, or after three?" Mark asked, releasing the slide with his thumb.

"Let's just shoot him."

"No! No wait I can-"

Weapons fire roared outside the storage facility, muzzles blazing and gun smoke rising. Torrak threw up his arms in a vain attempt to stop the hot lead pouring from the two blazing guns. Nothing hit him. The world was much quieter after the close range weapon reports, but not a bloody patch marred his body. Torrak brushed some white styrofoam disks from his arms.

"Blanks, dude, boy did we get you good!" Mark doubled over laughing.

"You shoulda seen the look on your face! You thought you were gonna die!" Mark staggered with liquor and laughter.

Torrak's scream was barely identifiable. Raising the mace he charged to crush their skulls. Both brothers responded with amazing agility in their drunken states, so much so that Torrak barely had time to realize he'd been shot through the left leg by a 9 mm in Matt's other hand.

"Back off!" Matt shouted, laughter gone. He stepped just out of arm's reach, 9 mm aimed at Torrak's chest.

"Drop what you're holding, or I'll put one of these ram-jet slugs through your other leg." Mark dropped the slide on an identical 9 mm handgun.

Torrak wasn't even sure where the second weapon had come from. Looking down at his leg, still not feeling the pain, Torrak could see a clean hole pouring blood on either side of his thigh. Softly muttering the words to a protective spell he felt the Mystic energy leave his body but never take form. The spell failed.

Torrak panicked. The two mercenary brothers could riddle him with bullets and there was nothing he could do about it. Pain finally reached his brain, and with it an overwhealming urge to escape. Fear drove home to override wound trauma. Torrak turned and ran.

Both twins gave him a single slug to remember them by and let him run away to die.

Mercenaries on both sides of the clearing waited nervously for the arms inspection to finish. Lined up in the center of the field were several giant robots and power armor to exchange hands, and two truckloads of small arms, explosives, and body armor to go along with them. Low fog prevented either side from seeing past the tree line. The members of First Strike wanted the sale over and done with before the fog cleared. They were selling weapons of war to the Coalition's enemy, the Army of the New Order.

"Here are the rest of the missiles for the X-500." Aken pointed to a row of 8 military style cases with American and German markings. "We had trouble converting NG missiles to Triax launch systems so we only used imports designed for the X-500."

"Check them." Drake motioned to one of his men.

"Self-guided, fire and forget, with a sixty mile effective range and let me tell you, these German babies will outperform anything the Coalition has. Faster and more accurate. Heavy yield explosive warheads, not quite as powerful as plasma, but just as effective."

"What about for the Titan?" Drake pointed to the camouflage-painted Titan-make combat robot.

"Would take some work, but you could fire these babies from the Titan's launch systems. You're already gettin' it with a full load of NG's, how much trouble were you expecting?"

"Lots. Do you have the mines?"

"Forty eight of 'em, just like you wanted. Over here."

Aken broke the seal on a large metal container and slit the packing foil with a retractable blade on his bionic forefinger. Reaching into the sawdust packing he pulled out a small sensor trigger mechanism and anti-personnel mine.

"Real nasty, these little suckers are. Little sensor here can be programmed to set off one or more mines at a time if it senses something as small as a jack rabbit or big as, say, a Skull Walker. Ain't powerful enough to punch through, say, Coalition infantry body armor, but going off about head level they'll sure do a number on 'em. Run four of these sweethearts together and kiss your troubles good bye." Aken kissed the mine and set it down on the case.

"Why is Donnovan selling off most of his heavy artillery?" Drake inquired, looking up at the giant Northern Gun Hunter robot.

"Gotta make ends meet, ya know. Liberty doesn't pay too good, but ya already know that. 'Course, just between you and me, this isn't most of his heavy artillery. He just bought some really sweet alien imports on credit, and he probably doesn't want them breathin' down his neck for the dough. Side's, yer gettin' a good deal on these older babies. We kept 'em up good, they're just not as good as some of the newer mechs."

"Weapons look good," one of Drake's Headhunters reported. "Couple of 'em need a little work, but most of 'em are okay."

"Fair enough for the price."

"And on the subject of price, you got the eighty million?"

"Seventy eight million."

"That was before you bought the two X-10s. You want the Predators, it's eighty million."

"Well take them both."

"Spoken like a true soldier of fortune." Aken held out his hand to accept a pair of universal credit cards, but Drake pulled them away and cocked his head to the tree line. The sounds of thrusters carried through the mist and fog, growing louder but out of sight.

"What's that?"

"Probably one of our A-7's on patrol." Aken listened, knowing knowing full well it wasn't the sound of a Sky King they were hearing.

The tree line on both sides of the clearing burst open with weapons fire. Lasers razed fleeing mercenaries and cut down Headhunters left and right. Dropping from the mist above, two Coalition SAMAS broke into the center of the clearing and started havoc of their own.

"Ambush!" Drake shouted, but both SAMAS turned and knocked the cyborg off his feet with converging rail gun bursts. Metal slugs ricocheted off heavy armor and caught Aken off balance. Rolling behind the leg of the Hunter, he narrowly missed drawing rail gun fire. Two hundred feet of open ground lay between himself and the nearest cover, already thick with smoke from returning cover fire. From one side of the field half a dozen Coalition troops made their advance beneath heavy suppressive fire from the forest. Looking around in dismay, Aken realized he was the only one left standing, his own Headhunters cut down where they defended their positions. Drake and his men were scrambling to one side of the clearing to escape the crossfire. Desperately seeking a way to escape, Aken sprinted for a fallen comrade and grabbed for the weapon in the dismembered hand. Metal slugs tore earth and lasers seared past to crater patches of ground all around him. Rolling over, belly flat on the ground, Aken saw SAM number 15 turn his way.

Chapter 13

Aken released the safety on the modified NG-E4 plasma ejector and held down the trigger. Plasma poured down on the Coalition exoskeleton in a rain of disk-shaped charges. The front of the power armor disappeared in a blaze of white hot flame and the entire area around it fell to misplaced charges. Aken yelled at the top of his lungs and sprinted at his foe without lessening the barrage. A laser beam scored his armor but he didn't register the burning pain.

The weapon stopped firing, barrel smoking and heat guard glowing. Metal fires burned at molecularly bonded armor and deep within the vital workings of the SAMAS. The weight of its ammunition drum and engines tipped it over backwards onto the rear maneuver jets where it blazed brightly, its pilot escaping in the form of steam.

Another laser beam collided with Aken's chest and took away layers of skin beneath the composite armor. If he was going to die, he was going to make sure he took a few of them with him. Slotting another clip from a dead mercenary's belt, Aken knelt in the cover of a blast crater and prepared himself for a last stand.

"Aken! Get your tail out of there!" his helmet radio cracked. Two of the six visible Coalition troops were dead and the other four pinned down by heavy suppressive fire. Running and weaving between blast craters, Aken sprinted for the piles of blasted foliage at the clearing's edge. The bark of a grenade launcher reached Aken's ears a split second before the ground around him was broken with fragmentation explosions. Launched by the ripple effect, Aken sailed through leaves and branches out of sight.

Adrenaline overrode all sense of pain and disorientation, the will to survive stronger than the urge to fight. The half dozen remaining Headhunters followed Aken's lead and fled the Coalition slaughter in the direction of Liberty.

Policemen in light urban style armor kept the curious and the violent from crossing into what was being called a crime scene. The barn doors were wide, letting all outside see the carnage within.

"How do you know?" Pritchett reached for the knife Greg was holding but he pulled it away.

"It's a Chi-town run, but the R and the double zero starting number means it was field issue, not urban. I'll bet if I check it, against the stolen equipment list, this will show up as part of the Cedar Lake lot."

"Computers lie, Lieutenant," the sheriff spoke without expression.

"Don't I know it."

"Betcha that mutant dude in your uniform did it," Mark nodded.

"Come again?" Greg turned to the pair of men that nearly matched his above average height and physique.

"Yeah, that gene-spliced thing with the grafted wings tried to get past us this mornin'. Torrak, one of them ANO mutants."

"Please excuse Matt and Mark, what they lack in manners they make up for in other ways." Donnovan shot the twins a dirty look. At 6'4'' and 200 lbs of lean muscle each, the brothers had done a bit of head busting in their time, and served as First Strike's first line of defense against magic and psychic threats.

"All I know is it looked like Coalition troops that ambushed us this morning and ripped off our hardware." Aken puffed on a ragged cigar.

"That's impossible. Ain't no way cuz we checked on them right after Torrak tried to sneak past us. All their SAMs and armor ain't been touched. Dead Boys inside guardin' their stuff too, they didn't go nowhere either," Matt shot back at Aken.

"SAM 15 and 117B were supposed to be on patrol this morning." Greg scowled.

"They ain't. Still locked up." Mark shook his head.

"Well, they were supposed to be, and somebody knew that." Greg reminded himself to track down Darren and Dave and chew them out.

"Well, we done our job and watched yer stuff. It didn't go nowhere." Mark chewed gum loudly.

"I'd say somebody's been watching your patrol schedule and wanted to make this morning's raid look like your doing, Lieutenant," the sheriff stated in his monotone drawl.

"It's a pretty easy guess who tried to get to your gear and frame you for the raid on my company this morning." Donnovan shifted his weight to his other foot. "But that still leaves us with a serious problem. I lost over twenty men and eighty million credits worth of hardware, and then there's the matter of my guard and, and all this." He waved his hand and looked about the barn.

"Excuse me, sir, there's a Cyber-Knight who says he can help us find out what happened." One of Donnovan's Headhunters pointed into the crowd of spectators.

Sir Renfield wore his ornate dress armor and blue cape with the crest of knighthood. Donnovan shrugged.

"It couldn't hurt. Bring him in," Donnovan grunted, too upset by the recent events to care who helped out.

Policemen opened the line for Sir Renfield.

"Morning, Sir Renfield," Greg greeted the Cyber-Knight with a handshake.

"Lieutenant."

"You two know each other?" Donnovan raised an eyebrow.

"You could say that." Greg offered, noting with satisfaction the look of disapproval on Pritchett's face.

"Always good to have a Cyber-Knight around, even if they're just passing through. Sheriff Morley." The sheriff extended his hand, for once showing a glimmer of emotion.

"You know something we don't?" Donnovan broke up the greetings.

"Not personally, but I have two friends who may be able to discover things others would miss. One is a gifted Mystic who can often sense imprints left on objects and places. The other is a Techno-Wizard with a pretty keen eye and knowledge of magic rituals."

"Are you going to allow this? His friends probably did all this." Pritchett pointed to the dead bodies.

"Hey, like Donnovan said, it couldn't hurt." Greg shrugged.

"Where are they?" Sheriff Morley asked.

"Over there. Van! Anja!" Sir Renfield motioned them past the police line with a nod of approval from the sheriff.

The round of introductions acquired Greg another disdainful look from Pritchett.

"You keep interesting company, Lieutenant."

"You want to find out what happened or not? You might not take much stock in what they say, but they will." Greg pointed to the crowd.

"I think you're putting too much belief in the ravings of a magic user and psychic, no matter what any of them think."

"That's okay, Captain, we're happy to lend a hand anyway." Van flashed Pritchett a smile.

"May I see that arm band, please?" Anja reached out and took the Coalition armband from the sheriff. "Is it okay if I take it out of the plastic bag?"

"Why?"

"I need to touch it before I can feel any imprint left on it."

"Very well."

Anja pulled the armband from the ziplock bag and sat on the ground with her back up against the tracks of the APC. Aken took a step away from her, giving Donnovan a look of skepticism. Anja's nose wrinkled and she concentrated harder.

"I don't understand. I'm not sensing anything, anything at all. In fact, I can't even read anything here." Anja looked distressed.

Van whipped out a device from his overstuffed belt pouches, two mechanical arms attached to a small hand-held box with numerous displays and L.E.D.s. Van waved it around, tapping buttons when it didn't respond.

"That's strange. Normally it would be picking up something, at the very least some psychic emanations or psychic energy in use."

"Maybe you're not using it right. Did you follow the direction on the cardboard box it came in?" Matt pointed to the device and blew a big bubble.

"Sorry, Mr. Van De Graf." Donnovan glared at the two brothers. "Matt and Mark have a way of disrupting magic and psychic emanations."

"Yeah yeah, now I suppose you're gonna make us leave so you can come up with another good story." Matt turned to Anja. "He always makes us. Wanna go find a nice quiet spot and —"

"Matt, Mark, take Smith and Todd and go find out where my eighty million's at." Donnovan barked.

"Only things we dig more than booze." Mark tossed an empty liquor bottle against the APC.

"And women," Matt added, winking at Anja.

"That's kickin' tail an' chewin' bubble gum," Mark stated.

Both brothers spit their bubble gum on the ground simultaneously and sauntered off. Anja blinked in wide eyed amazement.

"They're weird."

"You should see them when they're sober." Donnovan shook his head. "They accuse each other of seeing all the things they don't believe in when they're drunk or high on something."

"Yeah, then they shoot each other with blanks," Aken added.

"I know," Sheriff Morley stated gravely, recalling more than one "shoot out."

"Hey, it's working now." Van's device lit up and made a series of strange noises. The arms quivered at the sides of the box and tiny lights glowed dimly.

"Get that thing away from me." Pritchett growled angrily.

Van waved it closer to the captain intentionally and the arms extended to their full length. Lights shown brighter and a light bar on the box went from green to red. Van waved it closer to make sure it wasn't just some random evil thoughts getting a rise out of his meter. The tones went nuts, sounding louder the closer the device came to the captain.

"Hey, it likes you."

"Van." Anja gave him an exasperated look.

"Sorry. I'll put it away now."

"Please, Anja, continue. What does that armband tell you." Sir Renfield pressed through, annoyed at Van for goofing off.

The Mystic closed her eyes and held the armband with both hands. Everyone watched with interest. Even Pritchett found himself mildly curious what the woman would have to say, though he expected it to finger the Coalition for the crime despite the evidence otherwise. Psychics were dangerous, unpredictable at best.

"This has changed hands many times and had many owners." Anja looked at the armband and shook her head. "There's so many traumatic imprints it's hard to pick any one of them out."

"Can you tell who killed the livestock and murdered the children? That's my concern," Sheriff Morley urged.

"I'll try." She closed her eyes again, concentrating on seeing images in the recent past of the cloth armband. Suddenly a wave of graphic scenes filled with intense emotional turmoil washed over her. The images triggered horrible memories in her past and brought with them new waves of turbulence. Letting out a sharp yelp, Anja thrust the armband off her lap and crawled away from it out of reflex.

"You okay?" Van knelt by her, taking her shaking hand.

"I know who did this. He's filled with rage and evil desires. He's done this and much more!" Her voice trembled.

"Who?"

"It's Torrak, Van, it's Torrak!" Her body shook with fear, images of her capture and near death on the Shifter's altar of sacrifice imposing themselves over conscious awareness.

"He's not here, Anja, pull out of it!" Van grabbed both her hands and broke through the imagery with strong telepathic contact. "You're safe and it's over. You're safe." He spoke to her mind and she clung to him closely.

"Who is this, Torrak?" Pritchett asked.

"We had a run in with this D-Bee magic user about seven weeks ago near Akron," Greg answered. "I lost a man in a way like I've never seen before, and just about got everyone killed. All we know is this Torrak is some D-Bee magic user, and correct me if I'm wrong, Van, very much part of the Army of the New Order."

"Yep. Darren and I found that out the hard way."

"Thank you, miss. You've been very helpful. Fits what we already suspected. Of course I'll have one of my psychics verify what you've seen." Donnovan picked up the armband and put it back in the bag.

"It's Torrak. He's the one you want." Anja looked to Donnovan and then to the Coalition officers.

"So, you can tell us where this Torrak is?" Pritchett asked, surprised at not being fingered by the psychic and beginning to take some stock in Anja's claims.

Greg's jaw dropped in disbelief.

"I don't ever want to touch that thing again. I'm sorry."

"Understandable, I'm sure." Pritchett cooed soothingly. "In most cases I don't put any stock in psychic claims, but you seem reasonably trustworthy, for a magic user. Thank you both, and you too, Sir Renfield."

Pritchett shook the dumbstruck Cyber-Knight's hand. Greg's jaw dropped another notch. From his place at the edge of the crowd, Trenton seethed with anger that his mechanical body couldn't expend. The captain was now more his enemy than ever before.

"Please, if you can excuse me, I need some time to be alone." Anja got to her feet and excused herself, giving Van an apologetic look.

"So what are we going to do about this, boss?" Aken leaned against the headlight bank on the APC.

"Find out everything we can about where our hardware is at, then come up with a way to get it back without destroying it."

"We know where it's headed, let's do something about it before it's too late."

"Do what, Aken? We have responsibilities to uphold here. Even if we could take action we'd lose more trying to get our stuff back than it's worth."

"What, are we just gonna let them get away with all this?"

"I make the decisions, Aken. In a few days, after our new armament arrives, we'll deal with the Army of the New Order, my way. In the meantime we gather intelligence on their capabilities, possibly exercise a few strategic raids if the opportunity arises."

"I'm afraid we may beat you to it." Captain Pritchett spoke up loudly. "I have a score to settle."

"You know Zenjori's recruiting from every D-Bee village and nomadic tribe from here to the ocean?" Aken blurted out. "Dead Boys make easy targets."

"Since we're all jumping into this, I might point out to the captain that Zenjori Suka is my jurisdiction." Greg looked at Pritchett. "I've a task to complete and don't need someone else's misguided efforts getting in my way."

"What would be ideal here is if we could organize a joint, if only temporarily, alliance to eradicate this threat to all of us," Sir Renfield offered.

"A novel concept but it never works that way," Pritchett retorted. "Everyone always goes off and does their own thing." He glared at Greg.

"Do what you want. I don't care." Donnovan started walking away.

"Donnovan. Just one thing," Greg called after him. "Exactly what were you selling to the Army of the New Order?"

"You have scouts, Lieutenant, ask them."

"So do you. Don't you think it would be in both our interests to trade intell? We probably know things about ANO you don't. Shouldn't we find out what each other knows?"

Donnovan stopped and pondered the proposition for several moments, not looking at the waiting officer.

"Aken, tell the lieutenant what he needs to know." Donnovan walked away.

"Trenton, tell Aken what he needs to know," Greg called his ops sergeant over. "Talk to Sharp for the latest reports."

"Where are you going?" Pritchett caught Greg's arm.

"None of your damn business," Greg shot back, throwing the bionic hand off his arm and walking away. He was glad Trenton was the only man under him to see him disrespect the chain of command.

"I don't believe I heard you correctly, lieutenant. What was that you said?" Pritchett yelled, infuriated at Greg's total lack of respect. Discipline among the troops was getting bad enough without the horrendous example being set by Lieutenant Merrick. Something had to be done.

Greg increased his pace more for warmth than to avoid dealing with the captain. It was too cold out to be walking around in just a uniform. Fuming as he was over Darren and Dave's dereliction of duty, he barely noticed the crisp air or thinning fog. He ignored the fading voice of his commanding officer and tried to focus on the mission goal. Everything was so confusing. Nothing made sense anymore, not rank, duty, or objective. It was like going through the motions, having long forgotten the reasons for them. When at last he tracked down the two RPA's he was on the verge of doing something violent, but without any real reason to justify it.

Very few patrons visited the Match Head during the late morning hours and fewer still were present when Greg entered. Most of Donnovan's mercenaries had other things to do and much of the Coalition force was on active duty. The only two Coalition personnel in the room were sitting at a darkened corner beneath a dimmed lamp and surrounded by vacant tables. Dave leaned over his breakfast while Freya continued an animated conversation. Leaning on Darren's shoulder half asleep, Cyndiara's eyes fluttered open at the sound of Greg's boots on the wood floor. Darren chewed his hash browns slowly and looked up with bloodshot eyes laden with dark bags.

"Where are the two of you supposed to be right now!?"

"Ahhhuh, Lieutenant."

Darren winced. Dave winced. Cyndiara winced.

"Easy on the volume, sir." Dave mumbled, rubbing his temples.

"You missed the party last night, dude. Gibs threw a kegger and drank us all under the table." Darren smiled sheepishly and rubbed the bridge of his nose.

"We didn't travel halfway across the continent for you to party with Gibs. Why aren't you on patrol?" Greg moved forward menacingly.

"We'll get to it after breakfast. Eventually."

"Eventually!? What about right now?"

"Morning, Lieutenant!" Freya stood and took Greg by surprise with her cheerfulness. "Are you hungry?"

"No. No, I'm not hungry."

"Well, how 'bout ya just sit down here and I'll bring ya some fresh eggs and browns." she pulled out a chair for him to sit. Greg stared at the chair and at Henry's niece as if both were crazy. Freya patted the seat.

"I'm not staying."

"Relax a little while I get your food." she guided him into the chair. "Have some milk. You'll feel better." Freya poured him a glass of milk from the pitcher on the table, gave him a wide smile, and then skipped off into the kitchen.

Greg stared at the milk, unclear as to how he wound up sitting at the table in the first place. In a way, it was a good thing. Greg's anger began to subside, after all, he was actually hungry now that he thought about it. Dave's lovesick eyes followed Freya into the kitchen.

"Isn't she great, Lieutenant?"

"A real catch, Dave," Greg responded sarcastically, staring at the sandy-haired, freckled face of his RPA.

"I think I'm in love."

"Well that's a switch." Greg looked at the kitchen door. Freya wasn't necessarily ugly, more homely if Greg wanted to be polite. Freya had short brown hair, rather plain features, and was a bit pudgy, not Dave's usual type. "I thought you went for the buxom blond, no-brainer types."

"Who, me?"

"How long have you known her?"

"Four days."

"Four days and you think you're in love? Good, Dave."

"We're gonna git married."

"Don't get your hopes up. It might be a very short honeymoon."

"Are you married, Lieutenant?" Cyndiara asked.

Greg held up 10 ringless fingers.

"That doesn't mean much."

"No. Never been married. Why do you ask?" Greg was losing even more hostility with each passing minute.

"You seem like the kind to be married. The husband type. No offense or anything."

"None taken."

"You're not gay, are you?" Cyndiara kept the questions coming.

Greg looked at her eyes to see if she was joking, but she seemed to be serious.

"No, absolutely not. I just don't date much."

"Why?"

"Because it's going to take someone really, different to — Why am I telling you this?"

"I just asked," Cyndiara responded as though she'd been offended.

"Darren, did Sharp wake you and Dave up at 0600 for your patrol this morning?" Greg pushed the conversation away from the personal.

"Right on the nose. How could I forget." Darren rubbed his eyes.

"And what time is it now?"

"Like morning sometime."

"It's after 1100 and you're just now getting up for breakfast?"

"We hadda get a little sleep, sir." Dave shrugged.

"What concerns me more than you two skipping your patrol is that Sharp let you get away with it."

"Hey, don't knock Sharp, sir. He's doin' his job just like you told him to, we just cruised for more Z's," Darren defended his friend.

"How 'bout in an hour we just take Brian and Peterson's patrol," Dave suggested hopefully.

"How 'bout you finish your shift like you were supposed to and take Adams' and Peterson's patrol. I had to pull Brian into work on repairs and Peterson shouldn't be out there by himself. At least one of you would have to fly with him."

"Get Rachel to do it."

"PFC Brown is no more qualified to go out solo than Peterson."

"Neither is Lieutenant Sorenson and you put him an' Brown on 12 to 1800. Mike's been shot down down more times than any of us."

"Up until our last op Lieutenant Sorenson had an almost flawless flight record." Greg paused, trying to get himself worked up again. "Why am I sitting here arguing with you two? Stuff the rest of your food in your mouths and go!" Greg took a drink of milk.

Cyndiara laughed.

"Yer browns will be done in a jiffy." Freya reached out and dropped a pile of scrambled eggs on a plate in front of Greg. "Wipe your face." She dropped a napkin on his lap and scurried back into the kitchen. Greg wiped away his milk mustache and stuffed some food in his mouth.

"Well, Dave, if you can talk her into coming back with us to Chi-Town, you'll be a happy man." Greg plugged another fork full of eggs in his mouth, pretending not to notice the leery glance between his two RPA's. "I want you two to make a fly-by over Q-7 and see if you can pick up the trail of several large bots leaving Liberty to the north. If you lose the trail, go north by north-east sixty miles then double back and forth on your way back."

"That's not our usual pattern," Dave pointed out.

"I'm aware of that. If I'm correct, you'll draw fire from a convoy moving into the steeper hills to the north. Check in with Trenton before you go and he should be able to fill you in on what to look for."

"Woah, baby. Like, dude, I thought drawing fire was bad," Darren protested.

"It is and it isn't. Get me your best count on mechanized and troops, and any air power they've got. If things get too hot, hightail it out of there. Feel free to return fire, maybe make some hit and runs. The important thing is to assess the rebel army and wear them down if we can. Unfortunately I think we're up against more than we came prepared for."

"You shoulda been a specialist, dude. How come you're doing the intel and not Sorenson, not that I'm complaining."

"Cuz Sorenson's off with Lisa someplace," Dave muttered.

"Hmmm. Dave, is Lisa checked out on a SAM?" Greg's grey eyes twinkled deviously.

"As far as I know. She's cleared on the UAR-1 and the Skull Walker, but I don't know what she's like in a SAM."

"She's not touching SAM 15, not in a million years!" Darren blurted out. "Movin' a robot around in a repair bay an' test flyin' a SAM ain't the same thing as fighting. Two separate things. Some baby dragon pops up to play tag an' it really stinks when you don't know know how to tag back. Lisa's never taken a SAM into combat, not as far as I know."

"It was just a thought. Some added incentive for Sorenson to get off his butt."

"Lisa handles herself pretty good when the shit hits the fan," Dave defended his co-pilot and communications officer.

"Yeah, but it's lots different up close an' personal, not behind twenty tons of armor. You know that, dude."

"I agree, it would be putting her at risk. She's not ready." Greg poured himself another cup of milk.

"Here you go. Eat up." Freya dumped hash browns on his plate and left the steaming frying pan on the table. Dave grabbed her around the waist and pulled her down on his lap.

"You don't get freaked out much, do you Lieutenant?" Darren got serious.

"That depends on what you mean by freaked out. Even if I was, as an officer I can't show it. There's times when I might be just as scared as the next guy, I just don't let it take control. I can't."

"Don't ya get scared when all those monsters an' baddies come at ya?" Freya asked.

"There's different kinds of fear, and everyone reacts different." Greg pondered the question, and the fact that he was having breakfast with two derelict soldiers discussing things he shouldn't. He considered making up an answer and moving on, but then realized he couldn't remember the last time he really experienced fear.

"How does Dave react?" Freya asked teasingly.

"Dave's pretty much straight down the center as soldiers go." Greg leaned back and took a thoughtful pose. "Dave knows when his life is in danger, but I've never seen him lose control. Straight down the line, not too reckless, but not afraid of making a move even if it's dangerous. Follows orders, most of the time." Greg shot Dave a warning look.

"What about Darren?" Cyndiara asked, pretending Darren wasn't in the room.

"Now that's a different story. Darren's not afraid because he doesn't think he can die."

"Huh?"

"It's all a game, and death is just part of the game that doesn't actually happen to him. Sure, he recognizes danger and reacts to it, but it's not the same as fear. He doesn't know when he should be afraid. Death is something that happens to other people, not him."

"And I'm really good," Darren came back in a cocky tone of voice.

"Being good isn't what's going to keep you alive. Sooner or later that one mistake will be the last. What's kept Darren alive this long is the fear he doesn't let himself acknowledge, making him recognize his mortality, sub-consciously at least." Greg looked right at Darren. "You haven't let it blind you to what's going on in the fight. The times when you face death, you've used your fear instead of letting it control you. But you're still not in control of it either. The adrenaline rush, to cheat death and come out on top. That's going to wear off eventually, and then you'll have to deal with the fear. I wonder how much it will change when you've got something to lose." Greg's grey eyes drifted to Cyndiara, and the conversation sobered.

"What do you have to lose?" Cyndiara asked in all seriousness.

Greg had no immediate answer, silently searching his life for something he still believed in. Something he had to value.

"My life. A very strong survival instinct. That's built into everyone."

"Then why risk it? Having a life just to risk it is stupid."

"I'm not afraid to die."

"You do it just because you're not afraid?"

"No, and yes, I have experienced fear in ways none of you can dream of, but that's not the same as being afraid to die." Greg figured it was time to end the conversation, but continued on anyway. "You become numb somewhat, but with experience comes confidence, and hopefully, not recklessness. After you've been through enough, you're not really afraid of dying even though it's very possible. You look back and say, 'I've gotten out of worse, or taken on higher odds than this and won.' Sure, there's still fear, but you control it. First you have to face it, acknowledge it, then overcome it. If you're lucky it all happens fast. It's the situations when you have the time to recognize and face your fear, that's the hard part."

Greg continued his breakfast, deep in thought.

"Pritchett freaked, didn't he?" Darren recalled the unexpected retreat.

"Pritchett is a very brave man, and it's not a fake front. False bravery doesn't last a second, it gets stripped away and shows a person for what they are. Braggarts, and people who talk like there's nothing in this world they fear, are sometimes the most fearful people inside. They've never faced their fear, and danger has never stripped them of bravado until it's too late. Danger brings out the best and worst in a man. Pritchett's not afraid, partly out of the kind of real courage that counts, and partly out of ignorance. He's never had to face real fear, and when it happens he isn't sure what to do. He doesn't know how to face and overcome his fear because he's never done it before. The only way he can respond is the most basic survival instinct, fight or flight. As much as I'd rather not be under Pritchett's command, I will say this for him. He's not a coward."

"But you still haven't answered my question. Is the only reason you risk your life because you don't have anything to lose? Defending your home, people you care for, those are reasons to fight and die. I don't understand risking your life for nothing," Cyndiara pressed on.

"Thank you for the breakfast, Freya. How much do I owe you?" Greg ignored the question, finalizing the discussion.

"We got it, sir. How often do we get to have breakfast with you?" Darren flipped his card on the table.

"Keep an expense record, I'll see what I can do about reimbursing you when we get back to Chi-Town. You two ready to go?" Greg pushed his chair back from the table and stood.

"I guess," Dave mumbled.

"Sir, why are we doing this?" Darren queried.

"Because that's what we're out here for. Because I'm ordering it."

"No, I mean why are we doing this."

Greg stopped himself from blurting out "because it's our job." Somehow that didn't seem like enough motivation. Why was he out here?

"You know, a month ago I could have given you a twenty minute lecture on how we're fighting for humanity and trying to reclaim our world. But right now that doesn't do much for me, so why should I give you the same line? I know Zenjori Suka and the Army of the New Order have to go."

Cyndiara nodded. Darren wasn't done.

"I know that, man, Suka's got his coming. I mean, like what are we accomplishing with all these patrols and things we do just because some jack-ass back at Chi-Town wants us to. Why do it?"

"I could give you every official response in the book and tell you it's not your place to question, just trust and follow orders, but I'm not sure myself anymore. I've been in the military for eight years and never lost sight of the reasons I enlisted when I was 16. I wanted a better life than what I had in the 'Burbs, and to make a difference for mankind, change things that were wrong and do something more constructive with my life than waste away there. Now, now I'm out here doing some politically minded colonel's dirty laundry. I'm ordering men into life-threatening situations, but that's how orders work. I get orders, I obey them. I pass them on to you, and you obey. That's how it works."

"But why do it?" Cyndiara asked.

"I don't know. I expect both of you airborne within the hour just the same." Greg pointed at the two RPAs. "Hangover or no hangover, I need you on patrol and checking out what I told you to. I'll be flying south-east. Check in with me every hour on the hour through the comm link in Skull 41."

"Whatever."

"We'll talk more about this later, but don't pass it on to anyone else, understand? This was an off-duty discussion that didn't happen."

"I can hang with that." Darren nodded.

"And just to give you both some real incentive to keep on top of your duties, I will personally have you both thrown in Sheriff Morley's jail if either of you pull another stunt like this again."

Long, heavy strides brought Drake across the mercenary camp. Headhunters, D-Bees, and other warriors quickly moved aside for the giant 'Borg to pass. It didn't take an expert in psychology to interpret the cyborg's unfriendly intentions. Drake passed a group of new recruits and stepped up to the mechanic fixing a patch of armor on a badly painted SAM 117B.

"You little shit!" Drake lifted the terrified Operator up in the air, eye to eye. "You didn't convert the rail guns like you said!" He tossed the man to the ground and held up a scorched C-40 with his larger pair of arms.

Zenjori excused himself from orientation of the new mercenaries.

"Drake, is there a reason you're attacking Xevo in front of the new additions to our army?"

"This rail gun Tim was supposed to shoot me with. I told Xevo to put a power breaker inside so it could be switched down to a lower velocity. It wasn't supposed to do this to my armor!"

Drake pointed to the left imprint pattern on his otherwise perfect armor. One side was barely marked, but the left burst pattern bore deep into armor and sported sets of stress fractures.

"Xevo, did you install the power breaker in SAM 15's rail gun?" Zenjori inquired smoothly.

"I didn't have time! I would have done it but there were too many other things you wanted me to fix first. I was working on the jamming device with what you gave me. The kind of thing you want takes time. I'm really sorry about your armor, Drake! I can fix it. I'll do it first thing."

"You'll do more than that! You lied to me, you little —"

"Drake, calm yourself." Zenjori reached down and helped the terrified Operator to his feet. "We've just acquired over eighty million credits worth of hardware at the expense of one stolen SAMAS and five men. You deserve a bonus for a job well done," Zenjori praised his second-in-command.

"Not that it matters much since Torrak screwed up," Drake accused in a metallic voice that carried to where Torrak could hear.

The Gromek stood by himself, as always. Healed of his physical injuries, Torrak's humiliation scarred much deeper. His yellow eyes blazed with fury, and the words to an incantation came unbidden, just as Drake's array of three forearm rockets involuntarily popped up to fire.

"Stop!" Zenjori shouted, pushing Drake's arm aside and using an ancient mind calming technique to squelch the hostility around him. "Calm yourselves, there's no place for fighting here."

"Try and finish that spell, mage, and I'll kill you," Drake rumbled.

"Torrak, I wish you to do what you do best and summon a new army of demons. Demons for you to use to kill Coalition troops. I told you before and I tell you again, I'm not upset at you for this morning's incident. It couldn't be helped, and you did what you could."

"I don't want your pity and I don't need your lies," Torrak seethed, more humiliated by Zenjori now than before. Turning to leave, Torrak mumbled a threat. "Even 'Borgs sleep sometime."

"Drake," Zenjori warned. "No trouble. Not now, not here."

"Let me waste the magic user before he stabs us all in the back."

"Patience. I need something else from you right now."

"Yes, Suka San." Drake disarmed the forearm launch system and the protruding missile tubes slid back under protective armor plates.

"That group of Headhunters that just signed on with us. They have their own equipment and seem much more competent than most of the vagabonds we've been recruiting. I'm assigning them to Sledgehammer squad, along with the two X-10 Predators we just acquired. The Titan goes to Carnivore squad, but you get first pick of the troop weaponry."

"Thank you, Suka San. It looks like there are more recruits than we have weapons for. I assume the second-raters go to Kruno's command?"

"Lower your voice. Kruno knows most of his men are expendable cannon fodder, but they don't." Zenjori jerked his eyes at the milling squads of D-Bees and poorly armed frontier people. "Many of them want nothing more than room and board, and the chance to ensure their freedom by eliminating the Coalition threat." Zenjori dropped his voice to a whisper. "I have convinced them that if we send the Coalition States a clear message by destroying their advance spies, it will make Liberty safe for many years to come. If we succeed in retaking Liberty, that may not be too far from the truth. Make them feel like they're doing something heroic, not futile, please?"

"Sorry, Suka San."

"So then," Zenjori spoke loudly. "We have much to do yet today. J.J. and Kruno have located an excellent place to base our operations from. It will take us the rest of the day to pick up and move there. I want you to coordinate with Kruno and send a demolitions team ahead to begin laying a defensive perimeter. Use the X-10's to clear a good place for our headquarters. Carnivore squad will make up most of the line defense, leaving Sledgehammer as the acting mobile force to step in and retaliate wherever the heavy firepower is needed. Carnivore should be able to slow the Coalition down long enough for Sledgehammer to concentrate fire and eliminate them."

"The Coalition will not attack. If they discover our defenses, they will show themselves to be cowards. Donnovan and First Strike are not Coalition. They will attack us. I'm convinced of that."

"We may have to defeat both, but not at the same time."

"What makes you so certain?"

"The Coalition commander in Liberty has already had the seeds of suggestion planted in his mind. Notec has made sure of it."

Half-eaten bodies littered the ground between burned out cabins. Even without special training it was obvious to Greg that much of the burning was ignited by a few well placed plasma bolts intended to block off one side with a wall of burning structures. What wasn't as clear was the lack of healthy, adult bodies. Most of the victims were the elderly or very young. The few signs Greg could read told him at least sixty people had been herded the half-mile to the sea where their prints simply vanished at the rugged bluffs. No marks of any vehicles or thruster burns of aircraft could be found. Other than the village itself and a few sets of matching boot prints around the village, there was nothing to indicate who the attackers had been. Greg wiped charcoal from his hands on his uniform, still pacing the smoldering ruins. None of it made sense.

Why he'd flown clear to the ragged coastline he didn't know, perhaps just to see the ocean, and perhaps because he needed some time away from military regiment to think freely. Finding the village had been an accident, one Greg wished he could find an answer to.

He flew back to the coast again for a better look and discovered all the boats at a makeshift dock down the coast had been systematically punctured with some type of high energy blade. Something or someone wanted to make sure none of the villagers escaped. No bodies in the water. Things just didn't add up.

For lack of something better to do, Greg left the docks and flew out over the ocean. In the south-east he could see the rippling blue energy of a powerful ley line flowing out across the ocean. Below him the waves rolled on toward land. On the horizon a metallic spire thrust its head above the water, a reminder of past civilization lost. Greg had heard stories about how the coastal waters he now flew over had once been a sprawling metropolis that sank beneath the waves with the rise of Atlantis. Tidal forces and displaced ocean had struck the coast and obliterated the cities that once nestled up to the water's edge. Three hundred some years later the only reminder of past civilization was under water or twisted piles of rubble and overgrown ruins.

Greg skimmed the tops of the waves at dangerous speeds, testing the limits of his sanity just to see how far he'd gone over the edge. The total lack of fear pressed him to greater and greater feats of danger until a wave crest struck the exoskeleton's feet and almost flipped him over into the ocean. Pulling up and away Greg let the adrenaline rush through his veins again and embraced the forgotten sensations. For the moment he still held a value for life and his own survival.

Making a sharp U-turn he aimed the SAMAS towards the shoreline and rough-hewn bluff. A flock of giant, winged animals flew south along the shoreline but didn't seem to care about him, so Greg left them alone. Not everything that crawled through a Rift was bent on human genocide or craved the taste of human flesh. Some were just dumb animals that wound up trapped on an alien world, and some were creatures from Earth's past. The struggle for survival wasn't always a successful one, but mankind was still the dominant species and would fight to keep it that way. It was still too early in post-apocalyptic history to tell who would win.

Greg's mind tore apart years of Coalition indoctrination, questioning everything he'd ever believed in. The oaths of loyalty and duties of an officer seemed distant and meaningless. To defy the edicts he'd sworn to uphold was treason, but what made it all a cancer destroying his values was the fact that he couldn't find a reason to cure it. To spend eight years of his life dedicated to something and then lose it all in a matter of days terrified him, but the soul-searching went on its brutal rampage nonetheless. What did he really believe in? What would be the consequences of the choices he feared he'd make? Events were closing fast and time was fleeting; there was no way to stop his treacherous awakenings.

Anger and frustration possessing his mind and soul, Greg pushed the SAMAS to 300 mph and clipped treetops without concern for the danger. Miles of scenery flew past the speeding exoskeleton. A tree limb struck the unit's left leg and the air intakes inhaled twigs and leaves. A moment of panic snapped Greg back to reality and instant reactions saved his life. Pulling higher, then slowing to a cautious speed, He angled the SAMAS towards a small river and landed softly on the bank.

Scrambling from the humming power suit and throwing off his flight suit, Greg fought free of his clothing and dove headlong into the frigid water.

Nerve impulses whiplashed his senses with icy shock and his ears hissed loudly in his head. Heart-stopping cold arrested runaway thoughts and emotions, forcing reality back in check. Surfacing five yards out, Greg gasped as his body adjusted to the shock. His temples pounded, but crystal clear thought once again returned.

Giving into impulse, he filled his lungs with air and dove back beneath the surface. Powerful strokes propelled him along with the current. The natural thrill kept him going down stream faster and farther until his lungs screamed for air. Determined to press his limits a bit farther, Greg fought the current towards the bank, determined not to surface until he reached it. Rocks and submerged branches came closer, forcing him to weave in order to continue hugging the bottom. Something hit his shoulder, stopping a stroke.

Bursting from the crisp, flowing water, Greg gasped for air. Standing before him was a very beautiful woman.

Chapter 14

"Uh, excuse me!" Greg gasped, trying to find his footing in the water's current. Her waist length bluish-black hair clung to an athletic body of perfect proportions and her sun-bronzed skin was flawless. Greg didn't have but a moment to gawk.

The speed with which she grasped his wrist and locked him away at arm's length took Greg completely off guard. Her iron grip tightened and before he could apologize for his unexpected arrival, she'd forced his head beneath the water. At first Greg thought the reaction a bit extreme, but quickly realized it wasn't in fun. Lashing out with a powerful leg sweep, he threw her down beside him. Arm lock broken, he grabbed her wrist. She forced his arm back and split the back of his hand open on a rock jutting up from the stream, then wrenched her wrist out of his grasp.

Pushing away and attempting to put some distance between them, Greg was kicked in the chest with a foot he barely had time to see coming, sending new levels of pain through his numbed body. Old injuries added to new ones, the blood from his hand spilling into the river unnoticed.

"I'm sorry! I didn't even know you were here." He backed away as she crouched in the water ready to attack again. She paused, every muscle tensed for action, but her greyish blue eyes weren't focused on him.

"Easy, I'm not trying to hurt you." Greg glanced around to make sure he wasn't surrounded. "I ran into you by accident." He moved his hands in a calming gesture. "Really, you don't need to kick me anymore." He winced, looking down to see a bruise already forming over his heavily muscled chest. If it weren't for the muscle mass, her kick might have broken bones, Greg thought. Brushing wet hair out of his eyes he glanced around again to see what she was looking at. He was alone, standing in a freezing river with a beautiful woman that wanted to kill him. Greg started laughing so hard it hurt his chest from the ribs she'd just cracked. Her cold, expressionless mask turned to one of confusion.

"What is your name?"

Instead of answering she crept closer, like a cat stalking prey.

"Hey, he, hehehehe." Greg coughed as he laughed. "You could at least tell me your name. Wow, you've got quite a kick." He winced again.

She sprang. Greg was ready this time and deflected her foot to the side of his head. She paused a split second too long trying to keep her balance in the water. Grabbing her ankle, Greg tried to tip her over backwards. Instead he found himself holding her ankle above her head and the next moment he was underwater again. Time for a different approach, Greg determined, still finding the entire affair hilarious.

Latching onto her wrist with both hands Greg used a painful joint lock to force her away from him. Her other fist clobbered his jaw hard enough to jar his entire skull.

"Why do I always end up in fight with some psycho with no clothes!" Greg hissed through clenched teeth and threw his weight into her arm. Giving way and backing up before he broke her wrist, the woman allowed Greg to force her onto the muddy bank. Suddenly she went with the weight and slipped out of the lock in one fluid motion. Greg pushed her down hard.

"Listen, I'll just walk back to where I came from and you'll never see me again."

Slipping back into ankle-deep water, Greg tried to get past but again she struck with a precise kick. The force it took Greg to deflect the blows made him wonder if he hadn't met his match. He would have expected this kind of fight out of a Juicer or Crazy, but this woman was obviously neither.

"Why don't we just go back to Liberty and talk this over." He bruised his arm to keep a crescent kick from smashing his head. She'd moved in too close and Greg saw his opening. Feinting a knee strike, he caught her leg behind the knee and locked it against his waist. The last thing she expected.

His uppercut snapped her head back with bone-jarring force. Striking a woman wasn't his first choice, but she was going to kill him if he didn't. Instead of going limp from the blow, she slammed him in the nose with her forearm and Greg's eyes misted instantly without his consent. Desperation drove home and he threw her over his shoulder, following in with a tackle from behind. Both bounced off the moss-covered bank and slid into the water, but it was Greg who came out on top with a clumsy full nelson keeping her face just inches from submersion. He could taste the blood from his nose and see it dripping from his chin. Struggling to get away, the woman endured several seconds under water before Greg let her back up again.

For the first time in the engagement, he noticed the peculiar point of her slender ears. *Probably has D-Bee blood in her family history,* he summarized with disappointment. The hair and eyes weren't quite human, either. No wonder she was so wild. On the other hand, maybe she didn't understand a word he was saying.

"Do you understand American?"

No answer. She tried to get free again but Greg pressed down on her neck even harder.

"If you struggle, I'll push harder. It's already got to hurt, don't make me make it worse. Do you understand what I'm saying?"

"Yes."

"Okay, good, you talk. That's a start. I still can't let you up until I know you're not going to try busting my skull again."

"Release me." Her voice had a peculiar accent he didn't recognize.

"First answer some questions. Let's start with your name." Greg concentrated on establishing trust. He didn't plan to drown her, or let her up right away. "Its okay, make up a name if you want."

"Natarsha."

"Well Natarsha, tell me why I should let you up?"

"Leave. I won't harm you."

"That's what I'd like to believe. On the other — Oh, damn." Greg whispered.

Thrashing up the river 1500 feet away came a pair of horse-like creatures with what looked like horns and spindly arms. It was difficult to tells from so far away, but it looked like each had a nasty set of long claws at the end of each arm. Gregg's blood froze. The monsters sniffed the air and water and kept thrashing up the river.

"What is it?" she whispered.

"I don't know. They're too far away. At first I thought they were two riders on horseback, but they're monsters of some kind. Not happy kinds." Greg imitated Sharp's favorite monster description.

"The blood. They smell your blood."

Greg took a chance. Slowly he released his hold and they both sank deeper into the water. He could feel her muscles tense beneath him.

"I hear them. What do they look like?" she whispered.

"They're right there, coming up the river. Bigger than I thought, ten, maybe twelve feet tall. They look like a horses with a bunch of spines running down their necks and a pair of arms with claws. Horses don't have arms."

"Melech," she breathed quietly.

"They don't look friendly. I left my SAM running up the river, but they could probably run me down before I got to it. I think they heard me." Greg sank lower as one Melech stopped at two hundred yards and listened. Greg's heart pounded harder than ever. This was exciting. He was definitely nuts, no doubt about it now.

"They will find us by your scent. I can kill them. You must run."

"If you can't take on one naked man in the river you're not going to last ten seconds against those things."

"I have weapons on the bank."

Greg looked to the moss covered bank and noticed a bulky alien-looking rifle accompanied by an ornate jeweled sword.

"Are you sure?"

"Do not delay. Go now and do not come this way ever again."

"That won't be hard. I'm not even sure where the I am now anyway. Good luck!"

Pushing himself up and running away, Greg gave a quick look back to make sure she wasn't aiming the rifle at him. Both weapons were gone and she was nowhere in sight. The two monsters charged up the river, their beady eyes fixed on the only visible humanoid. Dodging through trees and tearing his way through thick brush, Greg ran for his life. The SAMAS purred quietly on the river bank next to his scattered clothing. Mindless of accumulated injuries, he pulled on most of his clothes and stuffed the rest inside the exoskeleton with him. The SAM's audio amplifiers picked up the scream of a dying animal downstream.

Blowing out a plume of water behind him, he flew just inches above the river. Passing the chance meeting site faster than expected, Greg launched the SAMAS above the treetops in a quick semi-circle. Blood stained the river bank and mixed with the flowing water. A headless Melech lay partly up on the bank. The other lay in a bloody heap entangled in some kind of glowing net. Natarsha was gone.

Switching optics to thermal scan he searched the forest for a human heat signature. Running with surprising speed away from the river was one human-sized warm spot. Greg angled closer and slowed to match speed. A definite shape and shades of orange and red designating body temperature took form. Greg banked the SAMAS away. She didn't want to be followed.

Getting his bearings by referencing the computer navigation system, Greg headed back for Liberty and tried to concoct a plausible explanation for his injuries. Events like this didn't happen in real life. Nobody would believe such a fantastic story, even if it was true. It had been true and he wondered if he would ever see the beautiful woman again — under much better circumstances he hoped. He smiled, then winced at the pain in his jaw and nose. Truth had proof. Fact was stranger than fiction.

Brian and Lisa stared up at Skull Walker 191, contemplating the one eyed robot in silence.

"I don't know how we're going to fix that," Brian spoke up at last.

Both technical officers wore dark utility uniforms with military insignias and looked out of place in the civilian-run mechanic shop. The large, six-story structure housed the most complete repair facility in Liberty and currently showcased a Coalition APC and Skull Walker next to an industrial-owned X-500 Forager robot used for hauling timber and construction. Passers-by did a triple take and then usually moved on due to the armed Coalition guards making sure thieves had second thoughts. Two Dog Boys harassed a pair of inexperienced technical officers from Pritchett's unit making repairs on the APC. Ever alert for psychics and magic users, the Dog Boys kept an ear to the doors for sounds of trouble. Lisa stared up at the gaping hole in the Skull Walker where the right eye/spotlight had been.

"Do you have any concept of how much work it's going to take to fix just the internal damage?"

"No. That's your job." Brian nudged her and gained her annoyance.

"I can't replace the spotlight. Not without an exact replacement or something about the same size. Then there's the transparent armor cover, that I can't imagine finding out here. Gizmo doesn't have any, does he?"

"We can always put an armor plate over the hole."

"That might work."

"Brian, can you bond an armor plate over the eye and make it look like a pirate's eye patch?"

"That's a great idea!" Brian brightened. "I could even bond a length of power cable on the outside to make it look like it was actually wearing the armor patch over its eye. That would look cool!"

"Just remember whose idea it was."

"Hey Giz!" Brian called to the shop owner up on the repair gantry around the X-500. "You got any 20 mm poly-bond?"

"Check the last row of slots in the shed!" The cybernetically augmented mechanic waved a diagnostic probe at the armor shed in one corner of the structure.

"Thanks. I'll put it on my tab." Brian took Lisa by the sleeve.

"C'mon, give me a hand. This stuff is heavy."

"Uh, Brian, how did you get to be on a first name basis with everyone here?"

"Uh, Giz's pretty cool. Most of the guys in here are. Besides, it's Pritchett's expense account, not mine." Brian slid open the door to the large shed and marched to the back. "40 mm, 30 mm, 23 mm, that stuff looks used, 21 mm, here we go, 20 mm. This stuff is heavy!" Brian rolled the sheet out on its tracked housing and tried to lift it.

"Do we really need 20 mm? That's pretty thick for just a patch. Don't you usually layer thinner plates?"

"The way Pritchett goes into battle?"

"Then what are we doing using this?" Lisa looked around the shed with a glint in her eyes.. "Where's the 5 mm poly-carbonate? It is Pritchett's can we're protecting, remember?"

"Don't tempt me."

"He won't know the difference."

"Yeah, but there's other people in the Skull Walker. If it was just him, well, maybe."

"You're no fun."

"I can't lift this. Go call Wreath for me, will ya?"

"Wreath?"

"The big D-Bee working on Sheriff Morley's ATV outside."

"Brian, how'd you get this place to let us use their facilities?" Lisa asked.

"I talked to Giz when we got here and we hit it off. I offered to show him how to bond a transparent molecular shell on an existing multi-layer composite. I'm helping him rebuild this really cool Pre-Rifts speeder."

"Did Merrick approve of you giving out Coalition technical secrets?"

"No, but Pritchett did. Sort of. He wanted me to supervise the repair efforts and I told him I couldn't do it without proper facilities and an expense account. He tells me to do what it takes to get Gizmo to let me use their facilities. He tells me the Coalition is sending more patrols out this way in the future and it helps to have a friendly shop to get repairs done at. I just took a little officer's initiative, and got what I wanted," Brian grinned.

"Sometimes you really surprise me, Brian."

"Yo! Wreath! I need some help!" Brian shouted and moments later the large D-Bee sauntered into the shed with a stupid grin on its bony face. Lisa couldn't decide if Wreath was male or female.

"Help?"

"Yeah, can you carry this armor plating over to the Skull Walker and leave it on the lift?"

"Wreath can do." The D-Bee ambled forward and carried the 300 pound armor plate out with one hand. Lisa backed away, not very trusting of the giant alien.

"What was that?" she whispered when Wreath was gone.

"I dunno. Wreath."

"Is it male or female?"

"I dunno. It's just Wreath. He, or she, is pretty good with machines, though. Not real smart, but it understands how machines work better than any mechanic I've ever known. Real good tempered, too. Giz an' I couldn't figure out why the particle beam cannon on this speeder wouldn't respond to a system diagnostic, and Wreath just walks up, feels up the speeder, and says 'you repair thing not understand. Part not understand. Machine say need new chip but repair thing not speak same talk. Fix chip.' Sure enough, Giz knows what he's talking about, we yank the diagnostic chip from the particle cannon and run it through a filter by itself, and we find a tiny fracture in the nano-circuit. It's not fried, so we'd never suspected it. No real way to figure that out without spending days de-bugging the entire system, but Wreath just touches the speeder and he knows. Pretty cool, huh?"

"I wouldn't want a D-Bee anywhere near my mech, especially one that thinks it can talk to machines." Lisa pointed to Wreath, who was holding a conversation with the Sheriff's ATV.

"Wreath's weird, but he's okay. A month ago I would have agreed, but I never met a D-Bee like Wreath before. I suppose there's got to be others out there that aren't all bad. There's gotta be some smart, good natured ones out there that don't wanna kill people, like Wreath."

Brian's blasphemy shocked Lisa further.

"I'd be careful who I said that around. I don't care, personally, but you could get into big trouble, maybe even C.I.S."

"I'm not stupid. Trust me, I'd know if I was being watched."

"Just like you did to Mike last time? Just like someone in our unit watched all of us?"

Brian's expression changed.

"When's the last time you checked Skull 41?"

"An hour ago. Before I came here. It's clean, and I ran the virus killer through all of Pritchett's robots and power armor again just to be on the safe side. I even downloaded — don't tell anybody — the transmission logs from the Enforcer and Abolisher and checked the records on all the SAMAS. I don't want a repeat of last time any more than you do."

"That's for sure," Brian agreed seriously.

Both stopped and looked at each other.

"The Skull Walker."

Leaving the shed at a run with memories of betrayal driving them to new possibilities, both technical officer sprinted for the one vehicle they'd never checked. Climbing the scaffolding and dropping into the pilot's compartment of the giant robot, they surveyed the internal damage momentarily before scrambling to action. Lisa found fewer internal systems damaged than anticipated.

"Brian, what's the code?"

"49174447. Then type in Mind Games." Brian pressed closer, leaning over her chair. "That's Pritchett's code, I didn't make that up."

"It needs voice authorization."

"No it doesn't. Pritchett's afraid someone might try an' override his code and voice print, so he's got the alarm rigged to voice authorization. Hit the switch under the seat." Brian reached between her legs and hit the concealed switch. Lisa looked at him with eyebrows raised. "Sorry." Brian backed away, embarrassed. "That wasn't my idea either. I didn't put it there."

"I was worried for a second."

"Voice code accepted," the female voice announced, and command functions became available.

"How did you get Pritchett to give you access to his vehicle like this. You must have done some major kissing up." Lisa cracked her knuckles and started typing in commands.

"He didn't want to at first, but after his techs kept screwing things up he wanted someone who actually knew what they were doing making repairs on his personal Skull Walker. He wanted it done yesterday, and so I didn't give him any choice. My way or no way. 'Course I didn't exactly say it that way, but you get the idea."

"This is what I expected to see." Lisa shook her head and stared at the screen. "Do you know the code for that?"

"Pritchett's got a code on the communications system too? Man, and I thought I was paranoid!"

"I could probably hack through it, but it might take awhile. Days, even."

"I got a faster way." Brian stood on the back of the seat and stuck his head out the top hatch. "Wreath! Wanna do me a really big favor?"

"Okay."

"Climb on up here." Brian grinned at Lisa.

"You're not serious."

"Why not?"

"It's your neck here, not mine."

"You want Wreath do something?" The large D-Bee stuck his head into the pilot's compartment.

"Yeah. Can you talk to the computer and get it to tell you what the access code is for the communications system?"

"Yes!" Wreath gurgled enthusiastically, then looked suspicious. "Why?"

"I forgot," Brian lied.

"Oh. Okay." Wreath concentrated hard. Lisa looked skeptical. "Code is star star star star star."

"Asterisk." Brian translated.

"Those are just used to cover up the real numbers, right?"

"Who knows. We're talking about Pritchett here. Maybe it really is just five asterisks."

"Here goes." Lisa punched the asterisk key five times and the communications programs activated.

"Thanks Wreath. I won't forget now."

"Okay." The big D-Bee grinned and climbed down the scaffolding.

"This is a mess." Lisa frowned at the screen. "The last time somebody ran diagnostics on this was over two months ago."

"You can make it look like we didn't do this, right?"

"That's easy. Used to do that kind of stuff all the time as a kid back in Chi-Town, before I got busted. I'm not seeing anything really suspicious, but I'm running the virus killer just in case." Lisa pulled a micro-laser disk from her belt pouch and slotted the clear plastic casing into the deck. A few quick commands kicked the computer into diagnostic mode. "This will take a few minutes, but we'll know if the systems have been infected."

"And that should give us a list of all transmissions covered up by the virus?"

"In theory. I only ran the program on an infected system once, to make sure it worked. It found the virus and killed it like it was supposed to, gave me a report, and added the vaccine to the anti-virus system in case someone tried to reintroduce it. It should work here, if Pritchett's Skull Walker received a direct transmission from you-know-who. The virus will have already erased itself from the reception log and blanked out the normal trace parameters, that's why we couldn't find it last time. My program searches for the files the virus erases, basically like following footprints. If the virus is here, somebody could be using the Skull Walker to relay long range transmissions without the communications system having any record of it."

"We're not gonna get ourselves messed over this time. I want that traitor bad!" Brian clenched his fist.

There was a traitor among them and the betrayal had cost the lives of many in the past. As self-appointed secret guardians, both Lisa and Brian were determined to find out who it was before any more deception cost them their lives. What differences they had with each other faded out of mind with a much greater threat at hand.

"We never discussed exactly what we would do if we found the virus," Brian pointed out.

"If it is here, I can purge it and restore all the systems it corrupted with the back-ups from Skull 41. We probably won't be able to recover past transmissions the virus erased though, just a list of blank spots.

"That means we can't pull up exactly what the transmission was?"

"No, but we have a de-scrambler this time." Lisa patted a pouch on her belt. The tiny device hadn't been easy to acquire.

"All we need is a complete transmission record and we can nail him. If only we could make the computer think the virus is still there, and let the comm system accept the incoming signal, except we make the comp record it and pretend like it sent it instead."

"You know," Lisa's eyes went to the ceiling in thought. "I could write a program that simulates the virus and accepts the scrambled signal from the traitor. It shouldn't be too hard since Cara and I had to break down the original virus to find out how it worked anyway. We make the transmission go through all the motions like it wants to, except, like you said, it really doesn't relay or transmit back to Chi-Town. We get a complete record of the transmission, the traitor thinks the message has been sent, Pritchett doesn't know about it, and all we have to do is run it through the de-scrambler and we've got the traitor."

"I'm just the engineer, you're the computer expert." Brian didn't mention that he'd gotten into Lieutenant Merrick's personnel files and looked up hers, nor that he knew all about her history of drugs and criminal record. Of all the members of his unit, Lisa was the one with the highest I.Q. Brian kicked himself for drifting down that line of thought again. She was taken. He was over that now.

"This is going to be lots of work."

"I know, but you can do it."

"At least you appreciate others," Lisa muttered bitterly.

"Uh, I guess," Brian responded, unclear what she meant by the comment.

"I mean, like you just don't take for granted that someone can do things you can't. You don't seem threatened by it, and you just work with it instead of against it."

"Yeah, uh, well, I never thought about it," Brian rambled, still unsure what she meant.

"Like, I mean if you knew there was something wrong between you and another person, you'd tell them, right?"

Lisa's line of questions seemed strange, and Brian couldn't follow the progression at all. Was it about him? Was it about them? What was she talking about?

"Well, uh, you know me and the Brian Adams School of Diplomacy. I just kind of say things without thinking first, but it gets everything out in the open."

"I just don't know if I should tell Mike or not."

"Oh. Ohhhh!" Brian finally grasped what the conversation was really about. Not computer programs, not him. "Why, is there something wrong?"

"We get along pretty good, and I really like him, and like the chemistry is good and all, but I don't know. Something's wrong, and I don't know if I should tell him."

"Why not? I'd tell him. I mean, If I was dating someone. A woman." Brian quickly corrected himself when Lisa's eyes sparkled mischievously. "Open mouth, insert foot." he said ruefully.

"The Brian Adams School of Diplomacy?"

"— and yoga, where your instructor teaches you to get both feet in your mouth at the same time."

"But you really think I should just talk to him about it?"

"First off, I don't know how you two get along together, and I don't really want to. But how can you resolve anything if you can't even talk about it?"

"Sometimes things resolve themselves. Nothing said is better than saying something you shouldn't. I don't know, I guess maybe I romanticized everything too much and now I'm disappointed because it didn't end up exactly like I thought it would."

"Uh, I'm gonna shut my mouth now."

"Do you think I rushed into the relationship?"

"Mmmmmmm." Brian pressed his lips together and put a hand over his mouth.

"You can talk. I don't think you could say anything that would totally shock me."

"In that case, yeah, I think you probably fantasized too much and then found out real life was different. No white knight in shining armor, or hero to sweep you off your feet. Just life."

"Thanks, Brian." Lisa put his hand back over his mouth.

"Mo Probmmmm."

"I just don't want it to end over something stupid."

"That I can identify with." Brian gently pushed away her arm. "You don't want to give up something good just because it didn't go exactly like you planned. You haven't been together that long. How do you know this isn't just some kind of phase?"

"Because every other time I've felt this way things never worked out."

"Did you ever stop and think that maybe the reason things didn't work out is because you never got past feeling like you do with Mike right now? Take it from someone who's done things without thinking them through, rash decisions can get you in to trouble."

"I'm having a hard time respecting him."

"Okay, now that's a different problem. Why? Because now you've got him? The fight is over and you won? You're bored now and looking for something else?'

"It's always been that way." Lisa tried to remember a time when it wasn't.

"Maybe, but it shouldn't always be that way. It's never going to change for you unless you, not someone else, does something different. You'll probably always be smarter and better at most things than the guys you date, so you're the one that has to get past it, not them. Give him a chance. The poor guy gets dumped and then you scoop him off the floor. He's got a long way to go to still. Let him get back up to speed before you kick him. You might get over this, and he might be what you're looking for after all."

"I didn't think you liked him?"

"I don't. He's an jerk. That doesn't change anything."

"You think I should give him another chance?"

"You want my opinion?"

"Yes."

"Don't make it some one chance kinda deal, then you'll just be looking for some excuse to dump him. Give it time, and really try to talk to him and work things out. If he's a jerk, then that's a good reason to quit. If he's cool with it and you can actually talk to him, then you might work things out."

"I'll think about it."

"Yeah, it's not like you're already on the prowl for someone else, are you?"

"No."

"So what do you have to lose by giving him some time." Brian's eyes fixed on the deck. "Whoa, is that supposed to do that?" He pointed at the blinking red box on the screen.

Lisa was all business again.

"It's here, Brian. The virus is here. Someone's been using Pritchett's Skull Walker to transmit." She started running her virus killer through its paces.

"Dang, and if this thing hadn't been shot up we proabbly never would have known."

"The traitor's getting smarter. They knew we wouldn't have access to Pritchett's command robot. Colonel Lyboc knows we're on to him and he's covering himself."

"Except we're gonna kick it this time."

"I really don't think even Pritchett knows he's being messed with. That really was his retreat order last time, but who knows what could have happened."

"What if he does know?'

"He doesn't, or he wouldn't have let you near his Skull Walker. I'm killing the virus." Lisa hit the last key and the sequence began.

"How long will it take you to write up an intercept program?"

"Several hours, even for something as simple as this. Plus I'll need to run a simulation before I try it on the Skull Walker. Could be twelve, fourteen hours."

"Do it. I'll make up something if Pritchett or any of his goons come around to check on us." Brian started climbing out.

"Brian, thanks. For being honest."

"No problem. I don't know any other way."

Seeing the world through the glowing eyes of Torrak made Van extremely grateful he'd chosen Techno-Wizardry over necromancy. The screen in his Mountaineer ATV played out what Torrak was seeing at that very moment, just like a badly edited film. Although the contraption couldn't impart what the subject was thinking, Van got the impression the Gromek Shifter hated every living thing he saw, especially the Elven Mage currently standing in Torrak's way.

Lip reading would have been useful, Van mused as he watched in silence. The Elven Mage he recognized as Credo, and the view narrowed from time to time whenever the Elf spoke. He seemed to enunciate the word Torrak strangely, with a visible emphasis on the latter syllable. He was drawing some type of circle on the ground and seemed to be explaining it to the Gromek. Van leaned closer to the screen and watched intently.

Anja didn't approve of magic "eavesdropping," as she called it, but Van figured what she didn't know wouldn't hurt her, especially regarding the winged Shifter. All afternoon she'd been meditating and wanted to be alone. Her only explanation was that it helped her reach new understandings with the world, and she hoped he would understand that from time to time she needed to be by herself. That, Van understood completely, and left her to it. He would deal with Torrak in his own way.

The Elf was milking a copperhead snake's venom into a glass beaker covered with what looked to be a stretched balloon. Judging from the amount of venom in the beaker, Credo had other snakes and had been working for quite some time. Shaking his head and laughing arrogantly, the Elven Summoner placed the snake back into a cloth sack and then proceeded to pour the venom out along the edges of the circle and across its center. Then, taking a large beaker full of a liquid metal, the Elf poured it into clay molds formed into symbols in two quarters of the circle.

Time was running out on the mystic charge, so Van powered it up for several more minutes by channeling energy from his body into the contraption's crystalline capacitor. The image brightened.

Now the Elf was making some strange hand gestures and appeared to be enticing Torrak to emulate him. Van didn't recall any of the circles he'd read about requiring such obscene movements, but the summoner seemed to be enjoying himself by making Torrak repeat them over and over. Suddenly Credo reached over and yanked a few tiny scales off Torrak's arm. In what looked like a calming gesture, Credo shrugged and stepped back into the circle.

Standing in the center of the circle, Credo appeared disoriented, looking around in his pouches for something. Exasperated, Torrak handed the summoner a pen. Thankful, and once again badly mispronouncing Torrak's name, Credo dipped the pen in a thick gooey metallic solution and started writing on the ground in the circle's center. Credo stood and his mouth moved in chant. The screen went blank.

Evening hours brought a thick mist beneath a darkening sky. Dampness soaked the pages of Kro-Mar's book, finally forcing him to put it back with the others in one of his waterproof bags. He couldn't wait until later that evening when he'd go back into Liberty where his alter ego was a celebrity. If he spent his days in dragon form he could spend his nights as a human and keep up the charade indefinitely, or at least until the humans bored him and then he'd just do what he planned in the first place. Return to his natural dragon form in a crowded area and scare everyone.

Somewhere in the distance the sound of a badly played flute reached Kro-Mar's keen ears. Curious as to who would be bothering the wildlife in the woods at this time of day, Kro-Mar leisurely meandered in the direction of the shrill notes. The tune sounded vaguely like 'she'll be comin' 'round the mountain,' but only vaguely. Kro-Mar cringed as several high pitched tones collided. That flute had to die.

Pushing aside tree branches, Kro-Mar crept closer to the sound. Belly scraping ground and tail lashing in anticipation, he stalked the one responsible for creating a cacophony. The notes stopped. and Kro-Mar froze.

"Hey, man, groovy costume."

Kro-Mar practically flew straight up, snapping branches and letting out a startled yelp that sounded like a rhinoceros. Ten feet away hanging upside down by a tree branch was a wild haired man in psychedelic painted armor. Kro-Mar stared in amazement.

"You wanna dance?" Delwin goaded Kro-Mar.

Kro-Mar roared and smashed a tree next to Delwin.

"Chill with the negative waves, man. Like, be one with nature and the cosmos, man." "Wow," he wheezed. "Wow, that spells MOM upside down. Groovy."

If Kro-Mar was confused before, now it was time to make sure he hadn't been Rifted to a dimension where this kind of thing was normal. He was a powerful dragon capable of mashing this brightly-painted idiot to a pulp. The wild-haired man should be scared for his life and either be fleeing or begging for mercy. Where in this simple equation did something go wrong?

"I am the great and all powerful Kro-Mar! Slayer of mortals and terrorizor of armies! None have stood before the mighty Kro-Mar and lived to tell of it!"

"Well whoopty todooodi woo who!"

"What?"

"Wow, man you got some way righteous colors." Delwin waved his hands at invisible colors of the dragon's aura.

"What's the matter with you? Don't you realize who I am?!" Kro-Mar wasn't angry yet, he was too confused.

"Yeah, man, I know who you are. You're like one of those dragons that breathes fire. I am what you call a Delwin Moonbeam, and I am happy that you and I are now meeting on this beautiful evening." The crazy man extended his hand. Kro-Mar stared at it.

"Why aren't you scared?"

"No, man, I've been Delwin for as long as I've been a Moonbeam. It runs in the family."

"What?"

Delwin cherry-dropped to the ground.

"Wow, man, you look much different now." Delwin tweaked his head from side to side. "How'd you do that?"

"I didn't do anything."

"You want I should make some pretty music?"

"No! No you should not make some pretty music!"

"What should you and I want to do this fine evening?"

"Do?"

"I am feeling like causing mischief. What should we do, my friend?"

The man had to be completely nuts. That in itself Kro-Mar found fascinating, not to mention the prospect of doing something naughty. He was beginning to like the wild-haired man.

"Mischief is good."

"We can find a Splugorth Slaver and tie its tentacles together, then make it chase us."

"Are you crazy!?" Kro-Mar couldn't believe he was hearing this from a human.

"Or trade all the furniture in somebody's house with all the furniture next door."

"He he he he he he."

"Or go paint town hall neon pink."

"You have a good sense of humor."

"Or we could steal the mayor's underwear and run it up the flagpole in town."

"Or run the mayor up the flagpole! He he." Kro-Mar giggled and Delwin went on with infinite possibilities for practical jokes.

For once in his life Kro-Mar forgot all about how superior he was, forgot about all the stuff he wanted, forgot about revenge and forgot about himself. Now he had a little buddy to play with and look out for, and the adventure was only beginning.

Varles Moden was known as "the Splugoth Demon Slaver" to the terrified colonies of the eastern continent, and the name hardly came close to describing the horrors he wrought. Slave raiders from Atlantis had been hitting the eastern part of North and South America for centuries, but Varles was one of the worst. Most slavers preferred to harvest a small percentage of a village or town population and leave the rest as stock to continue breeding. Varles reveled in the blood and gore of senseless slaughter.

Rising in the containment housing that physically linked him to the ornately decorated floating barge, Varles picked one of the weaker looking slaves to hurl the empty skull at. The Techno-Wizard implants throughout his body and head collated the sensory input from five large eyes fused with the barge and five more barrel-sized eyes floating nearby. Watching the slave's horrified expression from three separate angles, Varles purposefully aimed to injure, not kill. He enjoyed his food most when it could still struggle a little.

Towering ten feet above the twenty foot-long barge, Varles was the most fearsome thing any of his captives had ever seen. Magically augmented reflexes combined with heightened awareness kept the slaver at the peak of performance at all times.

The skull shattered the slave's left leg with astounding accuracy. Varles waved his eight tentacles happily and ordered the slave brought to him by one of his favorite warriors.

Hopping the five feet from the barge to the ground, an athletic woman strode into the group of huddled slaves. Though beautiful and well proportioned, all feared the woman almost as much as they did the slaver. She and the three others on the barge had been their captors, taking great delight in abusing any that got out of line. The woman wore a near transparent body suit, accented by jeweled bracelets and a spiked neck collar. Slaves themselves, the Altarain warriors served the slaver's every whim, from birthing to death.

Anisa kicked a slave that strayed too close, taking her time approaching the wounded snack. The man pulled himself away with his arms, hopelessly trying to escape the Warrior Woman. Her distinctive metal boot came down on his other leg and the glimmer of a smile broke her marble features. The metal helmet she wore covered her unseeing eyes, but she needed no vision to feel the pain she inflicted. Much like her demon master, the altarain's body was hyper-aware of the environment, surpassing the need for vision as most beings understood it. What was lacking in sight was more than compensated with her other senses and psychic awareness. Without a word, Anisa grabbed the slave's neck and with an iron grip, left him choking for air. She tossed him onto the barge where Varles' flesh body merged with the synthetic. In an effortless bound she hopped back on the ornately decorated barge and took her place at Varles' side.

Slipping lower into the slime-filled containment of the barge's center, the slaver inspected his dinner with the eye at the tip of his long staff. The symbiotic weapon looked down on the slave with an unblinking stare, what it saw its companion did also. Nearly as large as a human skull, the eye swam in a translucent fluid partly filling the large glass ball at the top of the staff.

"This one has much life in it," the staff purred telepathically.

A symbiotic link made Varles and the staff inseparable. If one died, the other would also. Varles poked at the gasping slave with a giant, clawed finger, trying to make his meal realize what was coming.

"Anisa. prepare my food," Varles ordered the silent Warrior Woman.

Anisa pummelled the slave with her fists and feet in a torrent of fury. Then with a quick fluid motion, she drew her dagger and killer her master's "food" before anybody had realized it had happened.

The other three Altarain Warrior slaves on the barge sat silent and motionless at their appointed places, not having gained favor in Varles' sight. By far, Anisa was the closest to his concept of the perfect slave.

Observing with distracted amusement, Varles moved forward to feast on his "meal". Twisting back and forth in the containment that linked him to the lower barge half of his body, Valres stretched out seldom used muscles that itched for combat. So few villages offered much threat to him and his slave warriors. At times he wished there were more foes worthy of challenging his supernatural powers. Other than one encounter with a mechanized being upon a mechanized mount, his battles had been won much too quickly.

One of the floating eyes watched an approaching Warrior Woman from a distance, zooming in on its own to provide Varles confirmation of identity in the darkness. Unlike the others she wore no thin body suit or slave collar, instead her clothing looked like that of a common wilderness scout with fur trimmed coat and thick, padded leggings. Perhaps the feature that distinguished her most was her long bluish-black hair. Normally Altarain warriors had no hair.

Plodding wearily to her master's barge, Natarsha concentrated on closing her mind to the mental probes the eye staff was sure to use. Guarding her thoughts had kept her alive for the eight months since her birthing. Early on, she volunteered for espionage duties, and was subjected to Bio-Wizard augmentation to make her appear more human to the towns and villages she spied on. Any chance to be away from the barge and Varles was taken, no matter how dangerous or risky. Natarsha hated him and the other Altarain Warriors with a deep burning passion she'd never been able to conceal. Still she obeyed, for death was the only alternative to servitude.

Only once had she contemplated escape, and for those thoughts she received torture that would forever scar her mind, though her body was healed. The scars in her soul went deeper with every village and town she spied on and then returned later to massacre. With every child she killed in its crib and living being executed on Varles' whim, her hatred for him burned hotter and the scars went deeper. Nobody ever escaped the rule of the Splugorth.

Navigating in near total darkness came as easy to altarains as walking in broad daylight did to humans. Vision was a foreign concept to beings that could sense the world around them without it. Touch, scent, sound, and taste filled in where sight was lost. Incredible psychic perception opened another level to the surrounding world. The Splugorth, ancient supernatural beings beyond human comprehension, had genetically altered and bred altarains for thousands of years as expendable warrior slaves. Birthed into captivity until death ended a typically short life of slavery. If Natarsha failed to please her master, another could easily be birthed to replace her.

Even before reaching Varles' barge, Natarsha could feel the intense suffering of the tortured slave and abused captives huddled before it. Anisa was enjoying the powerful emotions like a drug. Natarsha hated it.

Her encounter with the bizarre human that afternoon left her with some very strange impressions. Surrounded by pain and suffering most of her life, it took her completely off guard to be bombarded with new thoughts and emotions. Even brief excursions into villages and towns were full of fear and distrust, then to come back later and experience the hatred and pain during the slaughter only locked away anything meaningful in her life farther behind the iron doors she'd erected to shield herself from the memories. Why had the human with the Coalition power suit been so bold and fearless? He didn't know who or what she was, but even though she'd tried to kill him, there was none of the fear and hate she'd expected. His emotions had been jumbled and confused, but never like anything she'd ever experienced or imagined possible. She'd been acutely aware of his heart beating strongly against her back, another sensation unlike the quick, terrified beat of a heart about to stop. Why did it move her so deeply? Natarsha vowed to keep her questioning thoughts secret. She would probably be punished severely for not killing him anyway.

"You are late," Varles growled. "Explain yourself."

"I am very sorry, master. In order to keep up my disguise and appearance, I must bathe and wash my clothing from time to time. While doing so I encountered a warrior from the Coalition, outside his armor and mechanical suit. I fought with him but he overpowered me. A pair of Melech smelled his blood and he released me in order to escape. After slaying the Melech, I returned as quickly as possible to report this to you, my master."

"You were beaten by a human? A Coalition human!?" Varles snarled. Natarsha bowed her head in shame. "Come here, slave."

Hopping up onto the floating barge, Natarsha tried to keep from touching the blood-caked fixtures and workings. The entire barge reeked of death, as did Varles and the other warriors. Slime dripped from Varles' mouth and fell in a glop near Natarsha. He knew her aversion to the barge and its film of gore. She didn't cringe when a giant tentacle struck her from behind and forced her to her knees in the thickened blood and ooze, nor did she shy away from the device Varles pulled from its special housing on the barge and slowly stroked her face with. The hand-held device sprung open with an awakening cry and living tentacles eagerly reached out for skin to touch and mind to probe. Try as she could, Natarsha couldn't hide her fear of the Bio-Wizard interrogation device. Too many times she'd been subject to its horrid clasp and body-chilling powers. As if he knew how much she detested it, Varles stroked her face just enough for the tentacles to touch her mind and leave their cold imprint. At his command the interrogator could induce levels of pain and torture beyond the physical capacity to endure.

"Do you realize what you've done? You have informed the Coalition of our presence."

"He did not recognize me, master."

"I did not tell you to speak!" Varles clubbed her over the head with the interrogator. A thin line of blood ran down her forehead and across her cheek.

"She speaks with a forked tongue and doesn't say what she does-n't wish us to learn," the staff whispered to Varles' thoughts. "We should kill her and find another more suitable slave to take her place."

"Slave, tell me about this man and how many Coalition soldiers he has with him and I might make your death a shorter one." Varles ignored the symbiont, knowing it could be days, even weeks before he received a replacement spy from Atlantis. He needed knowledge now.

"There was just one. He came in a power suit and left the same way. He spoke of a place called Liberty."

"So the Coalition stretches its muscles and sets its sights on the east coast," Varles mused, thinking of the political power it would earn him to uncover a Coalition plot. "I've heard of the occasional patrol pressing this way, but I wonder if that is the case this time. I believe not."

"Shall I cast an Oracle?" the staff suggested, eye swirling in the sphere to give Varles a view of himself.

"Yes."

White and blue clouds formed where the transparent sphere fused with the staff. Swirling mists began to take shape in Varles' vision to become moving, fighting forms in black armor with the faces of death. Red eyes stared out from death masks and vaguely skeletal skulls. The Coalition soldiers were fighting on foot, and the scene closed in on an oversized suit of armor and a Coalition officer wielding a large plasma cannon. The Coalition attacker fired repeatedly, slaying a Warrior Woman that threw herself in the path to save Varles from the barrage. Sights and sounds of a raging battle swirled all around, but it was unclear who and where they all were. The Co-alition officer charged, leaping at the Oracle view until all that could be seen was the black skull and glowing red eyes. Mist passed before Varles' eyes — all his eyes — and the Oracle ended. Once again the sphere became transparent, the eye swirling down to view the kneel-ing Warrior Woman.

"You have failed in your task and displeased me very much," Varles rumbled. "Someday we must fight the Coalition, a possibility I've wished to endulge but only in the way I choose."

"Kill her, before she betrays us," the staff urged telepathically.

"What should I do to her, Anisa?" Varles asked, not wanting an opinion so much as a voice to make Natarsha fear.

"Torture her, Master, very slowly and painfully until she begs to die, then heal her and start all over again," Anisa chimed in a cold, unemotional tone.

"I've one task for you, Natarsha. If you succeed, I will allow you to live. If you fail, then you die slowly at my whim. Do not forget I can always find you." Varles leaned closer, slime spilling from the containment chamber and sliding onto the barge floor. Silently floating closer, a giant eye much larger than the others aimed an oddly shaped plasma cannon at Natarsha's head.

"Can you identify the man you encountered?"

"If I was near him again, master."

"Find him. Win his trust and steal his knowledge, interrogate him if you wish, but learn how many soldiers are with him and what types of robots he has. I want to know every detail, if he cannot supply that then find another to interrogate until you know everything. High Lord Tole will want to know every detail, and if your report is incomplete I will see to it you are placed in a transmutation chamber and left there for weeks, and whatever creature you've become when you are removed will be tortured slowly and eventually killed. Have I made my threats clear to you, slave?"

"Yes, master."

"And because you've already failed me once, I'm going to give you a taste of what your sweet life will be like if you fail me again." Varles breathed deeply, taking in the intoxicating aroma of fear as he lowered the interrogator to Natarsha's face. "Not a sound. Not one sound. If you so much as whimper we will start all over again."

Zenjori rubbed tired eyes and slowly stepped down from his command vehicle. Cold, damp air pervaded everything and made his joints ache in the morning. Being awakened at the crack of dawn didn't lift his spirits either, not after a long night of vigilant supervision of his army's placement. Zenjori didn't want or need a crisis.

"What's the problem this time, Kruno?" Zenjori walked up to the commander of Carnivore squad.

Notec Depi stood close by, vigilant of possible attacks on the mercenary leader. Already one death had slipped past the psychic's security measures, a death he'd for some reason not foreseen.

"Mornin' boss. I ain't sure it's so muchava problem, though."

"Then why did you wake me?!" Zenjori lost his usual composure.

"J.J. found somethin' this mornin' ya might be interested in lookin' at. Him an' Trench is lookin' 'round for that Elf right now."

"Kruno, are you going to keep standing there jabbering like a moronic hillbilly or are you going to tell me what you thought was so important that I needed to be roused from some much needed sleep?" Zenjori clipped abruptly, fighting to control his temper.

"I'll do better than that, boss, I'll show ya."

Zenjori gave Notec a nod of acknowledgement, then the three walked in near silence down a steep slope to a thick grove of trees. Somehow Kruno's spitting tobacco at every passing insect got on Zenjori's nerves more than it ever had before. It seemed reasonable to simply strike out from behind and kill the mercenary for the slightest offense.

"Better watch your head, boss," Kruno pointed up at the branches overhead. "This whole bunch of trees is 'fested with birds."

Hundreds of birds perched in the branches of the grove. Zenjori hardly took notice.

"That's infested, you idiot."

"That's what I said. Well there you have it. One dead D-Bee." Kruno pointed to a body laying next to a circle on the ground.

Zenjori stepped around the mercenary into the small clearing at the grove's center.

"Mornin' mate, guess we're too late for this 'un, eh?" J.J. greeted Zenjori cheerfully. Other than severely damaged armor, the Juicer seemed not the least bit worse for wear.

"What happened to Torrak?" Zenjori stared at the dead Shifter and the body of his vulture draped at his feet.

"Best we can tell that Elf wasted him an' moved his body here." Trench spat in the tracks around the circle. "No marks on the body, or that bird thing at his feet. They're both just D-E-D, dead."

"Yeah, weren't offed here, someone dragged 'em here," J.J. seconded cheerfully. "Just found 'em layin' next to that circle, 'long with all them flocks there." He waved his arm at the birds, but none flew at his urging.

"Credo. That damned Elf did this," Zenjori cursed.

"Who's Credo?"

"The Elf's real name, J.J."

"Oh. We found this note tacked on the body." J.J. waved a small paper. "Everything else is gone."

"What does it say?"

"Dunno, mate. Ain't real good at readin'"

"Give it to me." Zenjori reached up and snatched the paper away. The writing was surprisingly legible, in perfect standard American. Zenjori shot J.J. a look of scorn.

"What's it say?" Trench crowded closer.

"Peter Piper picked a peck of pickled peppers." Zenjori shrugged and read on. "If Peter Piper picked a peck of pickled peppers, how many pickled peppers did peter piper pick?"

"I don't git it," Kruno rubbed his bald head.

"It's a stupid tongue twister riddle." Zenjori waved the paper.

"I get it it. I know! A peck!" Trench answered the rhyme.

Suddenly the paper in Zenjori's hand burst into flame and turned to ash. The sounds of hundreds of birds flapping wings and taking flight reached their ears as wave after wave of them descended on Torrak's corpse. Hundreds of birds tore at Torrak's flesh and pecked thousands of holes in his deceased body. Kruno laughed a deep, hearty laugh.

"It's a joke! It's that Elf's idea of a joke! Get it? Peck?" The big mercenary nearly doubled over with laughter.

Zenjori didn't share the mirth.

"J.J.! I want you to track down that Elf mage and bring me back his head!"

"I dunno, Suka San." J.J. scratched the back of his head.

"For this Gromek I couldn't care less! But I will not be mocked! Twenty-five thousand credits! I want his head on a stake, you understand!?"

"It is kinda funny, Suka San. 'Sides, that Elf ain't no easy kill."

"Fifty thousand credits! Double that if you bring him back alive so I can make him pay!"

Zenjori grabbed J.J.'s drug injection harness to emphasize his point. Carefully and deliberately, the Juicer removed Zenjori's hands from the harness.

"I think I got ya now, mate. 'Scuse me." J.J. stepped back and casually walked from the grove, stopping just long enough at the armory vehicle to properly arm himself for an extensive journey. Since he'd signed on as a sniper and assassin for the Army of the New Order, J.J. never once witnessed the company commander lose his temper. In spite of all the ups and downs, the mercenary army had always been well-managed, and Zenjori Suka had always maintained a level of self-control that demanded respect. Until today.

He found Kreg sleeping soundly under the sleeping protection of another sentry. A swift blow the sentry's head ensured he would be sleeping awhile longer. The Glitter Boy stood without its pilot ten feet away. Silently the augmented assassin crept up to Kreg's mat and reached through the mosquito netting. J.J. pressed the button marked play on Kreg's walkman and tweaked the volume to full.

"Ahhhh!" Kreg threw the headphones off and sat up.

"Sorry, mate, didn't mean to startle ya."

"What the hell, J.J.?!" Kreg rubbed tired eyes and tried to smooth away wild hair.

"Listenin' ta more of that long hair music 'for ya went to sleep?"

"Yes, but not at 190 decibels!"

"Guess you've neva' been to a real rock concert."

"Just because you never sleep doesn't mean the rest of us don't." Kreg turned down the volume and put the headphones back on. Something about the juicer's gaze kept him from laying back down and going to sleep. Kreg pushed aside the mosquito netting.

"Never listen to much 'cept rock-n-roll, ya know?"

"Nothing wrong with rock and roll," Kreg said wearily. "But there was better music long before that. Ever hear of Tchaikovsky, Dvorak, Mozart, Beethoven?"

"Ah, Beethoven. He played some good rock-n-roll."

"Beethoven? He'd roll over in his grave to hear that. He was from the classical period, almost forgotten in Pre-Rifts time, and even more now."

"Some things ya just gotta forget."

"Why did you wake me up? It's too damned cold out to be talking music," Kreg grumbled.

"Juss thought I'd tell ya good-bye, I guess."

"Where are you going?"

"Don't matter much, just so's I'm not 'round here anymore. If you've got any sense you'll clear out while ya got the chance. Come with me, if ya want. Suka's flipped his lid, ya know."

"You're deserting?"

"Call it a career change. I got 'bout two, maybe three years left outta life 'fore all the chems get me, an' I don't want ta spend it workin' for no crazy man. Just thought I'd warn ya to git out while the gettin's good."

"I can't do that, J.J. You're my friend, and I'm not going to say anything, but I can't just leave. Zenjori's the only person who ever believed in me. I could have run out back in Free Quebec, and maybe I should have, but I don't have any place to go. If you want to leave, go ahead. I'm staying."

"Too bad." J.J. leveled his particle beam pistol at Kreg's head. "It's not personal."

"I thought you were my friend."

"Assassin's rule #1: Assassins don't have friends."

J.J. clicked off the safety, holding the aim steady but hesitating to fire. Kreg sighed, knowing he was dead. J.J. Suddenly put the pistol back in its holster and walked away, turning once and winking at the pale-faced pilot.

"Never was much good at either."

Free at last. Free from Torrak's constant bungling. Free of the mindless, unfocused agression and no outlet to direct it at. Free of the Gromek's failed ambition. Mind Crusher hummed happily at Credo's side. At last, one who could use his powers to the fullest and would feed him with the souls of many slain in ice cold blood. The future looked promising for his new wielder. In time the two would become forever linked, or at least until a better wielder came along. Mind Crusher recalled every one of its owners, although time was meaningless to the entity trapped within the rune mace. Credo would do very nicely, for now, but only for a lifetime.

Chapter 15

Gravel crunched under Greg's feet as he leisurely strolled down a logging road north of Liberty. The gravel was crushed waste of concrete and asphalt left over from Pre-Rifts times and was put to good use in the post-apocalyptic world. The recycled road surface helped during the icy winter months when giant logging trucks made the route despite the weather. Greg didn't know how far out of town he'd walked, but it was dusk now and the lights from a logging camp ahead were starting to shine in the distance. He cursed himself for not waring armor. The C-18 and MP-10 on opposing hips could handle most minor threats, but his newly purchased black trench coat and civilian dress wouldn't stop a bullet, much less the razor-sharp claws of some monster. Most of the logging trucks he'd seen that afternoon had at least one armed rider in case of trouble, and the actual logging sites he'd passed used giant robots for much of the labor, that doubled as defense against roving monsters from the wilderness. Liberty usually had advance warning of any sizable attacks coming the town's way, so Greg took solace in the fact that very few large monsters got past the outlying logging industry without detection.

He'd spent all morning with Sergeant Winters making sure his unit was ready to move out at a few minutes' notice. Even Pritchett had become obsessed with battle readiness and, to Greg's surprise, intended to lead a full scale assault against the Army of the New Order. Intelligence reports were incomplete, but definitely indicated the enemy was much stronger now. Dave and Darren's run-in with the enemy convoy the day before provided him with information he needed about the opposition air power. What worried Greg was the ease with which his two best RPA's managed to elude and damage a greater number of fast attack craft. It seemed as if Zenjori was daring the Coalition to attack. Any assault would be premature until he could determine what his unit was up against.

Then there was Brian and Lisa. He knew the two of them were up to something the second they started giving Pritchett a line of technical bull about 'the quad BCI tri-valve T66 plasma converting magnifier being out of sync with the electromagnetic induction field' in his Skull Walker. Supposedly, Pritchett's command robot would be fully operational by morning so the captain could lead the Coaition into battle with his one-eyed vehicle. Whatever the two technical officers were up to, he'd find out before they embarked at 1000 hours the next morning, just in case it was something that might get everyone killed. A little creative intimidation and pretending to know more than one did worked wonders from time to time.

Stumbling on a protruding root, Greg stopped long enough to fish a multi-optics band out of his coat pocket. Like a thick pair of seg-mented sunglasses, the bands were designed for use at night. Stopping once more to button up his coat, Greg heard another step taken in the gravel, a step he didn't take. Casually dropping the optics band over his eyes, he panned back up the road with light intensifica-tion. At first he didn't catch it, but on his second sweep he noticed a shadow that shouldn't have been there.

Continuing on down the road, he loosened the coat but didn't bla-tantly reach for his guns. If he was being followed, who or whatever it was might rush the attack if discovered. Greg turned the nob on the eye band to thermo-imaging and slowly looked back over his shoul-der while he walked. A human shaped heat signature stalked the edge of the road two hundred feet behind him. There was too much heat for body armor so he slid his hand over the MP-10. No sense vaporiz-ing whoever it was when wounding was an option.

Headlights from the last logging truck of the day splashed across the tree-line and then flooded the road. Hurling himself to the brush at the side of the road, Greg waited for the rumbling sixteen wheeled vehicle to make its crawl up the hill. His pursuer had taken conceal-ment behind a leafy bush at the side of the road still some two hun-dred feet away. Turning the optics band back to light amplification, he cursed his stupidity as the band cut out to prevent being fried by the abundance of light. If he could just get close enough to get a good shot off he was certain he could place a bullet to wound. If he missed the first shot, well, that's what fully automatic weapons fire was for.

The logging truck rolled closer, on its back several large tree trunks. Waiting until the heavy vehicle blocked the space between himself and his pursuer, he sprinted to match pace with the wheels and ducked under the protruding tree trunks to the other side of the road. Letting the noise of the vehicle cover his approach, Greg ran alongside the vehicle until he was closer to the heat signature, ready to duck back behind the logging vehicle and take the figure by surprise. He drew his gun, finger steady on the trigger and heart pounding with excitement, senses alert and muscles ready for action.

Moving unexpectedly, the form slipped away and back down the road, Greg doubling back and pushing to a sprint just to keep up. He almost got to within tackling range, but the heat signature went faster. Dropping to one knee, Greg fired the MP-10 at the running legs. The bullets showed up like tracers on the heat scan and disintegrated in tiny white auras about the lower half of the running form.

"What the ...?" Greg flipped the optics band to light amplification. Running down the road was a slim form in a dark fur-trimmed coat and hood. How could he have missed?

"Stop there or I'll shoot you in the back!" he shouted, flipping the selector to fully automatic.

The running figure slowed to a full stop. Greg stood and cautiously walked forward, looking around quickly to make sure he wasn't surrounded. As he moved closer he could make out the shape of a sword across the figures back. He stopped ten feet away.

"Turn around and keep your hands where I can see them."

In the green shine of the night-vision optics, Greg looked at the face beneath the hood. Finely carved features and a pair of soulful eyes looked back, the eyes not focusing on him in the dark.

"Natarsha? What are you doing here?"

She pulled the hood back, Greg twitching at the trigger as for moment he thought she was reaching for the blade. Her hair was tied back in a braid and fell down her back inside the coat. Greg looked around one more time just in case this was a trap.

"I followed you."

"Over eighty miles on foot since yesterday? Chasing down my SAM? I don't think so."

A spotlight from the logging truck swiveled back towards them. Apparently his gunshots had been heard over the sound of the engine. Greg stepped back to a tree trunk and pulled the blanked goggles from his head. The spotlight panned across Natarsha then swung back and narrowed on her. She stared straight ahead, oblivious to the glare.

"Hey, get out of the light."

Natarsha stepped closer than Greg wished and forced him back into the woods off the road. He'd seen her move fast before and didn't want to find his own gun aimed at him. The spotlight went dark and the sound of the vehicle lessened as it topped the rise and continued on the other side. Greg chanced placing the goggles back in his pocket and relied on his natural sight.

"There's no way you followed me from the river. How did you find me?"

"You spoke of Liberty. I came to find you," she spoke solemnly with an accent Greg still couldn't place.

"Why?"

"My village was burned to the ground and my people killed by monsters." Natarsha used her most convincing and rehearsed story line. "I have no place to go."

"Bull. Even I couldn't run eighty miles in thirty hours over terrain like that, and if I could, I wouldn't follow the person I tried to kill the day before. Try again," Greg snapped without thinking first.

"I, I wanted to apologize," Natarsha stammered out a practiced line very poorly. This was confusing her. He obviously didn't know who she really was, and deep down was enjoying the risk this confrontation came with. Her usual lines weren't going to work. She'd try something else before resorting to violence. Killing him would be too simple. She needed information.

"I, I am sorry I attacked you."

"Apology accepted. My apologies for rudely interrupting whatever you were doing buck naked in a freezing cold river. Now tell me why you're really here. You're a D-Bee, right?"

"I prefer Dimensional Being," she retorted hesitantly, remembering something she'd overheard at a village she'd spied on months earlier.

"Don't get ruffled. No racial slur intended. It's called slang," Greg chuckled. Somehow it didn't bother him one bit that she wasn't human. All the lessons and years of military indoctrination had gone out the window. This was all new and exciting.

"You can put that away. I am not going to hurt you."

"Glad to hear that. My face is still sore from yesterday," Greg laughed, never lowering the weapon from the target. "You want to start telling me the truth? Who sent you?"

Natarsha searched for something convincing to say but kept coming up with stupid questions instead. She could feel his distrust, but there was no anger or hatred with it. It would be too bad if he gave her no choice but to proceed with interrogation.

"I can not tell you what you want to know. That is all I can say. Accept it."

"Okay, for now." Greg carefully put his gun back in its holster. The danger was intoxicating him like a drug.

"I have come to warn you to leave this area at once," Natarsha blurted out without thinking, partly from sincerity and in part to win his confidence.

"Me? Why?"

"You and all the other Coalition soldiers. There is a threat that even a whole platoon of your men could not kill."

"Sounds interesting. Tell me more." Greg grinned, his mind made razor sharp by the possibility of death. Whatever her game was, he'd play it for all it was worth. This was fun, and besides, he couldn't remember the last time he'd spent time with someone unrelated to the military. Dangerous or not, she still had a powerful allure.

Natarsha took a step closer, still unsure if she should incapacitate him or not. The heat of his body reached her from the nearness.

"If the Coalition were to defeat this monster, it would. . . .." Natarsha bit her lip, horrible memories of past torture imposing on her present thoughts. She was torn between hurting and helping him.

"Let me guess. It would free you of his tyranny and you would be forever in my debt," Greg finished her speech in words she might actually have meant. Her expression darkened.

"You are mocking me." She stepped closer.

"No, but you're not giving me anything believable to go on. If you really needed help to free your village, why come to me?" Greg asked seriously.

"You are not afraid."

"Should I be?"

262

"Yes."

"Why?"

"Stop that!" She stepped so close she could hear his heartbeat and feel the warmth of his body. Her intent had been to knock him unconscious and drag him back to Varles, but she faltered. She could sense his features better now, somewhat fuzzy with the dense facial growth. The scent of new clothes and gun oil mixed with the stronger scent she'd followed. His heartbeat focused in her ears, a reminder of their first encounter. Natarsha knew she should strike him down. She didn't know anything else.

"You're beautiful."

Natarsha's hard expression changed to one of confusion. An almost dazed look followed. This man was crazy. She was wasting her time on this one. She'd have to find another Coalition officer to interrogate. This one didn't make sense.

"What are you saying?" she asked slowly.

"It's a compliment. You are beautiful."

"Not important."

"Sure it is. Are you hungry?"

"What?" She could hear the crisp sounds of some type of paper being torn.

"Hungry. As in food. You do eat?" Greg broke off part of a candy bar and held it closer to his face.

A foreign scent wafted past, enticing hunger she'd been ignoring.

"Yes. I eat," she snapped.

"Want some chocolate power bar?" Greg watched her expression carefully.

"Okay." She took it gingerly and nibbled a bite. It tasted sweet. Sweeter than any wild berry or fruit.

"You've never tasted chocolate before, have you?"

"No."

"Cake? Ice cream? Hot apple pie, microwave dinners?"

"No."

"Ever want to try?"

"That is not possible." She tried to focus on her mission. At least she'd won his confidence, she consoled herself, even if it meant doing the unexpected. If he didn't work out, he might lead her to a Coalition officer that would, and of course the prospect of new adventure had its appeal. Natarsha took her first full taste of chocolate. Greg beamed happily.

"You're trying something new for the first time. Take a chance. Experience new things."

"There is not enough time."

"I'm not doing anything important right now, are you?" Greg didn't wait for an answer. "It's a long walk back to Liberty, but nothing for someone who came over eighty miles in just about a day, right?"

"You must promise not to speak of this meeting."

"Who's going to believe me? This type of thing only happens in books and vids, not real life. You have heard of vids, books?"

"I, do not read." Natarsha almost gave up the truth.

"That's fine, most of my men can't either. I'm sure I can find a book or two in town to read to you."

"Good." Was all Natarsha could think of to say. The two edged back onto the road and walked side by side in wary companionship. On level ground Greg estimated her height at about 5'10'' and a full six inches shorter than him. On the other hand he'd seen her without the bulk of clothing, and knew the height was well proportioned and tightly muscled, very much how he preferred his women, not that there had been many.

"What do you do? For a living?"

"I'm a scout."

"Wonderful! I've been needing to hire a scout for a certain job." Greg watched her face for a reaction. It remained an expressionless marble mask.

"What type of job?"

"I'll tell you all about it." He handed over the other half of the chocolate bar.

Natarsha took it with much less trepidation. This was going to be her most treacherous mission ever.

"Stop staring. You look like an idiot." Nim nudged Cowboy.

The big soldier pretended he hadn't been looking in Rachel Brown's direction.

"I wasn't staring."

"Wipe your chin,.." Nim continued. "You're drooling."

"It's okay to talk to her," Bill assured him.

"You could go check her weapon again," Trenton suggested.

"Shut up. That's too obvious."

Rachel sat on the edge of Cowboy's hover rover and pretended not to overhear the conversation twenty feet away. All around there was excited chatter about the upcoming battle, everywhere but the group of four sitting on the fallen log by the road. They were all moving out from Liberty and making a one day trek north before assaulting an army more than twice their size. Pritchett's troops roamed about aimlessly, waiting to begin the dangerous journey while non-commissioned officers continued last minute checks of inventory and personnel. Finished with their preparatory responsibilities, Cowboy's friends tried to encourage the lovesick Corporal to show some courage off the battlefield.

"It's not like you don't know her, man. It's been over a month since she transferred from General Underhill's division. She probably knows by now."

"I've talked to her before," Cowboy defended his manhood.

"Yeah, if you call barking orders and runnin' drills talking," Nim responded sarcastically.

"Well if you don't wanna, I will," Bill threatened. "I can definitely go for the amazon type. Short brown hair, tall, buff. Look what you'd be missing."

"Cowboy's probably afraid she'll kick his tail," Trenton joked.

"I am not."

"Or maybe he's afraid Rachel's partner, Mathis, will punch his lights out." Nim untactfully jerked his mechanical thumb at the other CR-1 rocket team member.

Mathis tried not to turn his head at the sound of his name, sharing a hidden smile with Rachel instead. He almost matched Cowboy for height, but had definite African ancestry and a boxer's physique. It would be a close fight if Cowboy took the rhetorical challenge literally.

"All right. Lay off. I'll think of somethin'." Cowboy stood, gathering his courage. His three friends started a not so quiet cheer. "Shut up, I'm going."

"Corporal Wesley Nelson!?" Captain Pritchett yelled across the staging area and strode briskly in Cowboy's direction. "Corporal Wesley Nelson, correct?"

"Yes, sir." Cowboy squeaked out. His squad stifled giggles.

"Corporal, where are Sergeant Winters and Lieutenant Merrick?" Pritchett came to a halt before the shame-faced NCO.

"Sergeant Winters and Lieutenant Merrick are over there." Trenton pointed to a small group in the distance. He didn't appreciate having his rank ignored by the captain, even if it did give them all something else to kid Cowboy about.

"Yeah, over by those scouts. Sir," Cowboy seconded.

"Thank you Corporal, Sergeant." Pritchett nodded to Trenton and strode off purposefully with Sharky slithering behind.

"Wesley?" Nim spoke the name with a questioning look.

"You never told us your name was, Wesley," Bill chuckled.

"Corporal Wesley Nelson," Trenton chortled in metallic tones.

"Shut up! I didn't choose it, my parents did. I'll kick your ass if you keep callin' me that."

"Sure thing, Wesley." Bill dodged Cowboy's foot.

"You guys aren't ever gonna let me live this down," Cowboy mumbled and started walking away.

"Ohhhh Wesssley!" Rachel called out sweetly. "Come check my weapon sights again?"

Captain Pritchett focused on one thing, oblivious to the trail of embarrassment he'd sent Cowboy down. It was 10:15 and they weren't under way yet, over an hour behind schedule. He wanted to know what the delay was. For some reason he was feeling an unexplainable urge to make the attack.

Several members of First Strike gathered around Greg and Sergeant Winters, giving grunts of acknowledgment to Pritchett and leers of disdain to the bald Psi-Stalker on his heels. Pritchett noticed how un-regulation Lieutenant Merrick looked, and the haggard unshaven features that did not become an officer.

"Lieutenant, what's the holdup?"

"Intel. The schedule can wait. We're not engaging the enemy until I know exactly where they are and how to hit their defenses."

"I thought you and Lieutenant Sorenson already knew all that. Let's go."

"If you want to leave, go right ahead."

"You'll probably git 'tacked by a sploogie," A grizzled scout with one eye advised the captain, displaying rows of crooked teeth set in a scarred face.

"According to several trappers that just came in from Finton, there's something called a Splugorth slaver out there someplace. I haven't the faintest idea what that is, but it's bad," Greg translated. The grizzled scout nodded vigorously. "First Strike's got too many things to cover here to send out a force to attack this thing, so we need to be extra careful out there."

"Where's Lieutenant Sorenson? He's your specialist, what's his opinion?" Pritchett looked around for the other officer.

"Not here." Winters grunted.

"He's out scouting for a good base camp to stage our attacks from. Donnovan's scouts found us the exact location of Zenjori's army, and say he's entrenched in a good place. We have a preliminary count on his infantry." Greg nodded to the First Strike scouts and thanked them by name. Pritchett shifted impatiently.

"Then, assuming we leave now, we can make camp and assault first thing at dawn tomorrow."

"Like hell," Winters growled.

"We don't have enough intel for an effort. First we learn more, then we attack. No discussion," Greg stated.

"Fine. What are you doing about getting it?"

· "I've hired four local area scouts to get us to and from Zenjori's position without snags, plus to recon and assess the enemy position once we arrive."

"Do you trust the word of the locals?"

"No, not particularly, that's why I hired four and sent Sharp ahead to make his own report. If all the intel doesn't add up, I know who's lying." Greg smiled, wondering how Natarsha's report would compare. "Plus I plan to take a small squad in for a look around and confirmation."

"Well I'm trusting your experience to get us in and out as smoothly as possible," Pritchett spoke his confidence inspiring tone. Greg regarded him warily. "Keep up the good work, Lieutenant."

"Sure."

"I'll be in my Skull Walker when you're ready to leave." Pritchett left Sharky standing by himself until the Psi-Stalker realized his commander was gone.

The one eyed scout laughed heartily at the comical sight.

"Your captain is an idiot," the wolf-like D-Bee scout at Greg's left commented.

"I think I could be convinced to go along with that, my friend." Greg patted the D-Bee on the shoulder.

"Why do you take orders from him?"

"Rank."

"Rank? Is that the reason you follow a fool? Maybe it's time for a shuffling of the ranks."

"You know, Gammund, I think you have a point. Gammund has a good point, doesn't he, Jerry?"

"Hmmf." Winters grunted, disliking more and more the casual associations of his friend. But the D-Bee did have a point. "Give me the word and when Pritchett goes for his morning crap, he don't come back."

Brushing aside wild flowers to get a better view of the city ruins, Sharp nestled lower to the ground and hoped his jet pack wasn't sticking up above the hedge of shrubs. He could hear Darren's

SAMAS somewhere nearby and distinguished the sounds of a hover rover coming from the valley leading into the ruins. The sun was blocked by clouds and reduced the contrast in his view finder. His unit would be passing through the overgrown ruins shortly and Cowboy's hover rover was making the first sweep just in case there was more to the ruins than met the eye. Merrick didn't like sending the entire force anywhere with blinders on.

Rising lines of smoke in two places from the ruins meant there were a few semi-intelligent inhabitants, the smoke consistent with the type of small cooking fires a tiny nomadic band or group of primitives might use. On closer magnification the two smoke lines led back to two small, apparently abandoned camps. Dense overgrowth in the ruins obscured most of the view, but Sharp was fairly convinced neither camp slept more than a dozen. Just nomads, D-Bees, or primitives trying to survive in the wastelands.

"Sharp to Crawl 1. Looks clear."

"Roger that. Nothin' goin' down." Cowboy worked the rover's radio with one hand and played with his C-27 in the other. Bill stood in the rear and leaned on the heavy C-40 mounting. It had all been too long since they'd blown some monster or D-Bee to smithereens.

Sharp swept back and forth across the rough remains of the Pre-Rifts city. Vegetation made outline patterns of the old roadways. At one point in the past decade a fierce battle had been fought in one quarter of the city. The devastation pattern suggested a large group had surrounded and pulverized a smaller group taking cover in a standing structure. The misshapen center was just starting to grow back over small craters and strafing scars. Fallen trees and dead timber extended half a mile from the center, new growth taking the place of the old.

"This place is dangerous," a female voice whispered in Sharp's right ear. Sharp nearly popped straight up out of the bushes. Crouched beside him was a woman with a braid of blue hair and beige colored coat. Lieutenant Merrick had warned him to be on the look out for the new scout. She hadn't made one hostile move and Sharp felt intimidated by her.

"Don't sneak up on people like that. They might think you're going to do something unhappy to them."

"There is a dangerous being down there in the ruins waiting to kill your advance group," Natarsha whispered.

"Where? Tell me where it's at?" Sharp set the AQ-3 on high resolution.

"It will look like the rest of the forest except when it moves. It is large, twenty feet. It can be seen by the heat it gives off," Natarsha continued, feeling phantom pain from Varles' brutal torture wrack her body. She couldn't allow it to prevent her betrayal.

"Where? Where is it?"

"I do not know. It is too far away. Tell your advance group to change course. Tell your Lieutenant."

"Not until I know what's down there."

"I can not help you more than this," she clipped and slid away silently.

An uneasiness churned in Sharp's stomach. If she'd wanted to kill him she could have done it already. He felt as though he was being watched, but forced himself to begin a thermal scan of the city ruins. Living things popped up everywhere and grew in number every time he increased magnification. Living things of all types showed up as warm spots in a swimming pool of cooler colors. Larger ones stood out against the background and once he passed a humanoid shape running along with the wildlife and not disturbing a single animal.

"This is stupid. I don't even know what I'm looking for," Sharp thought out loud. "Which are monsters and which are just stupid animals?"

Something big passed through the image in his HUD. Sharp panned back and dropped magnification a notch.

"Sharp to Crawl 1. Back off now. Big bad monster 'bout the size of a house and three humanoids waiting in ambush ahead of you."

"We can take 'em."

"I have a bad feeling about this one, partner. This is not a happy monster."

Sharp enhanced the image and saw tentacles appear behind the heat-defined shape of Varles. The lower half of the creature met with a semi-warm base or hovercraft that seemed to float above the ground without disturbing a leaf or twig. The three humanoid forms moved silently through the fallen buildings and overgrowth.

"Merrick to Sharp. Where is the creature in relation to our planned course?"

"It's sitting on it."

"We can't afford a battle right now. Crawl 1, backtrack half a mile and proceed to point WP-14 by way of the river through west quad 19."

"Okay, sir, Crawl 1 out." Cowboy slammed the microphone down on the dash. "Where are we on the map?"

"I think we're someplace in east quad 4." Nim played with the map display, checking the waypoint path to find out where WP-14 was.

"Turn around," Cowboy ordered Cody, the rover's driver.

"We're not fighting?" Rachel pressed forward, bumping soldiers with the CR-1.

"Merrick says no showdown."

"Okay, now we're in east quad 4," Nim relayed happily.

The hover rover blew debris around its wake as it swung back on ground it had just covered.

"That wasn't there before." Bill pointed to a purple mist drifting over their path. The air around them rang out with high pitched war cries from all around. Things were moving behind every collapsed wall and overgrown tree.

"Go!" Cowboy shouted and the rover plunged into the purple mist.

Toxic filters kicked in to prevent poisonous vapors from penetrating full environmental armor. The cheers suddenly became angry, high pitched shouts. Dozens of tiny black things scurried out of hiding. Nobody waited for the order to fire. Destroying virtually everything in a radius from the craft the troops fired at anything that moved or might hide something that moved. Caught in their prank the tiny beings fled for their lives amid razed vegetation and descending ruins. Bill pursued one across barren ground with a steady stream of slugs from the mounted rail gun. Passing through the purple mist, advance team Crawl 1 emerged unscathed from the faeries' trap.

"Yeee Haw!" Cowboy cheered.

Leaping from an overhanging tree, a tiny black Bogie bounced off Cowboy's armor and landed on the dash. It popped up and bared its teeth, insect-like head snarling threats.

"Get it off there!" Cody did his best to keep it away as it scurried across the dash.

"Little piece of dirt," Cowboy muttered and smashed it up against the wind screen with his rifle's bayonet. The high frequency blade punctured the Bogie's hard exoskeleton and notched a mark in the windscreen behind it. Aiming the gun and Bogie away from the rover, Cowboy blasted it off the bayonet. The Bogie's scream ended abruptly in a descending charcoal fireball.

Once again, and to Greg's astonishment, Captain Pritchett acceded to the more experienced officer and gave over full control of the base camp security measures. After three tours of the camp perimeter, two equipment checks, and once over the provisions, Greg was reasonably sure the camp and coffee were secure. All robots and power armor were set to passive scans with no active radar for missiles to home in on. At ten miles from the enemy's position, either side was capable of taking advantage of the other's errors.

Action followed action without much time for reflection until the security task was complete. Greg's mind kicked back into its search for purpose now that the matter of survival was resolved. Destroying the Army of the New Order and retrieving the stolen data was unquestionably the objective. Greg couldn't seize motivation to drive himself to accomplish it, and without self-motivation he couldn't expect to inspire his troops. It was all like acting out a meaningless ritual.

Distant waves from a sonic boom rolled above the tree tops.

"Merrick to Skull 41. Who's being shot at?" He asked into his wrist comp.

"Darren," Lisa responded as if Greg should already know.

"Tell him to back off and not provoke anything."

"Yes, sir."

"Is Brian up there with you?"

"Right here, sir," Brian yelled from Cowboy's hover rover twenty feet away.

"No, sir," Lisa answered.

"Never mind, I found him." Greg marched to the rover, jumping a small fall-back trench to get there. Cowboy and Sharp sat in the rover playing cards and discussing the last western vid they'd watched.

"You need something, sir?" Brian looked up from his task.

"I want five type 1 fusion blocks set with remote detonators and a silencer for this. By tonight." Greg handed over his MP-10.

Brian dropped the clip and ejected the round already in the chamber before examining the weapon closer.

"Don't you ever clean this thing?"

"It's a Wellington caseless. I'm not supposed to clean a caseless, am I?"

"Caseless or not, you still need to run a bore brush down it after you're done shooting, and it wouldn't hurt to break it down for a good cleaning every three or four hundred rounds. You could get a misfire with this, maybe even a chain fire or barrel jam."

"I ran a box of 500 rounds through it getting used to the feel."

"Yeah, you'll want to clean it more often. Bullet throwers can be a pain in the rear sometimes, but they're pretty simple." Brian reloaded it and set the gun on the rover's hood. With a black bandana he tied his wild hair out of his eyes.

"Can you make the silencer?"

"10 mm's a cinch. I can screw mount it with a length of tubing and jury-rig something. How quiet do you want it?"

"Quiet enough to press against someone's back and not be heard twenty feet away."

"It's still going to make some noise, no matter what. I can make it quiet, but you're gonna be carrying a silencer four to six inches in diameter and about a foot long. If you'd asked before we left I could have made a good one, but out here I'm going to half to jury rig something. I'll have to drill holes in a metal tube and then pack it with insulation from a grenade case. You'll get about six or seven shots before the powder cruds up the sound holes and you gotta repack it."

"Never mind." Greg took the weapon back. "I'll use a Vibro-Knife."

"What do you need the fusion blocks for?"

"Recon. If the opportunity presents itself for sabotage I want to have the option available."

"We have type 2's and type 3's, but no type 1's. Nobody ever wants them.

"Figures." Greg glanced over at Cowboy's squad.

"If you don't mind my asking, sir, didn't you hire scouts for recon?" Brian continued working on repairing a patch of damaged body armor.

"The scouts may prove unreliable. They've all reported similar accounts of Zenjori's position and strength, but each had a different opinion about where he'd placed several power suits and cyborg units. Plus, nobody's found the Glitter Boy or the X-1000. An assault is too risky at this point." Greg leaned on the hood and absent-mindedly toyed with the power cord leading to Brian's tool.

"That's not helping."

"Sorry. Oh, I also need more of those laser targeting mechanisms and two more sets of multi-optics goggles."

"That's Lisa's department. What exactly are you planning?"

"Zenjori picked a reasonably defendable position on a bluff overlooking a small river and two creeks, covering three sides. The only way to reach the bluff is to cross the water and then fight an uphill battle. The fourth side is a steep, rocky embankment my scouts tell me is impossible for our robot units to ascend and just as bad for infantry in full armor. That leaves Zenjori with three zones to defend, assuming we had the men to lay a siege on that many fronts."

"What if a squad were to climb up the backside and pull their armor up behind them with ropes." Brian suggested.

"The sentries would have to be taken out first, and it still leaves the squad in a dangerous spot if discovered."

"The SAM's could cover them."

"Only if there was a force keeping Zenjori committed to defending the other three sides and we'd already established complete air superiority. Keep the ideas rolling, I'd rather not do the head-butt thing."

"No ore transports this time."

"Not this time," Greg laughed. "We're going for the subtle approach. Lieutenant Sorenson and I are taking a squad up the backside tonight to get an accurate count and find out where the rebel armor is. If we're lucky we'll be able to cripple their defenses."

"I'm glad I'm an engineer."

"If I don't make it back you'll be more than a technical officer." Greg smiled good naturedly. "Cowboy, Sharp!"

"Yes, sir?"

"Nap time. You're going to be up late tonight."

"On my mark," Greg whispered and nodded to Lieutenant Sorenson.

"Climbing."

"Climb on."

Two other soldiers watched Mike with awe as he began ascending with ease what they assumed was an unclimbable rock face. Night-vision goggles synthesized daylight to a certain extent but left shadows and dark spots in dangerous places for a technical climb. Moss covered rocks and decomposing stone made most forms of protection inadequate. Mike chose his holds carefully, stopping every ten feet to slip a small mechanical device into cracks in the rock and clip the rope through a carabiner attached to it. The climb undoubtably would have been impossible wearing full environmental armor.

As Mike approached the halfway point some fifty feet above the ground, he started having second thoughts about the safety of the climb. One false move and with the quality of his placements, he'd probably do a zipper all the way to the bottom.

Standing by to cover a hasty retreat, Cowboy and a squad of six observed the climb from a rise 1,500 feet away. They could see the five sentries guarding the sloping rise above the rock face, but none appeared to be aware of the climbers so far. Sharp waited patiently by himself in a sniper position to quickly dispatch any curious sentries. If things went badly, Cowboy and his fire squad could probably keep the enemy's hands full long enough for the others to escape while Sharp killed immediate threats to the four man recon team. The cold air made the sentries well defined targets to the AQ-3. The more he used the Pre-Rifts targeting system, the more Sharp was sure the optics and enhancement were superior to standard issue Coalition gear. With enhancement to full on thermo-imaging he could even see the heat from an armored sentry's breath show up in warm colors against the background. Then he saw the sixth heat signature moving its way closer to the sentries far from the climbers.

Greg was making his climb now, pulling up a second rope behind him for the other two to ascend. One fingerhold gave way and Greg went down, but the rope and body harness kept his descent to a few feet. Greg climbed on.

Sharp cut down a sentry with a silenced 7.62 mm bullet. A few more to go. Nearing the top, Greg slipped again.

That time he knew it wasn't an animal. The shuffling over the rock face stopped, but upon dropping a monocular nightvision system over his right eye, the sentry could make out motion no more than a few feet away. Cursing again he snatched up his rifle and stalked down the steep slope to the rock face.

"Think you could make more noise?" Mike whispered loudly as Greg pulled himself to the top and started securing the second rope.

"That's not the same thing as climbing on the wall."

"Really."

Hairs on the back of Mike's neck tingled and a foreboding sense of danger swept over him an instant before twigs snapped on the incline above him. Drawing a seldom used military issue .45 he rolled over and aimed the weapon at the sound. Pressing through the branches of a scrawny tree came the moving form of a large energy pulse rifle, followed shortly by the sentry.

"Oh man," Greg breathed, thinking very seriously about a speed rappel.

Something moved behind the sentry and in a quick, fluid motion his head jerked back and to the side with a distinct cracking sound.

His short gasp was silenced by a hand over his mouth and the same hand guided the body silently to lay against a tree trunk.

"It's okay, she's with us." Greg pushed aside Mike's .45. "I think."

"How did she get up here?"

"I don't know. Make sure that's anchored." Mike gave the second rope a tug and unclipped himself. He crawled up to where Natarsha crouched in the cover offered by the tree. "Thanks."

Natarsha nodded inside her hood.

"Why are you up here?"

"You hired me. I was listening to the plans of your enemy until I heard you coming. The one you call Zenjori is up there with his commanders," she whispered quietly.

"And nobody noticed you were there?" Greg asked suspiciously.

"No. They have placed many explosives around their camp and more also on the slopes they expect to fight on."

"Best two thousand credits I ever spent," Greg muttered, still a bit unsure how reliable the strange female scout was. He'd found his thoughts drifting back to her over and over during the past day, although there was something not quite right about her.

"You do not believe me. I will show you."

"Hold up." Greg readjusted his headset. "That's affirmative, Sharp, take the other two out. Yes. Yes I know she's here. Thanks for the timely warning," he whispered.

"Psst." Mike crawled up under the tree. "Here." He handed Greg a small pack pulled up from below.

"Natarsha, this is Lieutenant Mike Sorenson. Mike, meet one of our scouts."

"Natarsha." Mike nodded.she remained motionless and silent. "Clean job." Mike felt the neck of the sentry, then began removing the man's armor and affectations.

"What are you doing? You don't look anything like him," Greg pointed out.

"I don't have to. People rarely make eye contact at night, they just recognize familiar things and assume the person's identity. I've done this kind of thing before."

"There is another sentry near the rise leading to the camp of your enemy. There is another one guarding the vehicles they travel in and one sleeping near a robot."

"You've been up there?" Mike asked incredulously.

"Yes."

"Was there a very large hover transport there?" Greg asked.

"Yes."

Mike and Greg exchanged looks. There was a possibility of completing vital mission objectives without further bloodshed, assuming Zenjori kept the stolen disk or copies of it in the command craft. Natarsha tolerated the unusual level of noise created by the other two soldiers ascending the rope. Mike finished latching the last armor plate then closed his eyes.

"There's another person nearby," he stated.

"More psychic stuff, eh Mike?" Greg tried to rile himself up, but the usual distrust of psychics wasn't there. It made him feel strange, out of touch with a lifetime of fundamental military doctrine.

"It is one sentry. Alone. Your sniper cannot hit him." Natarsha spoke quietly, face shrouded beneath the hood.

"Show us."

Greg motioned the other two men to follow and then tried to emulate Natarsha's stealthy movements. Blood coursed through his veins as his heart pounded in his chest once again. The excitement of danger made him increasingly aware of the environment around him. He wondered briefly if he was becoming suicidal or just having some twisted fun.

In a small, natural hollow of land, a single cigarette lit the night with its glow. Protected from the cold wind, the sentry took a break from his long watch. Natarsha lay flat on the ground, motioning the others to stay back.

"I got him." Mike stood and walked boldly toward the sentry, holding behind his back an active high frequency blade.

"That you, Cole?"

"Hmm hmm," Mike snorted, striding casually up to the other man.

The sentry glanced up and appeared satisfied. Mike took two more steps and shoved the knife through the sentry's skull.

"Clear," he whispered sharply for the others to come in.

"Not very well equipped," Greg observed, noting the single, partially charged energy clip in the sentry's gun and the battered armor suit.

"Stay here, out of sight." Mike ordered Cody and motioned Peterson to follow.

With augmented cybernetic hearing, Mike could hear disjointed bits of conversation coming from the enemy camp just over the rise. Good placement, he thought to himself, protected from sniper fire by the natural contours at the top of the hill. Flickering lights played games with the shadows, making the forest seem alive. Natarsha led the way up the hill, never stumbling over vegetation or breaking a fluid grace. Every few yards she would stop the group and just sit listening to the surroundings. Conversation grew louder and more discernable from the background noise. The low hum of several robot vehicles indicated a state of battle readiness should there come an unexpected attack. Outlines of giant robot vehicles beneath camouflage netting could be seen beyond the flickering firelight. Magnification revealed the sleeping forms of enemy soldiers. Most slept fully clothed and at least partially armored. Sitting around a small fire near the circle of vehicles were the commanders of the Army of the New Order, and among them was Zenjori Suka. A light exoskeleton protected the man's body, but the helmet rested on the log beside him, leaving his head unprotected.

"What I wouldn't give to call in an air strike right now," Greg mused, fingering his C-18.

The weapon seemed to be calling out to be used. With one well placed shot he could slay the notorious mercenary leader. It would be too easy.

"Don't do it," Mike whispered urgently as Greg slipped the laser sidearm from its holster.

"We can end it. Right now, right here."

"There's no way to get away in time."

"We can do with four of us what's going to cost dozens of lives to do another way. Whatever happened to that risk everything attitude you pulled at Youngstown? Four lives instead of forty. Pretty fair trade in my book," Greg said a bit too loudly.

He shrugged and braced his right arm on his knee to steady his aim.

"Are you crazy? We'll all die." Mike flipped the safety back on.

"Probably." Greg flipped the safety off, wondering if he'd completely lost his mind. He wasn't afraid to die, nor did he care if he lost his life taking another. No heart pounding, no pulse quickening, no regrets. Did it mean it was his time to go, or that he'd gone over the edge?

"You don't have someone to go back to." Mike flipped the safety on. "I do. I don't want to die. Not here. Not now."

Emotional turbulence triggered Natarsha's hyper awareness and she dared open herself to it further. The two men were silent, each pondering the value of their lives. A thrill rushed through her like she'd never experienced. Answers to questions she'd never before considered flooded empty regions of her mind. Greg was searching for something Mike seemed to grasp, but what it was Natarsha couldn't comprehend. Flashes of anger, sorrow, and volatile emotions finally reached a level of equilibrium in Greg's mind. Natarsha was trembling from overexposure to foreign stimuli. When twigs cracked nearby and the foursome scrambled together into a ditch the close proximity and physical contact almost sent her into sensory overload. The sentry passed by without noticing the intruders.

"Shhh, listen." Mike cocked his head toward the campfire. Greg crawled partway out of the ditch, climbing over Natarsha in the process. He, too, cocked his head toward the camp.

"I can't hear anything."

"Stop moving. It's Zenjori. He's talking and I can't hear with you making noise. Be still!" Mike hissed. Jumbled words barely audible to human ears were amplified and deciphered through his cybernetic ear implant.

"What's he saying."

"Something about the Coalition. I've got to get closer."

Mike inched out of the ditch and slid into an awkward position mirroring the shadows. At 150 feet, every noise in the forest between himself and the conversation was amplified. Noise filters cut out insect sounds and other definable sounds to isolate the human speech patterns.

"— Way of repeating itself, as it did with the Third Reich, as with the United States, and as it has with the Coalition," Zenjori's hypnotic voice blared in Mike's ear. "The people became complacent, satisfied with the quality of their lives and wanted nothing to take that away from them. One of the very first things Hitler did was gain influence, and eventual control of the media, to control what the people knew. Book bans and censorship seemed acceptable costs for the life of freedom the people were given. Little by little personal freedoms were stripped away, each time in the promise of preserving the lifestyle the people had grown accustomed to. The media was controlled, so there was nothing but the official story and government views to be heard.

"One cannot argue with history. The people have, and continue to believe the lies propagated by corrupt governments. The Coalition States as lead by Emperor Prosek repeat history once again. The people are too stupid or lazy, lulled into complacency and voluntarily stripped of their rights."

"And then it's too late," a deep metallic voice added. Mike assumed it was the voice of Drake, the renegade Cyborg once a member of the Coalition military.

"It's like putting a frog in a pot of boiling water. The change is so drastic the frog will immediately leap out. Whereas if the frog is put in the water while it is still comfortable, and the temperature is increased gradually over time, it won't notice until it's too late for escape. Hitler was intelligent enough to look ahead and eliminate threats to his power. Once opposition within the government was neutralized, he used that government to slowly strip away personal liberties of the people, at the same time promising and delivering economic stability. The people believed this acceptable for the prosperity they enjoyed, not realizing they were supporting a maniacal dictator.

"Taking the guns away from the people made certain nobody but the military had power, because, ultimately, those with guns hold true power. Should any opposition arise, Hitler held true power and it was simple to crush any trouble, first by media and public opinion, then through violence. Control of religion, limited freedom of speech, government property ownership, all disguised as necessary steps to maintaining order in society. Over and over through history governments controlled the people, and over and over the people allowed it to happen out of ignorance and complacency."

"But most of 'em didn't even know it's happenin' to 'em." Kruno pointed out.

"That's what I just said," Zenjori snapped. "That's what ignorance is. And it's even more prevalent in the Coalition States than ever before. Emperor Prosek manipulates the people's fears with misinformation and fans the flames of racial hatred with lies and propaganda. What acts would seem unconscionable to commit on another living being are permissible for the greater good of the people. Atrocities committed in the name of self-defense are supported by the people who feel their lifestyle threatened. Racial violence is acceptable, after all, it's the D-Bees and aliens causing all the problems to begin with. From their point of view, it's the human's world and D-Bees don't belong here. It's a simple matter for the Coalition government to fabricate a threat, raise prices in the cities, infringe a little on the people's lives, then call it the work of D-Bees and rebels. The only way for life to return to normal is for the people to support new government intervention. The people don't know any better, they feel their lives and families threatened and support, even participate in acts of violence that might otherwise be considered barbaric.

"If the people knew the truth and hadn't already relinquished their power to enact change, then Emperor Prosek and the corrupt leaders wouldn't stand a chance of maintaining the control they have now. That is why we're here. That is why the Army of the New Order is here. To make certain the Coalition doesn't expand its evil influence and cause death to the innocent."

Up to that point, Mike found it hard to argue against the words he was hearing. He'd seen and experienced too much. Now Zenjori was burying his own history of sadistic violence by waving a flag of righteous calling. He must be playing up to new members of his army, Mike concluded. Anybody who'd been part of Zenjori's company for long knew the rebel leader didn't really stand behind the flag he waved. Mike wondered if they knew how black Zenjori's heart really was.

"Do you think the Coalition will attack us here?" an unfamiliar young voice asked.

"Kent, they killed your grandfather, murdered members of your family and invaded your hometown to massacre your friends. What do you think?" another voice Mike didn't know reminded the boy of a deluded past.

"I know, we all think it would be foolish for the Coalition to follow us all the way out here," Zenjori cooed. "And it would be foolish of them to attack us where we obviously have the upper hand, but such is the nature of their delusions. I'm certain that the soldiers we will be fighting have been brainwashed by the same lies as the Coalition people have. It's too bad, really, they have never known the truth and never will believe it even if told. They're misguided by the lies and hatred they've been around all their lives, and don't know anything but to do as their Emperor demands. One cannot reason with them, just try to defend one's own life from their violent intentions. It's not their fault they follow the orders of evil leaders. It's those leaders who care nothing for the lives of their own soldiers that will send them into battle with us, knowing they can't win. All we can do is fight and save our own lives."

"Their military commanders are poorly trained and have no experience fighting a real opponent," Drake commented.

"And those that do know how to fight have their hands tied, another case of history repeating itself," Zenjori went on. "What's sadder still is the lengths of disparity the Coalition will go to to ensure that their own military stays in line with the Emperor's propaganda. I could tell you true and verifiable stories of exactly what is being done to their minds. Chemicals that make a person susceptible to suggestion are put in their food and water. I have proof. Proof that the Coalition is willing to kill all of us to make sure it never falls into the hands of certain elements of their own government."

"What proof?" Another voice asked.

"In time, once we've dealt with more immediate problems. There is a 5th column in the Coalition, but it is too small and too late to counter the Emperor's control. That's why we must win a victory here, to ensure a chance at overthrowing Emperor Prosek's government when the opportunity arises. To—"

Mike cut the amplifier and slid back into the ditch. Zenjori's inspirational speech was making him sick, plus he was detecting a growing impatience among his companions. Natarsha squirmed free of any physical contact and attempted to recompose her thoughts while the two officers discussed battle plans.

"Natarsha, where are the guards stationed around the large hover craft?" Mike's question interrupted her thoughts.

"Two now. One inside, one outside the large hatch," she stated without moving.

"You're sure?"

"Yes."

"Peterson. Stay. If we screw up, cover our back sides the best you can then get your own back down the cliff." Greg shoved the sentry's rifle into the soldier's arms and followed Mike closer to the vehicles.

Crawling an inch at a time, Mike closed in on the sentry nearest the parked X-1000 Ultimax robot. Breathing quietly he got to his feet, testing the ground carefully before committing his weight to each step. One more meter. Almost close enough to slip an H.F. blade through the flexible joints of the sentry's polycarbonate armor. One more slow, careful step. The sentry still had his back turned. Mike brought the tip of the blade an inch from the sentry's neck and drove it through the light joint armor with one powerful palm strike to the pommel. Flexible armor stretched then sliced open and pushed through at the sentry's throat, the tip vibrating softly clear through the neck. Mike waited for dying convulsions to stop, then sat the body down against a tree and propped it up with his rifle.

A black form moved between the X-1000's legs and came to place the pilot's head in the dead sentry's lap.

"How's that for irony," Greg whispered. "Never knew what hit him."

Mike looked at Greg and began to wonder just how far gone the lieutenant was. Greg crouched down and pulled a small brick-sized explosive charge from his pack. Mike shook his head vehemently. Greg pointed to the Ultimax and grinned.

Using the robot's knee plate to help boost him up onto one giant arm, Greg climbed the twenty foot unit with a specific goal in mind.

Reaching up and under the heavy armor plating of the right shoulder rocket launch system he felt around for the flimsy metal plate covering the magazine access. Normally well protected from direct fire, the light covering wouldn't stop a fusion block from blasting through and detonating the rocket payload. Greg extended a tiny antennae for the remote detonator and slipped the charge in place. He couldn't suppress a few chuckles as he climbed back down to the ground. Mike pointed to a giant hover craft twenty feet away and mouthed the word "disk".

Three minutes later another sentry leaned against a tree trunk and a sleeping Headhunter was relieved of the obligation to wake up. Inside the giant transport both men switched over to infrared optics before searching for the disk. Missiles, cases of explosives, and heavy weapon racks were everywhere. Mike accessed the transport onboard computer and hoped the light from the vid screen wouldn't be noticed through the pilot's compartment windows. Less than ten meters away Zenjori sat in front of a fire preaching future glories of his army.

"Damn," Mike breathed.

The disk had been run on the computer and even had its own catalog file. The computer wanted the laser disk in drive G, but the tray was empty and no disk of any kind was nearby.

"Uh, Lieutenants. The scout just aced another sentry," Private Peterson reported over the radio. "Don't you think somebody's gonna notice pretty soon?"

"Thanks, Peterson. Stand by." Mike climbed back down into the cargo bay to discover much of the ordnance had been rearranged and gun racks emptied. Greg was placing his last explosive charge under a rack of missile cases.

"Got the disk?" Greg asked.

"No."

"I'd ask Zenjori where it's at but he's going to be atomized in a few minutes.

"We need to leave. Your scout just took out another sentry."

"Pretty smooth, isn't she?" Greg beamed, filling the rest of his pack with grenades and explosives liberated from the rebel magazine. He finished tying off a bundle of weapons and handed one fifty pound satchel to Mike. "No sense wasting perfectly good weapons."

All the way to the rock face and back to the parked hover rover, Greg felt the detonator transmitter calling out to him. He sat down on the hood and toyed with it like a kid playing with a new toy.

"C'mon, Lieutenant, lemme push it." Cowboy reached for the little device.

"I said no. It's mine." Greg pulled it away and stood on the rover's hood for a better view. The sequence was programmed at .25 second intervals between the X-1000 and the two in the transport. The other soldiers scrambled up on the rover not wanting to miss the fireworks.

"C'mon, push it!"

"10 seconds. 9, 8, 7, 6, 5, 4, 3 . . . do you think we should do it right now?"

Greg fought to keep control of the detonator.

"You're such a tease," Bill joked.

"For real this time. 10, 9, 8, 7, 6, 5, 4, 3, 2, 1. Boom."

Chapter 16

After the first distant concussion, it became impossible to delineate between remote charges and secondary explosions. Earth-shattering detonations rolled away from the hilltop in continuous report to the giant clouds of smoke and flame. Missiles hurled into the air by expanding gas detonated in rapid succession while explosives chain-fired across the ground from vehicle to vehicle. Sparks rained down from burning bits of armor turned into molten shrapnel.

In the silence that followed, a bright glow could still be seen lighting up the night sky above the rebel camp. Cowboy breathed a reverent replay, eyes aglow with delight.

"Hell yeah. . ."

Natarsha huddled deeper into the space between a fallen tree and a moss-covered rock. Sleep was a luxury to catch up on whenever the opportunity arose, and it had been days since she'd slept more than an hour or two. Varles would be expecting her to report back within the next seventy-two hours and would probably force her to ride into battle with him on the barge. She had all the information Varles needed to know before he attacked the Coalition. It would just be like all the other times when she'd spied on a village or group of travelers and then come back later with Varles to capture and destroy them. This time would be the hardest to endure.

The longer she associated with Greg and the others the more difficult it became to see them as just objects to be used and sold like cattle. The urge to spare their lives from Varles' tender mercies grew stronger every day. If only there was a way to make them leave without her master knowing. That, in itself, would be a rebellion to help make amends for all the horrid things she'd done at her master's command.

Time after time her mind returned to the memory of the closeness shared with Greg, an experience lacking the fear and hatred that she'd come to expect from all. She relived the experiences, the feel of his pulse and beating heart, the dangerous new emotions he instilled. Varles would make her pay dearly if he ever learned of those memories.

Resolving to wrap up her intelligence report the next day and return to the slaver the following night, Natarsha fell into a dream-filled sleep.

Fragments of X-1000 armor still glowed faintly by morning light. Trails of smoke rose everywhere in the blast site from shrapnel imbedded in trees, earth, and other vehicles. A Mountaineer ATV poured out black smoke from its last burning tire and nobody made an attempt to stop it. Scorched and dismembered bodies lay untouched where they'd landed. Any salvageable equipment had already been removed from the blast zone and the immediate area was abandoned due to moderate levels of radiation from destroyed nuclear power systems. Zenjori Suka looked over the smoldering site, clenching and unclenching his fists inside the armored exoskeleton.

"They have to pay for this."

"We've moved all unprotected personnel to the forward perimeter." Drake strode through the smoking ruins without concern for the radiation. "Sledgehammer is standing by in reserve position."

"And Notec?"

"Doing better. Colnae healed most of his injuries but doesn't know how to reverse the radiation or damage or replace his arm."

"How did they get in without anyone knowing!?" Zenjori shouted angrily.

If it hadn't been for the psychic premonition of Notec, his powerful psychic ally, the explosions could easily have killed everyone at base camp. Notec's warning and telekinetic force field gave just enough time for the mercenary commander to secure his armor and escape the epicenter of the explosion. The Mind Melter had almost lost his life and was now missing his left arm to a piece of shrapnel. Losing equipment and personnel paled in comparison to the blow to Zenjori's ego. His own men had fearlessly risked their lives to save his.

"We found our rear sentries half a mile away stashed in a ditch. Best we can tell, the Coalition sent a squad up the backside cliff and took our sentries' bodies with them when they left. Booby-trapped their trail as well. I lost a man to a grenade nest and several of my cyborgs were damaged trying to follow the trail."

"Special Forces?"

"Clean kills, good demo job, that would be my guess except our contact in First Strike didn't mention any Special Forces among the Coalition detachment." Drake stood beside his commander and looked around at the devastation. "Definitely not average tactics."

"How long until we have serious radiation problems?"

"A day or two, perhaps less for the line men. Radiation will kill them slowly later, and most of our men know that. Some are talking about deserting."

"Have you—"

"Of course. They know the penalty. I made an example of the ones instigating it."

"J.J. started this. Over thirty men unaccounted for now."

"Some may be around us. It's hard to tell." Drake poked a vaguely humanoid form at his feet. "Tech crew was in the Mountaineer. Xevo got his."

"Our options are limited now. We can't remain here for more than a day, and we can't hold out in a war of attrition because we can't make repairs or resupply."

"We still outnumber them better than three to one in armor and two to one in personnel, not counting the cannon fodder Kruno keeps in front of his Headhunters. Plus we have a Glitter Boy to pick off any of their heavy armor. We have the tactical advantage for an offensive."

"The Coalition isn't our only problem."

"First Strike?"

"Yes. We can hold our defensive position another twenty-four hours, through tonight and tomorrow morning. After that, we have no alternative but to attack. First, I want to do as much damage to the Coalition armor as possible. We may even make them retreat or aggravate them to attack. I'll need a coordinated attack, both air and missiles."

"We're pretty evenly matched for air to air combat and can pulverize them with a full-scale missile attack, we just won't have reloads."

"I don't want a full-scale engagement, just enough to trick them into putting their SAM's and other air units up. Once they throw up active radar, we fire a barrage."

"If the Coalition is nothing else, they are predictable."

"Look around. They're learning."

"Lieutenant Merrick! Lieutenant Merrick! Wake up!"

"What the hell?" Greg's sleep laden eyes tried to focus on what was dragging him from a sound sleep.

"Sky Kings and X-10's comin' in!" The blurry face shouted.

"What time is it?" He rubbed his eyes and sat up. Every muscle ached.

"12:30, sir. Can I take your SAM?"

"Peterson, if you so much as touch my SAM, I'll think of something really bad to do to you. Who's making the intercept?"

"Pritchett's flyboys. Lieutenant Adams told us to hold back until I woke you up," Private Peterson relayed enthusiastically.

"Adams is giving orders? Now I have to get up." Greg stretched and looked around for where he'd thrown his boots and radio. No more than 1,000 feet away an extended explosion shocked the air.

"Incoming!" Pritchett's voice blared over the loudspeaker. The sound of outgoing missiles rushed past and eight seconds later more explosions sounded. Greg leapt from the rover just in time to get flattened by the shockwave of a missile colliding with the Enforcer over a hundred feet away. Stunned and barely able to breathe, he watched the world with detachment. Soldiers ran for cover as starbursts radiated in sickening repetition against the armored body of Pritchett's Skull Walker. Missile trails streamed away from the smaller Enforcer as it desperately sought to save itself from incoming volleys of guided warheads. Debris floated downward from a blazing cloud of plasma where a SAMAS had once been.

Greg's SAMAS awaited less than thirty feet away, but it seemed like a mile in slow motion. His own voice sounded distant, like another person reciting the clearance code. Comm chatter buzzed like an angry swarm of insects in his head and it took an effort of will just to remember how to operate the communications system.

A single streamer appeared in front of the Enforcer just as the pilot brought up the arms to protect its body. Armor fragments flew as deadly shrapnel and the left forearm sailed up and over the robot's head to land just inches from the rover Greg had just left. Lowering the burning stump of its severed left arm the Enforcer's shoulder-mounted defense lasers converged on another armor-piercing warhead one hundred feet from punching through the weakened armor.

"Skull 41! What's going on?!"

"Missile barrage!" Lisa yelled over the radio.

"Who's painting us?"

"Nobody! Sky Kings are too far away and there's nothing on the ground."

"Cut your radar."

"What?"

"Shut off all active sensors and get away from the Abolisher!"

"I've got a lock on the source. Do I go silent anyway?"

Greg paused momentarily. To delay could mean destruction.

"Return fire. Four. Then go silent."

"Yes sir, four plasma warheads armed and away." Lisa hoped Brian's special modifications came through.

The rear-mounted launcher blasted fire trails to the ground as the missiles left their verticle housings and arced over the forest toward their targets miles away.

"Crap," Dave answered the weapon lock warning tone. "They just pinged us when you fired. Four incoming. Twenty-five seconds."

"Got 'em." Lisa switched to lock in on the incoming volley and launched the remaining two missiles to intercept. Swirling trails met in mid-air, expanding explosions visible before the sound returned. Missiles committed fratricide in a series of brilliant flashes but never reached the Skull Walker. Friendly missiles disappeared off the tactical screen along with the four enemy warheads. The first four ended their flight, sounds of explosions racing back to confirm the kill. Out of sight miles away, the rebel Titan robot blazed away in a pool of its own burning armor.

Desperately seeking to save itself from a similar fate, the Abolisher fired auto-cannons intended for bombardment. 144 mm shells sped past incoming missiles to crater distant hillsides. By the time the crew was able to select fragmentation shells and arm for proximity detonation, the rebel missiles found their mark. Staggering back, the heavy robot tried to stay upright as four high-yield warheads slammed it from the front. Like the dying scream of a wounded animal armor fatigued and tons of metal bore the Abolisher to the ground. The pilots lay inside, strapped in but too dazed to react from the fall.

Flames gushed out behind the CR-6 launcher on the Enforcer's left shoulder as it spent the last of its missiles to intercept another volley. Pounding shockwaves returned thirty seconds later from multiple plasma clouds above the tree line.

Hugging the treetops and relying on the sensor feed from the Enforcer, Lieutenant Merrick and the remaining SAM's took the enemy exoskeletons by surprise.

Looking around at the blasted armor and smoking fragments of the other robot vehicles, Dave breathed deeply and checked the damage assessment just to make sure he hadn't missed something. Not a scratch on Skull Walker 41.

"I don't think I'm going to complain about the missile launcher anymore."

Multi-color magic markers indicated the last known location of enemy personnel, robots, and vehicles on Pritchett's plastic covered map. Black arrows followed dips in topographic contours showing the captain's proposed advance lines and way points. In dark blue ink, a single line ran straight up the center of enemy positions. Captain Pritchett finished drawing out the battle plan and explained it to the skeptical officers around him.

"We pin him down on three sides so he can't move his troops without exposing one of his flanks. Fire squads one through six make the advance under the Abolisher's auto-cannons, allowing it to stay out of direct enemy fire while still providing support. Fire teams Saber and Fury open a corridor here for Lieutenant Merrick's unit to drive through and take the hill under cover fire from Skull 41 and Enforcer 790." Pritchett ran his finger up the dark blue line to the summit.

"This isn't a king-of-the-hill wargame back at Chi-Town." Greg leaned over the map, a challenging tone in his voice. "Three major flaws here. One, you don't have the Glitter Boy on your map. Two, there's at least two dozen cyborgs up there, and I don't see them on the map either. Three, I don't see your Skull Walker."

"After the SAM's have established air superiority, they will engage the Glitter Boy and the cyborgs as soon as they've been flushed out. As for Skull 191, it's too badly damaged to risk taking into combat."

"But you're okay sending in the Abolisher with 65% of its main integrity compromised and a crew with severe concussions? Your entire frontal assault plan is going to suffer at least 75% casualties, even if it works! That might win you points for reaching an objective in a simulation, but it doesn't go down too good out here."

"Casualties are inevitable, Lieutenant. I thought with your experience you would know that by now," Pritchett snarled, losing the diplomacy he'd been trying to extend.

"This isn't just an us vs. them scenario where we walk out in a field and slug it out. They have a superior position, higher numbers, and more firepower. The only thing going for us is technology and a few of us that know what we're doing, and that edge just isn't enough to win a slug fest. Your whole, whole attack idea is a piece of garbage.!" Greg grabbed one of the pens but Pritchett snatched it away.

"Very well, Lieutenant. I wouldn't normally take a Skull Walker with 25% of its structural integrity into a battle situation, but if it will save the lives of a few men it's worth the risk."

"You think that's it? Worth what? What risk? We're not not here to prove anything, are you?"

"Is that supposed to have some special meaning, Lieutenant?" Pritchett leaned forward and spoke in a low voice.

"Sir. You don't have to prove anything. We can do this another way and win," Greg spoke quietly so the others wouldn't hear. If the captain forced the issue to save face it would waste all their lives for nothing. Something of his diplomatic ability remained, but it was volatile and unpredictable.

"I am, of course, open to suggestions should anyone wish to voice them." Pritchett stood up straight.

"I've got an idea."

"Yes, Lieutenant Adams?"

"We could use snipers to take out most of their sentries and frontline troops before they have a chance to shoot back. Then we draw out their remaining aircraft and exoskeletons and lead them into a place where we can use the combined firepower from ground units to take them out. While it's still dark out, we rig something so the SAM's can airlift fire teams in from the backside and take the hilltop, avoiding the entrenched positions altogether."

"There, even Brian has a better plan." Greg invoked an irritated look from both Brian and the captain.

"Thank you, Lieutenant Adams. I think a more conventional plan is in order rather than having infantry play acrobat with flying exoskeletons."

"We shouldn't even be attacking them like this at all!" Greg pointed disdainfully at the map. "Given enough time we can do it with our SAM's and a platoon. Destroy their vehicles and mobility, then wear them down a little at at time. They can't resupply, they can't even escape without their transport vehicles, and we can just keep doing hit and runs then going back for repairs and rearming, something they can't do. They're not equipped to defend night assaults, so we might even be able to hit them again like we did last night. There's no reason to rush into a half-baked frontal attack."

"And what do you suggest we do if they launch another missile attack? We don't have anything left to shoot back!"

"First Strike does. All we need to do is keep Zenjori and his core army from getting away and wait for a joint effort. Zenjori knows he can't handle both of us and he'll either attack first, try to make a retreat, or stand and die. This attack isn't even necessary."

"I have to agree with Lieutenant Merrick. There's no need to rush into a premature assault." Lieutenant Sorenson stepped forward.

"Well thank you for presenting these alternatives, but my final decision has been made. We will proceed as planned, executing stage one at 2300 hours."

"I'm letting you know right now I strongly object to this command."

"Thank you, Lieutenant Merrick. Noted."

"And my unit isn't charging in anywhere until both the Glitter Boy and cyborg squad have been located and heavy support is present for suppression."

"That's acceptable. Winters will lead the advance unit to take the hill. At his discretion."

"My discretion tells me we've got trouble," Winters growled.

"I beg your pardon, Sergeant?"

"We've got trouble, sir."

"Well, Jerry, think it's time to play cards?" Greg encrypted the unofficial command.

"If we get a chance, I shuffle."

Hinged prongs slipped in the access ports of the back-mounted ammunition drum and unlocked the set pins holding it in place. Brian rotated the drum inside the feed casing counter-clockwise until it released the holding clamps, then put his foot against the SAMAS' left intake and yanked the drum farther out. It stuck. Brian pushed harder with both legs and gripped his loading tool harder. The drum refused to budge.

"Get out of there, you piece of garbage!" Brian gritted his teeth and pulled with all his might. It didn't move. "I don't need this! Get out!" He yanked harder. Something made a strange sound and Brian flew backwards into the hover rover amid a rain of metal slugs spewing in a fountain from the drum feed port. The stream of language leaving Brian's mouth attracted stares from clear across camp and laughter from the audience in the rover. Darren tried not to laugh at Brian's predicament. It was his SAM the frustrated tech was trying to fix.

"Hey, looks like you fixed the problem. Drum's not jammed anymore."

"It waits until after I get it out to do this!" Brian kicked the drum angrily and tried in vain to slide the metal plate covering the feed port in place.

"It's gonna be a pain pickin' up all those slugs when the sun goes down." Darren looked at the darkening sky. "Want some help?"

"Yeah, if you want to fly this tonight."

"Not really, but I can't let you get your rears kicked by a Glitter Boy, either." Darren started scooping up handfuls of metal slugs and dumping them on the seat next to Brian.

"I can't believe Merrick is making me drive a rover," Brian complained, finally controlling the damaged ammunition drum.

"That's cuz he knows you're not gonna freak and dump Cowboy and the rest in the first ditch you come to."

"No, he says it's to give me some front line combat training. I gotta earn my commission. Just because he came up through the ranks he thinks everyone else should. I'm an engineer, not a platoon leader."

"Dang, you sound just like this spaceman dude on one of my vids back home. Don't worry, buddy, you've been through some hair-raising stuff before. You'll do fine."

"Don't patronize me," Brian scowled.

"I could make Lieutenant. I just don't want to."

"The day you get commissioned I will truly know fear."

"No, seriously, you get to be an officer and then you get all kinds of responsibility, like they make you drive a hover rover up an enemy fortified hill and expect you to win, for example."

"I can handle going up against the enemy infantry, that's tough but not impossible." Brian stopped fidgeting with the drum and looked in the direction of the offensive to come. "Going up against the Glitter Boy? One shot and it's all over." Brian shook his head solemnly.

"It won't touch you. It's mine."

"One shot for your SAM and you're history too."

"Hasn't got me yet." Darren grinned with a roguish look. "If Merrick and Sorenson can keep the X-10's off my back, I can finish the Glitter Boy this time. Woulda had them Predators today except this thing jammed on me. Don't want that tonight."

"You got that right. We haven't even scratched it."

"I've been thinking 'bout it and figured we've been doin' it all wrong. What makes a Glitter Boy so dangerous?"

"The boom gun?"

"Exactly, the boom gun. Okay, follow me on this, we can blast all day and hardly tweak the armor, but all it takes is one shot from it and you're dead. But without its rail gun the Glitter Boy is just an almost indestructible walking armor suit that can't shoot back at you. All I gotta do is punch out its teeth and I can wipe it off the planet."

"Even if you cut the feed belt, its still got about a dozen shots left in the gun magazine. I know, I checked up on the schematics back at Chi-Town. Good luck blasting through the armor bonded around the barrel. It'll shoot you several times before you hit anything that counts."

"New angle. Hang with me."

"Brian, I need a plasma grenade."

"Why?"

"Okay, tell me what would happen if I put a plasma grenade down the barrel of the boom gun?"

"Nothing. Lever doesn't have enough space to spring and hit the fuse."

"But what happens when he fires?"

"The amount of time it takes the projectiles to accelerate down the barrel...wait a minute." Brian tried to review the physics in his head. "The boom gun doesn't work like a normal rail gun, in fact it's not even a true rail gun. It's a mass driver, using electromagnetic coils to accelerate a cluster of slugs, but the field decay lasts too long and it loses some velocity at the end of the barrel, not that you'd notice on your end. The electromagnetic coils set up a cascade effect pulling then pushing the projectile cluster as it moves down the barrel."

"No talk techno speak. American speak only."

"What's going to happen is the electromagnetic current is going to set off the plasma grenade at the same time it tries to accelerate the projectile cluster down the barrel. It's gonna fuse the metal slugs right to the coils!"

"I'm kinda hazy on the whole electromagnamate gizmo watchamacallit fusing thing. That's bad for him, good for me, right?"

"Definitely bad for him. The power relay circuit will kick over and shut down the gun so it doesn't fry the capacitor pack. That's genius!"

"I'm glad you thought of it, buddy." Darren slapped Brian on the back.

"They should have this in a manual some place."

"They probably do."

"Pick up the rest of your C-40 slugs while I go get some grenades and rig something for you to carry them in." Brian headed for Skull 41.

"Uh, whoah there, partner."

Brian shrugged and stared at the Skull Walker.

Running lights off in the darkness and flying just meters above the treetops, Darren fell into a wide-spread wedge formation composed of seven other SAMAS and a Sky Cycle. Making the advance on the ground were infantry squads followed at a distance by mechanized units. Perhaps the most crucial point in battle would be fought in the next few minutes. Achieving air superiority would determine whose ground forces would be shredded from above.

"Four Predators and four Sky Kings on approach. Thirty seconds to contact,." the lead cycle reported.

"Go to formation Charlie. Let's see if we can split them up some," Greg ordered. Having Darren as his wingman allowed some freedom in facing uneven odds. Darren had downed more exoskeletons than any of them.

"They're still holding vertical diamond." The Sky Cycle pulled ahead, easily outdistancing the winged SAMAS.

"Stay with your wingman. Red and Blue teams, engage the Predators. Yellow and Gold will take the Sky Kings. Cycle one, be ready to break off and intercept if they make a run for the bots."

"Fifteen seconds."

"Radar on, go loud. Break off and engage."

"Sir, two Sky Kings just broke off."

"Watch them. Don't let them get near our armor."

"Roger. Cycle 114 in pursuit."

The faster craft banked away and sped for the wayward rebel aircraft. As small, lightly armored VTOL aircraft went, the Sky Kings carried a threatening array of armament, more than enough to destroy a pair of crippled robots.

Cycle 114 cut the distance to less than a mile before slinging around behind the Sky Kings. One broke off the instant it was targeted and tried to circle back. The craft made a wide swing just as the Sky Cycle connected a high power, laser beam with one of its two rear jets. Plumes of flame shot from two holes through the damaged engine. The pilot fought to keep control of his craft and still avoid the laser beams passing through tail fins and maneuver jets. Jinking and weaving, it tried to break away from the cycle, once more being scored by laser beams.

The smart missile on course for the Sky Cycle fired from rebel robot units wouldn't get there in time. The Sky King pilot was about to eject when laser beams cut through the other thruster and blew out the controls. The craft veered around wildly to get caught by incoming rockets from the Sky Cycle. It blew apart in two distinct burning pieces before the lower half ignited its rocket payload and became a cloud of expanding gas.

Two seconds later, Sky Cycle 114 suffered a similar fate from the missile launched by a rebel robot. Armor and wings rained down from the shrapnel mist.

Closing on the unprotected Abolisher, the second Sky King was about to open fire when the giant robot started shooting first. Auto-cannons ill-suited for hitting maneuverable airborne targets were made even worse by sensory systems damaged by the missile blast radius. Damaged cannon mounts were sluggish on response, not matching the targeting systems inside the robot. The cannons were so far off target, the Sky King's pilot laughed, closing boldly to within 3,000 feet and scoring a direct hit with a pair of armor piercing rockets. The Abolisher's framework creaked from the stress of its own weight and repeated impacts, but held together. One shell hit the Sky

King's nose dead center, shattering the foreword laser and sending shrapnel back into the cockpit. Body armor kept the pilot alive and the rugged control system held together enough for the Sky King to change course. Making a wide, wobbly U-shaped turn around the Abolisher, the Sky King was fired on by each set of cannons in turn. Overconfidence and focus on his target cost the pilot his life as the craft took two more shells, one just beneath the cockpit and the other striking the pilot directly. As if defying its death, the pilotless Sky King took five more seconds to break apart in mid-air and scatter its remains over a three hundred meter burial site.

"Abolisher, come in Abolisher." Lisa tried to warn the damaged robot of impending doom.

"Abolisher here. We just splattered a Sky King!"

"Don't celebrate, get out of there. We're tracking four missiles heading your way! Think of something fast or bail out now!"

"They're not on my screens."

"Your sensors are damaged. You don't have time! Eject!"

"They're not showing up. Let me check the —"

Missiles tore through unprotected systems and scattered armor in all directions. Explosive shock slammed the Abolisher's crew into their controls as the supporting structure snapped and the robot collapsed on itself. The auto-cannon magazine chain fired an instant later and turned the upper half of the robot into a deadly fireworks display.

"Skull 41 to Merrick. I think we just lost the Abolisher."

"Merrick. Survivors?"

"I don't know. Infantry's going to need fire support in a few minutes and there isn't going to be any from the Abolisher. Pritchett says he wants the SAMs to do it," Lisa relayed.

"Tell Pritchett to order his troops to hold back until we've dealt with enemy air. We're busy. Merrick out." Greg veered away from a pair of mini-missiles.

"Those almost had ya, dude."

"Darren! Where are you going?"

"Take the one on the left, I got the one on the right." Darren pushed his exoskeleton to its top speed on a collision course with a Sky King.

"Well shoot at it, Darren!" Greg fired repeatedly at the Sky King closing on him.

The first burst tore a line of slugs up the nose. Taking evasive action, the Sky King banked up and to the left.

"Bad move," Greg breathed, elevating his C-40 to the computer-calculated lead ahead of the target's position. Like tracers in the night, metal slugs drew lines to the left and right of the weaving craft before connecting solidly with the underside and tearing away maneuver fins. Superb aerial expertise saved the pilot from losing the craft but left him open for attack. Two more bursts ripped the vitals from the Sky King's belly and sent the disemboweled craft to the ground.

Greg felt the surge of victory. Not a scratch on the SAM. Radar displayed SAM 15 and the last Sky King almost on top of each other. Greg followed Darren's heat trail with thermo-imaging and observed the quick and dirty way to down a Sky King. Flying twenty feet to the right of the incoming craft Darren simply stretched out the left forearm and hit the pilot in the head with a plasma mini-missile. The entire cockpit became a fireball and the Sky King blazed downward like a comet.

"Show-off," Greg mumbled.

"Somebody get this guy off my thrusters!" Peterson frantically dodged away from his stubborn Predator attacker.

The X-10 held the dogtail, intent on downing SAM 117B.

"I'm all over him, dude. Max out on speed and take him down to fifty feet vertical."

"You're on your own, Darren, I've got a fix on that robot launching the missiles." Greg veered away and streaked for an enemy Multi-bot.

"I can't shake him!" Peterson started to panic.

"Chill, dude, it's just an X-10. You're faster and more maneuverable." Darren slowly closed on the X-10 from behind. "Bring him down lower."

"If I get any lower, I'm going to hit a tree!"

"Nap time, pal." Darren rose up behind the slower power armor, noticing the complacent flight pattern. He took his time and slammed it with a mini-missile in the back of the head. Plasma washed over the upper exoskeleton and sent the rear wings in opposite directions.

Darren watched the Predators arms and legs in a slow crawl as it plummeted to the earth at over 200 mph. That kind of fall nobody walked away from.

"Thanks. Behind you, man," Peterson warned.

Two SAMAS from Pritchett's unit pursued a moder-ately-damaged Predator, besieging it with continual rail gun fire. Darren slowed and hovered in mid air, taking aim at the approaching exoskeleton.

"Hey stop wasting ammo. That thing's got twice the armor you do and it doesn't have to worry about reloading. Smart tactics, assholes."

"Up yours," Sergio spat back.

"Here, let me show you how it's done." Darren carefully sighted in the X-10's battered helmet and splattered the pilot's head all over the wing joints. The Predator sailed silently into the forest.

"That was my kill!"

"If you hurry you can get off a few shots at the one Taylor and Yoshi are chasing down." Darren dodged one of Sergio's wings as the two exoskeletons nearly collided.

"Too late," Private Yoshi declared triumphantly.

The remains of the last flying exoskeleton crashed to unsung burial grounds.

"Way to go Yoshi! You're equal with Sorenson now!" Darren threw the jab out at Mike, forced to fly wingman to Sergio.

"Cut the chatter," Pritchett's annoyed voice came loudly over the com. "You've got air superiority, now move in and cover the infantry assault."

"Where's your wing man, SAM 15?" Sorenson demanded.

"Probably beatin' the crap outta some poor, defenseless robot."

"Darren! Get over here and cover me!"

"Okay, I was wrong. Hold up, dude, I'm comin'" Darren's SAM sped for Greg's location.

Darren was feeling indestructible again. Three, okay, two and a half kills and the night was still young. Going up against a Glitter Boy wasn't so bad. Darren checked his left side to make sure the plasma grenade was still there.

Near the base of the hill, a fire fight was breaking out between advancing infantry and Zenjori's outer perimeter. Darren wasn't even sure what Greg was attacking until rail gun rounds and mini-missile trails passed each other on thermo-optics.

"Darren!?"

"I'm coming!" Darren made a bee-line for the localized fire fight on the hillside.

Greg's SAMAS was pulling tightening circles around a Multi-bot, one of two the rebels reportedly had in their arsenal. SAM 312 was getting close enough to avoid a missile lock but still had to avoid rail gun fire and the occasional mini-missile volley. Four troops on the ground protected the robot from close attacks and fired sporadically at the circling SAM.

"Take out the greatest threat first." Darren closed in while Greg drew fire.

One well-placed burst killed the hatch gunner. Laser fire from the ground turned his way but wasn't even close to connecting. Telescopic targeting and multi-optic enhancement did its trick and two of the ground troops stopped firing forever. Darren's SAM screamed a missile lock warning.

"Sir, do whatever yer gonna do right now."

Dropping onto the upper body of the Multi-bot, Greg stuck his left arm in the open top hatch and fired a single plasma warhead mini-missile into the pilot's compartment. Plasma flashed up the open hatch and spewed forth in a geyser of flame. Greg jumped to the ground completely satisfied the Multi-bot was no longer a threat. Even if anyone survived the enclosed blast furnace, which wasn't likely, there wouldn't be anything left of the control system. He finished off two panicked ground troops with close range rail gun bursts, armor splayed and bodies left wide.

"Dang, sir, why don't you kick some tail?"

"Glitter Boy!" Peterson's excited warning rang out on the comm.

Seconds later a sonic boom followed.

"SAM down!" Sorenson proclaimed.

"If someone hadda, go I hope it was Sergio," Darren mused out loud.

"SAM 916. Direct hit from behind. Pilot might have survived," Mike announced.

"Damn. Yoshi."

"You still want the G-10?" Greg lifted away from the burning Multi-bot.

"Yes sir!"

"I'll cover you."

"You're on. Rock-N-Roll!"

Pritchett looked at his tactical screen with jaw set and grim determination. The air battle had gone better than he could have hoped for and one rebel robot was down, but he couldn't pull the SAMAS away from the infantry to deal with the Glitter Boy now that his Abolisher was lost. His Skull Walker made a funny sound every time he moved it, and the pilot's compartment rattled and groaned every time the rail cannons fired. At least the enemy ground units didn't have the range to shoot back.

"Fire squad 3, you're clear to advance. The Samson P.A. in your path is down."

"Captain! That Samson ripped us good and the rest of us took collateral from a rocket."

"This isn't a vacation, Corporal, advance!" Pritchett shouted over the radio.

"Yoshi's still alive." The communications officer called up medical readouts on the power armor units. "Somebody's got to get her out of there."

More sonic booms echoed past.

"iSr! That Glitter Boy's slashin my s —"

"Fireteam two, hold on for another few minutes. Fireteam two do you copy. Come in Fireteam two."

"Sir, we got another problem. The rebels are moving their NG-Hunter into range." The gunner rotated the skull body and opened up on the distant mech. Two seconds later the Skull Walker shuddered and rocked back. Multiple warning tones screamed and a new icon flashed brightly on the damage display. A grinding sound accompanied by a continual vibration followed.

"Radiation leak! Not critical but gotta shut down quick!" The communications officer tried to silence the nasty sounds coming from some place in the robot's undercarriage.

"How did the Hunter hit us!?"

"Farther up on that hill. More drop time for the slugs. If it hits us one or two more times, it's over. We have to retreat and shut the reactor down!"

"Turn us around and get the Walker away!"

Slugs impacted the skull's upper half and ran a line down the side. The sound coming from underneath increased dramatically. Every running step jarred the frame and stressed damaged workings.

"85% structural damage! Environment functions breached!"

"Skull 41! Do something about the Hunter!" Pritchett screamed, expecting slugs to tear through the pilot's compartment at any second.

"790's on it!"

The communications officer turned and gave Pritchett the news.

"One more hit and we're through."

Enforcer 790 sprinted across the river and up the opposite embankment. The Glitter Boy had stopped firing and the infantry assault had punched through the outer defenses. Coming down the embankment at a dangerous speed came the giant Hunter robot, furious that the Skull Walker had moved out of range. The pilot was so intent on finishing the damaged Skull Walker, it didn't notice the smaller robot springing for it.

Corrinne ran with one-minded focus, the Hunter getting larger and larger on her HUD. The Northern Gun manufactured Hunter towered almost twice the Enforcer's height as it barreled down the hill, and outweighed the smaller mech two to one. In a fair fight the Hunter would have little trouble ripping apart a damaged Coalition Enforcer without missiles and missing a hand. Corrinne never played fair.

Planting the right knee firmly against the ground, Corrinne slammed the Enforcer's left arm stump against the Hunter's overhung chest. Bracing the Enforcer's shoulder for impact and latching onto the Hunter's crotch with the robot's right hand, she prepared to put the bigger mech down. Metal screamed from the impact. In one fluid motion Corrinne pressed off the ground with her left leg and hurled the giant Hunter robot over her head.

The resounding impact of the two colliding robots was nothing compared to the sound of the thirty-some ton Hunter slamming to the earth fifty feet down the hill. The huge turret-mounted rail gun drove its barrel into the ground, the momentum of the sliding robot snapping the cannon from its turret housing. The crew was too dazed to know what had happened and could only wait for the robot to stop. Corrinne was on it before a natural dip in the terrain halted its downward furrow.

Grabbing hold of a rear exhaust port and placing the full weight of her Enforcer on the sprawled Hunter, Corrinne began dismembering it with continuous fire from the shoulder mounted rail gun.

"Two hostiles, six o'clock." Jameson swiveled the sensor turret and spun the top shoulder lasers to cover the Enforcer's rear. One of the enemy troops got off an ion discharge before lasers converged on his damaged body armor and cut him in half. The other rebel turned to run, but received similar treatment.

"If all we get is a few scratches out of this, I won't feel cheated," Corrinne commented.

One enemy robot wasn't ever getting up again.

"SAM 612 just ran into the cyborg squad. SAM 29 is down and the borgs are shredding it on the ground," Lisa reported Yoshi's wingman lost.

"Your corridor is clear, move in!" Pritchett ordered. The loss of troops on both sides was appalling, but the inner perimeter was buckling and Zenjori had played his hand.

"Fireteam Saber, counterattack and drive that Samson back! It's killing us!" a frantic cry from Fireteam 5 blared over the radio.

"We have visual, stand by. Moving in now."

"No! This is Winters to fireteam Saber. Back off and hold the corridor! Take the Samson after we pass!"

"Disregard that order, Fireteam Saber. Advance and engage," Pritchett countermanded.

A section of hillside to the left of the assault corridor lit up in crackling fury. The cries of Fireteam Saber ended quickly.

"You ran yer team into a minefield! It's on the map!" Winters shouted over the rover's radio.

"My tactical displays are out!" Pritchett yelled back, more sickened by the blatant mistake than the cost of lives. In the confusion of battle, these things happened, he rationalized.

"Sorenson to Fireteam 5. Keep your heads down. I've got your Samson."

"How many cyborgs?" Lisa inquired, Skull 41 starting up the hill behind Brian's hover rover. With all the carnage on the hill, not one challenger had confronted them. Fireteams Saber and Fury were supposed to have cleared it, but the lack of defenders was eerie.

"Half a dozen, maybe more." Pritchett didn't know. "Move in before I suffer more casualties!"

"Where's the rest? That's about half the number of cyborgs they have."

"Corporal Andrews, Sergeant Winters, I am at the limit of my patience! Do not become cowards this close to victory!"

"Listen here you D-Bee lover!" Sergeant Winters wound up. Pritchett hadn't left his Skull Walker since the meeting and the chain-of-command was still in place. "When I get back there, yer gonna be one sorry son of a ...!"

"If you don't follow my orders, I assure you, you won't be coming back!" Pritchett shouted.

Through a wall of smoke and flame the rover burst upon a burning clearing. Along its edges and charging through the flames like predatory demons came two dozen fully armed and heavily armored cyborgs.

Chapter 17

Oblivious to the battle raging below him, Darren flew fearlessly into the jaws of death. The Glitter Boy swivelled its mass driver up to meet him. Coming in faster than planned, Darren avoided the flechette round and collided with the stationary armor unit.

"Great plan, Darren." Greg flew past to engage a Titan combat robot protecting the Glitter Boy's flank.

Alone against the Titan robot, he started by blowing the sensor turret to smithereens with his last mini-missiles. If it couldn't see him, it couldn't hit him. After that, it was like shooting fish in a barrel.

The Glitter Boy hardly budged at the impact, its grounded pylons and rear stabilizer jets compensating for the loss of balance. Darren winced at the pain running through his body. Face-to-face with his nemesis at last.

Kreg looked at the skull-like helmet of his adversary, knowing for certain he was up against a madman. What kind of sane person would run a SAMAS into a Glitter Boy? Pushing the SAMAS away with his left arm, Kreg swung the rail cannon down with his right.

"Coalition incendiary delivery service," Darren announced cheerfully on the amplifier and pushed the plasma grenade down the barrel.

It rolled back out onto the ground.

Kreg fired.

Air collided where the projectile cluster had been and cracked the air with a sonic boom. Darren didn't want to know how close he'd just come to dying. None of his damage sensors informed him of missing body parts so he assumed he was still in one piece. The grenade lay on the ground, pin still in place.

"Guess it's the hard way." Darren grabbed the barrel of the boom gun and pushed it aside, pointing his C-40 at the shoulder swivel mount. Mushroomed slugs flew back to strike his gun and arm, ricocheting off the dense armor at the joint. Chrome splayed wide in a jagged line around the critical location. From somewhere outside his range of view, a powerful punch shattered the tiny spotlight below his right shoulder and sent the SAMAS back onto its thrusters.

Darren could have sworn the Glitter Boy intentionally aimed its rail cannon directly between his SAM's legs. Full thrust engaged, Darren flung the power armor into the air, flawlessly swinging his legs up and over in an acrobatic stunt worthy of any performer. The earth split in the smoking patch of ground left by the thrusters. Two hundred slugs burrowed deep.

The boom gun sailed in a slow spin out behind the Glitter Boy.

Kreg knew something was wrong the instant he lost the visual targeting lock from the gun, and the way the right armor and shoulder had jerked wasn't at all right. Looking over to where his right hand held nothing but air, Kreg felt his skin go cold. A clammy sensation washed over him. The boom gun was gone.

"Ha! Got you now, sucka!" Darren fired two perfectly aimed bursts and then got the shock of his life.

The rear ammunition drum on the Glitter Boy's back sailed off into the woods on explosive jettison. Crouching down then leaping upward with jet thruster assistance, the Glitter Boy went airborne.

Darren was still pointing the rail gun at the ground when the larger power armor grabbed hold of the thrust intakes on either side of Darren's head. The SAMAS' hover jets slowed the fall some, but not enough. The Glitter Boy crashed down on top and slammed the SAMAS' maneuver jets into the ground. The jets choked and died. Holding Darren down with one armored hand, the Glitter Boy raised the other for a hay-maker.

"Nobody told me these things could jump let alone fly!" Darren tried to recover from the mental shock.

Darren's head jerked to the side inside the padded helmet when the Glitter Boy's fist crashed down with enough force to smash an engine block. Molecular bonded armor strained and his helmet working bent under the stress. Darren swung with his left and clocked the Glitter Boy upside the head. It hardly budged.

Another weighted punch drove the optics systems closer to Darren's face. Darren swung back, barely marking the dense armor plating.

"This isn't working," Darren observed, grabbing the Glitter Boy's incoming fist with the SAMAS' left hand.

The strain pushed the exoskeleton to its limit, grinding servos and stressing stabilizers. Trying to free his right arm in vain, Darren watched the left be inexorably forced back.

Shifting his weight over the SAMAS, Kreg pulled away his fist and latched onto Darren's hand with the large chrome alloy extension of his own. Clenching his fist in the sensor control glove so hard it hurt, he began crushing the SAM's light armor.

Pain registered slowly at first, but got steadily worse. Darren knew his wrist wasn't supposed to bend that way, nor were the bones and sinews of his hands supposed to all come together in one place. The jets were still stalled out and the rail gun was pinned against his body, barrel aimed someplace near the Glitter Boy's heavily armored leg. Doing the last thing he could think of, Darren pulled the trigger as fast as the weapon could fire. Metal slugs ripped at the Glitter Boy's chrome knee over and over, each time coming closer to reaching the vital workings inside. Darren cried out in pain as the larger power armor tightened its grip on his hand.

The series of warning tones in Kreg's helmet and HUD cut short the urge to mangle his enemy. He slammed the SAMAS one more time for good measure after releasing the twisted hand. Pulling off the SAMAS too late, he felt super hot hydraulic fluid spill into the lower right leg and drench the light armor he wore. Staggering back on the weakened leg joint he prepared himself to launch one more time before the SAMAS could get up and fire. Hydraulic fluid ran down the mirrored surface from the wounded knee like a trickle of blood.

Struggling to get the SAMAS upright without the maneuvering jets, Darren felt as though the exoskeleton had gotten much heavier. His left hand and wrist were in agony and the clammy feeling creeping along his flesh told him he could lose touch with the real world at any moment. Already his equilibrium was failing and the surroundings wobbled more than he did. The Glitter Boy was coming at him again, and Darren brought up his arm too late.

Several tons of force slammed him back off his feet and onto the rear jets again, jarring debris loose. A restart of the thrusters started them smoking and spitting, just enough to get the SAMAS upright and blow clear the stoppage. He was knocked down again, the Glitter Boy giving no quarter.

"I'm getting my tail kicked by a Glitter Boy that doesn't even have a gun." The thought made him mad. Once again the thrusters sputtered and put the exoskeleton back on its feet.

Reacting on instinct, Darren fired another burst at the weakened knee and received a nasty ringing in his ears from a two-fisted punch to his head in return. The world spun and his rail gun jerked another misplaced burst. Both of the Glitter Boy's hands latched onto his gun and ripped it away, feed belt and all.

Like a third person in the back of his mind making him do things without conscious thought, Darren bounced upward and flamed the jets to clear debris. The broken control mechanism swung the exoskeleton clumsily out of the way of the Glitter Boy, but barely enough to escape its airborne flying tackle. The right thruster choked and Darren hit the ground again.

Kreg landed wrong, putting too much weight on the damaged right leg. The weight of his heavy armor bore down on the weakened frame, bending it at the knee in the opposite direction it was supposed to bend. His leg fractured horribly inside the unit. Agony so intense it took his breath away rushed to Kreg's brain and swept the will to fight with it. Frantically he rolled over and tried to reach the leg and bend it back into place, but there was only so much mobility offered by the power suit. Lying on his back, he looked at the bent leg and screamed in pain.

Staggering to a halt a foot from the Glitter Boy's head, SAM 15 bent over to look at the dying power suit, then raised a foot to repeatedly smash the face plate. Sensors and targeting systems blanked out and the displays blinked on and off each time the armored foot came down. Kreg was worse than helpless.

"Stop! I surrender! I surrender!"

The foot crashed down again.

"Please! Don't kill me! I surrender!"

"I don't care. You deserve this." Darren heard himself speak with authority.

The armored foot struck again.

"I give up! Just bend the leg back and I'll get out! I promise! I'll tell you everything."

Darren paused. He was barely in touch with reality. It took several seconds for Kreg's words to sink in. Walking to the bent leg he yanked it with the SAM's right hand.

It moved about a foot. Kreg screamed. Darren put his weight into it, managing to bend the knee joint into a somewhat horizontal position.

"Get out or I'll bend it back the way I found it."

"You'll kill me."

"Yeah, just like you wasted my friends and slaughtered those towns and villages. Get out."

Locking clamps released pressure around the arms and legs inside the Glitter Boy and the head unit tilted back as the front body section slid down and outward. Gasping at the pain, Kreg pulled himself from the Glitter Boy. Through the SAM's night vision optics it looked like the pilot's leg was soaked with blood through the flexible armor suit. Kreg dragged himself free, thankful it was only hydraulic fluid coating his armor. The inside was already swimming in blood.

"Don't kill me."

"Why not? I saw the vids. I was at Youngstown. I know what you did and you're going to pay," Darren's befuddled mind rattled on without slurring a syllable. Motive and logic didn't agree with each other.

"You don't understand. We were paid to attack those towns and villages along the Tolkeen border. We were paid by the Coalition to do it. Your money. Your guns. I need a doctor, please!"

"Lyboc paid you off to make sure the skelebots went through."

"Skelebots?" Kreg coughed, laughing hoarsely. "Zenjori was wiping out villages long before I joined him. destroying resistance so your own army could come in and take over, each time getting closer to Tolkeen. I can prove it. Get me to a doctor and I'll tell you how. Zenjori has a disk."

"What about the disk? Where is it?"

"He keeps it on him. You got set up. Your own government set you up to get wasted like the rest of us. And they're putting stuff in the water to make everyone believe what they're told, messing with your vids, it's all on the disk."

"You're lying. There's a list of fifth columnists on it. I know. I saw the intel reports."

"The list isn't complete. Most of it is proof of what the Coalition is doing to its own people. Get the disk for yourself. Lyboc wants you to kill us and destroy it so nobody knows what he paid us to do. Your captain knows."

Giant clouds of flame and smoke blew skyward from the assault corridor, less than a second later the repetitive sound concussions followed. The buzzing sound in Darren's head became louder, not just because his head hurt. His systems were warning of something coming down the hill toward them. Kreg collapsed on the ground, panting to stay conscious.

"SAM 15 to Merrick, over."

No response.

"SAM 15 to Merrick, over."

No response. Nothing on the radio at all.

Greg's SAMAS, somewhat the worse for wear, came skidding to a halt from a direction Darren wasn't looking. In the exoskeleton's arms he carried a very large mirror surfaced rail gun.

"Did somebody lose this?"

"Sir, my radio isn't working." Darren switched over to the voice amplifier as Greg had.

"Neither is mine. Something's jamming our frequencies. We have to go. There's an X-500 and the other Multi-bot coming down. I think we're losing."

"Where's the Titan?'

"Up the hill with its crew splattered all over the smashed controls. You going to make it?"

"I'm not feeling so good. I got the Glitter Boy." He pointed.

"I'll pat you on the back when it doesn't look like it'll knock you on your can." Greg looked down at Darren's twisted left fist. The helmet didn't look so hot either.

"What about him? He told me all kinds of stuff about the disk."

"Can you carry him?"

"I think so."

"Stay with me, Darren. You can collapse after we get back to camp."

Crashing timber up the hill turned both heads as the X-500 came closer. Its infrared spotlight bathed them and the belly turret angled down. Coming around behind it, Kruno's Multi-bot added its firepower.

"Forget him! He's nothing without the suit! Go!" Greg shouted and lifted out of the ion beams paths.

Charged particles blew up vegetation and blackened earth in a six foot swath beneath him. Sputtering flame and disintegrating earth helped propel Darren away from a rail gun burst. He bounced once to retrieve his rail gun then went airborne, two robots rushing the pursuit.

"Wait! Don't leave me like this!" Kreg wailed.

Kruno laughed. One giant robot foot ended Kreg's misery.

"Drive them back. Don't let them escape," Zenjori commanded quietly. Observing the battle from near the hilltop, he'd watched his outer lines fall to the Coalition onslaught despite the casualties he inflicted. Little remained between faltering inner lines and his position. Calling the battle a victory was premature. He'd lost too many power armor units to survive another organized assault, but the Coalition had lost their only chance to win. The casualties to his army he could afford. The Coalition could not.

"Kruno's forces are decimated." Notec marked off the outer perimeter on the battle map, then marked off several sections of the inner defense ring. "He's got two robots and some Headhunters counterattacking here, but our defenses are gone."

"Special thanks to the late Mr. Xevo for his radio jamming device. The Coalition is going right where we want them and they don't even know Sledgehammer squad is coming."

"Drake's probably loving this," Colnae commented, leaning back in the hover rover's seat and watching the pyrotechnic display from a distance.

"War is hell, and the Coalition is going to know what hell is."

"Oh man," Dave sighed.

"Skull 41 to Pritchett! Too hot! It's too hot!" Lisa shouted over the radio and knocked a cyborg off its feet with a converging rail gun burst. Four more moved in and returned fire. "Come in! Come in!"

"Git back!" Sergeant Winters barked at Brian, but the hover rover was already banking into a u-turn.

"They're turning around!" Dave watched the hover rover fly between the robot's legs.

"Skull 41! Git the hell back! There's too many!" Winters shouted into the radio.

A loud static noise returned.

Backing away from the onslaught, Skull 41 drew the most fire. The forward laser turret was blasted to a scrap metal appendage and both spotlight eyes turned to hollow sockets. Blinded and dying fast the Skull Walker stumbled to the side as its undercarriage buckled under its own weight.

Concentrating firepower on the heavy Coalition mecha, Drake's cyborg squad slammed through in a vicious counterattack. The four remaining legs collapsed and the mangled skull crashed down. Sending sixteen cyborgs in pursuit of the rover, Drake detailed the rest to finish off Coalition troops pushing through Kruno's lines. Drake chortled in a ominous rumbling voice and aimed his Wellington mini-missile launcher at the disfigured skull.

Explosive bolts blew the top section from the Skull Walker and ejection seats fire skyward instants before a plasma warhead slagged through frontal armor and caught the reserve magazine in the back of the pilot's compartment. The Skull Walker blew apart from the inside, opening up like a flower with burning petals of metal.

"We gotta go back for Lisa and Dave!" Brian shouted.

"Like hell," Winters grunted, climbing over the seat to exchange fire with pursuing borgs.

Laser beams and plasma charges flew both ways wreaking havoc on both sides. Bill fired continuously with the mounted C-40, more than once clobbering his teammates in the helmets with the barrel as he went from target to target.

"That one's got a launcher!" Bill cried out, spotting a partial conversion cyborg dropping to one knee with a shoulder-mounted rocket tube.

"Not for long." Rachel steadied her CR-1 on Cowboy's shoulder and fired a plasma warhead mini-missile. The borg exploded in a series of expanding flame balls, the magazine on its waist and back igniting.

"Reload!"

"Hold still!" Mathis dropped the missile as Brian swerved to miss a falling tree.

"Get the four-armed one!" Cowboy shouted, firing the last charge in his canister at Drake.

"Got 'im!" Bill swung the rail gun and knocked Cowboy face down in the rover. The feed belt jerked and the rail gun spat metal slugs into the heavy cyborg's armor. Drake caught his balance and swung his Wellington over to put the laser dot on Bill's chest.

Smoke shot from behind the launcher and all Bill saw was the smoke trail coming directly at him. Plasma expanded in a blazing sphere on impact. White hot flame seared over the occupants of the rover, burning armor and weaponry. Expanding gases blasted Rachel headfirst out the back of the rover and launched Bill into the rover's path. Brian latched onto the controls to keep from flying out and tried to keep the craft from crashing.

A second mini-missile bore down, killing instantly the wounded soldier brave enough to command the smoking rail gun. Winters sailed out of the second explosion to find the rover no longer beneath him. Striking a tree trunk, it smashed through and landed, awash in burning tree limbs. The cyborgs closed in.

What was left of Fireteams Saber and Fury opened fire just in time. Exchanging devastating barrages of fire, both sides pounded each other to a halt. A Coalition hover cycle was blown to bits along with its rider and one of Drake's cyborgs fell to converging rocket volleys. Trenton pulled together the last of Fireteam Fury and pressed back. Draining his last energy canister, Trenton switched to forearm rockets and traded mini-missiles with the closest attacker. Trenton won the exchange.

Under the hail of death, Winters charged the nearest cyborg and planted a fusion block on its armored chest. Caught by surprise, the cyborg panicked, swinging its rifle to get the Coalition soldier away.

The timer counted down from eight but Winters was too pissed off to care. To the utter astonishment of the borg, Winters grabbed the oversized plasma cannon from its bionic arms and blew off its leg. The body slammed to the ground.

"Sarge! Sarge! C'mon!" Cowboy stood his ground to cover his sergeant's retreat.

The rover tipped precariously out of the burning foliage and veered over two troops trying to get back in. Winters pushed off the fallen cyborg and sprinted for the rover. An athletic dive that defied his mass landed him against the red hot armor of the C-40.

"Git movin', Brian!" Winters shouted without checking to see who was driving.

Soldiers piled back into the smoking rover and helped the wounded in behind them. Clumsily heaving his body over a hover jet, Cowboy accidentally clobbered Winters. The rover lurched, spewing flames from damaged skirts and jets. Fireteams Saber and Fury fell under withering fire, with not more than a quartet surviving to flee with Trenton away from the advancing cyborgs.

Retreating down the hillside across the devastated battlefield, the Enforcer gave its last aid to cover the retreat. Rail gun and lasers blazing the Enforcer picked lead targets, but was only able to slow the counterattack.

For the first moment, Winters felt the pain of his injuries filter through. Scorched plates of armor were mirrored by burns of skin beneath, and his shoulder hurt badly, from what he wasn't sure.

"Cowboy! Head count!"

"Cody and Rob never made it back in and we're missing Bill and Rachel! Mathis isn't here either! He was running back to get Rachel!"

"Brian! Where's Shepard!?" Winters noticed the melted and empty seat next to the blasted radio.

"Right here!" A soldier in marred black armor announced from the driver's seat.

Winters rolled over and looked carefully through blackened eye pieces. Instead of the flanges of an officer's helmet the plain black surface of a grunt's skull-plate sat behind the rover's controls.

"Where's Brian!?"

"I dunno!"

"We can't leave 'em up there, Sarge!"

"Shut up, Cowboy!" Winters barked.

A long range laser beam cut through a damaged chest plate and exploded a soldier's innards back through the hole.

"Haul outta' there, Shepard!"

"Jenson just bought it!"

"Get down in the rover and pray!"

War stunk. Too many people got killed and too many were forgotten. Sharp had done his share of killing, but now it was time to save a life instead. Communications were dead and somehow things had gone very wrong. Worse yet, the Skull Walker hadn't come back down from the mountain inferno. There was no way Sharp was going to leave anyone behind. Not this time.

Slotting his last energy clip, Sharp secured his JA-11 and jetted full-throttle to where he'd seen a SAMAS go down earlier. He dropped through an opening in the trees just in time to hear the SCMS give its warning.

Two D-Bee Headhunters, each at thirty degrees from him. The compressed tactical from the targeting system showed exactly where the threats were. Firing a burst from the hip, he ionized one before he could fire. The second stood near the downed SAMAS, using the up-turned thrusters for cover. Sticking a bulky forearm mounted weapon over the smoking armor unit, the Headhunter blistered Sharp's shoulder with charged ions. Calmly and deliberately, Sharp went down on one knee and blasted off the exposed arm with a well-placed laser beam, then used the jet pack to bounce over and finish the enemy with close range ion charges. Another tone sounded from the AQ-3 to let him know the clip was empty and the internal canister was in use. No time to waste.

Someone had already pried the SAMAS open and dragged the pilot out onto the ground. Sharp didn't know who she was but recognized the insignia on her uniform. One of Pritchett's RPA's. The only thing he could see wrong with her was the trickle of blood running down her face from a cut above her eye. A chilling thought occurred to him. Zenjori was taking prisoners, otherwise this RPA would be dead by now.

Gently picking her up with both arms Sharp retained hold of his JA-11, draping her legs over his gun arm. The balance would be tricky in flight. No mistakes.

Impact hit his body with bone-jarring resonance. His head hurt and his back was numb. Things were flying around him out of an explosion from behind, his ammo belt, radio, and jet pack splintering into bits of shrapnel. Sharp staggered forward but for some reason didn't fall. The world spun around for him and he turned to see a light Terrain Hopper exoskeleton thirty feet away. It wasn't a deliberate action but survival instinct pulling strings deep within him. Looking down the bore of a grenade launcher, Sharp couldn't help but wonder if there was life after death.

The element of surprise worked in Sharp's favor. Nobody took an armor piercing grenade in the back and just turned around to see what hit him.

Sharp's unconscious aim took over, concentrating firepower on the upper body and head of the exoskeleton. Writhing to get away, it bounced up, hitting its thrusters and then crashed a second later its pilot blinded by charged ions erasing his retinas. Sharp's semiconscious mind sent him trudging down the hill and away from the assault corridor. The idea of getting away and saving a life, played over and over in his mind. Get away and survive.

Endorphin patches on both sides of Darren's neck more than compensated for the pain. In fact, he was feeling just dandy. The remnants of the Coalition force were at the base of Pritchett's Skull Walker.

Three undamaged hover rovers idled by themselves several meters away, ready to convey the personnel to safety. A pair of technical officers, the only two left, worked feverishly on sealing the leak in the Skull Walker's nuclear generator. Word was the Army of the New Order was regrouping for one last counterattack to finish them off. In Darren's drugged happy state it didn't seem to matter.

Military flashlights clipped to shoulder harnesses served as the only illumination for the emergency meeting at the Skull Walker. They had five minutes at best to decide the fate of the M.I.A.s. Five minutes to decide if the ones left behind were as good as dead.

"I don't leave my men behind! Not until I know for sure!" Greg shouted at the defeated and haggard captain.

"We don't leave our pals behind," Cowboy voiced, glaring at Winters.

"There's nothing we can do for them." Pritchett spoke evenly, eyes tired.

"I've got good officers and men missing in action. I will not leave until everyone is accounted for, dead or alive."

"My men are out there too, Lieutenant. You don't think that bothers me?! We don't have a choice. If we're here when the rebels counter-attack, we'll all be dead."

"And Jerry! You left how many men up there!? What is the matter with you?!"

"Now you wait one minute! You can't talk to me like that! Not after all we've been through! Ya know I'd bust my tail to save anyone in yer outfit! Treat me with some respect!" Winters shouted back. "You think I had a choice?! It ticked me off I hadda leave my men behind!"

"Sergeant Winters was right to pull out when he did. He saved the lives of most of your men, Lieutenant." Pritchett reasoned.

"I don't need yer help you cowardly D-Bee!" Winters tore into Pritchett with such vehemence that the Captain took a step back.

"As you were, Sergeant Major."

"Yer own men gonna take you out some day . Don't you ever think yer ever gonna git away with what you pulled today."

Quiet murmurs followed, but nobody took their eyes away from the faceoff. Winters already had his gun drawn, pointed at the ground at his side. Pritchett blinked first. He considered asking Winters if he was threatening a superior officer, but the question seemed ludicrous the way Winters' dark eyes bore into him. Pritchett knew his life would always be in danger now.

Rail gun fire sounded nearby and Peterson sailed in for a clumsy landing with a damaged SAMAS. The left thruster flared out brightly, almost knocking the exoskeleton into the group of officers.

"Sorry. There's something makin' it do that. I couldn't get anyone on the radio."

"What's going on, Peterson?" Greg stepped away from the SAM.

"They're comin'. X-500 and a Multi-bot, and more borgs than I could count. We gotta move. They still got missiles left. I saw 'em."

"How far?"

"Half mile, less now. I shot at 'em and got back to warn you cuz the radio's down. Lieutenant Sorenson and the Enforcer are tryin' ta slow 'em down some."

"Victor! I need the Skull Walker running now!" Pritchett yelled to his tech officer.

"I've got it held together with tin foil and chewing gum, sir."

"Whatever works. Power up, we're leaving."

"We can make it back to Liberty by afternoon if we haul," Nim announced.

"And leave our buds here?" Cowboy pushed his friend.

"We don't even know if they're alive! We're soldiers. We fight and some of us die. Face it, man!"

"Merrick, I'm not going to order you to withdraw, but you should know what your chances are." Pritchett turned and began marshalling the remaining troops into the hover rovers.

The rest stopped and waited for Greg to give the order. This was the kind decision Greg hated.

"You say we go after 'em and we're with you." Cowboy straightened up to his full 6'7'' and squared his shoulders.

It would be ordering a death sentence to stay. Greg knew it. His men knew it. He could see it in their eyes and yet he knew they would follow the order if he gave the word. Something clicked deep within his soul. The leaf began to turn.

"Load up. We'll organize search parties as soon as we're clear of the counterattack. After that we can stage search and rescue from Liberty. We will get our people back."

"You heard the Lieutenant. Git moving." Winters exchanged a lengthy look with Greg.

"What about the other rover? It's not gonna make it." Nim pointed to the trashed military vehicle.

"Put Jenson at the controls. Give him a grenade."

"Jenson deserves a proper burial," One of the soldiers shot back.

"We can't leave him for the magic users." Trenton urged.

"We can't do anything for him. Maybe this way his death won't be for nothing," Greg spoke sympathetically.

"The rover?" Nim asked.

"Trap it. Good."

Sorrenson's SAMAS plopped down in the camp looking more like a mutilated hunk of trash than an exoskeleton. The ground trembled at the approach of the enemy robots.

"We have to—"

"I know. Take the boom gun off my SAM then fly escort for the others," Greg ordered the other lieutenant then rushed to SAM 312.

Pritchett's Skull Walker and the rovers pulled away into the darkness.

"Peterson, you're with me. Darren, escort."

"Yes sir."

"You got any ammo, Peterson?"

"Uh-huh."

"Be generous with it. Pretend it's X-mas and you're Santa Claus bringing hunks of metal to all the bad boys and cyborgs."

Misplaced weapons fire came over the treetops even before the two exoskeletons lifted off. Two robot vehicles suddenly appeared less than 500 feet away and at their feet came over a dozen cyborgs.

Rail gun nearly empty and systems operating at 10%, the Enforcer wobbled backwards on weakened legs, shuddering with each step. Corrinne knew the robot wasn't going to make it, but was determined to continue hurting the enemy until the very end.

It took only a moment to know when the end had come. When the missile warning tone sounded, Corrinne pulled the ejection lever. Two ejection seats blew skyward from the fractured robot as two missiles impacted. Parachutes blossomed above the fiery wreckage of the burning Enforcer.

"Peterson!" Greg shouted over the loudspeaker to his wingman.

"What!?

"No more Santa Claus. Grab the Enforcer crew!"

"Yes sir!"

Greg banked away from incoming plasma bolts and tried to beat the cyborgs to one of the descending parachutes. Coming down hard, the Enforcer's co-pilot bounced once and groggily tried to free himself of the harness. Greg almost knocked him down by mistaking a tree stump under the parachute for the pilot.

"Get over here!"

He didn't have to ask twice. Practically jumping into the SAM's arms, Private Jameson clung on for dear life. Greg gripped the rifle and flew straight up above the tree line. Far away, Peterson's thrusters could be seen making a hasty retreat, two legs sticking off to the side where legs usually were not.

"Good going, Peterson. I'll have to make you an NCO someday," Greg commended the dead radio and then hit the jets in pursuit.

Thirty seconds later a localized mushroom cloud rose above the trees where Jenson made his last stand.

Stumbling down a steep embankment, Sharp splashed noisily into the creek at the bottom and came face to barrel with several Coalition weapons. A tiny light cupped in someone's hand lit the darkness enough for him realize he wasn't going to die.

"God, Sharp, we almost shot you." Lisa let some light slip through her hand so Sharp could recognize her.

Several other armor-clad figures came out of the shadows, one sporting a stylized officer's helmet.

"Something's wrong with my radio," Sharp blurted out, getting a hush from several troops.

"We're being jammed." Brian lifted the face plate of his officer's helmet and looked down at the RPA Sharp was carrying.

"Oh."

"That's Private Yoshi." One of the soldiers pointed.

Sharp knew the young soldier was also from Pritchett's unit by her armor alone, but didn't recall a name.

"Man, shut up, Gerald," Private Robert Rollings hissed. "You want them borgs comin' after us?"

"Were you followed?" Brian looked over Sharp's shoulder into the darkness.

"I dunno," he responded, still dazed from the grenade concussion.

"We better get farther up the creek," Brian advised, leading the group of survivors to a cleft between a stump and a large boulder.

Sharp still stood holding the injured RPA.

"You okay, Sharp?" Lisa asked, shining her light on his back. "Oh my god. What happened to you?"

"Grenade. I think. Good thing Merrick made me switch over to the electric model. I think my radio's fried, too."

"You can put her down, Sharp." Brian took out his own light and carefully illuminated a spot on the ground.

"Oh." He gently put her down, feeling pain spring back to his arms and neck. "Will she be okay?"

"I don't know." Brian looked her over, feeling for obvious broken bones.

More sounds of the battle traveled up the small valley.

"We're all gonna die! We're gonna die!" Private Gerald stood and aimed his C-12 at dark shapes.

"Man, get the hell down, Gerald!" Private Cody Nelson yanked the panicked soldier down, wincing at the painful burns he'd received when thrown from Brian's rover by an exploding mini-missile.

Nobody in the huddled group had escaped the battle without some injury to show for it. More weapon reports and explosions reached the group.

"Farther away that time," Lisa observed.

"They're leaving us! They're leaving us here to die!"

"Hey!" Brian looked up from administering first aid to Private Yoshi. Gerald's faceplate was down but Brian didn't need to see his expression to know the soldier was about to lose it. "Private Ben Gerald, right?"

"Yeah, yeah."

"They aren't going to leave us. We're going to make it, okay?"

"Yeah, yeah okay."

Brian went back to checking the RPA. It didn't appear as if there were any broken bones or serious injuries, but he injected her with a dose of nano-robots to make sure there weren't any internal injuries. Other than the nasty swelling above her eye, she appeared to be okay.

"She'll live, right?" Sharp leaned over, lifting his faceplate for a better look.

"Yeah, Sharp, she's probably just got a concussion."

Brian patted his friend on the shoulder. Private Yoshi had a blend of Asian ancestry, something Brian hadn't noticed during the examination. It suddenly became clear to him why Sharp was so concerned. The scene brought back painful memories in Brian's mind of soldiers left behind, and his heart went out for the torment Sharp must have experienced.

"Sir, Lieutenant Adams, what do we do now?" Private Nelson asked.

It took a second for Brian to realize he was the one being addressed. Taking his eyes away from Yoshi he noticed everyone was looking at him, grave faces expecting him to make the next decision. Suddenly he felt sick, a pit growing in his stomach and moving up to the back of his throat. Brian's mouth went dry. He looked from face to face, realizing each was depending on him for strength and direction. Their lives, all their lives, were resting on his shoulders, a responsibility he'd never wanted or anticipated. The decisions he made now would decide who would live and who would die.

"Brian, Lieutenant Adams, you are the ranking officer here." Lisa's intent gaze locked on him and he returned it for a long moment.

Her support gave him the strength to break the freeze on his body and mind, replacing the knot in his throat with a tingling sensation that ran through his entire being. It was all up to him now, like it or not, and if he didn't get them to safety, nobody else would. Throwing off doubts to his own abilities, Brian formed orders with natural fervor.

"All right, then, here's what we do. Private Gerald, I need you to do something important and help Private Nelson carry Yoshi here. Have either of you been trained in first aid?"

"No."

"Not really, sir." Nelson glanced at Gerald.

"That's okay, just be careful with her head. We're going to move up this creek a ways and try to re-establish radio contact. If for some reason that doesn't work, we'll work over to this ravine I saw on the map and use the hills to cover us back to the river. From there we can pretty much find our way back to Liberty, right, Corporal?" Brian nodded to Sharp.

"Uh, uh, yeah. That should work."

"What if they come after us, sir?" Private Rollings asked, displaying his partially melted C-14 rifle.

"As soon as we put some space between us and them, Corporal Andrews and I will check the weapons and fix what we can. In the meantime, give Corporal Andrews a quick inventory of what each of you has."

"What do you want me to do?" Dave asked, nursing an injured leg among other bumps and bruises.

"You and Li — Corporal Andrews have worked together before. Help her keep track of the inventory."

"Yes, sir." Dave smiled thinly.

Brush and twigs rustled somewhere down the creek. Flashlights went out and the group crouched lower, listening to the sounds. Footsteps in the water continued intermittently, then receded.

"No more than one or two," Sharp whispered.

"They probably heard us, man." Rollings peeked out from his position behind the stump.

"If they did, and they're not ours, they'll come back with more." Sharp checked the readout on his his weapon. Eight charges remained in the cell. Nowhere near enough.

"We need to move, now." Brian flipped his light back on, covering it partially with his armored palm. All eyes fixed on him in expectation.

"They'll track us. Easy."

"I know, Sharp."

"Maybe someone should lead them away from us." Lisa suggested. "Make an obvious trail out of the creek for them to follow."

"I know."

Brian hated his position at the moment. To send someone as a decoy was an almost certain death sentence, and each of them knew it. Worse still, Brian knew if he gave the order it would be followed. He wondered how Lieutenant Merrick had done it all those years, knowing he was ordering a man to his death. The sickening feeling returned when he wrestled with the best decision. The only one of them who could pull this off and have a glimmering chance for survival was the one person he least wanted to send, his best friend and companion since childhood, Sharp. He looked at his friend, both men understanding what it meant.

"Okay." Sharp nodded slowly, dropping his faceplate and hiding a wince of pain as he rose to his feet. "Make sure she makes it, Brian."

"She will." Brian nodded. "We all will."

Sharp nodded, the full understanding of what he was about to do sinking in. Without another word he crossed the creek downstream and started smashing through the brush on the other side.

Lisa choked on a lump in her throat and looked at Brian in the dim light. He dropped his faceplate and locked it in place so none could see the tears.

Victory cheers rose with the morning sun. A costly and hard-fought battle was over, and the Coalition was soundly defeated. Exactly how many escaped didn't matter, it was the piles of dead bodies and wrecked mechanized units that testified to success. Laid out on the ground were the spoils of war; Coalition weapons and captured prisoners to be dealt with however Zenjori Suka saw fit.

"Suka San, we think a few escaped up the north creek," Drake announced quietly, not wanting the prisoners to know any of their friends had survived.

Damaged patches on the cyborg were blasted away, but Drake was still in his prime. He hadn't been able to kill the last stragglers or the Captain's Skull Walker. That really pissed him off.

"How many?"

"Could be four or five. On foot."

"Send one of your cyborgs and four or five experienced Headhunters after them. I don't want them finding their way back to Liberty."

"Yes Suka San."

"Notec, Colnae. I need you two on medical detail. We're moving away from the hill and we can't afford liabilities. Heal the ones who can still fight. Be quick with the others." Zenjori tossed a pistol to Colnae.

"Yes, Suka San." The mage grinned.

"Yo! Boss! Got ya some more P.O.W.'s." Kruno tossed a beaten prisoner into the dirt along with two others wearing the same uniform and insignia.

Rachel moaned and tried to get up, but the abuse her body had taken was too much. Mathis looked at her with swollen eyes. All Bill could do was lay where they tossed him, the front of his uniform melted to his skin and much of his body covered with burns.

"Yes. I see that, Kruno. It appears your men have already taken a few liberties."

"Spoils of war. Ya know the rules. Check this out." Kruno held up the chestplate to Bill's armor.

Much of the composite was melted and the ceramic cracked around the impact mark.

"Mine?" Drake asked.

"Yep. Direct hit with a scorcher and the guy inside ain't dead. Gotta hand it to them C.S. egg-heads, eh?"

"I know why that one is laying on the ground almost dead, Kruno, but was it necessary for you to injure the others without my consent, spoils of war not withstanding?"

"Black one busted Trench's nose." Kruno kicked Mathis over, beating Trench to it with some obvious glee. "Didn't hurt the woman. Not much anyway." He laughed.

"How wonderful," Zenjori stated, deadpan expression masking his annoyance.

"Watcha gonna do with them others?" Kruno pointed to the other four Coalition prisoners lined up on their knees.

"They're not from the same unit as these three. My guess is these three are the ones that paid us a surprise visit the other night. I think we'll let young Mr. Tristan decide their fate. Kent, come here, please." Zenjori waved Kent Tristan away from the weapon's pile.

The teenage boy skirted around the prisoners with a mixture of fear and hatred. Zenjori put his arm around Kent like a father would a son.

"Kent, what do you think about these Coalition troops we captured?"

"I, I don't like them." He glared.

"And you shouldn't. See the insignia on those four over there? See the emblems on their uniforms? Do you recognize it?"

"Yes," Kent hissed through clenched teeth, tightening fists and shaking with fear and anger.

"They're the same ones who killed your grandfather, tortured and killed all those people in your town, and probably did all those horrible things to you. You have a right to hate them. Now is your chance to make things right. Avenge the death of your grandfather and make them pay for what they did."

"Kill them?"

"If you want." Zenjori turned to Kruno and held out his hand. "Gun."

Kruno turned to Trench.

"Gun."

"Man, I just cleaned it." Trench spoke in a nasal tone, a bandage over his nose to stop the bleeding.

He handed over a sleek 9 mm. Zenjori put the weapon in Kent's hand.

"Do what you want to them. As quickly or as slowly as you think they deserve."

Kent strode forward and pressed the barrel against a soldier's forehead.

"Oh god." Sweat ran down the soldier's face and he closed his eyes to what was coming.

The other prisoners watched in horror, wondering if they were next. Kent faltered.

"Go on, Kent, they killed your family. It's the right thing to do."

"He's using you, man!" Mathis yelled. Trench kicked him in the head.

"Look at the emblem on the uniform, Kent. You remember, don't you?"

Kent fired at the soldiers head.

"Way to go, kid!" Trench cheered.

Kent went down the line, one after the other execution style. Zenjori had to pull him away before he killed the three soldiers at Trench's feet.

"Them too!"

"No, not that way." Zenjori pried the gun out of Kent's hand.

"Why not?!"

"They should all suffer for what they inflicted on you, and all those innocent people. Justice must be done. You can help, of course, if you wish, but they will suffer for their deeds. Quite grisly."

"I don't care. I want them to suffer."

"Bring the injured one over to that tree. I'm sure we can find a spot on his body that hasn't been burned yet." Zenjori produced a pen-sized welding torch.

"Your sick!" Mathis spat blood at Zenjori's feet.

"For that, you get to be last. Sick is what you'll be when I'm done with your friends."

Rachel moaned, trying one more time to get away. Trench moved to kick her back down. Mathis moved suddenly and the mercenary was on the ground before anyone knew what happened. Mathis put his knee against Trench's back and ripped a grenade from the mercenary's belt. The pin fell to the ground in front of Trench's broken nose.

"Come now. A grenade is not the weapon you need to kill me." Pushing Kent behind him, Zenjori put his helmet on and aimed the .9 mm at Mathis. Kent and the other rebels backed away for safety.

"No! Don't shoot!" Trench pleaded.

Mathis looked at Bill. Bill pushed himself up into a sitting position.

"Do it." He fell back, hacking out a hearty laugh.

Mathis turned to his teammate of many years. Rachel nodded solemnly.

Mathis dropped the grenade.

Chapter 18

Long shadows invaded the cavernous regions of Gizmo's shop. The setting sun triggered extensive banks of mercury lamps to drive the shadows out of every visible corner of the six-story structure. In the harsh, truth-telling light stood Pritchett's Skull Walker, supported by the repair gantry like a giant, wounded arachnid. Lined up against one wall were damaged SAMAS and a score of malfunctioning energy weapons. Pritchett's two technical officers sat blurry-eyed at repair stations, attempting to resurrect the remains of several C-27 plasma cannons. The usual pair of guards outside the facility were absent, replaced by a dozing pitbull Dog-Boy and two lieutenants. Greg appeared remarkably more alert than Mike, but both wore haggard, lean expressions of fatigue.

"I hate to think of what it's going to take to fix 191." Mike stared at the mangled robot.

"More than you or I will ever make. That's Pritchett's concern, not ours."

"We don't have enough to cover repairs to the SAM's, not with Brian and Lisa missing."

"Infantry's our first concern, then fixing the SAM's. We can get two of them out on search patterns fairly quick. The Skull Walker's not going anywhere. As far as the cost, I've got us covered," Greg reassured.

"What did you do? Sell a SAM to First Strike? We don't have the budget for those kind of repairs." Mike's eyes narrowed with suspicion.

"Hated to do it, but I sold Darren's trophy and some of the rebel weapons to Giz. Not many units can withstand the boom gun's recoil, but Giz says he knows a mercenary with a rebuilt G-10 that's missing a gun. Pritchett can go to hell if he thinks he's getting a cut of the take." Greg grinned.

"Is that how you're going to explain your actions at your court-martial? You just armed another Glitter Boy. You realize that, don't you."

"I'm worried, can't you tell?" Greg's gray eyes flashed dangerously.

"Are you . . ." Mike's question trailed away and a sting of fear struck with him Greg's smoldering gaze.

"Crazy? No. No, for once I think I'm really starting to take control."

"You're risking a lot."

"I haven't even begun to take risks. Hey! Giz!" Greg called the shop owner.

The cyberneticaly augmented mechanic strode over with an uneven gait caused by his mismatched bionic legs. In combat, Giz couldn't compete, but in the shop, his extensive augmentation was a local legend. Giz never carried tools. He was one.

"Evenin' gents." Giz lifted a transparent welding screen so both mismatched cybernetic multi-optic eyes could inspect the two officers.

"How long would it take to fix SAM 15, completely?" Greg put his hands on his hips, towering above Gizmo's lopsided form. Giz turned around and focused one of his eyes on the exoskeleton opposite him in the garage.

"Well, that arm and hand are a painful sight, might be it takes me longer than you think. Body work's a breeze, but head not simple and parts I have none. How soon will you be needing it?"

"Rush job. I will be needing it tomorrow morning, if possible."

"Then price is high for help I have not." Gizmo turned back around to face his customers. "Your repair persons have not returned?"

"No, they're, missing at the moment. That's why I need the SAM fixed, fast."

"I will hurry, then. Like your repair persons, I do. Offered red-haired one job, you know, but he could not accept. Regrettable."

"We don't know if he's alive, Giz, but as soon as the exoskeleton is done we'll start searching."

"Your captain and sergeant borg talked of search earlier, but not agree. Sergeant cyborg very angry at captain, but then get quiet and tell to speak at different place when other sergeant walk in. Sergeant major, wide shoulders for clean man, then climbs gantry and looks around like he thinks nobody is watching him. Goes inside Skull and does not come out. I don't ask questions."

Mike and Greg exchanged looks.

"What would Trenton be doing talking to Pritchett?" Mike queried.

"Didn't ask," Giz answered.

"You're sure it was my Full Conversion sergeant?" Greg asked. "Pritchett has two borgs that look similar."

"Sure as I have two eyes. He and captain left when black sergeant major arrived. He is still in there, ask him." Giz pointed to the Skull Walker.

"That's odd. When I did a background on Winters, he didn't come up as a qualified pilot, or engineer."

"He's not. I don't think he even knows how to use the onboard systems." Greg shook his head.

"Communications?" Mike cocked his head at the Skull Walker.

Greg's brow furrowed and he started marching for the scaffolding.

"Maybe he doesn't have to know how."

"Wait! Quietly," Mike advised and began carefully ascending the gantry.

Hand over hand in rhythmic motion, both men climbed to where the open hatch could be seen below them, then slowly down to the Skull itself. Inching his head over the edge, Mike's cybernetic ear strained to hear any sounds that might clue him to Winter's actions. The sound of an access panel being replaced and screws locked into place came in too loud for comfort. The red glow of emergency lights was the only light coming from inside.

Greg gave a questioning look. Mike signaled for both to enter on the count of three and ran the time on his fingers.

Winters banged his head on the command console as the two new occupants made a clumsy landing on loose access plates behind him. Straightening fast and rubbing his head, Winters contemplated his situation. Neither officer said a word.

"What the ...?" Winters stepped closer, confrontational nature coming out strong.

"What are you doing in here, Sergeant." Greg's lowered head and fixed gaze gave him a sinister appearance in the flashing red glow of the emergency lamps.

"None of yer business." Winters reacted to the intimidation.

"Sergeant Major. The lieutenant asked you a direct question. Answer it, for your own good," Mike demanded, wondering if he was playing good cop/bad cop, or if it really wasn't play at all.

"I was looking for the captain. That's all." Winters went to move past and discovered Greg's hand latched in an iron grip on his wrist.

Strength went against strength, but Greg's hold remained strong. Mike pulled a flexible light from Winter's other hand.

"You done?" Winters growled.

"That isn't an explanation, Sergeant. What are you doing in here?" Greg didn't blink.

"Merrick, please. Sergeant Major, we know you aren't qualified to be operating the systems in this machine. We know you were doing something under the comm panel. Are you going to tell me or should I check it?" For some reason Mike was finding the interchange amusing in a distant sort of way.

"Somebody hadda do it!"

"Do what, Sergeant?" Greg tightened his grip, muscles bulging and knuckles white. Winters refused to acknowledge the pain.

"And ta think I figgered you'd back me on it."

"Is there something I should know before I open this?" Mike crawled under and started twisting the locks.

"Just don't mess with the console."

"Ohhh boy." Mike inched his head inside the opening and looked inside with the flexible light to find exactly what Winters had been doing. A type 3 fusion block with its timer set for one second and holding. Several wires ran from the comm breaker circuit to the detonator on the explosive device.

"Pritchett never woulda' known what hit 'im." Winters pulled his arm away as Greg lessened the vice.

"We thought this was something else, more serious, Sergeant." Mike's muffled voice came up from under the console. "You didn't wire this fusion block to anything else, did you?"

"No, just the power switch."

"Power switch? How did you know which was the power switch?" Greg asked suspiciously.

"Traced them lines on that 'chematic thing on the back of that panel. Turned it on an' off a few times ta make sure. It woulda worked if you hadn't screwed it up."

"I'm impressed, Jerry, for taking such initiative. I'd be proud of you except you'd probably have just killed one of Pritchett's techs instead. Good thinking."

"That wasn't the power switch." Mike stood and handed Winters the fusion block.

"Huh?"

"You were wired to the anti-tampering circuitry designed to fry the computer in case of capture. I haven't a clue why we're not all blown to pieces right now."

"You realize, Sergeant, that I'm supposed to report this." Mike looked disapproving.

"But you won't," Greg shot back and pulled the fusion block out of Winters' hand. "You're going to help us wire it to something only Pritchett would touch."

Mike looked at the fusion block and back down at the console, seriously considering the consequences of altering the chain of command, and wondering how close he'd come to receiving a similar fate on his previous mission.

Clanging chains struck the outside of the Skull Walker, and the rattle of heavy steps on the upper catwalk caused a triple response of drawn C-18's aimed at the open top hatch. Greg slipped the fusion block into his left hand while training his sidearm at a section of catwalk. A second set of footsteps moved much quicker across to the rear section of the robot and then stopped.

"There's three of them" a voice whispered from above, followed by audible sniffling noises. "It's Merrick and Winters, and someone else."

"Are you certain?"

"Yes. It's them."

"Lieutenant Merrick? Sergeant Winters? This is Captain Pritchett."

"We thought you might be someone else," Greg lied, holstering his weapon and shooting Winters a look.

Pritchett's head popped over the hatch.

"Ahh, Lieutenant Sorenson. What are the three of you doing in my Skull Walker?" He asked politely.

"Privacy. Open spaces can be dangerous security breaches," Mike covered smoothly.

"We're discussing our patrol schedule and rescue options, any objections?" Greg noted the way Pritchett's eyes lingered on the fusion block in his hand, but decided to leave the captain wondering.

"No, actually that's a good idea. As senior officer I should have been informed of this meeting, but if you'll bring me up to date on your plans we can start our discussion where you left off. Sharky, go stand guard," Pritchett ordered and climbed into the Skull Walker.

Winters mumbled some inaudible string of words under his breath.

"Status. I have four functional SAM's, two of which aren't going anywhere until after a complete overhaul. Mine and Darren's, 312 and 15, should be back in top form within seventy-two hours," Greg said, starting with a mechanized assessment. "You have one SAMAS. Number 612. It looks better than anything I've got right now. I don't see why we can't field one SAM for search and rescue right now."

"My pilot, Sergio, has been up for over twenty-four hours. Sending him out now would be foolish," Pritchett contended.

"We have other qualified pilots."

"I'll go," Mike volunteered.

"Just a minute, Lieutenant, 612 is attached to my unit." Pritchett felt uneasy about giving up the one working piece of armor he had left.

"It's going to be at least eight to twelve hours before we can send out an organized search party. There are other things we can do in the meantime, and getting a fix on our MIA's as soon as possible is a top priority."

"I agree. Believe me, Sorenson, I'm sympathetic, I know you have a personal interest in making sure any MIA's are rescued." Pritchett sounded sincere, referring to Mike's involvement with a technical officer in Merrick's unit. "I can assure you I will do anything I can to aid our search and rescue operation. Merrick, how is your wounded RPA, PFC Corley?"

"Darren's hand was fractured in several places and his wrist was broken, but the doc said he wouldn't lose it. Doc had him under a pretty heavy anesthesia for surgery. Told me Darren wouldn't shut up the entire time, conscious or not. I can have him back in action tomorrow. He's the best RPA we've got. Not that it will matter much by the time we get mobile." Greg mumbled the last part, feeling claustrophobic all of a sudden.

"Dr. Alverez's attitude worries me. Do you think Corley may have said some things he shouldn't"

"Darren always says things he shouldn't." Greg started smiling, anticipating the irritation he was about to cause. "He said some interesting thing about you and Colonel Lyboc." Pritchett's features darkened.

"Really?"

"Of course it was most likely just the drugs talking. I don't think the Glitter Boy pilot knew what he was talking about. He couldn't have known anything, right?" Greg started tossing the fusion block in his right hand. Pritchett tried not to notice. "Guess we'll never know, will we?" He waited for the captain to compose his response.

"I'm glad to hear your RPA is going to be all right, that means we can send out SAM's in pairs instead of solo. We'll schedule the first shift for 0800 tomorrow. PFC Corley and my man, Sergio."

"We're shorthanded, not desperate," Mike countered. "Sending the two of them together may be a mistake."

"I'm sure they can be professional long enough to handle it. Both have friends out there, and the added firepower might become necessary for a hostile extraction. The rebel army is still out there. Two RPA's stand a better chance than one."

"I wouldn't be surprised if only one of them comes back." Greg stared at Pritchett, still tossing the fusion block. "I'd be willing to wager on who it will be."

Pritchett scowled.

"Regardless, a cooperative search is in order, and it needs to be more than a pair of SAMAS," Mike demanded, getting irritated at Greg's unprofessional behavior himself.

"I'll have Sharky take my Dog Pack out in the morning" Pritchett offered. "No solo actions, please. We can't afford any more losses."

"Afford? Funny, you being concerned with price now." Greg's tone became dangerous. "Everyone has a price to pay, Captain, some more than others. We've already paid ours. What about you?"

"I'm going to pretend I don't know what you're talking about, Lieutenant, you're obviously very tired. Let me restate my position on our common, and immediate goal; Rescuing any and all MIA's and fortifying our position here in Liberty." Pritchett tried to meet Greg's gaze, but finally looked elsewhere.

"Fortify?" Greg couldn't grasp the concept of orders and objectives anymore. "Fortify with what? For what?"

"We ain't got nothing left." Winters didn't mention the secret stash he'd set aside for Pritchett's timely removal.

"Let me assure you, Sergeant, that what I have is available for your use as well. I have two C-40 ammunition drums and several cases of ordnance in my APC, plus the reserve here in the cargo bay." Pritchett pointed to the cluttered rear bay of his Skull Walker. "What's more, I have a crate of mini-missiles and fusion blocks stashed in storage that we haven't even broken the seals on. We have no shortage of supplies."

"How generous."

"We're all out here together, now more than ever. Let's try and remember that," Pritchett admonished diplomatically.

"That all remains to be seen." Greg reset the timer on the fusion block and handed it back to Winters. "Some of us have memories we'd like to forget."

Heat from the small fire was directed by a stack of logs and overhanging rock, warming the body of the resting RPA. Two others huddled closer to the fire, though it hardly did much through their full environmental armor. Private Yoshi was awake and in fair spirits, joking with Dave and Private Gerald about far off places and times.

Perched on a small ledge ten feet above the creek at the bottom of a steep ravine, the Coalition troops took refuge in the natural hollow created by a giant tree that had fallen and ripped a gap in the embankment with its upturned roots. The cold mist still reached them in the ravine, but at the moment, water and warmth were taken care of. Food and safety had yet to be attained.

Brian and Lisa sat on the small rock ledge examining the few weapons and explosives they'd managed to salvage. A few energy clips with charges left, several C-18 sidearms, two TX-5 projectile pistols, and a pair of type 2 fusion blocks lay on the rock slab. Brian forced a fabricated metal piece to a C-14 Firebreather in place and carefully tested the pump action. Something inside popped along with the sound of clinking parts and loosed springs.

"Wait, no, Brian. . . " Lisa grabbed his arm before he could hurl it to the opposite bank.

"That's the fourth time now!"

"Maybe it's just broken, like I said before." She pried it away from him and set it on the rock out of his reach.

"I know exactly what's wrong with it, I just need my tools," he grumbled, holding up a warped assortment from his kit. "Problem is they all pretty much look the same. Melted."

"That leaves us with one working rifle. At least most of the sidearms are okay.

"Yeah, lots of good those will do if they find us. We'd almost be better off throwing rocks at them."

"You sure the fire was a good idea?" Lisa lowered her voice, not wanting the others to hear her questioning his orders.

"It wasn't a good idea, but it was the only way to keep Yoshi from going into hypothermic shock. I think Gerald and Nelson dropped her in the creek on purpose."

"It wasn't the only way." Lisa's eyes laughed.

"Oh please, not that again."

"You had five volunteers. Six. I might have done it."

"No way. I know she's the only one without environmental armor, but it wasn't an option then, and it isn't one now."

"You're no fun," she teased, pouting and letting matted blond hair fall down over part of her face.

"Not that I would have minded watching you strip down, or anything. Private Yoshi's not that bad, either."

"Should I be jealous?" She nudged him. "You looking at other women now?"

"C'mon, Lisa, why do you always do that?" Brian reached past her and picked up the C-14 again.

"What?" She batted her baby blues, for once not intentionally.

"You know it's not like that anymore. I already feel stupid about the way I acted, you don't need to keep teasing me about it."

"Sorry, Brian, I guess I thought you could joke about—." Lisa stopped and reworded. "What am I saying. Sorry. Really, I'm sorry."

"Now you really had to go and make me feel like an fool," Brian sulked, taking the weapon apart again.

Lisa went back to filing shrapnel out of a TX-5 barrel, not sure what to say.

"Would it help if I ordered you to go keep Private Yoshi warm?" He spoke up, trying to hide a smile.

"Now see, there you go again! What am I supposed to think?"

"All right, so the joke's on me. Just take it easy, okay?"

"Okay, but only if you make it an order, Lieutenant." She smiled.

"Yeah, yeah that's right." He went back to his work.

Lisa readjusted her earphone and fiddled with the wires leading to her helmet on the rock beside her. There hadn't been any more transmissions, and they hadn't broadcast calls for help themselves in case the rebels might be eavesdropping. Either help was too far away or simply non-existent. Lisa looked back over at the soldiers now in Brian's charge. She knew Dave could handle the stress, as could the two veteran troops Brian had sent out to dig trenches and set booby traps. The other two needed the most support, Private Gerald was a raw recruit and Private Yoshi was an RPA seldom exposed to danger outside a power suit or robot. Things were going well, a bit too well under the circumstances. She knew Dave had someone to go back to, and that the fire to survive would help carry the others. And then there was Brian, who they all drew strength from whether he knew it or not. He wasn't the same person she'd met months before.

"I think I'm going to break up with Mike," Lisa stated out of the blue.

Brian paused in his work, but didn't look up.

"Why?"

"It's not working."

"We had this discussion before."

"And I've thought about it some more. I don't know if it will ever work. He's still in love with his ex-fiancee, you know. I knew it all along, I guess. I should have expected it, catching him on the rebound like I did. I'm, I'm not even sure what I expected. Or wanted."

"That doesn't mean it can't work out. Believe me, I know, there's no perfect relationship. You gotta work at it, sometimes more than others." Brian kept working. "I still think he's an fool, though."

"I wonder if he made it."

"Sorenson? He probably got himself shot down, like always, but knowing him he'll survive. He always does."

"I just don't know how to make it a clean break."

"Well, if and when we get back, and assuming he's waiting there with open arms, just do what your heart tells you at the moment. Your real feelings won't lie. Not much else you can do."

Lisa watched Brian sort out the parts and begin patiently reassembling the weapon for the fifth time.

"You did really good last night, you know."

"I didn't have much choice." He glanced up at her and over at the trio by the fire.

"No, I mean it. When it all came down, you did good."

"Well, don't tell them this, but I was just doing the first thing that popped into my head most of the time. I just pretended like I knew what I was doing. What else was I supposed to do? Your life's in danger, you just do the first thing you can think of to survive."

"Maybe that's part of the reason. What did you think about last night, when your rover was hit and you thought you were going to die? What were you thinking?"

"I don't know. I'm not even sure I was really thinking about anything. I just knew I didn't want to die, and I grabbed Nelson 'cuz he was closest to me and we ran until we came across Rollings hiding behind a fallen tree. Heck, I didn't think much after we found you and Dave, and Gerald. I just did the next thing that came to mind. It worked, I guess, but I wasn't thinking much until I had the time to figure out what was going on."

"That's not really what I meant," Lisa tried to explain herself. "I mean, okay, when the Skull Walker went up, and I was above it floating back down on my parachute, it couldn't have been more than twenty seconds, but all these things kept running through my head all the way down. Kinda like those stories you here about your life passing before your eyes. It was real, only it kept happening over and over. And it wasn't Mike I was thinking about."

Brian stopped his work and looked into her eyes, trying to read the signals that words hadn't expressed. A crackling of branches up on the other embankment ended the moment.

"It's just us, Lieutenant." Private Rollings edged down the steep slope, using trees and branches to ease his descent. Behind him Private Nelson mimicked his action. Lisa made Brian lower the C-14, making him feel stupid for aiming a broken weapon at his own troops.

"You all done?"

"Yes, sir, but it was a pain. How come we had to dig full-size trenches if we ain't gonna even use 'em?" Rollings asked.

"Same reason you put the broken weapons facing out and covered the trenches with branches." Brian got up, pouring the C-14 parts into a belt pouch for later assembly.

Rollings helped Nelson reach the ledge across the creek, then got a running start and scrambled up behind him to join Brian and Lisa. Both were dirty, armor caked with mud.

"I know why we put the guns there, sir, to make them think there's actually guys in the trenches. But it took forever to dig 'em out as deep as you told us."

Brian and Lisa moved to the fire, sitting on roots from the tree. The two veterans came to a halt and immediately plopped down near the fire to rest, pulling off dirty helmets to lean on.

"For one, we might actually need to use those trenches. Two, did you rig the fusion blocks like I said?"

"Yes sir."

"Well, this is what I was thinking." Brian shot Lisa a quick smile. "If you just shot the heck out of an enemy trench and weren't getting any return fire, you'd still have to go check it out, right? To be sure, just in case you didn't see all the enemy soldiers or they were playing dead. You'd have to be sure, right?"

"Oh, oh yeah!" Rob Rollings brightened. The buzz-cut soldier had already managed to smear mud on his cheek.

"So they make sure nobody's in the trench, and whamo!" Cody Nelson smacked his hands together.

"Trip lines all set?"

"Yep, but the grenades ain't gonna do much. All we had left was Gerald's wussy firecracker H.E.'s."

"At least we'll have some warning."

"Right, sir!" Nelson saluted, leaving mud on his forehead.

"Nelson, is that C-12 working?"

"Yes sir."

"Telescope?"

"On the fritz. Spots good, but I ain't sure on the aim."

"Get up on the lookout point where I told ya to go when you were done." Brian did his best impression of Sergeant Winters minus the colorful language.

"Yes sir!" Nelson hopped up and started climbing back up the side of the ravine.

"So when's our take-out gonna be delivered?" Dave flexed his leg, trying to keep the injury from stiffening up so bad that it kept him from walking.

"Funny. Anything on the radio yet?" Brian turned to Lisa.

"Nothing."

"They can forget their tip," Dave joked.

"Looks like we're probably going to have to hoof it back to Liberty." Brian looked at the small squad. Nobody had escaped without some type of injury, minor or not. He'd never checked his own bruises and burns, afraid it might make the others worry or think he was weak. Winters never showed pain or weakness, neither would he. Brian tried to imagine Lieutenant Merrick giving orders and what he would do in this situation.

"How far we gotta walk?" Dave asked, wincing in pain. He hadn't dared remove his armor for fear of never getting it back on.

"One, two days maybe, depending on how fast we go. Bet you're glad you stuck with that old plate-style instead of switching to the new soft suits all the RPA's in Chi-Town are using."

"I'll say. Leg would be busted for sure."

"That means you can walk. Are you going to be okay to travel soon, Private Yoshi?"

"I think so. My head hurts. Sometimes I think I'm going to puke."

"That's fine." Brian didn't show his concern. "I'm sure Ben here will be happy to act as your crutch if you need it."

"Sure thing." Private Gerald beamed.

"Man, this is gonna take a miracle." Dave shook his head, casting a good natured smile around.

"I could do with a miracle about now." Lisa looked up at the overcast sky. "Whatever gods are up there, we'd really like to go home now, please."

"What do you think happens to us when we die?" Yoshi asked, looking directly into Brian's brown eyes.

"I don't know, I guess nobody does, really. Some people say you walk into this light or something like that, but from my own experiences, I've been hit in the head so hard I saw all kinds of lights. I don't know how accurate that is."

"Do you believe in an afterlife, or some kind of god?" She pressed the issue, treading on ground generally shunned by the Coalition.

"Yeah, like the Pre-Rifts cults?" Rollings asked.

"I know about those Pre-Rifts religious cults, we all do."

"It was the magic users, wasn't it Lieutenant?" Ben nodded. "They used their magic to make people think they were performing miracles because there really wasn't any magic back then and the people didn't know they were being tricked. All the people back then did what they said 'cuz they thought they were gods."

"Freya believes in some Pre-Rifts god." Dave joined the discussion. "She says he created the whole universe and used all this magic to help people way back in ancient times, like before electricity, vids, or any other technology."

"Right." Brian sounded skeptical.

"So what do you believe, Lieutenant?" Yoshi fixed the question and her gaze on Brian again.

Years of indoctrination told him all the right things to say and arguments to give, but somehow he couldn't stomach repeating those lines when he looked into her dark eyes and saw the passion for life behind them. If what he suspected about her head injury was true, she was dying.

"Truth is, Yoshi, I don't really know what to believe. Gerald's right about the Pre-Rifts cults, most of the so-called miracles were just magic users trying to trick people, we know that now. Some people believe in this reincarnation thing, where you come back reborn in a new body. I'm not sure how that's supposed to work. To me that sounds kind of depressing, like I'd have to go through all the same crap growing up again, over and over. Besides, if I had past lives, how come the previous me doesn't keep the present me from making the same mistakes again? See what I mean? It's real confusing.

"Other people believe in a god, or groups of gods, like way back in ancient times they supposedly lived at this place called Olympia, or something like that. They believe these of gods watch over them and do miracles when they pray to them. I'm not sure how that's supposed to work, either, but it's kinda scary if you really think about.

"Personally, when I look at the complexity of human life, or any life, for that matter, and all the wonders of the universe, including magic and other stuff we don't understand, I really can't just believe it all happened by some freak chance. Now whether it was some great, powerful god that started it all or something else we don't understand, I don't know. It all had to start someplace."

"What about after death? What happens then?" she asked.

"I don't know." Brian paused, realizing the blasphemy he was speaking, but he just couldn't bring himself to lie. Not now, not to her. "I'd like to think it doesn't just end, like you're dead and that's it. That's actually more scary and depressing than believing in some weird afterlife thing. Some people believe if you're bad to other people, you go this hell dimension. It's supposed to be this place where you burn and get tortured forever."

"Oh, so that's where that comes from." Rollings nodded understandingly. "Go to hell. I always wondered what Winters really meant."

"I'm not even sure Winters knows, he may just be repeating it because everyone else does. Those same people believe if you're good to other people, you go to this other good dimension where you get to live forever. Problem I have with that is, it brings you back to some kind of god or being that decides who was good or bad, and that kinda sucks. You're right back where you started with the whole god thing. I don't know, Yoshi. Personally, yeah, I'd like to think there's this afterlife thing where your soul goes when you die, at least someplace better than this world. It's kinda up to what you want to believe in, I guess. Which god or gods or no gods you believe in and whatever happens after that is, well, it's all unknown. I don't think about it much."

"I have." Dave grew somber. "Actually, just about every time I go into battle I wonder if there's a god out there."

"Me too." Rollings nodded.

"Like you said, I'd like to think it's not just over, that there's something better after," Dave went on. "Freya says, if you believe in some god and when you die you find out you were wrong, it's no big deal. But on the other hand, if you don't believe, and in the end you're wrong, well then you're pretty much hosed."

"That's very insightful, Dave." Lisa smiled. "I believe we'd better get you back to your woman fast, before you start sprouting wings and quoting ancient Pre-Rifts texts."

"So I take it you don't —"

An explosion cut short Dave's question and jarred all to battle alertness. The echo faded away up the ravine.

"One of our traps." Rollings looked at Brian.

"Grenade." Brian stated, snatching up his helmet and the pile of weapons to play quartermaster.

"Lieutenant Adams! Lieutenant Adams, this is Private Nelson. Come in!" Cody's voice came in on the comm.

"Adams here. What's the situation, Nelson" Brian did his best to sound in control, like Merrick always did. He looked over and saw Private Gerald kicking dirt on the fire. "Gerald! No! Stop doing that!"

"They'll see the fire!"

"No, they'll see the smoke if you keep trying to put it out! Leave it alone!"

"-up the hill!"

"Sorry, Nelson, 10-9?"

"There's two of 'em, plus one more, I think, covering them from the trees as they're goin' up the hill."

"Don't give away your position yet. Which hill?"

"The, uh, north one. Opposite bank from you, sir. There's one in the trees. Shootin' some kind of particle beam at the trench up there."

"Only three?"

"Maybe Sharp got a few," Lisa whispered, making Brian think of something he was trying to forget.

"Only three so far, sir. I can't see the one in the trees very well, there's still too much smoke from the grenade."

"Give me a description of the two you can see." Brian finished handing out weapons and motioned for Lisa to gather up the rest of their gear.

"Headhunters, it looks like. Some bionics maybe, but their Gladiator-style armor's lookin' real bad and one of 'em's got a busted rifle on his back and's carrying a pistol. Their helmets are messed up bad, probably blast right through them with a C-18 if ya got close enough. Other one gots an ion rifle, Triax make, I think. Front load E-clip."

"Good eyes. Keep watching for others and don't give away your position."

"Yes sir."

"We can take 'em, sir." Rollings held up a high frequency blade in one hand, a C-18 in the other.

"Okay, Rollings, for right now I'm making you my corporal, okay?"

"Yes sir!"

"I don't know if it will stick when we get back, but for now consider it official. You take Gerald with you up to the fall back point on the ridge and be ready to finish those Headhunters off if the block doesn't get them."

"Yes, sir." Rollings motioned to Gerald and took a running leap across to the other embankment.

"Hey, Corporal Rollings, quietly. Don't make a mistake."

"Right, sir."

Private Gerald repeated the leap flawlessly, and received the exact same reprimand for the noise from the new corporal. The two moved up the embankment more quietly, still making enough noise to make Brian cringe.

"Nelson to Lieutenant Adams."

"Go ahead, Nelson." Brian signaled Dave to help Yoshi up the ravine, tossing him the last grenade. "Hope you don't have to use it."

Dave nodded and helped Yoshi to her feet.

"Them two Headhunters is mosta' the way to the trench. Guy in the woods shot up there a few more times, but still hasn't come out. Which of the two do I shoot first? The one with the rifle?"

"Neither. You've the only rifle we have. Save the firepower in case we need it."

"Yes sir. Oh man, sir, we're screwed."

"What? What happened?"

"It's a borg, sir, it's a borg down there. Oh, man, and another Headhunter. No way we can take a borg, sir."

"Just hold position. Maybe it will lose a leg in one of the trenches. Where is it going?"

"Moving over my way. Wait, it stopped and they both ducked back into the trees. I can't see them, but they're shooting at the trench on the other side now."

"If they make it past the trench, snipe at them and keep moving so they think there's more than one of you up there. Aim for optics and weapons, try and bring them down to our level."

"Right, sir, disable first, kill later."

"Lisa and I are going to find a spot on the bank opposite you and take potshots at them once they start trying to get you, that way maybe you'll have a chance to get off a few good shots. Make every shot count."

"I know, sir, I only got eleven left."

"Hey Cody, this is Rob. What are those Headhunters doing?" Rollings asked over the comm, waiting before crossing an open space between clumps of dense brush.

"They're checkin' on the trench we dug up there. One of 'em's skirting the tree line and makin' sure there's nobody waitin' to snipe 'em when they check the trench. Movin' good, these guys aren't dumb."

"Rollings, stay down until you're sure of a kill. Your best judgement, Corporal." Brian tried to bolster morale as he and Lisa worked their way down the ravine. The time for long range planning was gone, now it was shoot from the hip tactics. His heart pounded so hard it made his ears throb.

"Man, what happened? That Headhunter just dropped into the trench an' nothin' blew." Nelson watched the man with the pistol examine what was left of the defensive position after several particle beam blasts had altered it. "Too much dirt got in it. He's holding up part of the C-12 and waving so the borg down below can see it. Man, they're onto us, sir."

"No they're not. They're just onto the bluff, not us. We still have the element of surprise. They don't know we're actually still here." Brian hoped.

"Yeah, sure enough, sir. Cyborg and the other Headhunter are walking over to the other trench, or what's left of it."

"Now's your chance, if you think you have a shot."

"Yeah we —"

The detonation on the north ridge knocked leaves from trees and brought an avalanche of pine cones down the banks into the ravine.

The sharp sonic shockwave echoed for what seemed like seconds before fading away in the rolling hills and steep ravines.

"Holy smokes, sir, I think we got one. I wasn't watchin' but there's just a big cloud of dust over there now. Must have gone off after all!" Nelson proclaimed.

"Rollings, make your move while the other one is trying to figure out what happened."

"Yes sir!"

Brian plopped down between a pine trunk and the steep edge of the embankment, trying to pick out where the cyborg and Headhunter would ascend the slope to reach Nelson's position. He and Lisa carried C-18 sidearms, powerful for their size, but hardly enough to hurt a heavily armored cyborg. The best they could do was distract it so Nelson could hit his mark with the rifle. Brian pointed to a spot twenty feet up the bank and Lisa started climbing to her assigned position. No sense in them both being in exactly the same place.

"We got 'im, sir! Scratch one more rebel," Rollings joyously announced.

"Good work. What about the rifle?"

"Triax. Piece of crap. Got a few charges in it, but range and balance are toast."

"It's better than what you had. Find a good spot and wait for Nelson to start taking shots at the borg. Once he's got them committed to coming after him, you and Gerald fire at will."

"Yes sir."

Brian felt elation, despite the immense danger. He'd flunked infantry boot camp twice, when all one needed to pass was the I.Q. of a common houseplant and the ability to aim a gun where someone pointed. He'd been told he didn't have what it took to "make the grade" because he always had a "yeah, but" for every order a sergeant gave him. He'd never thought he had what it took for front-line combat, and concentrated on his technical talents. Merrick had told him he picked him for the "yeah, but," although he expected Brian to follow orders anyway. The "yeah, but" never quite left him, though he'd learned to hold his tongue. Now all the crazy ideas that came up every time he got an order were his orders to give. The plan was working, although not quite as anticipated and far from over. The strangest thought popped into his head, and it seemed so incongruous it made him chuckle. Cara couldn't call him a wuss anymore.

"Sir! Stupid scope is way off!" Nelson complained. Treetops behind him popped and descended from weapons fire aimed in his general direction.

"Take it off and go hard sight if you have to." Brian still couldn't see where Nelson was taking fire from.

"Man, Gerald, your rifle stinks. I missed three times!"

"Then give it back," Private Gerald returned over the comm. It was his rifle, after all.

"Come over here and get it."

"Take your shot and fall back, Nelson."

"I'm already on it, sir. Got the cyborg once in the neck, I think. Somebody already smacked it upside the head with an ugly stick before I got it. Its optics looked pretty fried, and the Headhunter with it ain't gonna be winnin' no beauty contest."

"Sounds like Sharp's handiwork. Concentrate on its head," Brian ordered, still at a loss as to where the sporadic particle beams and ion blasts were coming from. More energy beams cut through the trees down in the valley, originating someplace on the north side.

"That you, Rob?" Nelson's voice sounded worried.

"Yeah. Popped that headhunter a couple times 'fore it got its head down. He's lookin' right at me now. Got 'im! Popped up to shoot and I can swear he ain't there no more!"

"Good shooting, Rollings!" Brian praised, looking to Lisa and shrugging. She shrugged back, still unable to see where the battle was.

Two more particle discharges sounded so close Brian could smell the ozone. The far ridge showed two puffs of smoke and descending foliage where the beams had struck.

"Where the the borg go? I can't see it no more," Nelson asked.

"I don't got it either." Rollings answered. "I lost track of it when I was shootin' the Headhunter. I can hear it shooting."

"It ain't shootin' at me," Nelson announced.

"It's over by me and Lisa." Brian spoke quietly.

"Where?"

"In the bottom of the ravine." Brian slowly switched positions to look down the embankment.

A willow tree popped back in place near the water and through it stepped a large, Partial Conversion Cyborg no more than thirty feet from Brian's position. It carried a large particle beam rifle with multi-optics scope, and its belt was ringed with long power clips for the bulky weapon. It turned its back to Brian and sidestepped along the water, firing charges at the opposite embankment. It stopped again to change clips and then fired two more shots at the other side.

"What it shootin' at?" Nelson's voice sounded loudly on the comm. "I ain't anywhere near there."

Brian waved at Lisa and pointed to the borg, but she waved an emphatic "no" back at him. Brian pointed to his own helmet and then at the borg. She repeated her gesture. He held up three fingers and started counting down, then turned to aim his C-18 at the back of the borg's mangled skullplate.

Lisa shifted position for a better shot. Pine cones and dead branches slid down the slope into the bushes to the borg's left. It glanced over, then whirled around.

Brian pulled the trigger as fast as he could, laser beams colliding with chest, arm, neck, and head armor in a wild chaotic pattern. When Brian finished emptying the clip, the cyborg took its time and aimed its particle beam rifle right at Brian's head.

Two sets of laser beams burned through the willow tree at the bottom of the ravine and converged in rapid-fire fashion on the wounded armor plates of the cyborg's head. The beams ceased. Missing most of its head, the cyborg crashed to the ground in a pile of blood and scrap.

"Sir, I still can't see it," Nelson complained.

"Me either, sir," Rollings announced from the ridge behind Lisa.

The willows rustled again. Following the borg's heavy prints, a humanoid patch of shrubs and foliage moved silently to confirm the borg's demise, a Coalition C-18 in each mud and moss-covered hand. The distinctive point of a rifle stuck through the shield of overgrowth on the figure's body. It was Sharp.

"Sharp, Sharp, is that you?" Brian scurried down the embankment.

"Yep," was the weary reply.

The Coalition sniper collapsed and fell into the creek, staining it red with blood.

Van pressed the fan speed control to high and wiped the sweat from his brow. The small fan bolted to the interior of his Mountaineer provided the only environmental control without him having to go push a button in the pilot's compartment. *That would be too logical,* Van mused at his disjointed thoughts and continued working in the stuffy compartment.

A thin line of smoke lifted from the point where solder and circuit met with heat. The crossover was almost done, and then it would be time to test one of the most devious, and dangerous, creations he'd ever constructed.

"Yo! Dude! You in there?"

Three loud knocks struck the outside of the vehicle. Van blistered his finger on the soldering iron.

"Damnit!" Van flung it away from himself and stuck the blistered finger in his mouth. "Whath do you wanth?!" Van asked through the lightly armored skin of his Mountaineer.

"I like need to talk to you a sec," Darren answered back.

"Just a minuthe." Van glanced at the red L.E.D. clock before opening the hatch. 2:15 am. Why would someone be up at this time of night? He must have forgotten to shut the main doors to his rented shed.

Darren looked like a wreck. Disheveled clothing and plastered black hair contrasted with green eyes that remained remarkably alert for what the appearance portrayed.

"Whath?"

"Take your finger out of your mouth."

"Oh."

"Can I come in for a sec? I need a big favor." Darren looked around suspiciously.

"Yeah, sure." Van backed up and cleared a pile of scrolls from the other seat bolted to the carpeted floor. Darren looked once more outside then closed the hatch.

"I heard yoru unit got messed up."

"Yeah. I got the Glitter Boy, though." Darren heid up his bandaged hand and took the seat facing Van.

"I took a look at one of the G-10's First Strike has. Those are some tough units."

"Dude, something smells really bad. Uh, Van, your soldering thing is like burning a hole in the carpet." Darren pointed to the floor. The blackened tip of the soldering iron lay in a pool of boiling nylon.

Van snatched the cord from the power pack and flung the entire device out the door onto the concrete floor. Cool air from the re-opened hatch slowly replaced noxious fumes.

"Isn't that bad to breathe?"

"I'd imagine. Better leave this open for awhile to air out."

"Dude, I like need your V-med thing." Darren looked around the cluttered compartment for the distinctive looking glass salt shaker.

"Sure. Here." Van pulled the device from a belt pouch and handed it over, knowing full well Darren couldn't make it work.

Darren waved the device over his injured hand but the flashing lights and whirring sounds were absent.

"I think it's busted." Darren shook it harder.

"Actually, it's just not charged. I don't think it's such a good idea to use that to heal your hand. Remember last time I used it to heal that lieutenant of yours? Soresson, or something like that?"

"I don't care. It hurts and I don't want to be drugged out of my skull this morning on S & R. I gotta go look for some of my buds that didn't make it back and I gotta be able to use my hand."

"Who's missing?"

"Sharp never made it back, and lots of others you don't know. Worse, I gotta go out with Sergio. I can't even sleep until I get this fixed."

"If I use the V-MED to heal your hand, assuming it works, I'm not going to have to explain it to your C.O.'s handgun, am I?"

"Chill, dude, Merrick's cool, and if any questions come up I'll just say the Cyber-Doc did some weird stuff when he operated on my hand. I'll even wear the cast whenever I'm not in my SAM."

"Okay." Van shrugged and took the device back. "This won't work very well unless the Cyber-Doc already fixed any major damage."

"Yeah, he like put all the bones back where they were supposed to be already."

"Hold your hand still."

Whirring sounds accompanied by spinning lights emanated from the Van De Graf Medical Enhancement Device and a strange sensation ran from the the tips of Darren's fingers all the way up his arm. Directed magic energy from the Techno-Wizard device knit fractured bone and healed abraded tendons. Black and blue sections of mangled flesh and medical incisions faded to normal beneath the bandages and light polycarbonate cast.

"Wow, that feels way better."

"One of these days I'm going to get around to marketing this baby." Van put the V-MED back in its case on his belt.

"Oh. Now that's a crime." Darren spied a remotely recognizable C-14 laying on Van's makeshift work table. "What did you do to it?" He reached over and carefully examined it.

"Made a few more modifications."

"No way. You can't even slot an E-clip in this anymore. How are you supposed to fire a grenade with these wires and gizmo things in the way?" Darren followed the mesh of cables running from the 20 mm grenade launcher to the disassembled guts of what used to be an interactive video game entertainment center.

"That's just to test it. The finished version will have a removable screw-on cap that fits over the grenade barrel and feeds directly into the system. It should be all modular when its finished. All I have to do then is take off the interface cap and I can fire grenades like normal."

"As opposed to blowing the cap off the barrel when you fire?"

"No. Theoretically it should be sent directly at the target I'm aiming at on the screen." Van powered up the vid screen and finished hooking up the modified video game interface.

"I know some dude who blew away his vid screen with a shotgun, but a grenade's pretty harsh, don't ya think?" Darren was having fun teasing the Techno-Wizard. Magic practitioner or not, most techies were fun to tease.

"Well cross your fingers because I haven't tested it yet."

"What's it supposed to do? Waste vid screens?"

"Earlier I modified this grenade launcher so I could teleport a grenade directly to a target when fired. Solved quite a few problems and then I thought, why bother with a targeting system. Simply put, I can hit any target if I know exactly where its at. Then I got this idea to build a device to track and view people and locations remotely, like a crystal ball, only better and not so hokey. I planned to use it to find Zenjori Suka and see what he was doing so Sir Renfield could get together a force to go take him out. But then I got another idea."

"Wait a minute. You can like just say some magic and see whoever you want on the vid screen?"

"No I need to have met the person, and know who they are, then I program a tracking chip, and if they're close enough, then I'll see where they are on this map program. Once I've got a fix on the person, then I can see what they're seeing at that particular moment. I haven't worked all the bugs out, but it worked on Delwin. Then I ripped the guts out of that interactive game set, including the little plastic gun you aim at the vid screen and shoot targets in the game with. Hooked the emitter up to the weapon sight on the C-14 so where I aim the gun on the screen, that's where the grenade will go, assuming I'm in range of the real action."

"Shemarrian dude. Are you telling me you can just type in someone's name, and have them show up on your vid, then just sit here and frag 'em?"

"It's scary, actually, but yes. It is very energy intensive and there are some limitations, but overall this is a very safe and accurate way to kill someone from miles away and without warning or trace. I've already programmed some chips for Zenjori and a few others we both know."

"Could you use it to find Sharp?"

"Now that's an idea. Let me disconnect the C-14 just in case. How far away from here is Sharp supposed to be?"

"Like a whole mess of miles."

"If he's within this thing's range we should be able to locate him and see what he's doing. If he's not dead, that is. Let me set up a chip for that. Actually, let me try and see if I can locate him first without a chip. I wrote a program for stuff like that, but never tested it."

"If you can just get me close, I can find him in the morning. Sharp's pretty smooth. I'd give him better odds than everyone else we're missing. Fire it up, man, let's see the techno-magic thingy work!"

"Okay, I've got him on the comp, and about everything I remember about him. Any personal information you want to give me will help."

"Now just give it some juice, visualize a little, and. . . . . . "

"What does it say?" Darren squinted at the blinking type as if narrowed vision would improve his literacy.

"Target not acquired."

"Damn."

"Like I said, I don't even know if everything is working right. I haven't ever tested it without programming a locator chip first, and I've changed a few things around to hook up the C-14."

"Can you test it on someone you know will show up?"

"I could run it on Pritchett. It worked when I tested the chip." Van's eyes glittered playfully and the smirk was back on his face.

"Where can I buy one of these? I know someone back in Chi-Town I'd love to keep an eye on."

"You can't use it without the right, psychic frequency, we'll call it. You're not attuned right to make this work for you. However, if you need some help, I might be willing to run it for you."

"Pritchett's a good start. Gotta test it, right? Not that we'd ever want to see what he was doing or anything."

"Of course. We'd never eavesdrop."

Van typed in "Pritchett" and channeled energy from his body into the receptor circuitry and bank of modified chips beneath the keyboard. The screen blinked, then flipped through a series of maps to show a blinking red icon directly over the north-west section of Liberty. More energy primed the mystic circuitry to lock in the view from Captain Pritchett's eyes. The screen fuzzed, then a crystal clear image came in.

Troops and borgs surrounded the captain, along with several mutant Dog-Boys from the pack. Sergio nodded affirmatively and then Pritchett turned his head to a pit bull Dog-Boy leading the remainder of the pack.

"Where's the sound, man?"

"I must have forgot to hook it back up."

"I wanna hear what he's saying!" Darren moved closer to the screen.

"Isn't that one of those mutant Dog Packs you guys use?"

"Only some divisions use them. Merrick doesn't like them. I don't see Skarky anywhere, and he's usually either with Pritchett or the Dog Pack. Man I wish I could hear what Pritchett is telling them."

"That looks like one of those storage places you guys rented to keep your hover vehicles in. I recognize the metal support by the door." Van pointed to the image on the screen at the edge of Pritchett's vision.

"Dude. How long would it take to hook this up to the C-14?"

"That's a Coalition Captain."

"You said yourself it's untraceable. The perfect assassination. C'mon, I'll frag him if you don't want to!"

"I'm too tired to go through all this again with everything hooked up. I've been working on it for over eight hours and some of the parts still have to be powered up before I install them. Think of it like having run twenty miles and then needing to rest. Tomorrow maybe, after I get some sleep."

"We're on then, as soon as I get back from S & R. I'm gonna tell Merrick that you might be able to help us find Zenjori and our MIA's. I don't think he'll freak too much if he finds out, just so he doesn't know all the magic details. After that we take out Pritchett."

The screen died out and the view faded.

"I'll think about it." Van yawned.

"Ya know, I just thought of something. Is there like a record button on this thing?"

"No. Not yet. I could hook it up to a vid recorder I guess."

"Don't. If I see any vids of me an' Cyndiara, I'll know exactly who to hunt down for my royalties."

"I'd be more worried what Cyndiara would do to me, if you know what I mean."

"Do I ever." Darren grinned. "Tomorrow afternoon sometime. Laters!"

Darren hopped out of the Mountaineer and headed for the hotel a few blocks away. For a moment, Van contemplated testing the viewer one more time, not that he'd actually record it or any such thing. Opting for a safer alternative he locked up and made his way back to crawl in bed with Anja. It wasn't as tough as he'd thought it would be to respect her principles of purity, there were so many more important things to concentrate on. Just the same, now that Darren had planted the idea, he'd have to test out the viewer merely for curiosity's sake. Blackmail wasn't his style.

Normally Sharky wouldn't have passed up the opportunity to slay an unsuspecting mage and drink his life force, but this situation was different and he twisted his body deeper into the shadows as Van locked the shed and trudged away.

It hadn't just been luck that he was there to overhear the conspiracy to kill his commander. He'd been following Darren anyway, and when magic energies in the area altered slightly he moved in closer to learn why. Whenever magic manipulated the flow of ambient energy around it, mystic currents burned off and left a scent so strong it was difficult for the Psi-Stalker to resist. It took a great deal of restraint to conceal himself instead of feeding. Prudence payed off and he was rewarded for his self discipline. Pritchett would be pleased with him, especially if his report had a few self ingratiating details added. With gleeful intent Sharky slunk off to brief his captain.

"Lock on me one more time an' I'm really gonna kick your tail!" Sergio threatened for the fourteenth time in two hours.

"I don't understand either. It just keeps doing it without me. Must be a damaged system. Targeting glitch." Darren tormented his wingman. He'd give it fifteen minutes this time and then weapon lock SAM 612 again. Sergio didn't have the guts to face him one-on-one and Darren knew it.

"There's nothing here. Let's move on."

"That about finishes the first sector. Check in and take the east end of the second sector," Darren ordered.

"It's your turn to check in."

"Yeah, but I'm in charge. You do it." Darren was starting to think there might be something good about the whole command thing after all. Merrick had put him in charge, so why not take advantage of it.

"Jerk."

Sergio veered in the direction of the mid-morning sun coming through overcast skies. Cruising low and at a seemingly slow pace, the exoskeletons methodically searched for survivors with frequent radio messages and thermo-scans. A bank of dark clouds moved in from the north-west and threatened to dump rain in less than an hour. That would complicate the search.

"Darren, are you getting anything on your radio?"

"No. Just you."

"I think I see a smoke signal about 6,000 feet north-west of me," Sergio reported. Maybe there's someone over there."

"What was your first clue, Sherlock, the pillar of flourescent green smoke and frantically waving dude in the open field?" Darren closed in with telescopics.

"I got trees in my way"

"Wow, pretty good guess on the range. They're not responding on the comm."

"Maybe their radio's not working."

"Looks like CA-1 armor from here. One of our boys. How'd they get this far south-east without a vehicle?"

"I saw 'em first so I get to report it."

"I'm going down for a chat. You stay up and watch for bad guys. Wipe that brown stuff off your nose while you're at it."

Circling the column of green smoke Darren looked for signs of a trap. It wouldn't be the first time Zenjori had used stolen Coalition equipment to fool his adversaries. The Coalition armor was obviously one from Pritchett's unit and appeared undamaged. Slung over the soldier's shoulder was a C-12 rifle that kept slipping down every time the soldier waved his arms. Why wasn't he using the comm, Darren wondered. Leaving his rail gun ready to fire Darren hovered to a stop opposite the small field from the Coalition troop. The armor looked too new, and something didn't feel right. The soldier suddenly dropped to the ground.

His exoskeleton jerked violently to the left as wing fragments flew past Darren's face. Tactical warnings screamed in his ears and the HUD readouts flashed a red blinking wing on the diagnostic. There'd been no weapon lock yet something had just blown his right wing off at the joint.

Now there was a weapon lock.

Darren hit the booster jets and flung the exoskeleton away from an incoming mini-missile. The fragmentation warhead blew shrapnel back up into the jets and added blinking yellow lights on his diagnostic display. SAM 612 shot past overhead as the ground broke open in five places and Pritchett's Dog Pack was unleashed. Before Darren hit the ground, one mutant Irish Setter was shredded by the C-40. The trap snapped shut.

Dropping to one knee and quickly reloading the CR-1 launcher, Sharky watched with growing dismay as SAM 15 ripped his ambush to bits. Working in a smooth circular fashion, the damaged exoskeleton never missed its mark. A back hand splattered the German Shepherd's head and a short jet flash burned away areas of exposed flesh on the black lab. Nimbly sidestepping bolts from the pit bull's C-27, the exoskeleton made short work of the alpha dog by simply smashing its thick skull into its body cavity with the tip of the rail gun.

Laser fire from behind scored a line of holes in the main jet thrusters, but Darren was too occupied with removing a doberman's arm as it reached out with forearm claws to notice. He cracked the skull of the howling mutant animal and whirled around to deal with the human soldier by the fading smoke signal and burnt Dog Boy.

Sharky shouldered the launcher and sighted in, but a terror suddenly overcame him like never before. It was a new presence so dangerous and fearsome it made SAM 15 seem insignificant. Sharky slowly turned to face the source of his premonition; an irate Great Horned Dragon lowered its head and stared down on him. One last terrible scream left Sharky's lips before a scaled claw crushed the air from his lungs. Kro-Mar eyed the Psi-Stalker momentarily, then silenced him forever by decapitation.

Splashes of purple paint covered the scope on the soldier's C-12. Looking to his right in confusion, the soldier's black face plate became orange. A swooshing sound followed the shotgun report and something flying very fast slammed the soldier to the ground.

Delwin Moonbeam.

"My gun! Mine mine mine mine mine mine mine!" Delwin wrenched the weapon away from the stunned man. Bouncing to his feet, Delwin flipped the selector to fully automatic fire and emptied the clip.

Darren was finished crumpling the black lab before the C-12's clip was empty. Smoke from the blast crater wafted lazily through Delwin's wild, multi-colored hair. A form roughly the size of a Mac truck lumbered up behind the crazy man. Darren's confusion was put on hold momentarily when another weapon lock warned him of an incoming mini-missile.

Kicking off the ground, Darren's exoskeleton was caught from behind in an expanding cloud of shrapnel. New lights joined the diagnostic display accompanied by a pleasant female voice.

"Rail gun feed belt damaged. C-40 not functional."

"Not now, babe! Don't ditch me now!" Darren pulled the trigger repeatedly with no effect.

Looking down he could see the shredded end of the feed belt hanging just inches from the ground. The C-40 was nothing more than an expensive club now.

"You shouldn't have messed with me. I'm gonna waste you!" Sergio gloated over the radio. Darren's SAMAS stood shrouded in drifting smoke and settling dust, but telescopic enhancement revealed its apparent lack of firepower. Sergio readjusted, course and came in for the kill, eyes focused on the targeting dot lined up with Darren's head. SAM 15's left arm came up but the mini-missiles never left the launcher. Something else was in the way.

Huge wings and hundreds of scales filled Sergio's view and blocked his mid-air path. In a move that could only be described as a flying belly flop, Kro-Mar launched himself at his prey. Sergio had nowhere to go.

Mass to mass, the SAMAS lost. Stunned by the bone-rattling impact, Sergio was only dimly cognizant of what happened next.

Prying the exoskeleton out of the earth where he had landed on top of it, Kro-Mar released his past frustration on the man-made construct finally within his grasp. Time and time again the little mechanical beasties had foiled his best laid plans and extensive repertoire of spell magic. In the end, success was achieved with tactics the average stone age neanderthal could have devised. Kro-Mar clutched the exoskeleton and pounded the skull-like head with his bare fist.

Watching the almost cartoonish action unfolding before him Darren briefly considered expending his last two mini-missiles on the overly animated dragon, but concluded from past experiences that it would only tick the beast off. Darren looked to Delwin for a distraction, but the bizarre man seemed unworried by the fact that a very large dragon was pounding in the head of a SAMAS no more than a few feet away. At last a cry of victory from Kro-Mar ended the pummeling and the dragon held up the mangled exoskeleton in exultation.

"I got it!"

It didn't take a techie to figure Sergio's probable condition. One look at the SAMAS and Darren knew the RPA was the least of his concerns. The big, grinning dragon holding it like a rag doll was looking at him now. Fighting it without a weapon was ludicrous, and running away seemed unlikely. Darren gambled.

"Oh, uh wow, I'm like really scared now. You just killed the best pilot in the entire Coalition States! You must be the great and powerful Kramer!"

The dragon's exultant smile darkened. He knew who this human was.

"Kro-Mar!"

"Oh, oh yes, the great and powerful Kro-Mar! Word of your greatness has spread. All fear your name."

"Really?" Kro-Mar puffed out his massive chest. "Well of course. I, the immortal Kro-Mar cannot be defeated by mere mortals, especially one like you. Private Darren."

"Uh, you like know my name?" Darren really started to worry.

"Of course. Now show me how to make it fight." Kro-Mar thrust the mangled SAMAs at Darren.

"You know my name?"

"Dragons know everything, stupid human. Show me how to make it fight."

"Everything except how a SAMAS works." Darren was hoping he could give the dragon a reason not to kill him, but instead the monster stepped menacingly closer.

"Show me how to make it fight!"

"Uh, no problem, Kramer, I just didn't think one so powerful as you would need a crummy exoskeleton."

"It's mine now. Make it fight."

"Actually, I don't even know how I'm going to get Ser ... Admiral Sergio out of there, much less how you're going to fit inside."

"I can fit."

"I think you broke it."

"Give me yours then."

"Uh, mine's broken too, see?" Darren tossed the rail gun down. "Can't fly or fight with this one either."

"Show me where to get one that works and show me how to make it fight."

"Uh, sure thing. Just as soon as I find my pals, we can all go back to Chi-Town and I can get a brand new one for you."

"Hey, man, I heard about your friends, man." Delwin sidled up to Darren's SAMAS.

The familiar multi-colored shotgun was slung over his shoulder instead of the immensely more powerful C-12 he'd just liberated from its former owner.

"Uh, Delwin, now is not a good time to chat. Kramer, the big dragon right there, could eat us both any second now," Darren whispered loudly.

"Kro-Mar's my soul buddy, man. We're like one with the cosmos, experiencing the wonders of this universe, man. Kro-Mar's not gonna eat ya, man, are you pal?"

"I'll think about it." Kro-Mar didn't want to drop out of character. "Humans don't taste good raw anyway."

"Glad to know that. If you don't mind, I'll let you both get back to your wonders of the universe and I'll be going to look for my friends."

"No, man, like we can help you find your friends. Your friends are our friends, man," Delwin offered.

Kro-Mar sat down and tried to figure out what protruding part would make the exoskeleton open, suddenly disinterested in Darren and his predicament.

"I don't know, Delwin. I'm out here in the middle of nowhere with a weaponless SAM and you and the mighty Kramer," Darren thought out loud. "Pritchett's pack and only RPA just tried to kill me. I think I'll just hoof it back and report all this," Darren spoke sarcastically.

"That's okay, man, we'll find your friends for you. It wasn't them, was it?" Delwin looked around at the corpses of former Coalition warriors.

"No, definitely not. Actually, I'm not even sure I want to risk calling this in on the radio. I gotta think of something. If I run into Pritchett's goon squad like this I'm screwed."

"Here, man, you can use mine," Delwin offered his shotgun.

"No thanks, dude, uh, my hands are too big. See, finger won't even fit inside the trigger guard." Darren held out an oversized, mechanical extension of his own. "I really appreciate the offer, though. I need something bigger."

"Use that one." Delwin pointed to the exoskeleton in Kro-Mar's grasp.

"No! Mine!" Kro-Mar held onto the exoskeleton possessively.

"Kramer busted it." Darren pointed to the skewed angle of the rail gun barrel.

"Oh yeah, man. So why don't you just take one of their guns?" Delwin looked past Darren to the outer edge of the clearing.

Turning around slowly, Darren watched a pair of tall, female D-Bee riders approach on massive cyborg mounts.

Chapter 19

"You are trespassing on Shemarrian tribal land!" one of the female warriors shouted, dismounting and pointing a very large rifle at Kro-Mar.

"Leave at once or die!" The other warrior swung an identical rifle over and attached a feed belt to a pack on her back.

Darren did a tripletake, one to gawk at the very large proportions of the upper torso anatomy exposed on the warriors bodies, and another to gauge the height of the newcomers at about eight feet, equal to his SAMAS. Both had elaborate helms and body armor that was hard to distinguish from their bodies.

"Step right up, step right up, don't be shy, you too can have the deal of a lifetime!" Delwin rattled off in his announcer's voice, sauntering bowlegged to Darren's broken rail gun.

"You have thirty seconds!" The warrior on foot followed Delwin with her weapon while her cyborg mount pawed the earth with giant mechanical claws and brought two shoulder mounted weapons level with Kro-Mar. The beast's tail lashed angrily behind it as the ten foot tall cyborg creature prepared to pounce.

"Yes, for only 29, 99, 9, 99, 9999999999999, 99, you can have this pristine, right off the production line, Coalition C-40 rail gun. Now I'm sure you're asking yourselves, how can Delwin offer such a great weapon for such an amazing price?"

Kro-Mar sized up the situation as Delwin continued his used car salesman's spiel and the Shemarrian warriors counted down from thirty. They had really neat looking guns, without bends or broken parts. Kro-Mar wanted one.

"16, 15, 14, 13 ..."

"I am the great and powerful Kro-Mar! Lay down your weapons and I may spare your miserable lives!"

"9, 8, 7, 6 ..."

"Uh, Kramer, let's like, leave." Darren backed for the trees.

Kro-Mar chanted spells. Delwin added a free dicing and slicing paring knife to the bargain.

The Shemarrian Warriors leveled their weapons at the most dangerous intruder.

Leaping the clearing in a single bound, Kro-Mar tripped on the Shemarrian mount charging him from the opposite direction. Sprawling headfirst, he came to the end of his furrow right under the nose of the second rider and mount. Both blasted him at point blank range. The sonic concussion bent the grass around both warriors.

Delwin ceased the dealing, engaging his jet pack and aiming himself at the warrior on foot. Psychedelic armor impacted a body of much denser composition, bringing the airborne crazy to a jarring halt. Unfazed, Delwin latched onto the Shemarrian's rail gun and kicked off her chest, attempting to dislodge the weapon from her grasp.

Confusion and aggravation vied for prominence on the Shemarrian's face, unsure how to interpret the crazy man's behavior. Self-defense mechanisms kicked in and she extended sharp claws from the armored gauntlet of her free hand. Sinking the claws into the multi-colored jet pack, she flung the man away from her and prepared to do the only sane thing in an insane situation. Kill the lunatic.

Alerted to the motion by a pair of antennae protruding from her head and helmet, the Shemarrian warrior was still too slow in responding to Darren's body block tackle. The impact threw both to the ground, Darren felt every bone in his body rattled by the unexpected mass of his opponent. The rear jets on his SAMAS kept it from being rolled on its back, and allowed him to grab hold of the Shemarrian's rail gun in the struggle. He pulled back, struggling to wrench the weapon away. Instead he was pulled off-balance when his exoskeleton tried lifting the Shemarrian off the ground.

"Dang, lose some weight!"

One Shemarrian antenna flew from her head as Delwin hacked wildly from behind with his saber, shouting incoherent references to the Shemarrian's family origin. The distraction bought Darren the moment he needed and he placed one foot against the warrior's waist and pushed off with all the exoskeleton's might. The long rail gun came away from its owner and Darren staggered back to regain his balance. From somewhere on the warrior's right gauntlet, a pair of laser beams burned a mark in the power armor's chest.

Delwin's rendition of a weed-wacker on amphetamines finally removed the ammo drum from the Shemarrian's back and carved the head and shoulder armor. She slashed at him with her claws, finding most of her hand missing due to a similar slash from her mad attacker.

Darren took the opportunity to assess the stolen weapon while Delwin played ring-around-the-clearing with the infuriated Shemarrian. A quick glance to the center of the clearing revealed an insane dragon thrashing the rider and his mount. Gun, feed belt, ammo drum, and other more vital parts of both flew in every direction. The other cyber-mount was on the far side of the clearing, readying itself to charge the preoccupied dragon. Darren had a few seconds to figure how the weapon worked before attack was returned his way. The weapon was just about the right size for his exoskeleton, and balanced for one handed operation, but with double triggers and trigger guards getting in the way. Darren squeezed his armored fingers into place and a deafening thunder accompanied the unexpected recoil of the gun.

"That was loud!" Darren's head throbbed from the sonic concussion.

While the report was longer and less detrimental than a Glitter Boy's boom gun, the Shemarrian weapon still made his ears ring and the air tremble. Fingers now in place and wary of accidental discharges, Darren tried to aim the foreign weapon at the injured Shemarrian desperately attempting to kill the crazy in psychedelic armor.

Attempting to guess the sighting without computer targeting aids, his first two shots missed completely. Each time the weapon jerked and rolled back with the recoil, a counter balance and recoil suppression system compensated for the massive kinetic discharge. Not knowing how many shots he had left, Darren took careful aim and blew the Shemarrian's head off her armor-plated shoulders.

The body hit the ground, spewing sparks and jerking involuntarily. Delwin yelled something unintelligible, when the body sprung back to its feet and lunged blindly at where Delwin had been a moment before. Wires and mechanical workings of the neck joint extended where the head should have been.

Darren aimed at the damaged body, visually taking note of what seemed to be bionic implants exposed by Delwin's chaotic attacks.

"Get away from it, Delwin!" Darren shouted, but the crazy man was already jetting to the place Kro-Mar had hurled the other Shemarrian's rail gun.

Another blast knocked the cyborg warrior to the ground and nearly cut it in half, but it returned to its feet and started wandering in Darren's direction. One more flechette projectile caught it in the chest, scattering mechanical parts out the back. An instant later the cyborg disappeared in a massive explosion, taking with it a fifty foot patch of clearing. Darren looked at the new weapon with awe.

"Damn! Where were you when I needed you?!"

In the center of the clearing, Kro-Mar's fighting style would have made any prehistoric cave man proud. With every appendage, wing, and even spiked head, he thrashed the rider and mount, blindingly venting his rage on any part he came in contact with. Forgotten were spells and devious plots, plans and greed for new toys. Kro-Mar was not a happy dragon.

His rage reached new levels when the other cyborg mount leaped on his back and sunk four spine-like appendages from its side into Kro-Mar's scaled skin. Mass for mass about the same as the dragon's body, the cyborg creature blazed away with shoulder mounted weapons and tore into his back with a mouth full of razor sharp teeth. The weight of the cyborg creature dragged Kro-Mar over backwards, rolling both into a patch of smoking earth left by the Shemarrian's demise. Spurred on by the turn of events, the other rider and mount leaped into the tumble, claws and cannons flashing death.

For once in his life, Kro-Mar's teleportation ability served him well. Vanishing from the mass of flying claws and blasting weapons, he reappeared at the far edge of the clearing. He took a moment to regain his composure, noticing the relatively minor injuries he'd received in comparison to the damage the Shemarrian mounts were inflicting on each other. Kro-Mar smiled, renewing his barriers and making loud, throat clearing sounds to try and get his opponent's attention.

Darren watched the two mounts tear each other apart, the Shemarrian rider attempting to order them apart. This was too good to be true. Darren aimed his forearm mini-missile tubes at the trio and caught all in a pair of expanding plasma spheres.

Any question as to the Shemarrian's true nature was gone when the white hot balls of flame faded away. Fully mechanical features and chromed facial components were all that was left of the cyborg's living charade. Damaged severely and sporting exposed mechanical components from every joint, the two mounts tried to disentangle themselves.

"Hey! Over here!" Delwin shouted from one end of the clearing, holding onto a gun that was bigger than he was. The Shemarrian warrior turned in the saddle, retaining some vestige of sensory input.

"Hey! No! Wait! Delwin, don't fire that—"

"Wheee —"

Delwin's proclamation of glee was first cut short by the sonic concussion of the rail gun, and ended completely by his rapid recess into the trees at the end of the clearing. Both he and rail gun made rapid departure by recoil.

"— gun," Darren finished his unheeded warning.

Judging by the recoil his power armor absorbed when the weapon fired, Darren could only imagine the unpleasantness of riding one into a clump of trees.

Saving himself from a worse fate, Darren put two more rounds into the least damaged cyborg mount before it could free itself and turn in his direction. Darren was about to finish it when huge wings blocked the line of sight.

Coming down between the mounts, Kro-Mar threw every bit of strength into lifting the riderless cyborg mount into the air and using it as a massive malformed club to repeatedly smash the other one. Limbs, legs, and spines flailed helplessly as the cyborg found itself the unwilling weapon of destruction to its partner.

"He he he he he he," Kro-Mar rumbled. Now this was fun, breaking things. "He he he he —"

Suddenly, explosive shock waves knocked Darren down on his thrusters. In rapid chain fire the two cyborg mounts and Shemarrian warrior became flying shrapnel and expanding balls of fire.

Bits and pieces of armor rained down randomly in the clearing, leaving Kro-Mar standing in a blackened crater wondering what he'd done wrong. Darren started to laugh, scenes of too many Pre-Rifts

Wile Coyote cartoons flashing unbidden to mind. Kro-Mar stood frozen in posture, blackened from head to foot, charcoal scales falling one at a time from his body and turning to puffs of ash upon hitting the ground. Everything hurt, including parts of his body he didn't know he had. This was not fun.

Self pity took second place when Kro-Mar saw Delwin wander back into the clearing dragging the rail gun with one arm, the other hanging loosely at his side. Delwin dragged the Shemarrian weapon back to the edge of the crater.

"Whoa, man, like where did all the pretty birds come from this fine morning?" He waved at invisible sparrows chirping loudly around his head. "Here's your gun, man."

"Are you okay?" Kro-Mar came down on all fours, slinking his head to Delwin's side.

"Oh yeah, man, just need some quality time."

"Dude! What happened to your arm?" Darren overcame his intimidation of the dragon and crossed the clearing to Delwin's other side.

"Hey, it's doin' some funky things." Delwin wrenched his body from side to side, his broken arm flapping back and forth. "That's far out, man."

"Delwin's hurt bad." Kro-Mar looked over at Darren.

"Yep," Delwin seconded, flapping his injured arm with his good one.

"You probably shouldn't be doin' that, Delwin," Darren advised, no expert on medical procedure, but figuring the less you moved a broken arm, the better.

"Hey, buddy, let me fix you up." Kro-Mar gently picked up the crazy man in charcoal black claws and laid him on a patch of flat ground.

Darren stared in amazement as the fearsome beast worked magic spells to heal the injured crazy.

"Today is definitely going to rank in the top 'ten weird days' of my life."

Unfamiliar freedom of movement and the foreign feel newness of a brand new environmental armor suit gave Greg a feeling of satisfaction. Breaking in a new set of armor always took time, but this was the first set of non-Coalition armor he'd put on in his life. While still heavy and somewhat restrictive, the Explorer armor felt good, as did the change to a brand new NG-LG6 over/under laser and grenade launcher rifle. Even the clothes beneath the armor were different. As Greg left the outskirts of Liberty he shed more than just his Coalition uniform and insignia, but a lifetime of service and outstanding military career with it. He wasn't going back.

On his back was a pack containing all he needed to survive in the wilderness. He had no clear destination in mind or goals to achieve, but that very thought filled him with a new energy. Everything out there was new, an entire world to explore and adventures to find. He was no longer responsible for anyone but himself, and for the first time in many years, free of the burden of command. The decisions he made would affect him and him alone. No orders, no schedules, just the sky and the earth and everything in between to experience.

Watkins, the owner of the general store, had been quite generous in his bargaining. Of course the man had approached him first with the proposition of opening some under the table arms trades, something Greg had first found amusing but quickly took advantage of. His own armor and several Coalition weapons would turn up missing, and he hoped it would be assumed some D-Bee in town had finally done him in for good. With any luck, Watkins would have the sense not to sell the hot merchandise in Liberty and help aid the rumors of Greg's disappearance. In the end it didn't matter; MIA, KIA, AWOL, DOA, they all meant there was nothing for him to go back to.

Greg chuckled to himself when he remembered his encounter with First Strike on the way out of Liberty. He'd been urged at gun point into the back of an APC where Donnovan apologized for the ruse and wholeheartedly supported Greg's initiative. Donnovan proceeded to play several recordings he'd gotten of conversations inside Captain Pritchett's cabin, though he officially denied any type of surveillance.

Captain Pritchett had on a number of occasions plotted with his "goon squad" on ways to eliminate Greg and his entire unit, but each time opted not to take action because certain objectives were not yet accomplished. Greg had laughed out loud upon hearing the captain claim "Lieutenant Merrick has gone native," wondering if Pritchett could actually read his mind or was merely predicting the future. Donnovan seemed to think the whole situation was funny.

Offered a handsome salary to go mercenary as an advisor, Greg had to turn Donnovan's offer down. He'd commented on how all Donnovan really wanted was someone with inside intel on Coalition operations, and he'd do better paying off Lieutenant Sorenson. Donnovan claimed to sincerely want Greg as a member of First Strike, that the mercenary company could use someone of his experience and leadership capabilities. Greg had regrettably refused, stating he needed time away from a military structure and following orders, but he'd be sure to look up First Strike if he ever changed his mind. Shaking hands with the mercenary leader at the north edge of town, Greg couldn't think of a happier end to one chapter of his life.

Looking up at the patterns of stars shining through the clouded sky, he contemplated activating the modified night vision system he'd just had installed in the armor's helmet. The rugged logging road was difficult to read in the dark, but clear enough to navigate without artificial aid.

"It's a clear night on the road to nowhere," he spoke out loud, adopting a quick, steady pace he could maintain for hours. He hadn't gone more than fifty paces when a vaguely familiar female voice stopped him in his tracks.

"Lieutenant Greg Merrick."

He slowly turned and spied the silhouette on the road behind him, not sure weather to be overjoyed or worried.

"Natarsha?"

"Yes."

"How did you know it was me?" He walked back to her.

"Your voice."

"So much for getting away scott free."

"Where are you going?"

"Wherever this road goes, and then who knows? Want to come?"

"I thought you were in disguise, to spy on your enemy or to look for your missing people. I was not sure it was you."

"So you hang around outside of town just following strangers around?"

"Only you," Natarsha stated boldly, still deciding if she should follow through on Varles' orders just yet. The man was to be captured and returned for interrogation by Varles himself. How she did it was her prerogative.

"Then I'm in luck. Shall we?" He waved a hand down the road.

"What?"

"Go see the world, explore places we've never been, do things we've never done, experience things we were never allowed to experience before." Greg spoke for himself, not realizing the torment he was inflicting on the Altarain spy beside him.

"You are, leaving? Just leaving? What about your Coalition? What about your missing people?"

"The Coalition can go to hell for all I care, and my missing people are probably dead. You remember Sorenson? He found most of our, their, MIA's killed execution style. There's nothing for me to go back to. I'm on my own now."

"I do not understand. You are Coalition."

"Was, was Coalition. Not anymore. Turned over a new leaf, have a whole new life ahead of me. The Coalition is a thing of the past."

"But your missing are not dead."

"What?"

"Some still live. They travel a few miles from here." Natarsha laid the trap, still trying to decide between leading Greg to Varles or actually showing him where the missing Coalition personnel were.

"You know where they are? How many?"

"Yes. Eight of them, two injured badly. A powered armor suit. Another two are with them. Not Coalition. A dragon, and a man who smells strange."

"Alive?"

"Yes."

"Damn. I didn't need this." Greg walked to the side of the logging road and sat on a stump, removing his helmet and resting his head in his hands.

"What is the matter? You are not happy." Natarsha never even turned her head or moved from the road.

"No, I'm not. I mean yes, I'm happy they're alive, but this changes everything now."

"You do not want to go to them?" Natarsha was afraid to open herself to his emotions, this man was testing her will as it was.

"No! No I don't. I had everything worked out. I wasn't going back. Now, now I have to."

"Why?"

"Because if they were dead it wouldn't matter, but now I know what Captain Pritchett has planned and I can't let them walk into it. Winters, Jerry I knew would take care of business once I was gone, Donnovan was going to tell him the score. My men don't deserve to find their way back, only to have that bastard find a way to kill them."

"You will be saving their lives. This is good, yes?" she asked in her foreign accent.

Greg looked over at her, still finding it unusual that she always held conversations without ever looking at who she was speaking with, nor ever making eye contact.

"Yes, but if I go back there I'll be stuck with the task of finishing Lyboc's dirty work, sorry, the Army of the New Order, and dealing with Pritchett before he kills me and my unit. I was so close!" He put his head back in his hands, long hair falling down off his shoulders.

Natarsha edged closer, positioning herself for the blow that would render him unconscious. She wouldn't get a better chance.

"Life above duty."

"What?" She asked in response to the unexpected statement.

"Life above duty. It's a new value, one that took a while to realize. A balance. I don't think you'll understand what I mean."

"No."

"In this case, I must return and finish my job in order to save the lives of my men, even though some might die in the line of duty so others might live. Show me where my personnel are."

"You will follow?" Natarsha asked, but her mind was on the two new concepts of value.

"Yes," he got to his feet, replacing the helmet. "Lead the way."

"Are we there yet?"

"Gerald, I'm gonna kick your tail if you ask that one more time." Corporal Rollings turned to menace, the private with his fist.

"Chill, dudes," Darren warned behind them, Sharp's body draped over the SAMAS' arm and new weapon.

Their bizarre escort had vanished someplace miles back, not to Darren's surprise. Delwin and the dragon were the most unpredictable duo he'd ever encountered. Thankful as he was for them leading him to the MIA's, reliable traveling companions they were not.

"I was just kidding that time," Gerald whined.

"Shut up and stop dragging Yoshi's butt on the ground," Nelson complained.

"Everyone take it easy." Brian prayed he had one nerve left for his squad to get on.

Sharp kept mumbling directions that didn't make sense and the trial of malnourishment and many miles traveled had worn them all into the ground. Even Lisa had taken her turn carrying Yoshi when the RPA mysteriously collapsed into a coma. Her idea of a stretcher hadn't worked, and they were still carrying the wounded pilot between two mobile soldiers. Brian couldn't think of anything else to say that would keep the squad on the move, and in the end simply led by example. It was all he could do to make himself move on, but it was enough to keep them mobile. Dave leaned on his shoulder more heavily than before, his swollen leg compressed tightly in the armor casing. No food and no rest had taken its toll.

"Yes, Private, we're almost there," Brian retorted for the ten millionth time.

"How come I don't see any lights then?"

"Gerald, I'm gonna kick you so hard you —"

"Easy, Corporal." Brian was thankful his new NCO was far more aggressive than he. It gave him a gauge to control his own temper. He had no idea where they were, or how far from town they were, just that Darren said they were going the right direction according to the SAMAS' navigation system.

Something moved in the bushes, stopping Brian and Dave in their three legged tracks.

"I got thermo," Darren stated, seeing a warm body signature thirty feet from the clump of bushes.

"Lieutenant Brian Adams!" The closest bush stood.

"Uh, man am I tired." Brian blinked.

"What are you doing leading a convoy without a proper point man?" Greg dropped the bush and stepped out, removing his helmet and shining a light on his own face for them to recognize.

"Lieutenant Merrick!" Lisa cheered joyously.

"Oh, man, are you a sight for sore eyes." Brian let Dave find a place on the ground and rushed forward to confirm the good news.

"Hey, watch it!" Dave yelled from the ground.

"What are you doing dressed like that?" Brian asked. "Where's everyone else?"

"Thought I'd have better luck finding you on my own, in disguise, so to speak."

"Uh, dude, sir, there's somebody like over there in the bushes, in case you don't know." Darren pointed the new rail gun at the heat signature.

"That's Natarsha, the scout who found you. It's all right, you can come out."

Natarsha came to stand ten feet behind Greg, her uneasiness increasing with each passing second.

"You're gonna call for a rover, right, sir?" Nelson laid Yoshi on the ground and joined the reunion.

"Afraid not. We need to keep your safe return a secret for the moment."

"Then you know, sir?' Darren inquired.

Greg took in the damaged exoskeleton and lack of accompanying wingman.

"Looks like there's a bet with Pritchett I intend to collect on. Tell me about what you know a little later, Darren."

"We all know, sir." Lisa nodded at the SAMAS. "Darren told us how Pritchett tried to have him killed."

"Then I don't need to explain why I'm out here in disguise and your survival depends on your secret return to Liberty. What happened to Sharp?"

"He's pretty messed up, sir," Brian explained in technical jargon. "We don't know what happened to his armor, but we think he got shot up pretty bad and had a tree fall on him. I hit him with the IRMSS, but he needs a hospital."

"And that is, who?" Greg pointed to Yoshi.

"Private Yoshi, one of Pritchett's RPA's."

"Oh yes. She was shot down by the Glitter Boy. How is she?"

"I, I think her brain is swelling, or something in her head, from the bump on her head." Brian tried not to alarm the others. He'd expected her to be dead already. "I don't know how to fix that."

"Go now."

"Huh?" Brian turned to Natarsha.

Greg turned to read her marble features. The unsolicited suggestion was not anticipated.

"Go, now!"

"Why? Is there something we should know about?" Greg looked around in the darkness.

"Yes. We are being watched. If you value your lives leave now, and never travel this way again." Natarsha urged, feeling the presence of something hideous observing them. What the eye saw, Varles saw.

"Yes, but —"

"Go! I must leave you before it's too late. Go!" She stepped back into the darkness and was gone.

"You heard her, people." Greg heaved Yoshi over his shoulder. "I know you're tired but don't lag behind. If Natarsha thinks there's something bad out there, we don't want to find out what it is."

Buzzing mercury lamps bared the survivors to the harsh light of reality. Van's shed housed the returning Coalition MIA's and officers alongside the highly modified Sky Cycle. Van stared numbly at Darren once again, trying to contemplate the logic that started the chain of events up to where he stood. His Mountaineer ATV parked alongside the Sky Cycle served as a temporary emergency room for the wounded. Somehow, the entire situation seemed surreal.

"Hey Van, don't look so dazed, dude."

"Do you know what you've done?"

"Hey, it's like I said. Merrick's a righteous dude, he won't say anything about your cycle. We just needed someplace safe to go."

"And the first place you associated with safe for the Coalition, as in not risky or dangerous, was here?"

"Sure. I figured you'd still be up screwin' around with one of your gadgets, and there you were."

"Apparently."

"So, dude, can you move your Sky Cycle back a few feet so I can fit my SAM in here?"

"Why not? In for a penny, in for a pound," Van muttered an ancient saying he'd picked up from one of his instructors at Lazlo. The two men pushed the shed door open.

"I'll be right back." Darren darted outside, leaving Van standing there face to face with Lieutenant Merrick.

"Nice armor," Van commented.

"I thought so, only without all the magic crap you corrupted yours with." Greg let a thin smile through to let the Techno-Wizard know he wasn't really serious.

"So, anything else I can get you? A throw rug, some donuts, maybe?"

"I apologize for the sudden intrusion, Van, but Darren said we could trust you not to tell Captain Pritchett where we are."

"He's at least partially right."

"As far as I'm concerned, this little gathering is strictly off the record."

"That's okay with me, if you know what I mean." Van's eyes jerked to the stolen Sky Cycle.

"Darren also mentioned some type of weapon you were building to assassinate Zenjori Suka."

"Wow, Darren's been sniffing the glue again." Van rocked back on his heels, wishing Darren was back so he could insert his boot in the RPA's backside.

"Yo, Van, check out the new rod!" Darren walked the exoskeleton into the shed, wielding the Shemarrian rail gun in one hand and brandishing a large feed belt and drum with the other.

Van's jaw dropped. Forgotten was the violation of his privacy and invasion of his workshop.

"Jeez, Darren, how did you get that?"

"Long story. It involves Delwin Moonbeam, Admiral Sergio, and a really big dragon with lots of sharp teeth named Kramer. Kramer has the other one."

Van and Greg shared a mutual confused stare.

"I've been looking everywhere for one of these." Van fondled the gun.

Darren sat it down on Van's worktable and backed the exoskeleton into the corner before exiting it.

"It's not linked up to the SAM, and it still fires, so it must have its own power supply. Feeds from clips or belt to drum. Shoots these things." Darren set a large projectile casing on the worktable next to the enormous weapon.

"Oh Darren. Oh buddy, oh pal, oh friend of mine."

"I do need to keep it, Van. Van?"

"That's fine, I just need to spend some quality time with it to find out how it works." Van caressed the curves of the alien weapon.

"I'd leave you two alone, except I wanna make sure you put all the gizmos and whatchemecallits back in this time."

"So it's safe to say we've earned our keep?" Greg asked.

"Sure. Whatever. Stay as long as you want."

"Thanks. Darren, help me with the door?" Greg motioned to the large opening and lack of concealment. The two heaved the metal chain and let the heavy door come down in place. Just before it hit the ground, Greg stopped it with his foot and let it down slowly.

"There's someone sneaking up on the shed," Greg spoke quietly to Darren and handed over his MP-10. Putting on his helmet and throwing open the side walk-in door, Greg aimed his rifle at the figure frozen in mid-step.

"Oh come on, Merrick, like I don't know you're hiding my girlfriend and our MIA's in a Techno-Wizard's garage." Sorenson stepped into the light in front of the doorway.

"How long?"

"Since you walked into Watkins' general store and never came out." Mike grinned, looking back into the shadows down the row of sheds. "If I'm busted, you might as well come out too, Aken."

There was a long pause, then the First Strike mercenary left his cover and came over to join them under the light, a wide smile on his face.

"Man, is everyone lurking about in the dark tonight?" Greg shook his head, looking around for more shadows to appear.

"Change of heart, Merrick?" Aken asked, shifting his rifle strap to the other shoulder.

"Yeah, I know too." Mike smiled. "I thought about joining you, but figured you'd rather go it alone."

"Since everyone seems to know everything I do," Greg took a deep breath and glanced at Mike, "No real point in going soft now. Aken, tell Donnovan I've reconsidered and I'll accept his offer if, he can move my troops someplace safe and make sure nothing happens to them."

"You sure on this, Merrick?"

"This time, yes."

"I'll let him know. Don't wander too far off, I wouldn't want to have to follow Sorenson around to find you again." Aken patted Mike on the shoulder and jogged off into the night.

"Making more deals, I take it?" Mike asked.

"More than you know. Come on in and join the party, I know at least one person in there who doesn't hate your guts." Greg opened the door to the barrel of his sidearm.

"That's so reassuring." Mike stepped back.

Greg pried the MP-10 away from Darren.

"Man, sir, I though you said we were gonna make it look like an accident."

"Later, Darren." Greg went along with the gag just to see Mike's expression.

"Mike!" Lisa's voice carried across the shed.

"Lisa!"

She ran across the bay to him, meeting him at the door. The greeting hug and kiss looked a bit rigid. Darren opened his mouth but a disapproving shake of Greg's head shut him up. Brian stuck his head out of the Mountaineer door, then went back inside without a word.

"You made it back." Mike held her shoulders and looked over her disheveled clothes and fatigued, worn face.

"Brian got us back. We didn't know if you were alive or dead."

"I'm so glad to see you!" He hugged her tightly.

She pushed away from him.

"We need to talk," she said seriously.

"There's plenty of time for that."

"It's important. It's private." She glanced at Darren and Greg. Neither moved.

"There's an empty shed a few rows back."

"Don't go far." Greg held the door open for them. "I may need you back here in a few minutes."

"Goin' for some of that —"

"Shut up, Darren," Greg ordered, waiting for Mike and Lisa to exit the shed before closing the door behind them.

"Man, sir, you were thinking the same things I was."

"Not likely, and at least I have enough sense to know when to shut up."

"Yeah, but you gotta admit you wanted to say something." Darren gave him a crooked smile.

"Lieutenant." Brian came to a stop in front of the pair. "Can I talk to you a minute. It's important."

Darren started laughing, eliciting a chuckle from Greg as well. Brian's already haggard features went darker.

"Ignore him, Brian, Darren's been up too long. What's the problem?"

"I didn't want to say anything in front of them, but Sharp and Private Yoshi aren't doing well, and I don't know exactly what's wrong with them. They're going to die if we can't get them over to the Cyber-Doc."

"Not possible. Several men are still there, and Pritchett has a posted guard to make sure nobody harms them. We take them there, Pritchett will know, and then we have a worse problem."

"But they will die if we don't," Brian pleaded. "They probably should be dead already. Even Dave's out of it. Probably going to lose his leg, if he's lucky."

"Well, Van's got this —"

"Darren," Greg's voice warned.

"Right." Darren shut up, glancing over to see Van watching the conversation intently. Greg looked at the far wall and took a deep breath.

"Darren, your SAMAS is damaged bad, it probably needs a good cleaning before anyone works on it, right?"

"Uh, no, sir?"

"You're not understanding me. It's going to take you and several others at least fifteen minutes to drag your SAM over there and clean the dirt and shrapnel out of the workings, right?"

"Uh, yeah, sir?" Darren wasn't sure what he was playing along with yet.

"That's what I thought. Cody, Rob, uh, Private Gerald, come here please."

Three tired soldiers filed out of the Mountaineer and came to a symmetrical line, waiting for new orders they were expected to carry out.

"Yes, sir!?" Corporal Rollings saluted.

"Lieutenant Adams wants you to help Darren with SAM 15."

"But —"

"Don't you, Lieutenant" Greg cut Brian short with a hard gaze. "It should take about fifteen minutes."

"Whatever."

"Yeah, yeah it like froze up on me and Brian, Lieutenant Adams wants it over there in that corner." Darren caught on.

"Man, I just wanna sleep."

"Later, man, right now we gotta get all the dirt out of all the widgits and whosamacallits before Lieutenant Adams can fix it."

Grumbles and complaints assisted the exoskeleton to the other corner where Darren continued a line of bull any used car salesman would have been envious of. Brian stared at Greg hard, his numb brain starting to comprehend what was taking place.

"Van, you're going to be all by yourself for about fifteen minutes." Greg turned to the Techno-Wizard and jerked his eyes at the Mountaineer."

"Uh, yeah." Van nodded.

"Good, because Lieutenant Adams and I are stepping out for about fifteen minutes, and then we'll come back in and make sure we didn't accidentally misdiagnose our injured personnel. Come on, Brian." Greg opened the door and waited for Brian to reluctantly step outside the shed.

Greg shut the door behind them and paced to a dark shadow away from the light. Brian clenched and unclenched his fists, following Greg and never breaking his granite stare. He stood in front of Greg, boring into him with angry eyes. Greg didn't blink. At last Brian's gaze wavered and his shoulders slumped. He looked back at the door.

"I know what you did in there."

"You did a good job, Lieutenant Adams, bringing back our people. As far as I'm concerned you earned those lieutenant's bars."

"That means something, coming from you, I guess." Brian didn't look at him.

"But there's more to being an officer than doing and saying the right things. Sometimes it's about not knowing, not saying anything or doing anything."

"I never thought I'd see you pull a Sorenson." Brian sounded disappointed.

"Sorenson doesn't understand what you and I do. Looking the other way isn't the same thing as overt action. Rationalize it if you have to. You really didn't see or hear anything, and we're outside, so we don't know anything for sure."

"That's just as bad."

"If you had full knowledge, it might be. I may or may not recall several situations where I did the same for you, Lieutenant Adams."

"Brian looked up at the larger officer, recounting instances where Greg had looked the other way or not asked specific questions to allow certain vital actions to take place without his direct knowledge. But it was different then. It didn't involve a magic user doing unthinkable things to his friends. It was worse this time.

"But how, how, can I look at them the same again, knowing what I know? That almost makes it worse. Every time I see them I'll always wonder if it's really them, or if they are going to do something that magic user is making them do."

"That little facade in there was for your benefit as well as Cody and Rob and the other one. It wasn't for me. That way they can honestly say they have no knowledge, and you can always claim I ordered you outside for a briefing and that you didn't hear or see anything. How you deal with your own imagination is something to keep to yourself. Like an old commander of mine once told me, keep your field talk and your city talk separate."

"I can't keep a clean conscience that way."

"You do what you have to do, Brian, but you know as well as I do the difference between what we're taught and what we know. You've been in the field long enough to see the truth with your own eyes. That doesn't mean everything you know is wrong, but you can add an element of truth to your thoughts and opinions, whether or not you say it out loud."

"What are you trying to tell me, sir?" Brian asked wrestling with his own demons. "That magic users and D-Bees are just like us and they didn't really do all those things we know they did?"

"You said it, not me. I have no doubt that magic users have committed atrocities they're credited with, you and I have seen our share to support that. But that doesn't mean every magic user and every D-Bee is bent on murdering you or killing babies on an altar. Some of them aren't half bad, once you get to know them. Some of them, some, aren't much different than you or I." Greg spoke treason, and for the first time in his life, accepted the concepts.

"Wreath."

"What?"

"Wreath. He, she, it, is this D-Bee that works at Gizmo's. At first I wouldn't go near it, but after awhile I started forgetting to be wary of it, and then I realized I was thinking of Wreath as just another person. That bothered me at first, then I just forgot to think of Wreath as a D-Bee at all."

"Then you understand what I'm trying to tell you."

"But it isn't the same here. How can I trust that magic user?"

"I don't, not completely. I don't know if I ever will. Every time I walk down the street and see a D-Bee or magic user, I wonder if I'm going to have to fight them. But it's changing, slowly. But think, Brian, you brought those wounded back through the wilderness, through all types of hazards, when it would have been much easier and probably safer for everyone if you just ended their misery and moved on without the added risk. Why did you do that?"

"I wanted to save their lives."

"And you were willing to risk your own and the life of every man in there to do it. Would you rather Sharp, Dave, and Yoshi all die, now, rather than take one more risk?"

Brian thought awhile, knowing the correct answer wasn't the one he really felt. Better to let them die than let a magic user turn them into something not quite human. Somehow the Coalition edict didn't seem worthy of the price.

"How do you do it, sir?"

"What?"

"Do what you know is right but pretend to believe what you're supposed to believe."

"It's not easy, don't ever think it will be. But you're a crusader, Brian, you have the fire in your blood to do what you think is right and make choices for the better. You just need to temper it to work around the system, not against it."

"Kind of what we did when Lyboc tried to court-martial Sorenson?"

"Only a little better planned and not quite so obvious." Greg smiled. "You have the potential to become an outstanding officer, one that can make a difference from inside and still hold onto what you know is true. When you go back to Chi-Town you'll have a real opportunity to make a difference that not many others ever get."

"You sound like you're not planning on going back." Brian stared at the door, not wanting to make eye contact.

"There's lots going down tonight, more things you're better off not knowing about. There's a good chance I won't be coming back."

"You can't just leave me out of it now, sir. I know too much already."

"Your responsibility now is the lives of the men and women you brought back. You have to make sure they make it back to Chi-Town alive. You may even have to reign in Sergeant Winters, not an easy task, but he's a stand-up NCO who won't ever leave you hanging when it gets tough. By morning you may have more responsibility than you ever dreamed. Can you handle it?"

"I don't know, sir."

"I think you can." Greg put his left hand on Brian's shoulder. "You brought back our MIA's over fifty miles through hostile territory. You can get them the rest of the way home."

Sounds of an approaching APC prompted Greg to look at his wrist comp.

"That was fast. A little too fast." He strode over to the shed door and banged loudly. "We're coming back in, now."

Greg gave it a few seconds before opening the door. A First Strike Iron Maiden APC rounded the corner, its bank of lights temporarily blinding Brian.

"Get everyone together and have them ready to move out. First Strike is going to find a place for everyone to stay while we work this thing out with Pritchett."

"Darren too?"

"No. He stays. Get your wounded. Hopefully they aren't as bad off as you first thought. After all, you said yourself, you didn't know for sure what was wrong with them." Greg winked, holding the door open for Brian.

Headlights cut out as the APC clanked to a halt beside the shed. Aken popped his head out the top hatch while two mercenaries dropped the rear door and moved out to cover the dark streets.

"Your people ready to go?"

"Just about. Careful on the triggers, Eddy, Rock, I've two more wandering around outside someplace, oh, there they are." Greg pointed in the direction a Headhunter's weapon was aimed.

Mike and Lisa approached the shed walking several feet apart. As Lisa passed beneath the light to go inside, Greg could see tear stains on dirty cheeks. Mike halted by the door and didn't follow her inside, his usually alert eyes dead and shiftless.

"Looks like you were wrong, Merrick." Mike gave Greg a rueful smile.

"About?"

"There being somebody in there that doesn't hate my guts."

"I'd laugh and point, except I haven't had any for longer than you." Greg grinned, trying to cheer up the sullen espionage officer. Mike exhaled deeply.

"I'd trade places with you in a heartbeat."

"You want something to do to take your mind off it?"

"What did you have in mind?" Mike asked suspiciously, a flicker of light returning to his eyes.

"A little assassination, consorting with magic users, everything that will get you court-martialled again."

"Who's the target?" Mike asked, not sure if Aken could overhear them.

"Targets, my friend, targets."

Drawn shades and dimmed lights shrouded Pritchett's mystery meeting in secrecy. There were so few left in his unit, and many of them were wounded or couldn't be trusted. The small gathering in his cabin were the few he still trusted and knew would perform the grim task ahead without question. Indeed, once the proposition was laid out, it was he who was forced to be the voice of reason, reigning in more drastic suggestions.

"I don't understand, sir, why not end it all tonight? Why take the chance?" Pritchett's newly promoted NCO, Sergeant Nabian, urged from across the table.

"Because First Strike is still here and my contact tells me they're watching to make sure Merrick's men aren't harmed. In a day or two, First Strike is leaving Liberty, and that's when we should finish Winters and all the rest. Safer that way. I hadn't counted on First Strike getting involved. That sets us back."

A Full Conversion 'Borg entered the room, shaking his head to the question Pritchett was about to ask.

"No sign of Sergio? Sharky? My Dog Pack?"

"Nothing. They haven't reported in."

"My contact in First Strike tells me SAM 15 and its pilot came back hours ago. I'm not sure how it happened but it seems Merrick's ace has bested our ambush." Pritchett sat down, wooden chair groaning loudly under his weight.

"You already said it, sir, Merrick, , and this Techno-Wizard are conspiring to assassinate you. Tonight possibly. We have to take them out!"

"I know, Sergeant, I know. I wish they'd completed their assignment first. We won't have a chance to do it until our reinforcements arrive."

"We can do it quietly, sir. Do all of them," one of Pritchett's corporals suggested.

"That's right, sir, take out the whole squad before they know what happened."

"Now isn't the time for that, but soon. If they were all to leave Liberty and be away from First Strike, perhaps. It's truly a shame. Some of Merrick's men are just good soldiers following orders."

"But if we don't get them, they'll get us." Nabian countered.

"Perhaps. Perhaps if we simply remove Merrick and Winters, the others will fall in line."

"You don't really believe that, do you sir? Some of our own men are more loyal to Merrick than us. We have to deal with them, too, before our reinforcements get here."

"In time, but not right now. Once Merrick is gone we'll have another chance to test their loyalty."

"Merrick doesn't know yet, about The Company?"

"Not that I know of. I don't think it would make a difference if he did."

"That's why that magic user and Merrick have to die, tonight!"

"Very well. See if you can sneak our weapons out of lock-up and then take them to the edge of town in a hover rover. Next time Merrick or any of his people leave town, we'll be ready to make sure an accident happens."

Parked within the surging currents of a ley line outside of town, Van's Mountaineer ATV attracted a flurry of energy arcing and snapping at the devices inside. Darren's empty SAMAS stood parked outside, a jury rigged feed belt running from the back to the Shemarrian rail gun. The four men inside the ATV were magnets for the ley line energy, but none more than Van. Energy cascaded up and down Van's modified armor and arced to equipment he was readying. Greg and Mike shared uneasy looks about what they were doing, but neither was willing to back out.

"Okay, Van, one more time," Greg pressured.

"I've explained it to you twice already," Van complained, making the last adjustments to the C-14 and vid screen.

"But this time, put back in all the stuff you left out. I want to know exactly what's happening, and don't give us any more lip about special widgets and gizmos and all that technical crap. I have a technical officer. I've heard all that before."

"Okay, if you really want the whole truth."

"Yes. Every bit of it."

"Just remember, it's an experimental device. A prototype. I've never tested the complete system before so it might not work now. The reason we had to do it on the ley line is because it helps boosts the range of this thing and gives us a better chance of success. This vid screen, for lack of all the widgets and gizmo jargon, can be mystically powered, by me alone, to first locate then remotely view an individual I've personally met and can visualize in my head. I've refined a few things since Darren saw it, so all I have to do is type their name in on this locator keyboard system, like this..." Van typed in Zenjori Suka. "Then run a search. I've already programmed him into this recognition system, made up of re-programmable chips. A flashing red dot indicates Zenjori's location. The chip board was my own invention, I don't know if it —"

"Fine, it's fantastic, what happens?"

"Well, I power the device, with magic, for the mystically impaired like yourselves, and there he is!" Van pointed to the screen. Fuzzy images started to appear, a map program indicating contour lines in terrain and locations of Pre-Rifts towns and cities. A flashing red dot showed Zenjori's location.

"Man, we coulda' used one of these things before," Darren commented.

"What now?" Greg pushed on.

"We go to first person perspective." Van typed in a few commands, neglecting to inform the observers of the magic channeling taking place. "And there you have it."

"I see a cyborg, some bald Merc, and, others. Where's Zenjori?" Mike searched the live scene on the vid screen.

"You're watching the world from his point of view. This is what Zenjori is seeing at this very instant."

"That's incredible." Greg watched in amazement, disregarding momentarily how the whole operation was taking place.

"Turn up the sound, dude, we can't hear anything." Darren looked for a volume control.

"I never got that working right. Something with the spell and circuit conversion. I'll have to start all over and build another one I think."

"No sound?"

"Uh-uh. Like I said. This is a prototype. I think once I work some of the bugs out, I'll start from scratch and build one right."

"And you can do this to anyone?" Mike asked, starting to comprehend the implications.

"In theory, yes and no. There's some limitations." Van didn't want to discuss the details.

"But you can do this to Pritchett?" Greg asked.

"We already did, dude. Like I told you." Darren grinned happily.

"Got it programmed and everything, just waiting to go."

"This is incredible. So now, how do we shoot him with this, what used to be a C-14?" Greg handled the modified weapon.

"Careful, some of those wires are just clipped on, I didn't solder everything yet."

"Sorry."

"This is the tricky part." Van examined the weapon to make sure it was still okay. "I rigged this grenade launcher to shoot anywhere I aim on the screen, like a video game only in real life. See, everywhere I point the gun, that little red dot is where the grenade will hit."

"I don't get it. You're just going to blow yourself up." Greg looked at the barrel.

"No, because these sensors here and here at the end interpret the destination I target, and this device here in the barrel, again lacking proper description, uses energy I put into it to bridge the gap between the gun here in my hand to the location I point to on the screen. It teleports the grenade directly to the target, for all practical purposes appearing out of thin air. Completely undetectable."

"Do you have any idea how dangerous that thing is?" Mike asked, sobered by the possibilities. "Do you know what could happen if that thing fell into the wrong hands, or worse yet some Techno-Wizard without your good judgement manages to duplicate it? When we're done tonight this thing should be destroyed." Mike didn't finish the part that ended with Van not being left alive to teach anyone or make another one.

"I don't think so." Van started to feel nervous. He knew showing two Coalition officers his greatest invention yet was a bad idea.

"Nobody's going to smash your gizmo thing," Greg reassured. "But I have to agree. It should never fall into the wrong hands."

"I wasn't planning on selling it. As a matter of fact I've been working on ways to protect against it, just in case I'm not the only one with the idea. I think I've got some foolproof ways to build protection into armor, vehicles, houses, and stuff like that, I just haven't built any yet."

"I think if there were more than one of these, we'd have known by now." Mike shook his head.

"Hey, dudes, we gonna waste some rebel butt here or just keep talking about it?"

"So, Van, how do you hit Zenjori with a grenade, if what we're watching is from his point of view?" Greg pointed to the screen.

"Easy. We can shoot regular grenades, or ones I've specially modified just to drop a few feet in front of the person. Been working on all kinds of grenades, projectiles, mines, both magic and normal. You name it."

"Any chance you can make this thing work in reverse?" Mike asked. "Say on, a hard disk, for example."

"Doesn't work that way, but that's an interesting idea. I wonder if I could —"

"Later, Van, let's do this." Greg compared a 40 mm grenade from his own rifle with the 20 mm grenade from the C-14. "Too bad you didn't make it into something a little more powerful."

"I just built it into what I happened to have laying around. It doesn't need to be powerful, though, not for what we're doing tonight. Maybe when I build a new one I'll use a gun like yours. Wow, I could build it into all kinds of guns!" Van's face brightened, thinking of the possibilities.

"It doesn't look like Zenjori is wearing a helmet." Mike examined the view closely. The mercenaries were sitting around a fire. "Judging by the unobstructed view, right Van?"

"That's my guess. One grenade ought to do it."

"Heck, just spray down the whole camp while you're at it," Greg admonished.

"Can't do that, not if you want to hit Pritchett tonight, too. It's very energy intensive."

"How will we know if it worked?" Mike asked.

"If the screen goes blank and we can't locate him anymore."

"I'd like something a little more solid than that."

"Feel free to fly one of your SAM's up to where this is at on the map and get all the evidence you want to take back with you. You can blame it on infighting among the rebels. Make up whatever story you want, the important thing is that skum-bag won't be hurting anyone else." Van selected a fragmentation grenade and loaded it into the weapon.

The other three men took a step back, edging toward the door of the ATV.

"What?"

"It's not that we don't trust you, dude, but, ya know, just in case all you do is blow up your vid screen."

The Mountaineer jerked and rocked to the side.

"Jeez! That wasn't me." Van set the rifle back in the holder.

The side door ripped open and several weapons came in the doorway; rail guns, laser rifles, and plasma cannons.

"Everyone file out slowly or we'll simply massacre you all inside." Pritchett's voice came in loud with voice amplification. He repeated the order several more times more serious consequences attached.

Mike left the Mountaineer first and was relieved of his sidearm by an armor clad grunt. Darren followed, already weaponless and without armor, his SAM under guard. Greg just about started reaching for his rifle, but slowly picked up his helmet instead before joining the others outside. Van was the last to leave, casually slinging his helmet behind him as he left. It took several seconds for the searching soldier to remove and pile the belt load of gadgets he was never without.

"What is this about, Captain?" Greg sized up the odds.

There were two Full Conversion Cyborgs and eight soldiers, all with battle worn armor but weapons at the ready. Then there was Pritchett himself, a Partial Conversion Cyborg in battle armor, leveling a C-27 plasma cannon at Greg's head from fifteen feet away. Two soldiers stormed the Mountaineer to make sure there was nobody else hiding inside, and then made several trips to pile weapons and ordnance at Pritchett's feet.

"Consorting with magic users and plotting to kill a superior officer. My my, Lieutenant, too bad you had to bring these others in with you, but they were killed along with you as co-conspirators."

"You moron! We almost had Zenjori Suka!"

"And I'm sure I was next. Oh don't look surprised, Sharky told me all about your little plot to kill me and my officers, then take over my unit. Of course I knew why you and this magic user came out here." Pritchett motioned one of his cyborgs who then tossed an incendiary charge inside Van's Mountaineer.

"Better move."

Pritchett waved his barrel for the four prisoners to distance themselves from the ATV. Flames engulfed the interior and blossomed out the open door as the intense fire destroyed the vehicle. Van watched it go with sadness, more disappointed at never testing the device than distraught by its destruction. Flames leaped higher from melted hatches and plexiglass view ports.

"And you, Corley, I should have killed you long ago. I don't know how you got out of my ambush, but you aren't walking away from this one."

"Kramer."

"What?" Pritchett cocked his head.

"Kramer. Big dragon that ate Sharky. Same dragon's probably out there watching us right now." Darren looked confident.

Pritchett's men looked around warily, but never dropped their guard.

"Sorenson. You were dead the minute you left Chi-Town. You just took the easy way out and now I have to clean house."

"What's that supposed to mean?" Mike asked, feeling naked standing there without armor or a weapon.

"Did you really think Lyboc picked you for your abilities? You may have done well consorting with magic users and D-Bees in Minnesota, but you're more or less a screw-up, a disgrace to the uniform."

"Wait a minute." Greg paused, grasping concepts too obvious he couldn't believe they eluded him until now. "What's your connection to Lyboc other than watch-dogging our butts?"

"Watch-dogging? You still don't get it. I was to let you and your unit do the dirty work for me, only stepping in if you couldn't handle it, as is obviously the case. You knew where the rebels were for days and never did anything about it. You forced me to get involved."

"If you would have left us alone, we'd have gotten Zenjori and his damned Army of the New Order and been out of your hair long ago!"

"That may be true, but you were never going home. Not from the start. In fact you're already dead. An entire company and platoon of SAMAS are on the way to secure this territory and finish what you couldn't. Now I have to make sure the Army of the New Order is completely destroyed and the data they stole is never recovered. You've made a lot more work for me, Lieutenant Merrick."

"Who, what the hell do you mean we weren't going home?"

"Come on, Lieutenant, you didn't think Lyboc would let you back into Chi-Town knowing what you know, do you? In the event you did recover the data disk, I was to be sure of its safe return, without your assistance, because officially you and your entire unit would have been killed in action during the recovery. You failed, we failed, put the blame where you want, it doesn't matter. By the time my reinforcements arrive, your entire unit will be KIA or MIA, and any dissenters you've created among my men will be dealt with likewise. I tried to find a way to keep some of your men alive, Lieutenant, I might even have just reported them dead and allowed them to live, and I still might. At least you'll die on your feet, not like that magic user there when we finish with him."

Fire light danced off the weapon barrels and black finish armor of the Coalition execution squad, mingled with shades of blue from the crackling hues of the ley line.

"Sir, uh, sir. There's something behind us." One of the soldiers tapped Pritchett on the shoulder and stared.

Pritchett turned slowly, noticing the fixed stares of the prisoners in his sights.

"Don't move." A 'Borg glared at Darren, thrusting his rail gun toward him.

Darren didn't budge, not even noticing the menacing weapon. Visible in the light of the ley line and burning ATV was something more horrifying than Darren had ever seen.

"What is that?" Pritchett's voice betrayed no fear, but the sinking feeling in his chest and stomach was like none he had experienced before.

Gliding silently, several feet above the dew-soaked grass came a demonic monstrosity. Twenty feet in long and over ten feet from the base to the demon's giant skull, the Splugorth Slaver made its approach. Green slime dripped off its cybernetically enhanced body and long tentacles as it rose higher in the containment housing at the center of the barge. Its left hand wielded a massive staff with an enclosed eye floating in a thick solution at the top. Attached to the slaver's right arm was a weapon with a bore the size of a human head. Floating around the barge were drum-sized eyes, silently taking up positions to view the impending battle. Atop the ornately decorated barge were five female warriors, each clad in a near-transparent skin-tight body suit and wielding a range of bizarre weapons and magical jewelry. Four of the women wore metallic helms that glinted bronze in the ley line's blue light, solid eye guards covering sightless eyes.

The fifth slave warrior sat to the creature's left on the barge, the only one not wearing a helmet. Bluish-black hair fluttered about in the unnatural breezes flowing across the barge. Riding with the Splugorth Slaver into battle was Natarsha.

Chapter 20

Varles Moden rose higher above his link to the barge, virtually shaking with anticipation. Through the eyes of the barge, staff, and remotes, he could view the battle from every angle and collate the images to better command the action. All too often his prey was far too weak to offer any resistance, but here was a risk that gave him a tingling sensation he rarely felt. The Coalition force ahead was dangerous to be sure, but not impossible to defeat, especially since the ley line energy would enhance his magic. Spurred on by the heightened level of awareness, the demon urged the barge to greater speeds.

Floating eyes picked out the aura of the one human that was to be spared immediate death at all costs. Varles had special plans of torment for the one human Natarsha cared for. The others could be captured or killed, it didn't matter so long as the battle lasted long enough for his enjoyment.

His spy had betrayed him, though she believed the secret was safe from his interrogation. As punishment her for her failure to bring him back with her, he'd made her shed her human clothing and don the attire of a slave, forcing her to ride with him into battle against the humans she was secretly trying to save. The battle itself would be a brief diversion compared to what he had in store for his wayward slave and the human captive to be. Natarsha would be forced to inflict days, even weeks of torture on the human male, and when he finally expired it would be her turn to suffer the fate of her betrayal. Varles relished the pain and suffering he would cause, the mere thought of it bringing an emotional high.

But first there was destruction and chaos to be had.

Breaking the vice-like grip of fear holding his men entranced, Pritchett whipped around to Greg. He paused a moment, then reaching down with one arm, he picked up Greg's heavy weapons and tossed them back to him, then turned to face the oncoming menace. His back to his prisoners and the pile of weapons, Captain Pritchett fearlessly strode to meet the demon.

"Fire! Fire you bastards! Fire!" Pritchett charged, running, throwing off fear and replacing it with anger. Anger at the fear he'd felt in the Glitter Boy's sights. Anger at the fear and intimidation Lieutenant Merrick had revealed. Anger at his failures and the men he'd thrown away in war. Whipped into a battle frenzy of heroic proportions, Captain Pritchett screamed his war cry, snapping soldiers back into action. The charge of the slaver was joined by borg and armor-clad troop, going to meet the foe in a blaze of glory.

Lightning fell from cloudless skies, bursting a soldier's armored shell, a cloud of steam exploding from the burning armor suit. The charge continued, weapons blazing and beams striking down the demon's magical barrier and cutting into barge and Slaver alike. Another flash of light and crash of thunder left a steaming husk of armor where a soldier once had been. Rail guns, and energy weapons continued the onslaught unabated, slaying the Warrior Woman that flung herself in the path of incoming fire to save her master.

Battle cries never died as the Coalition fanned out to avoid the Slaver's kamikaze path. All but one cleared the barge's way, as Pritchett finished an energy canister and slotted another mid-stride. Bionic legs drove his body into the air as his eyes narrowed on the massive being atop the barge. Armor met the semi-organic plates of Varles' body, the Coalition Captain slamming into him at the combined speeds of forty miles per hour. Varles viewed the black death mask and red eyes of his attacker from the eye of the staff.

"The Oracle. . . . " The staff whispered in Varles' head.

A vicious kick with a mechanical leg sent the Warrior Woman to Varles' right over the ornate shield and off the barge. The human ducked a blow from Varles' slimy claws and yanked a small brick-sized block from his belt pouch. Letting out another war cry, the Coalition warrior prepared to slap the explosive mark of death on Varles' chest. Tentacles wrapped around Prichett's legs and arms and he was flung from the barge, fusion block landing on the ground before it could be set.

The hail of fire commenced more intensely than before.

Greg stood by the other three men, rifle held loosely in his arms. The turn of events was more mind numbing than before. He looked to his right and left and realized the other three were looking at him. He cycled a grenade loudly in the rifle.

"Give 'em hell."

Greg's battle cry joined the rest as long strides carried him into the fury of combat.

Darren darted for his SAMAS while Van rushed the pile of confiscated equipment to retrieve his gadgets. Mike watched the battle in a daze, standing alone and unarmed while the Coalition forces faced down the demon from Atlantis.

Two Warrior Women were on the ground, working a circle from one Coalition soldier to another, leaving some entangled in glowing nets and others in disjointed piles of armor and body parts. Plasma blades flashed and drew burning lines in armor. Laser and rail gun fire bore down on the deadly slave warriors, impacting invisible magic barriers that beguiled the the attackers' deception of vulnerability. Amid the carnage Varles picked his targets, firing flaming balls from his right forearm weapon. The flaming spheres seemed to home in on their targets and in a flash of steam, devour armor and flesh as one.

Sergeant Nabian yelled and fired wildly one-handed with his laser rifle, his other arm resting in the grass at his feet, cauterized at the shoulder by an Altarain plasma sword. Beams broke through magic barriers and scored patches in the Warrior Woman's body suit. In one fluid movement she lashed back, taking the tip of his gun with one stroke and Nabian's head with the backstroke. Fingers trembled at the weapon's trigger as it reached the ground. The warrior's magic barrier was back before Greg could reach her.

Firebolts and laser beams from the barge burned glowing pits in a cyborg's thick armor, returning its attention to the slaver. Mini-missiles from its forearms flared up and surged plasma over the mystic barriers of the barge in rapid strobes of light. From behind, the blade came down into the borg's thinly armored neck. Plasma splayed the cyborg's workings and flared through bionic supports as the Warrior Woman drove the tip home, the weight of her body pressing down to the hilt. The borg reached up to grab her leg on his shoulder. Plasma charges ran down the blade to the tip buried where armor wasn't. A graceful backflip landed the Altarain three yards away before the blazing metal fires within the cyborg brought it to the ground.

Greg joined the last Coalition soldier on his feet to drive an Altarain into the grass with continuous fire. Grenades expended and clip empty, Greg liberated Nabian's H.F. saber from his body and strode to the Altarain closest his position.

Laser blasts ceased a second later, a fire ball consuming what was left of the last soldier in a spark of burning armor and super heated mist.

Sonic assault followed the sudden impact that depleted Varles' magic barriers on the second strike. He'd heard that sound before. Spying the exoskeleton several hundred feet away near his fourth floating eye, Varles pointed and an Altarain sprinted toward her chosen foe, ignoring the battle of blades taking place just feet from the barge.

Kinetic force knocked the Altarain clear off her feet and into the dirt. Bouncing up without a scratch she renewed her magic protection and charged again, erratically changing course and closing the distance to her target. Fifty feet now, with the blade slicing air with white hot plasma. Something flew through the air and she avoided its trajectory. The object landed meters away, but its effect halted her instantly in her tracks, metal boots stuck unyielding to the ground by some work of magic.

Van and Darren gave no quarter. Rail gun and ion beam destroyed magic barriers and ended her slavery to the Splugorth.

Incoming fire followed Darren's movements and hit the exoskeleton from the side. Rail gun flechettes spilled on the ground from the severed feed belt. Only one round remained in the Shemarrian rail gun.

Greg let the Altarain slide off the end of his blade, never once seeing the marble expression on her face change, even in death. Black marks scored lines in his wounded armor, but now he was no more than twenty feet from the barge. Fireballs left the slaver's blaster and chased down Darren with unwielding intent, but the eye of the staff was on the lone figure before the barge.

Two Altarain Warrior Slaves remained on the barge, but only one ripped Greg's heart from his body and left him with nothing else to live for.

"Finish it!" He shouted. "Just do it!"

Varles languished in the ferocious emotions around him and the dramatics before him. It couldn't have come to a more exciting finish.

"Anisa. Bind my new slave," he gurgled.

The Warrior to Varles' right stepped to the edge of the barge holding weapon to subdue the human.

The struggle inside her ended. Better to die than live and continue existence as she knew it. Natarsha stood and unslung her ornate plasma sword.

"Betrayal is at hand," the staff warned.

Plasma cut deep in the staff's head, spilling life-giving fluid and reaching optic flesh. As Natarsha struck it with all her might.

Black blood and innards splayed wide from Varles' chin all the way down to the slime-filled vat beneath him.

Anisa whirled on the betrayer. Natarsha's metal boot sent Anisa off the barge to face the mercies of the enraged human below.

Varles reeled back, body mortally wounded and fear violating parts where fear had never been. The staff's marred view of the world showed Varles what his wounded body was too slow to stop. Eyes floating above the battle turned inward to witness the plasma blade's arc.

Wounds burst forth organs and intestines Varles' body came apart from the venting rage Natarsha unleashed on its symbiotic staff. Blow after blow creased the staff's eye and ripped away its life. Tentacles thrashed wildly and arms twisted as Varles' body became nothing more than a compilation of shattered bone and disassociated flesh. One vicious lash split the eye and rent Varles' brains from his fractured skull. The barge came crashing to the ground, imbedding itself in soft earth that became its grave.

Greg looked up at the plasma blade pointed at his head, wielded by the warrior he could not defeat. Anisa paused at the shudder behind her, metal boot shifting on Greg's chest before she delivered the finishing blow.

Super heated air passed above him. Plasma came in waves from just out of Greg's line of sight, erasing the invisible barriers a little more with each strike. He rolled away from the downcoming arc.

Captain Pritchett walked back into view, slotting another canister and pressing the attack. But it wasn't his cannon that ended the Altarain's life. Sensing the moment of collapse, Natarsha struck the instant before the mystic barriers failed. Anisa's head, helmet and all, landed at Greg's feet, the expressionless veneer for once revealing a look of surprise.

Five barrel-sized eyes turned as one above the battlefield and fled the scene to the east.

"Stand aside, Lieutenant. I've got this one." Pritchett shouldered the plasma cannon and aimed the barrel at the one remaining Warrior Woman.

Natarsha let the mystic barriers fade and turned off the flaming blade. A flash of pain and it would all be over. No more death. No more pain and suffering. Victory achieved and freedom won. A lifetime of memories to forget in the blissful embrace of death.

A body stepped between her and the instrument of her absolution.

"No." Greg stood weaponless, his body the only protection he could render.

"Are you mad, Lieutenant? Quickly, before she takes your head with that blade."

Pritchett took a step closer, the battle had awakened more within him than a sense of courage, it had brought to life values long forgotten in years of military service. It was time to make amends.

"You can't kill her, Captain."

"What's the matter with you, Merrick? Do you want to die? It's a D-Bee. It's killed, who know what it's done, and it's going to kill you too if you don't let me finish it."

"No."

"Forget what I told you about Lyboc and those stupid orders. They're wrong, and Lyboc can go to hell. Please, step aside so we can end this and get our people to safety," Pritchett pleaded, popping the face plate on his helmet so the officer could see he was sincere.

"You can't kill her."

"Then do it yourself." Pritchett pulled his C-18 and tossed it to Greg.

Greg looked at the familiar weapon in his heads. He'd seen it all his life, but it felt foreign to the touch and alien in his grip.

"This one lives. She has a name. Natarsha. She's not an it." He removed his own scarred helmet and met Pritchett with an unwavering gaze.

"Don't make this harder than it is, Lieutenant. We can still leave. Both of us. Our men. It doesn't have to end this way over a worthless D-Bee that's committed atrocities worse than you or I will ever know."

"It's not just about that."

"Please, Lieutenant, finish it. There's still a chance we can both walk away and save our careers. We can both get the people that count on us back where they belong," Pritchett pleaded, his sincerity undeniable.

Greg flipped off the safety and checked the charge. The clip was full.

"I'm not going to kill her, sir."

"Then step aside."

"That isn't going to happen either."

"Don't make me do this. Please, Lieutenant. Greg." Pritchett brought the still smoking end of his plasma cannon level with Greg's head.

"I'd rather not have to do this either, sir." Greg brought the C-18 up and pointed it at Pritchett's exposed face.

"I wish it could have been different. All of it. From the beginning," Pritchett breathed.

"Me too."

Pritchett's head snapped back, a line of blood riding down the brim of his nose and down to his mouth from the small bullet hole in the center of his forehead. His eyes lost their fire and glazed as his body relaxed. He let out one last sigh and crumpled to the ground.

Turning slowly as he lowered the laser pistol, Greg looked past Natarsha to the tree line. Mercenaries of First Strike approached the mangled barge with weapons drawn, but Greg's eyes traveled to the man handing a smoking sniper rifle back to its owner. Donnovan casually crossed the battlefield, armed bodyguards warily accepting

Natarsha's presence. She stuck the plasma blade in the ground and flung off the belt. The tension lessened.

Darren brought the SAMAS to a halt behind Greg while Van bounced from one joyous discovery to the next among the barge's wreckage.

"Man, that was intense," Darren exclaimed.

"Where were you, Darren?"

"When? While you were doing showdown in the old west with Pritchett or before?"

"Both."

"I was getting my SAMAS crispied by them giant fire balls. Then when I saw you playing Clint Eastwood with the captain I figured I might chance a shot, but I kept thinking, what if he pulls the trigger on reflex."

"Well, Merrick, no more encumbering loyalties, I hope." Donnovan gave Natarsha a bizarre look and stepped over Anisa's corpse to speak with Greg.

"Tell me something, Donnovan, what made you so sure Pritchett's trigger finger wouldn't just twitch a couple times before it hit the ground?"

"I wasn't sure."

"Guess I know what I'm getting into right up front this time."

"At least you can honestly tell your men you didn't kill the captain here. It clears you of blame, assuming you change your mind and decide to go back."

"Thanks."

"What do you want done with, with this woman here."

"Not my decision. It's hers."

Greg turned to look at Natarsha. She stood surrounded by weapons, trembling slightly.

"Well?" Donnovan addressed the Warrior Woman.

"I suspect she's been through more than you or I know. Give her some time. I'll vouch for her." Greg pushed a gun barrel in another direction.

"Whatever you say, Merrick. She doesn't leave until I get a decision."

"There's a few hours before daybreak." Greg touched her arm and she jerked away involuntarily.

"So?" Donnovan raised an eyebrow.

"By then you'll have it."

Daybreak on the battleground revealed a new fervor of excitement. Word had gotten back to Liberty that the Coalition had killed a Splugorth Slaver, and that the commanding officer of the visiting forces had fallen with his troops to achieve victory. Several scientists and scholars were arranging to have the dead barge and demon remains transported to another location for further study, although there was some discussion over many artifacts that had gone missing before the science team arrived.

Attempts to keep Natarsha's part a secret were as successful as a screen door on a submarine. Within hours the entire mercenary company knew, and by noon so would most of Liberty, although none really knew the exact details or had a convincing description of the former slave warrior. So far, she'd been silent, never once responding to the polite questions asked by more adventurous scholars and scientists. Van's unending barrage of questions had to be forcibly stopped by guarding mercenaries, who at last resorted to physical threats to make the Techno-Wizard go away. Questions about interrogation methods, scientific study, and even revenge surrounded her future existence. Nobody had ever spoken with a slave warrior from Atlantis and lived to tell of it, so little fact was known.

Greg finished discussing options with Lieutenant Sorenson and squared away his personnel before he returned for Natarsha's answer. He found her under guard in a small clearing adjacent to the battlefield. Sitting on a large stump, she didn't move a muscle when he sat beside her.

For a long time nothing was said, neither sure what to say. Oddly enough it was Natarsha who ended the silence.

"Why did you risk your life to save me?"

"I'm not sure." Greg leaned back on the stump.

"It does not make sense."

"I've been doing lots of things that don't make sense lately." He looked over at her, still noting the elongated ears.

She still wore the transparant body suit, adorned with spiked neck collar and jeweled wrist bands. Instead of the revulsion he expected to feel, knowing what she was, there was instead a warmth and feeling of kinship.

"Everything I have ever done I did because I had to. I do not understand you. You just do things for no reason."

"Well, okay, I'm not being completely honest. With myself either." He let out a long sigh. "Ever since we met, granted it was not a fantastic first impression, I've always wondered who you were, what you were really like. Running into you gave me something to look forword to, something to grab hold of and value when everything else was crumbling away around me. That's a long-winded way to say what I mean. Maybe I just wanted someone to hang out with, someone not associated with the military, someone who I could just do things with, and, probably more."

Silence returned, each mulling over the drastic changes in their own lives.

"What now?" she asked, face never showing a glimmer of emotion.

"Depends on what you want to do. Let me rephrase that. Going into town like you are now is out of the question. First Strike is afraid that if people discover who and what you are, there will be a mob situation. Oh, and you probably don't want to go to Chi-Town. Other than that, the sky's the limit."

"What about all those things you said last night on the road?"

"See the world? Explore new places? Do new things? I'm game if you are. You need to try new things, like having fun. Smiling, for example."

"That is new. Yes."

"To start, let's get you out of that outfit — not that I dislike the overall look — and find you a new set of clothes. New clothes for a new life. A shower or bath wouldn't hurt. Then you can spend some time thinking things through. Sound okay?"

"Yes. Where will you be?"

"There's still things to do. I could use a nap, but that isn't likely for awhile. I'll stay with you until I can work something out with Donnovan. Clothes, food, someplace to stay."

"He wants an answer. What are you going to tell him?"

"One question. Do you want to go, or do you want to stay?"

"I go where you go."

Greg stopped the words on his tongue at the unexpected answer. He stood. She stood.

"Do you mean that?"

"Yes."

"Then I'll tell Donnovan we stay together. I'm valuable to him because I know things about working in and around Coalition territory. He's probably planning to raid Coalition outposts in Missouri for supplies and weapons, and wants my knowledge of operations. As long as I don't push it, I can probably make sure nothing happens to you while we're still here. You may even get away with walking around town dressed like the rest of us mercenaries, I doubt anyone will know the difference. Life as a mercenary, that's new to me too, but it should be exciting."

"Yes." A hint of expression crossed her features.

"See, there, there is a woman behind the marble mask." Greg reached over and touched the tip of her chin.

She didn't jerk away.

"Hey, Fetter!" Greg called the nearest Headhunter, already trying to remember the names and faces of his new comrades.

"Yeah, wassup Merrick?"

"Get Donnovan on the comm, will you? Natarsha and I would like to speak with him."

Haphazard wiring led to the external speaker on Kruno's Multi-bot. The mercenary leaders gathered with Zenjori to listen to the comm signals relayed to them from a First Strike traitor. Mercenaries were mercenaries, and even the best of them would consider anything if the price was right.

Discussions over the slain Slaver and battlefield wreckage dominated the conversations, but occasional tidbits about the Coalition were revealed as well. It seemed the Coalition force had won back some trust from the townspeople in slaying the demon. More covertly, there were some discussions over the price for intact borg components and slightly used Coalition hardware. Once the conversations drifted to the practical joke someone had played on the Mayor of Liberty, involving some personal undergarments run up the town flagpole and tied off at the top so nobody could get them down.

More disconcerting was the talk regarding the officer now in command. A lieutenant was wheeling and dealing with mercenaries and the local mechanics shops to refit his squad for battle. Still more disturbing was the mention of a Coalition convoy that might or might not be returning to Coalition territory. The implications were clear. More Coalition forces would return if the convoy was permitted to get back and make a full report.

"Suka San, we need more information on what they have left," Drake offered his opinion.

"Can't be much more than an acre of turnips," Kruno declared, removing his coon skin cap to rub an itch on his bald scalp.

"Whatever they have, we've emasculated them," Colnae added.

"Magic user's right." Drake nodded. "They have no mechanized, just troops and a borg or two. Sledgehammer is still intact, and Kruno's got a few new recruits and worthless Headhunters to throw at them."

"Drake, one of these days I'm gonna—"

"Quiet. Both of you." Zenjori reached the point where he could barely tolerate his advisors. With exception to Notec and Colnae, the whole lot could go to hell. But they were right. If a Coalition return party got back and reported, while a second force held the fort at Liberty, there would be many more Coalition forces arriving to hunt him down and destroy what was left of his mercenary army.

"How many days until First Strike leaves Liberty?"

"Two or three. No replacements," Notec advised, his brown, wispy hair thinner than before. The same mutations that gave him his incredible psychic powers were taking their toll on his health. The missing left arm was more a psychological blow to push him over the edge. Radiation poisoning was slowly eating away his insides and there was nothing he could do to stop it.

"We still may get our chance." Zenjori paced, calculating things he needed to secure. "What is Liberty doing for defense?"

"Not sure zactly, boss, but they's figgerin' to run a sheriff and some deputies and set up a militia." Kruno chewed on a wad of tobacco.

"And of course the Coalition scored points by helping defend the town from the Slaver they killed," Colnae added. "That couldn't have been easy."

"There's no way the Coalition can remain in Liberty. First we ambush and destroy whatever convoy they're sending back, then we hide and wait for First Strike to leave Liberty." Zenjori still paced. "Once they are gone there won't be anyone stopping us from moving back in and liberating Liberty from the Coalition."

"Orders?" Drake rumbled.

"We move. west by south-west. We'll make camp at the ruins of the rail station we camped at on the way to Liberty a month or so ago."

"And from there we're just a few clicks from the river the road crosses. Perfect ambush site." Drake let out a synthesized laugh.

"By tonight I want to be in position to strike."

Brian tried to focus sleep swollen eyes in the bright lights of Gizmo's garage. Some food, a few hours sleep, and a shower helped dramatically improve his condition from thoroughly thrashed to just thrashed. Lisa leaned on his shoulder and yawned. Both were back in dark utility uniforms.

"I'm going to just go to sleep right here, okay?"

"We can't. Lieutenant Merrick wanted us here for something. Wake up."

He snapped his fingers in front of her face. Standing in the doorway they both looked up at the Skull Walker. It looked far worse than they last remembered it. Lisa started laughing.

"It's not funny." Brian got caught up in the sleep depraved humor as well. "Really," he laughed. "It's not funny. We have to fix that."

"Red-hair!" boomed a voice from the other end of the garage greeted. Brian's head slowly turned around. The giant D-Bee let go of the ATV it was holding, much to the muffled dismay of the cyborg mechanic still underneath it. Wreath leaped across the bay and snatched Brian up like a rag doll.

"Woah, hey. Oww. Oww! Wreath put me down, that hurts!" Brian tried to subdue the D-Bee mechanic's enthusiasm before the hug gave him whiplash.

"Red-hair not dead!"

"Red-hair's gonna be dead if Wreath doesn't put him down."

"Oh." Wreath set Brian back on the grease-stained concrete. "Wreath sorry."

"Glad to see you too."

"Wreath!" Gizmo yelled from a worktable covered with SAMAS parts. He pointed a finger at the ATV and pair of legs flailing beneath it.

"Uh-oh. Wreath done bad." The D-Bee looked positively ashamed and loped back to become a living vehicle jack once again.

"My guess is a male. A he."

"Lieutenant Merrick!? I didn't see you come in," Lisa exclaimed in surprise.

"Morning, at least I think it's morning, sir." Brian saluted.

"Twelve hundred hours. Sorry to drag you up so soon after what you've been through, but there's more to be done and you two are the only ones who can do it." Greg came to stand between them.

"What happened to your uniform?" Lisa asked, checking out Greg's civilian attire.

Heavy black jeans, a lumberjack-style coat over a green long-sleeved shirt, and thick-soled work boots. He'd shaved and tied his long hair back, but Lisa could tell he hadn't slept for a long time by the way his eyes squinted in the light.

"Uniform's at the cleaners."

"Don't you ever sleep, Lieutenant?"

"You know better than that. Officers don't get to sleep."

"Bust me back to private. I could use a few days of nap time," Brian joked.

"Is it true what we heard? About Captain Pritchett being killed by some demon last night?" Lisa asked.

Brian watched his reaction closely.

"Yes. Not to speak of ill of the dead, but it did solve a few problems for us."

"You had nothing to do with it?" Brian asked suspiciously.

"Oh, I had something to do with it, but we were fighting on the same side for once. Captain Pritchett died very bravely."

"Is it true you convinced some Warrior Woman, slave warrior, or something like that to turn on the demon and help you?" Lisa continued the questions.

"Something along those lines. You'll probably never meet her. That's not what I had you two roused out of bed for though." Greg changed the subject. "We're gearing up for the return trip, leaving sometime tomorrow. Hopefully early if Giz and his crew finish repairs on the hover rovers in time."

"Then, we are going back?" Brian sounded dissapointed.

"You have other plans?"

"No, well, I was just asking." Brian wasn't sure if he should share his doubts in front of Lisa. They hadn't talked since they got back. Brian wasn't going to bring anything up unless she did first.

"Here's the question for both of you. In your professional opinion, what's the status of Skull Walker 191?"

"Forget it sir."

"I'll second that." Lisa added.

"Will it make it back, more specifically?"

"If we were back at Chi-Town and I had a full gantry and crew, I'd toss it in the scrap heap for spare parts. It's a full rebuild job, from the chassis up. Frame's warped, plating's got more rivets than anything else, and it was like that before it got the it beat again."

"Can you fix it?"

"Sure, give me two or three months and an overhaul deck, but it's not worth it. It needs to be taken apart and completely rebuilt."

"Lisa?"

"Most of the internals are still good, at least last time I checked."

"Give it a once over and then give me a decision. Two possible options. Either you find a way to get it back to Chi-Town or we scrap it here."

"Uh, sir, what exactly do you mean by 'scrap it' here?" Brian asked.

"That's one of those things where I send you and Lisa out for some R & R and when you get back, the Skull Walker's gone."

"Oh. One of those things again." Brian nodded knowingly.

"Get to work. It may be your ride back to Chi-Town." Greg walked over to discuss the ongoing repairs with Gizmo.

"Shall we?" Lisa motioned to the Skull Walker.

"I should have just told him to scrap it so we could go back to bed." Brian mumbled, slowly approaching the gantry-supported mech.

"Put your headset on," Lisa reminded, adjusting hers before climbing the gantry.

"Right."

"We can get this done in about thirty, right?" she asked over the headset.

"You mean pretend like we're looking it over and then tell Merrick to scrap it?"

"You're catching on, Brian. I'm proud of you."

"We'll give it a once over like we're supposed to, but we both know this thing is shot." Brian crawled up a second gantry and started examining the robot's undercarriage while Lisa started calling up diagnostic systems inside.

"Hey, Brian, isn't this thing supposed to be powered down?"

"It should be, why?"

"Must be running on battery backups then. Main core is off and there's an open plate on the floor that's supposed to be covering the power pack. Somebody really messed things up in here."

"Probably Pritchett's techs. What's the charge on the battery?"

"71%."

"Kick the motor over once, will you?"

"You're not supposed to run that on batteries. The motor will eat the cell," Lisa advised, finger poised above the engine start button.

"We aren't going to run it, just start it, let it idle, then shut it off right away."

"Why?"

"There's some stress fractures under here that weren't here before. Real bad ones. Don't even need to use a structural analyzer to see them. Robotics are probably okay, but the lucifer joint is bent and I can see the bearing through the vetter seal."

"Okay," Lisa tried to remember her schematic courses. As far as she could recall, the lucifer joint was what connected the skull body to the robotic undercarriage. "How long do I let it run?"

"Ten, fifteen seconds."

"Okay." She hesitantly pushed the button.

Grinding and scraping noises accompanied a harsh jerk of the robot, then quieted down to what sounded like a mechanical esophagus trying to swallow a rusted car chassis. An unusual vibration made circuits and optical cables dance inside the Skull Walker. Lisa shut it off after six seconds.

"All right. Let's go get some sleep." Brian pushed himself off the smaller platform and swung onto the main ladder.

"What's wrong?"

"Motor mounts are busted. Four, at least." He climbed to the top of the Skull Walker and dropped through the open hatch.

"That's bad?"

"Bad doesn't come close. Oh, heck, that shouldn't be like that." Brian pointed to the open floor plate and immediately knelt for a closer look.

"So we just sit here awhile then go tell Merrick to scrap it."

"What the heck is this? Chewing gum?" Brian pulled his hand away with a gooey substance trailing behind it. He wiped it off on the floor plate.

"Don't ask me. It's not mine."

"Man, this must have been hit harder than we thought. I saw the blast marks outside. More rail gun hits. Lots of them. Nuclear power pack's got a seal on it, not a good job, but we're still good on rads so it must have worked."

"How did the power core get damaged? It's in the safest place on the whole Skull Walker."

"Impact shock, probably. Busted the hydraulic supports and bent the vetter seal off the lucifer joint. Broke the motor off its mounts, that might have bounced up and slammed the power pack."

"I'm glad I wasn't in here when that happened."

"I could fix it."

Lisa frowned.

"I could fix it with a full crew and a few weeks," Brian amended.

"So it's sleep time." Lisa pulled her headset down around her neck.

"Shouldn't be too hard to explain to Lieutenant Merrick. We'd have to yank the skull off the undercarriage just to get at the motor. Sounded like the trans gears are stripped too, plus the left drive bolts will need to be replaced or rebuilt."

"Are you making that up or could you tell all that just from listening to it?"

"I dunno." Brian ran his fingers through wild red hair. "You work around these things long enough you just know, without really thinking about it. Yeah, there's no way we can get this ready in less than two weeks, and that's just to make it move. Actual repairs, well, it's not worth it."

"How long have we been working?"

"Just a few minutes. Merrick will tell us to check it out some more if we tell him the Skull Walker's headed for someplace I don't want to know about. Guess you might as well download the hard drives and yank anything we don't want falling into the wrong hands."

"The transmissions!" Lisa's head snapped up.

"What?"

"I'm glad you reminded me. We never got a chance to check the transmission logs!"

"I can't believe I forgot all about that!" Brian had plopped down in Pritchett's command chair, scrambled out so Lisa could do her specialty. "Sorry."

"I'll get the voice switch this time." She teased. "Okay, here we go, comm system, asterisk, asterisk, asterisk, asterisk, asterisk, and we're in."

"There's a whole bunch of them!"

"Those are normal logs, the ones we want won't show up here. Wait a minute." Lisa stopped scrolling and backed up a few screens. "That's CFC-1."

"Who's Pritchett calling on that frequency?"

"Not just transmitting, receiving, too. Ran through the command scrambler and everything. Audio and video signal."

"Let's see it!"

"Hold on, it's not that easy. There are command codes."

"Should I go get —"

"Leave the poor man under the ATV alone. I've got it covered." Lisa grinned and held up a laser disk.

"Pritchett's command codes?"

"No, just my key." She inserted the disk in the comm deck and called up a file search on another console. "While I was in here I figured I'd be creative, so I used an old program Cara and I used to make ATM machines store I.D. codes every time they were entered. All we had to do was come back later with a key and retrieve the files, and we had all the account numbers and codes for everyone that had used the ATM machine since we inserted the program." She smiled deviously. "Too bad you're so honest. I could teach you a thing or two."

"I forgot about that, too!" Brian missed the playful jab altogether. "I still have Pritchett's expense account!"

"Really?" Lisa looked even more devious, blue eyes sparkling. "Brian, my lifelong friend."

"Hey, don't pull a Darren on me. We're not stealing the creds," Brian warned.

"How much is left?"

"Lots."

"How much!?"

"I'm not supposed to tell anyone."

"Afraid Pritchett will yell at you? C'mon, Brian, slide the rules this time!" Lisa urged.

"A little over 21 million."

"Don't you mean 17 or 18 million?"

"Stop tempting me. Besides, it's probably less now for all the repairs Giz has been doing while we were gone."

"How much could that be?"

"Half a mill, maybe."

"Like I said. 17 million left. C'mon, you know you can get Giz to stretch a few numbers, that way you'll be clean when we get back."

"Stop it. Don't you have things to be doing?" Brian pointed to the console.

"We'll discuss this later." She winked.

"The computer?" He pointed again.

"Yes sir!" Lisa saluted and returned to the console. "Ha, it worked like a charm. We can get into anything Pritchett accessed since we've been here last."

"Hold on a sec." Brian climbed half way out the top hatch then dropped back in. "Coast is clear. I just wanted to make sure Merrick, or someone else wasn't listening."

"Here it is. Elizabeth."

"That's the CFC-1 password?"

"Who's Elizabeth?"

"Maybe his wife, or a relative. I never thought about that." Brian sobered, realizing there was somebody waiting for Pritchett's return to. Brian had nobody, but still hated knowing that grief that was waiting for someone back in Chi-Town.

"It accepted it. I'm calling up the first two communications that occurred on CFC-1. This was two days ago."

A hated face appeared on the screen as the log played back. Colonel Lyboc was apparently in some dark room with lots of blinking lights and computer banks. The discussion between Pritchett and

Chi-Towns head of Espionage Division was primarily one-sided. Pritchett reported Merrick had gone native and discipline was non-existent, then asked for a date when reinforcements would arrive. Lyboc explained in little detail that the relief expedition was on its way and would be arriving within the week. A full company and platoon of SAMAS were coming under the command of a Major Ratello, who would be overseeing the construction of a communications center for both Coalition and civilian use.

When the recording was done playing, Lisa downloaded it onto another disk.

"If there's another company on its way out here, we can just wait until they relieve us and then go home. What's Merrick's rush?" Brian pondered.

"He probably doesn't know. This is CFC-1, even a lieutenant doesn't have access to that."

"Yeah, and he and Pritchett weren't real close, either. You're right, he probably doesn't know about our reinforcements."

"Does that mean we actually have to fix the Skull Walker?"

"Probably. What's the other one? Wow, that was yesterday. Less than twenty-four hours ago." Brian looked at the other CFC-1 communication Lisa had highlighted.

"2100 hours."

"We weren't even back yet."

"Let's see what it is." Lisa put the communication record on the main view screen.

Uneasiness became concern, which evolved to confused dismay as the communication played on. Lisa froze it and checked the charts that were being sent on the same signal to confirm what she was hearing.

"What's Pritchett talking about? All of Lieutenant Merrick's unit MIA or KIA, and all dissenters taken care of?" Brian stared at the casualty chart.

"That's what he said. See, here we are. MIA." Lisa pointed to the chart on the smaller screen.

"Yeah, but that makes sense, and so does the casualty report for his own unit, but how come everyone else is KIA? Getting a little ahead of himself, don't you think?"

"Darren's KIA, Merrick's KIA, even Sergeant Winters, Cowboy, Nim, Cody, everyone except Trenton."

"Then Lieutenant Merrick was right. Pritchett really did plan on killing all of us."

"We don't know that for sure. Probably, though. Let's see the rest of it." Lisa hit play.

The communications log continued on to a discussion between Colonel Lyboc and Captain Pritchett regarding the Army of the New Order. Lyboc laid out instructions and ended with the promise of regular supply drops once the captain completed the mission.

"So they finally send a whole company and armor platoon to finish this." Brian shook his head. "Should have done that from the start."

"Brian. You missed it. Lyboc told Pritchett not to capture the disk but to destroy it and kill anyone who knew about it."

"Well, that must mean —"

"Right! How did Pritchett know about this disk that Zenjori Suka supposedly has? Lyboc mentions it like Pritchett already knows what he's talking about. That means Pritchett had to know all along."

"That bastard!" Brian thought it through. "He was supposed to make us get the disk then kill everyone who knew about it. He wasn't just attacking the rebels because of the problems they started, he was after the disk. Now I wish he was still alive. Then we could wring some answers out of him."

"I know. Wait, we still might have something. I haven't checked the other transmission logs."

"You mean—"

"The ones I need you to go get my computer for. The case is at the bottom of the lift. I didn't bring it up because I thought we'd be going back to bed soon."

"I'll get it." Brian scrambled out.

With prying eyes gone, Lisa worked through the convoluted sequence on the computer that would bring up the secret transmission logs from their hiding place. She held her breath for several seconds, staring at the two blinking files that contained communications records sent to the Skull Walker by the traitor within her unit. Worse yet, there were two receptions that her program had netted and kept from being relayed to the traitor. Four chances to catch the person responsible for the deaths of her friends. Brian returned with her lap top computer and case.

"Here." She took it and started setting it up on the pilot's seat, then pulled out a long, thin fiber optic cable and linked it to the computer and pushed the other end into a jumble of wires and circuits.

"Isn't that a head jack cable?" Brian asked.

"Yes. The scrambler circuit was designed for use with a cybernetic implant. You don't know how hard it was getting this thing to work."

"You found a transmission from the traitor?"

"Four."

"Four?!" Brian asked wide eyed.

"Two, actually, two from the traitor and two the Skull Walker received and was supposed to relay to the traitor. We got both."

"Boy, we're gonna nail him." Brian slammed his fist into the palm of his hand.

Lisa pulled a tiny circuit from a protected hard case and inserted it into the jury-rigged jack attached to the cable.

"In theory, this should work."

"Theory?"

"I tested it the best I could with what we got out of the Enforcer, but it's not the same thing. I have to make the Skull Walker communication system and simulated virus program think it's relaying the transmission, but instead we rout it through this and crack the scramble."

"Well do it!" Brian practically climbed into the seat with her, brushing shoulders and making body contact that would normally have seemed awkward. Neither seemed to notice, or care.

"Cross your fingers."

The communications played over the main screen, followed by a short audio summary and report at the end of each transmission. For

424

both soldiers there was elation, but their hearts still sank into their stomachs.

"Brian?"

"Uh-huh?"

"We've gotta show this to Lieutenant Merrick."

Brian nodded, making eye contact for sincere collaboration, then climbed from the Skull Walker.

Trenton suspected something was wrong when he was summoned to a meeting of the remaining Coalition forces. What he expected and prepared himself for was not the reception he received at Gizmo's garage. Every member of the unit and two SAMAS closed in around him, weapons trained to kill. Forbidden to carry his weaponry in town, Trenton was essentially unarmed. There was no way out of this.

"Time to pay the piper." Lieutenant Merrick stepped into the ring of death, the only one there not in Coalition attire. Greg wielded his new rifle instead.

"I don't understand. What is this?" Trenton feigned ignorance in his best synthesized innocent tone.

"Yer gonna be dead, that's what," Winters growled. "I shoulda left you out there for the Glitter Boy."

"What —"

"We know it was you who sent the retreat signal through the Enforcer at Youngstown. Just like we know you're the traitor who's been working for Lyboc all along, Trenton." Greg sounded dissapointed.

Trenton's body slumped, armor plates dropping over sloped shoulders and defeated posture. The borg began to shake, rattling joints and battle-worn armor.

"Why, Trenton?" Brian asked, C-18 sidearm poised reluctantly for attack.

The large bionic body shook harder, attempting to relieve the tortured soul within of guilt a flesh and blood body could have shed in tears. Clanking sobs and tearless sorrow did little to relieve Trenton of the secrets he harbored and memories of the lives his betrayal had cost. For the man and machine there was no release from torment.

From behind the circle of confrontation, Anja bit her lip and leaned against Van for support. Despite the synthetic body, a living soul was trapped inside it, anguish transcending the artificial enclosure to touch her mind with its human emotions.

"We intercepted and decoded your transmissions intended for Lyboc, Trenton." Lisa spoke compassionately. "We also intercepted the transmissions that were meant for you. We just want to know why?"

"I didn't want to," Trenton wailed in a deep metallic voice. "But he put this thing in my head! I didn't even know it was there until we got back! I just did what he told me so I could get the Glitter Boy for what he did to me!"

"Bull. You an' Lyboc been screwin' us from the start," Winters menaced.

"No, no I swear I never met him until after the Glitter Boy took away my body and made me into this, this thing!" Trenton looked around, unable to project sincerity on the skull-like features on his artificial face. "I wanted revenge, for what the rebels and the Glitter Boy took from me, a life I can never get back! When Colonel Lyboc came to me, all he wanted was for me to watch and keep recordings of Lieutenant Sorenson. He told me Espionage Division suspected Sorenson of being a rebel spy and I would be helping all of us by watching him. I didn't even know what happened until we got back and I got out of Full Conversion acclimation. It was days before I started figuring out what had happened, and then I got scared what would happen if I said anything."

"You knew I wasn't guilty." Mike stepped closer in a battered SAMAS. "You could have said something!"

"Colonel Lyboc got to me first and told me what happened to borgs that didn't fit the profile, how they were used for experiments in R & D. He said I'd done good, and that it wasn't my fault the Glitter Boy got away. He said I'd have another chance to finish it. He arranged it so I'd be promoted to sergeant and set up false records in case anyone tried to find out. He said I was his insurance the next mission would succeed and the rebels would be killed. That's all I wanted!"

"Then how do you explain your transmissions!" Greg stepped closer, gray eyes flashing. "You sent detailed reports along with your recordings!"

"It was the only way to make them pay for what they did to me." The borg rattled again. "Colonel Lyboc fixed it so I could access the implants in my head and control the systems he'd had secretly built in. He didn't trust the captain either, and I was to make sure that if you didn't finish the rebels, the captain would." Trenton looked closer at Greg, red eyes glowing dimly. "I believed in you, sir, but the captain took over and got everyone killed. The magic users made him do it." He jerked up, looking over soldiers heads to the pair in the back. "They made him do it!"

"No they didn't, Trenton. Pritchett was being manipulated by Colonel Lyboc, just like you were." Mike's tone was angry. "Captain Pritchett planned from the beginning to kill all of us, wheather or not we destroyed the Army of the New Order. Lyboc played you and you fell for it!"

"No, no I would have stopped him. I sent reports of how he was being controlled by the magic users. Lyboc would have known the truth if I had to kill him."

"You never got the last two orders from Lyboc," Lisa stated.

Trenton turned toward her slowly.

"What orders?"

"We intercepted and decoded them with a chip just like the one in your head." Given an affirmative nod from Merrick, Lisa continued. "The first one came in at 0600 this morning. At 0900 you were supposed to eliminate Captain Pritchett and any remaining members of his unit, for treason against the Coalition States, revealing secrets to the rebels, and consorting with practitioners of magic. Your charges, Trenton."

"But, but, Pritchett was already dead this morning."

"Yes, but Pritchett had already sent a report to Lyboc and told him that all of us were dead. Lyboc thought Captain Pritchett had already killed everyone one of us except you."

"I, I don't understand."

"You were being used as a pawn, fool!" Mike practically shouted.

Greg raised a hand to calm him. Lisa continued her explanation, not for Trenton's benefit but for the rest of the soldiers around her.

"Lyboc wanted you to kill Captain Pritchett and the rest of his unit because he thought everyone else was dead. The mission failed, so Lyboc has you and Pritchett clean it up. The captain kills us, you kill the captain. The only one left is you. The only left who knows anything."

"I still don't understand. Why would Lyboc want everyone dead?"

"Because we know what he's done and he doesn't want any witnesses!" Mike shouted, but calmed down with a look from Greg. "You stupid fool. Back in Chi-Town we're already dead, and if Lyboc lets you go he'll have to answer for it. He's got to kill you too."

"That brings me to the second order, coming in a few hours ago." Lisa added. "There's a company on its way to Liberty even as we speak. Lyboc wanted you to brief the commanding officer, a Major Ratello, on the status of the Army of the New Order and ensure that the new field commander finishes the job. I'll bet this Major has orders, too, just like you, except Lyboc probably told him you were a rebel spy to be shot on sight. As far as Colonel Lyboc knows, you're the one last loose end he has to burn."

The borg shook uncontrollably, finally collapsing on his knees under the barrels of his squad mates. Fingers left their places hovering above triggers and barrels slowly pointed to earth, men and women he'd served with taking pity on the traitor in their midst. At last, Nim trudged forward, patting the borg's metal plated shoulder with a bionic limb of his own. He understood the loss that could drive a man to acts of depravity. Trenton was still his friend.

"You're a fool, Trenton." Winters lifted his face plate to berate the borg as only Winters could. "First you git yerself shot by a Glitter Boy, then you mess with everyone else to git revenge. Ya shoulda thought with yer real brain, not them things they put in yer head."

"I would tear them out if I could. You know that, Sarge." Trenton looked up at Winters, a shadow of the real Trenton coming through the synthesized voice.

"Those things are still in there." Mike pointed with the power armor's rail gun. "We don't have any other way to be sure." He took aim.

"Back off," Greg ordered.

Mike's anger was arrested, though for an instant he contemplated how easy it would be to kill Merrick. The rival officer wore no armor, and a SAMAS could kill a man with its bare hands, rail gun or not. The intimidation he felt from the other officer made him all the more angry.

"There's always the Cyber-Doc," Brian suggested.

"Take too long and he's not trustworthy. My way is faster." Greg motioned to Van.

Stepping through agitated Coalition troops and mindful of the uneasy stares, Van approached the borg.

"Please, Lieutenant, don't let him get in my head," Trenton pleaded.

"I'm not doing anything magic. Purely technical," Van lied, pulling out a box with blinking lights and beeper to use as a ruse to cover his real intent.

"No way!" Winters thrust the barrel of his plasma cannon inches from Van's face.

Cowboy and several others mirrored the action.

"Cool it, Sergeant." Greg pushed the barrel down. "All of you."

"Yer not really gonna let the caster mess with Trenton, are you?"

"C'mon, Lieutenant, Trenton's a screw-up, but that's too much," Cowboy complained.

"Give me another option and I'll take it. Either we blast Trenton's head apart to make sure we get what Lyboc put in there, or we let this, technician, tell us where it is and we have Brian and Lisa take it out." Greg looked around at the faces of his men. No alternatives presented themselves.

"Yer not gonna let the magic user open him up, right?" Cowboy asked.

"Not unless we have to, right Van?"

"Yeah, right."

"Man, Greg." Winters looked deep into Greg's eyes, then stepped back shaking his head.

Van waved the box around the borg's head and hit the button to make it change sounds and switch patterns of lights.

"What's he doing?" Cowboy fingered his rifle.

"Oh, this? This is a brain magnifier that reads the coefficient frequency pulse off the armature bands and lets me know where the equality regulator circuits meet with the mental crossover network." Van laid it on thick, reaching out with his mind to search the mechanical and electrical systems of the cyborg.

"Oh."

Brian gave Lisa a questioning gaze but she just shrugged.

"The resonance inhibitor seems to have taken some damage." Van showed the blinking box to Winters as though it would make everything clear.

"Where's that brain screw thing?"

"Let me localize it."

Van hit more buttons and waved the box over Trenton's head and upper body. He searched for the scrambler/descrambler circuit and setup Lisa had used and tried to pick it out of the unfamiliar blend of artificial body systems and bionics. Electrical and mechanical systems linked to the borg's brain in ways normal circuits did not, and he was finding it more difficult to isolate the machine from the man than any mechanical device alone. Finally, something matched the assembly pattern he searched for and he narrowed in to confirm it. The circuit was there, linked to three others he knew nothing about and brain implants he couldn't read at all. The entire setup was tied into implants inside Trenton's brain, protected inside the containment unit. All that had to be done was to sever the circuits from the controlling brain implants.

"I found it. It looks like my brain magnifier has found what you're looking for, see?" He waved the device around for all to see. Some nodded in agreement.

"Okay," Brian moved closer, ignoring the random blinking lights and beeping sounds of whatever Van had called the thing. "How exactly do we get it out?"

"I can draw you a schematic to follow."

"Great. Do that."

"Sure thing." Van stepped through the crowd and set the box on the hood of an ATV and began scribbling on a note pad, glancing up from time to time at the sensor device for confirmation. He handed the notes to Lisa and explained as best he could the recommended procedure for removal, including a whispered reference to the other three circuits tied to the scrambler.

"Thank you." She moved away a bit too quickly and confided with Brian on what tools to use for the operation.

Troops mingled about restlessly, some still keeping a close watch on the two magic users in their midst. Mid-afternoon sunlight shown down on the event taking place on the street in front of Gizmo's garage, nervous passers-by wondering why a squad of fully-armed and armored Coalition troops were surrounding the kneeling borg on the street.

Greg ensured the removal process was under way before approaching Van and Anja.

"Thank you, again, Van." He shook hands in plain sight of all.

"You're welcome, especially for our little exchange earlier." Van winked.

"That, well, you were very generous. I might have thrown that stuff away or destroyed it like the rest of the gear." Greg was careful not to give away too much in the presence of the others, though most kept a wary distance. Natarsha had insisted on destroying the warrior suit and shackles, along with any other paraphernalia that linked her to slavery under the demon. The sword Greg had snatched before she went on her purging rampage, and for some reason the medallion she'd worn wasn't harmed by heat, explosions, or even high frequency blades. Knowing Van had an intense curiosity for such things Greg visited the Techno-Wizard on his fundraising and organizational tour, figuring on picking up a few credits for the peculiar medallion and ornate sword. When Van offered an exorbitant six figured amount, Greg quickly accepted, figuring he was probably being taken, but didn't have the time or inclination to haggle over what he thought was worthless junk. They both came out of it happy and none the wiser.

Anja looked at them both suspiciously, then tugged on Greg's sleeve and motioned him close with her finger.

"Yes?"

"Come talk to me before you see Natarsha again," she whispered in his ear.

Greg snapped back up to his full six foot four and corner-eyed the Mystic with blood-shot suspicion. Van shrugged and mouthed the words "It wasn't me."

"How did you know?"

"I visited her," she stated matter-of-factly.

"That's not possible. One, because nobody but a few people know where she is. Two, very few people know her name. And three, there's a guard watching to make sure nobody makes the connection, or visits."

"Just promise me you will talk to me first."

"I think I have to, now."

"We'd better take off." Van noticed soldiers taking a closer interest in their conversation.

"You know what hotel we're at?" Anja smiled.

"I know. Thanks again, Van."

"Sure thing."

Tension levels dropped as soon as the two practitioners left the vicinity and Coalition troops were again left with only their own to worry about. Brian was ranting about how he was an engineer, not a doctor, while Lisa kept pointing to the notes and the splayed mass of circuitry and inner working of Trenton's head unit. The brain was nestled deep within the armored chest, safe in its containment unit and linked to the synthetic systems that were its body. Finally, Lisa just ripped out four tiny circuits with a pair of pliers — accompanied by a horrified scream from Brian — and set them on the work cart. Trenton complained loudly about not hearing anything until the two technical officers managed to put one of the circuits back and reassemble his head the best they could.

"We got it, Lieutenant!" Lisa shouted, cheers from the troops drawing looks from both up and down the street. Winters walked over to the tool cart and picked up one of the tiny circuits.

"When we git back I'm gonna ram all three of these down Lyboc's throat."

"Tools too, Sarge." Nim leaned over Winters' shoulder and picked a particularly nasty looking wrench from the rack.

"Them too. Pack 'em all up for special delivery."

"All right, everyone, listen up," Greg shouted above the noise.

Winters smacked Private Peterson in the back of the head to shut him up.

"Our convoy leaves tomorrow morning at 0800, but we need to have a serious meeting tonight before that," Greg went on, attention again centered in his direction. "Be back here at Gizmo's at 2000 hours. Check in all your weapons and gear with Lieutenant Adams before you go. Do not take it with you. I'm talking to you, Cowboy."

Several laughs and jabs went in Cowboy's direction.

"If you have any unfinished business, now is the time. We won't be coming back here."

Greg watched the faces of his men, his speech in part to decide who he needed to have a private talk with.

"What's stage time?" Winters asked.

"0600. Please, everyone be sober tonight at 2000, we're going to discuss some very important things that will affect the rest of your lives. Get drunk after the meeting if you want, not before."

"Sure thing, Lieutenant!" Cowboy cheered. He'd been in the bar since they got back from the last defeat, drowning the memories of someone he was never going to see again. The cheerful face was a drunken front.

"Dismissed. All except Darren, Sharp, Dave, Peterson, Jameson, and you, Corrinne." Greg looked to the RPA, now more a part of his unit than she ever was to Pritchett's.

"What did I do?" Joel Peterson looked hurt, his curly brown hair and brown eyes giving him an innocent look he'd learned to use.

"Nothing except visit Reaverton's book store one too many times."

"I wasn't reading, anything! I swear! I barely know how to read!"

"I know. I also know Reave has an attractive step-daughter."

Joel Peterson blushed.

"I know everything, Private." Greg smiled.

"What's this about, sir?" Dave asked.

"You and Darren probably already know. All of you follow me back to the paint shed. We have things to discuss."

Chapter 21

Weird looking orange puffy things paraded around a glass bottle full of neon yellow magic markers. The throbbing beat of the little orange feet on the emerald green tiles got louder and louder until Brian's head exploded.

Staring down at the dirty shop rag on the APC's dash, Brian tried to bring his mind back from REM into conscious reality. He hadn't meant to doze off, had he? The noises from outside the APC were getting louder, speech and the sounds of metal doors coming down and being locked in place followed. He turned his head from side to side and discovered muscle groups he didn't know he had could be tied into knots. Looking to his right he saw Lisa in a similar state apparently also aroused from REM inflicted lapses. She smiled and cocked her head, then mirrored Brian's reaction to discomfort.

"Ow," she complained. Looking through the new APC viewport, she saw personnel assembling for the meeting and checked her wrist comp for the time. "1955."

"Already? What happened to the last two hours?" Brian checked his own comp to confirm the time.

"I don't know. You said something about yourself in the third person and put the rag down as a pillow. I knew we had to finish the checklist, but I couldn't focus on the numbers so I just closed my eyes for a second to rest them."

"I hope nobody saw us." Brian looked out the viewport.

Cowboy and several other soldiers pointed and laughed.

"Too late."

"Now we're going to hear about it all the way back."

"I don't care."

"You've never ridden in a rover with Cowboy before."

"I still don't care. As long as there's a hot bath and a soft bed at the end of it, I can take anything."

"Lieutenant's here. We should probably get out there now."

"You know what this is about?

"No."

Brian glanced out the side port to make sure the Skull Walker was still there and not "scrapped" while he was asleep.

"I think I do." Lisa rubbed her eyes and looked into Brian's. "Think about it. We're all supposed to be dead or MIA. Lyboc thinks we're all gone. He doesn't know we're coming back."

"Boy will he be surprised."

"And what do you think he'll do?"

"He can't kill all of us."

Lisa gave him an "oh really?" look.

"Okay, so maybe he can. I'm too tired to think that far ahead."

"I wish we had more time. I can't think of a way to beat him this time. With the evidence we have we could sink him. Maybe. If he doesn't get us first, which he probably will, and that's still assuming whoever his boss is cares."

"Lieutenant Merrick might have a plan."

"He's climbing up on the APC's ram prow to talk to everyone. We better move."

"Back way."

Brian grabbed her sleeve and pulled her through the length of the APC and out the rear hatch so they wouldn't have to face the assembled soldiers from the front. Brian and Lisa slipped around the side and tried to look inconspicuous.

"Quiet, everyone, please." Greg stood on the raised ram prow and addressed the survivors. Lisa hadn't ever seen him look so haggard. "This an unofficial, off the record meeting, so for the time being, all comments, suggestions, and opinions are encouraged. Some of you I've already talked to, but for the rest of you what I'm about to say should not be taken lightly." He paused, looking into the eyes of personnel he'd known for years and ordered into battle many times. His face grew sadder. "We all know, at least in some part, what Colonel Lyboc, head of Chi-Town Espionage Division, had planned for us. It was he who ultimately got many of our friends killed at Youngstown, and what he didn't finish then, Captain Pritchett was supposed to finish here. But we're not dead, we're here, and now we have to decide what to do next.

"If, and I say 'if' because it is a choice, if we decide to go back to Chi-Town, there's a good chance Lyboc will arrange some accident to cover up his mistakes. Right now he thinks we're all dead, Chi-Town thinks we're dead, and probably many of your families have been given the bad news. We're all to be swept under the rug and forgotten, at least that's what Lyboc wants. In fact, the reinforcements on their way here now may intercept us on the way back and make sure there's nobody to implicate Lyboc. He's not likely to take our return sitting down."

"He's gonna hafta' take it." Winters held up a case containing the circuits recovered from Trenton and got several enthusiastic cheers.

"Even if, by some chance, you do manage to make it back to Chi-Town alive and try to confront Colonel Lyboc, you probably won't make a dent in his lies. He'll have you disappear one by one until there's nobody left who knows. Best case scenario, you make it back in one piece and retire, then disappear someplace with your families where he can't find you. Stay in the military and I guarantee you'll be on the next flight to the Tolkeen front-lines and ordered down the enemy guns."

"What are you saying, sir?" Cowboy asked. "That we should just go back and give up, after all this?"

"No, I'm saying you probably won't have a chance to fight, not the way you and I, and most of us here know how to fight. If he finds out you're on your way back, you probably won't make it all the way. Whoever decides to return is taking a serious risk. Fact plain and simple, you will most likely be killed."

"Hey now, what do ya mean by whoever's goin' back?" Winters looked around at the faces of his men for the ones that looked like they had desertion tattooed on their foreheads.

"You don't sound like you're going back, sir," Brian pointed out, making long eye contact with the officer he looked up to.

"I'm not."

Murmurs and gaping jaws passed through the soldiers like a plague. A few just stared, others gawked, but most talked among themselves in disbelief.

"You're just kiddin' us, right, Lieutenant?" Cowboy asked hopefully, rubbing his short cropped spiked hair.

"No, I've given it a lot of thought, and decided no to go back."

"You ain't 'fraid of nothin', not ever I've seen. You ain't losin' yer guts cuz some Colonel wants yer hide?" Winters asked, watching close for the answer he could already read.

"I'm done with the Coalition military, but for reasons of my own. What each of you needs to think about is what you really want, and decide if it's worth the risk to go back. Decide if serving the military is what you want."

"Yeah."

"Jerry, you have a wife and family. You have a reason to go back. Many of you have lives to go back to, things that are worth the risk, and I don't blame you. That's what we should be fighting for, our families and our freedoms. So if you have something or someone worth going back to and risking your life for, then do it."

"I'm not going back either." Mike Sorenson spoke up, leaning against a structural support in the back. "I have nothing to go back to."

"Me an' Dave are stayin' too," Darren added, not wanting Sorenson's pessimistic view to be the last word. "Me an' Dave got hunny's we gotta look out for here. But most of you have normal babes back home, so just think it over."

"Any other AWOL, deserting grunts I gotta beat some sense into?" Winters looked around with hostility.

"Nobody's beating sense into anyone. This is a personal decision everyone here needs to make between now and 0800 tomorrow morning. I can't stress to you how important this decision is. It will affect the rest of your lives. Give it some hard, honest thought and then decide if you're returning with Sergeant Winters, or staying behind and starting a new life." Greg's eyes lingered on Brian and Lisa, but he said nothing more, listening to the varied responses from the Coalition troops.

"Yer dead serious 'bout this?" Winter's eyes bore into Greg's with a hurt fury.

"Dead serious."

"Then you just live with what yer makin' here." Winters looked around at the Coalition soldiers talking among themselves.

"Does anybody else have something to say?" Greg asked. They quieted down but no response came back. "Then we're done here. Last night in Liberty, please spend it wisely. Staging starts at 0600, anyone who doesn't show, I'll know their answer. Everyone who plans to go back, get there in time for a briefing and weapons check. It's a long trip back."

Playing cards lay untouched on the table in the small cabin. Cowboy stared at them over the top of several empty beer cans, blurry eyes seeing memories instead. Sharp was staying behind. He'd never be there to cheat his squad out of everything they bet anymore. Bill was gone, his D-Bee jokes lost forever. Then there was the last, and most memorable game he'd played in the back of a covered rover with Rachel the night before the attack. His first, and last, game of strip poker. Tears welled up in his eyes and he downed another beer in one hard gulp, throat choking involuntarily. Nobody could see him cry.

Cody and Robert argued about they should do to Trenton when they got back. Nim and Sergeant Winters discussed some secret plan with other loyal members of the Coalition special ops unit. Cowboy didn't care. There was nothing left for him to go back to but the eternal war and countless battles to come.

Alcohol-numbed wits drove the pain to his heart and pounding rage burned hotter than anything had ever stoked his emotions before. He'd left his friends on the battlefield, not knowing if they were alive or dead. He couldn't go back without knowing, or his memories would haunt him forever. Unable to express in words the war inside, Cowboy stood and tore the table from its bolts on the floor. Through a haze of rage he vented, table smashing the cabin window and sailing out into the courtyard. The room went silent as the giant whirled around to face the group.

"We left them out there!" He hollered, pointing at the shattered window.

"Just what is yer problem, Corporal?" Winters stared at the window and back at Cowboy.

"We left them behind! We're not leavin' until I find out if they're alive or dead!"

"Calm down, man." Nim had never seen his friend like this before.

"Go to hell. All of you!!" Cowboy grabbed Cody by the shirt and hurled him across the room. "You left her behind!"

"Git yerself in line, Cowboy!" Winters stood and shouted.

"You!" Cowboy's wrath turned on Winters. "You ordered us to leave her behind! I'm gonna kill you!" Cowboy lunged, taking Winters and the other table with them into the bunks. Fists and feet flew wild and both men tumbled back and forth before Cowboy managed to get a handhold and fling the the husky sergeant into the next set of bunks on the other side of the room.

Cowboy's threat took on new meaning as he rushed across the room, casually hurling Robert out the window to meet the broken table. Mindless aggression drove blow after blow into Winters' body, the sergeant returning as good as he got to no effect.

Grabbing Winters' arm, Cowboy swung him across the room into the other set of bunks, following up with a kick that sent the sergeant between the beds into the remnants of the second table. Cowboy leapt after him.

A table leg struck Cowboy in the side of the head, pausing his drive to murder. Winters swung again, wood splintering and skin breaking in a line from Cowboy's jawbone to the back of his head. His eyes glazed, but the pain within made him oblivious to the punishment of body. Clutching Winters by the throat, Cowboy's knees finally buckled and he took Winters with him to the floor.

Breathing heavily and wheezing from traded blows, both men remained crumpled where they fell. Cowboy's rage reached its end, releasing the well of emotions fueling it.

"They're dead, Cowboy." Winters almost sounded sympathetic.

"No, no, we left them."

"They're dead."

Cowboy's enormous body was racked with sobs he couldn't hold back anymore. Tears came in uncontrollable waves as the sorrow took over. Winters put his hand on Cowboy's shoulder, tears welling up in his own eyes and his heart rising to his throat. The squad watched on.

When there were no more tears left, Cowboy raised reddened eyes to the only family he ever knew. Some swallowed hard, others fought back tears of their own.

The moment was broken with Robert climbing back inside the broken window dragging the table behind him.

"Man, Cowboy, I thought these windows were bullet-proof."

"They are." Winters grunted, a short chuckle bringing relief to the tension.

"I don't think we're gettin' our deposit back." Nim looked around the room.

"Don't matter. We're all goin' home tomorrow. All of us."

Sounds of a shattering window and a ruckus in one of the cabins sent Brian to the window of his rented housing across the yard. Fully furnished with beds and decor, the cabin assigned the technical officers had individual rooms and far more privacy. Lisa rolled over on her bed to see where Brian had gone.

"What was that?"

"Cowboy and his squad I think," he answered, satisfied that it was just another of their frequent brawls. He returned to the bed and laid back down on the covers. "Sharp told me about the hall wars the grunts get into back at Chi-Town. East hall versus West hall, or something like that. Glad I don't have to live with the jarheads."

"It takes people like them to fight a war," Lisa commented.

"Yeah, when things get really heavy it's nice to have them around."

Neither technical officer had spoken much since leaving the meeting. Going straight back to their cabin they'd both somehow ended up laying side by side on Lisa's bed, grateful for the companionship but each lost in their own thoughts.

"They're all going to have hangovers in the morning. That will be fun." Brian spoke sarcastically to the stucco ceiling.

"You've decided to go back?"

Brian rolled over to face her, taken by surprise at her question. He hadn't really thought about not going back.

"Why? You've decided to stay?"

"I don't know yet. It's a hard choice."

"I know what Merrick was saying was probably true, but I keep thinking there's got to be a way to work it out so we can go back and Lyboc still gets what's coming to him."

"Me too, but then I start doing what you do. I ask myself if it's worth it. Sure, there might be a way, but is it worth it?" Lisa rolled onto her back and stared at the ceiling.

"Everything I've ever known is back there. Sharp and I grew up in the Coalition youth program and joined the military to make a difference. All my stuff is back there, my friends, well, some of my friends, my best computer, my leather jacket."

"You're thinking about that?" Lisa rolled over to face him again.

"I like that jacket. I won it in a street fight with the Stone Heads."

"For crying out loud, Brian, if that's all you're worried about I'll buy you another leather jacket."

"That's not really what I meant. The jacket has memories of places and things I've done. It's all back there. My whole life."

"You're willing to risk your life for that?" she asked, their eyes meeting in the semi-darkness.

"I could make a difference back there. I know things now, things I didn't know before. Just because the system has flaws doesn't mean you just abandon it. Somebody's gotta take make changes from within, or it won't happen at all. I could do that."

"You could, but you don't have to." She rolled back over on her back. "I know what you mean about your whole life being back there. But it's different for me. I have some friends, my bike, but I hate my parents and I've never been one for working within the system."

"I noticed."

"Don't you ever think about what it would be like to start all over fresh? You know, a clean slate?" She rolled back to face him. "A whole new life to make what you want of it?"

"You are thinking about staying."

"Maybe." She looked deep into his eyes and reached over to take his hand. "I was thinking I'd wait and see what you were going to decide first."

Brian pulled away and put her wrist back on the bed. She looked hurt.

"What's wrong?"

"Lisa, please, not like this."

"What do you mean?"

"You're on the rebound, and as much as I'd like something to happen, I don't want it to be because you're looking for someone to fill Mike's place, or well, you know. Besides, I don't even know what I want. I like you. We've got something good going now. I don't want to blow it."

"You're not interested anymore?" Lisa was unaccustomed to being rejected, especially when she really was putting her heart on the line.

"I am, but not like this. Let's just take it one day at a time for awhile. See how things work out."

He noticed the tears welling up in her eyes and the hurt expression on her face.

"Don't be upset. Please. It's just that if you and I do get something going, more than we have now, I want it to be for the right reasons, so it will last."

"I suppose I had this coming," she choked out and rolled with her back to him.

"I'd answer that, but I'd probably just put my foot in my mouth again."

"Shut up, Brian."

"Okay." Brian rolled on his back, mentally challenging his principles to make sure he hadn't just blown his one and only chance. His convictions were still there, but he hoped he was making the right choice. He lay his values through the fires of truth to search for the ones that could stand the forge and tip the scales one way or the other. The big decision was hours away, and it would irrevocably change his life forever.

Weariness threatened to overcome him before he reached the small camper that was to be his home for the next few days. Greg stared at the two steps leading up to the narrow door and tried to work up the energy to ascend them. He'd spent the past twenty minutes talking with the First Strike mercenaries at the edge of the small mercenary encampment on the fringe of an old R.V. and shantytown that made up Liberty's slums. Usually practiced at remembering names, he couldn't recall them now, nor exactly what he'd just talked about. He looked around to make sure he wouldn't be walking into the wrong dwelling and looking down the barrel of some D-bees alarm system.

Most of the north slum area was clear of inhabitants, but transients, nomads, and the very poor still lived among the crudely constructed dwellings and Pre-Rifts R.V.'s. Donnovan seemed to think it was safe to stash Natarsha there until she was suitably presentable to blend with society. The twenty foot R.V. had no engine or tires, but it had electricity via an extension cord leading to some junction nearby, heat, and running water, the latter being somewhat dependent on the weather. Best of all, a loft and bed inside the R.V. awaited him. All Greg cared about was the bed.

Now past 3:15 in the morning, he'd finished squaring things away for the returning convoy and eventually escaped the well meaning conversation with Anja. There was still no clear explanation on how she'd found out about Natarsha — Greg suspected Van — and even less covering how Anja managed to have a talk with the former slave warrior. Still, the Mystic had lots of good intentions and advice, most of which Greg hadn't understood, in part from sleep deprivation and from the Mystic's oblique references to many topics. She'd kept saying things about how Van respected her purity, or something like that, and compared it to how Greg should treat Natarsha. About the only thing he remembered well was her repeated urgings for him to be patient and understanding, that Natarsha had nothing to relate to the world as he knew it. He'd never expected things to be easy — nothing ever was — and took her advice to heart as best he could. Promising to return when he was awake, Anja had finally let him go.

Two hours of sleep, if he was lucky. He stared at his wrist comp again, then to the pair of steps. The ground beside them was relatively flat, inviting him to abandon his foolish quest for a bed and embrace the ground in all its flatness. No, it was too cold for that. He gave himself a cause to make the ascent, and stumbled into the darkened R.V.

Natarsha sat on the ragged couch, back straight in a rigid posture. Bathed in moonlight from the opposite window, she wore the outfit he'd had on the first time he'd met her on the logging road north of Liberty. She'd bathed and rid herself of every item linking her to her past. Beyond her on the tiny table was the glint of a blade. Anja had said something about it, but he couldn't remember what exactly. He was too tired to care.

"Is it cold in here to you?" Greg noticed the temperature inside was only a few degrees warmer than the frigid weather outside, his breath frosting in the air.

"Yes."

"There's a heater." He crossed past her and flicked the switch on an electric heater where the microwave should have been. The heat took effect immediately, warming the air to more bearable temperatures. "Better?"

"Yes."

"I must have forgotten to show you that."

"I did not want to touch anything. This is very old. The walls have felt many things."

"I think it's a Pre-Rifts R.V. called a Winnebago. People used to drive around the country in them." Greg leaned over and picked up the knife. It was dull, rusted and the six inch blade was broken at the tip. It was still sharp enough to harm or kill.

"Where did you find this?"

"Here." She pointed to the sagging couch.

He set it back on the table and trudged the few steps to the ladder that led to the small loft bed. Ordering tired muscles to action, he rolled up onto it and let the soft, lumpy mattress do its best.

"Flat. Sleep." He mumbled, eyes and mind reaching for dreamland.

"What?"

"It's a sleep depravation mantra. Flat. Sleep. You know, that couch folds out into a bed. You do sleep, right?" He spoke to the warped fiberglass roof inches above his face.

"Yes."

"Good. One thing we have in common. Good night."

"You are not afraid I will kill you in your sleep?"

"What sleep. I have to get up in two hours."

"The blade is sharp enough."

"I talked to Anja. She said she spoke with you."

"The Mystic."

"Uh-huh."

"What did she tell you?"

"I don't remember."

"And you are not afraid?"

"I'm too tired to be afraid. Get some sleep." Greg closed his eyes to welcome dreamland when her voice snatched it away. Her words carried across the fog in his brain and made thought return.

"I was willing to die."

"So was I."

"I wanted to die. I wanted it to be over. When I realized you had saved me, I did not know what to do. I cannot express the sensations."

"Near death experiences sometimes make you appreciate life. I know."

"When I found the knife, I was going to end my own life, but the will inside me kept me from doing it. I thought about attacking you when you returned, forcing you to kill me, but you did not deserve that. The things I have done will not let me rest. I do not know what to do."

"You can leave any time, go anywhere you want. It's your life now. If you need time to work things out, do it. I understand."

"How could you? I have done all the things people hate me for, and many far worse. I am everything you should fear and hate, and the horrors I have committed on other living beings is a pain I cannot express or free myself of."

Greg rolled over on his side and made out her face in the dark. The marble mask was gone, replaced by trembling lips and a forlorn expression. She'd been alone with her thoughts all day. He didn't know what to say.

"I've been in the Coalition military eight years, and in that time I've done many things I'm not proud of and sent many, many men and women to their deaths on the orders of my superiors. I have to live with that, and move on, or it will eat me up inside. I keep busy, so I don't have to think about it, but that's not a solution, it's just a shield. Move on to something else before the past catches up."

"How?"

"I wasn't offering that as good advice. It's not."

"Then how?"

"I don't know. I hit the gym, lift weights, run in the morning, do endless laps in the pool until I'm too exhausted to feel the anger or pain. It's a poor substitute, but it's kept me sane."

"That is what I will do as well."

"We can do it together." He rolled over onto his back. "Just not tomorrow. Today. Whatever it is right now. We can start running and working out some other morning."

"I do not want to be in here. I need something to do."

"Can you handle being around people and blend in?"

"I know how."

"Want to come with me in the morning? Watch my back? I might need a bodyguard, just in case my sergeant is up to what I think he's up to."

"Yes."

"Good." He yawned. "Now lay down and repeat after me. Flat. Sleep. Flat Sleep."

Greg was sound asleep before the third repetition.

"Cowboy! What the hell do you need eleven fusion blocks for!?" Brian's tirade reached the inevitable point in the ritual of arming.

"You don't understand, buddy, I need them!" Cowboy leaned over the folding table and pointed to the cases of ordnance stacked behind Brian.

"Me too!" Cody seconded.

"You can't possibly carry that many, even if you could use them all!"

"Hey, that's what we all bought these duffel bags for."

Cowboy's squad tossed large, identical blue duffel bags on Brian's table.

"I can't believe this. I can't believe you're serious. Look at your belt, Cowboy. Both of you. All of you! You've got two, three, four, six fusion blocks on you already!"

"I need more."

"What the hell for!?"

"And we need some grenades, too," Nim added.

"And none of them wussy firecracker H.E.'s. We want the good stuff." Robert pointed to one of the cases.

"You know what, forget this." Brian threw up his hands. "Here, go ahead. Help yourselves. It's all leftovers from Pritchett's APC, so go ahead, take whatever you want!" He gestured wildly at the stacks of military cases.

The lights in the soldier's eyes came on as though it was too good to be true.

"Really?"

"Go right ahead. Take the whole case. Heck, take all the cases! I don't care!"

Brian sidestepped the charge and left the scene before he got trampled. Like a pack of starving wolves, the soldiers of Merrick's special ops unit descended on the stack of ordnance. Brian walked over to where Lisa leaned on the front left wheel of the Coalition APC. A smile on her lips infected Brian as he leaned on the wheel with her to watch the squad devour enough ordnance to arm a company.

"Winters is going to be mad," Lisa chided.

"He can try and take it all away from them if he wants."

Sunlight was just peeking through early morning clouds as the Coalition convoy prepared to move out at the edge of town. An unusual number of First Strike mercenaries were present, along with the wilderness scout Lieutenant Merrick had hired days before to spy on the rebel army. The woman was like a shadow to Merrick's movements, never far and never in the way. Brian looked around to see who was missing, and was surprised to see most everyone was there, if not gearing up to leave then saying last farewells and trying to ease tensions. Cowboy and company were going through the final stages of arming, each with bulging duffel bags and loaded from head to foot with explosives. Brian noted with a smile the empty cases strewn around his makeshift station. They'd taken everything, even the wussy firecracker high explosives.

"You know if one of them goes up, it's going to chain fire and kill everyone," Lisa observed.

"Yeah. I'm actually going to miss all this."

Lisa's head snapped over to catch Brian's gaze.

"You've decided not to go? You're in uniform and armor."

"I haven't decided yet. And so are you. That means you're going?"

"You'd better make up your mind. They were supposed to leave ten minutes ago."

"So you've decided to stay?"

"You tell first," she prodded.

"No. You go first."

"Same time." She counted the seconds with her hands to get Brian to speak.

"I have decided to sss, goo, sss" They both waited for the other to finish.

"This isn't working," Brian commented.

"Pick a number between one and ten?"

"How is that going to decide who goes first?"

"If you're within five, you go first. If you're more than five off, I go first."

"I'll just pick five."

"Oh yeah. Okay, one in twenty."

"That's not fair either. Percentages. And how do I know you won't cheat?"

"You think I, why Brian, after all this time?" She faked being insulted by his distrust.

"Absolutely. I know you would cheat."

"Better tell me fast. Here comes Lieutenant Merrick." She looked over his shoulder.

"I'm not going to fall for that one."

"Brian, Lisa, have you checked in with Winters yet?"

"Hi, Lieutenant."

"Told you," Lisa chimed.

"I'm only Lieutenant if you're planning on going back. After that, I don't exist."

"Actually, sir, we haven't decided yet." Brian eyed Lisa and felt his heart flutter as the moment of truth approached.

Merrick towered over him in his scarred Explorer armor, helmet in hand and sidearm in holster. His long hair blew in the breeze and the usual unshaven look was back. The tired, drawn lines on his face were still there, but the spark of life flashed in his gray eyes. Brian almost felt self-conscious, having showered, shaved, and pressed his uniform and polished his armor.

"You haven't decided? Cutting it down to the wire, don't you think?"

"Well, sir, we were thinking about it." Lisa looked at Brian.

"Okay, fine, who do I think I'm kidding?" Brian stood up straight, taking control. "Sooner or later I'm gonna say the wrong thing to the wrong person and my career will be over. I know this."

"And?" Greg prompted.

"So I guess that means I'm," Brian looked into Lisa's blue eyes and saw the answering fire. She nodded. "We're, staying. Both of us," he finalized.

"Glad to hear it." Greg's hand slammed Brian on the shoulder.

"Thanks, sir."

"No 'sirs' anymore. It's Greg Merrick now."

"Yes sir, okay Greg." The words sounded strange to Brian.

"You two better say your good-byes while you can. It's for good," he admonished.

"Thank you, Greg Merrick." Lisa smiled and reached up to kiss him on the cheek before grabbing Brian's hand and dragging him to the gathering at the hover rovers. Greg watched them go, seeing a joy both were experiencing for the first time.

Squads coalesced loosely and eyes traveled in Greg's direction as Sergeant Winters walked over to join him at the APC.

"About ready here, Sergeant Major?" Greg leaned on the APC, making eye contact.

"Ready when you are, Lieutenant." Winters stopped a foot from him and leaned on the armor plating.

Greg watched the pitifully few survivors of the ill-fated expedition prepare to go their separate ways. Arguments and counter-arguments went nowhere, but the remaining forces each believed strongly in their own paths. Twenty-one personnel of a force starting out well over one hundred. Twenty-one returning home to the lives they knew. It saddened Greg to see how few of Pritchett's force remained. A mere eleven of seventy-four from the beginning of the journey, with only seven returning home. His own unit had survived the perils of betrayal and combat mostly intact, now to be split apart forever by a force nobody could ever have predicted. Twenty-one brave souls returning to face a vicious betrayer, and most likely, death.

"Ya know, Lieutenant, some of yer men are very concerned about you."

"That's a good start, Jerry. You come up with that approach or did they?"

Neither looked at each other.

"Some of 'em seem ta think them magic users you been hangin' 'round got their mangy hooks in ya, makin' ya do things, like abandon yer country an' all sorts a crazy stuff like that."

"I suppose you set them straight."

"Oh, I tried. I told 'em yer juss bein' stupid and you'd come 'round when the time crunched." Winters waited for Greg to meet his dark gaze.

"I'm not going back, Jerry. My own free will. My decision." He looked at his old friend with sad determination.

Winters looked around to see more First Strike mercenaries than he'd expected, and the scout with the blue hair hovering near the squad that was supposed to take Greg by surprise. His hand trembled on his holster in anger.

"Got yer new pals here, eh? Gonna go with 'em and turn traitor after all."

Greg reached down and unsnapped his sidearm, never breaking eye contact with Winters. He knew the man too well.

"So now what? You gonna throw down? Aim that thing at us to make us think yer serious?"

"I've never pointed a gun at anyone in my life who I wasn't willing, at the time, to kill."

Winters worked his jaw, angered that the plan was never going to work now. Memories flooded back in his mind, adding weight to Greg's words.

"You aimed a gun at me, once."

"I know." Greg waited.

Winters' shoulders slumped slightly and he stepped back, nodding at the message he'd received.

"So that's the way it's gonna be."

Greg extended his hand. Winters stared at it.

"For old time sake, Jerry."

"For old times."

Jerry Winters clasped the hand of his life long friend for the last time, then turned and signaled his men to abort the planned kidnaping. Seconds later, Sergeant Winters was barking orders to the returning convoy, never once looking back.

The Coalition APC spearheaded the convoy out of Liberty and back into the wilderness. Silent waves of farewell were the last to be seen of the returning hover rovers carrying loyal troops back home.

Out of sight of each other, both parties felt suddenly alone.

Chapter 22

Slow, deep breathing kept a steady tempo. Natarsha listened to Greg sleeping and smiled to herself when she thought of the sleep depravation mantra, as he called it. The place was still too foreign for her to sleep any measurable amount of time so she sat on the orange and brown couch and tried to block out the sensory overload.

Tobacco smoke left its unmistakable odor imbedded in the walls of the R.V., and the scents of mildew, rotting wood, and other unknown things were starting to fade into the background. The couch and every object she'd touched in the R.V. was old and worn, each with imprints left by centuries of tenants. She was still acutely aware of the sounds of the surrounding, sparsely populated shanty-town. Dogs barked, and by the tones she could tell the warnings or greetings they imparted. There was a rat nesting in the unused air conditioning unit in the ceiling of the R.V., leaving its home periodically in search of food for its babies. Every so often a voice or conversation would come over from the tenants of the shanty-town, but she sensed no ill will focused on her. There was some curiosity, but none of the fear or loathing she expected. Most didn't care.

Her first day of real freedom had been extremely difficult to adjust to. Being surrounded by the activity of a full-fledged town was almost unbearable. So much going on, so many sounds, scents, and emotions all jumbled in one place. The inhabitants tuned out their surroundings and concentrated on one thing at a time, a habit she would need to adopt herself, especially being far more attuned to the environment around her. There were times during the day when she'd felt as though she couldn't take it anymore and the urge to flee to familiar wilderness surroundings became almost overpowering. Every so often, Greg would take her aside and ask her how she was doing. She'd lie. Staying near her guide of the strange new world, she'd found herself drawing on his strength and stability to pull her through, though he most likely never knew it.

Being present when the Coalition forces went their separate ways was both terrifying and enlightening. The threat of violence and the conflicting flood of emotions present had been difficult to sort out, but the rebirth of the ones who stayed behind had been breathtaking.

If they could leave behind everything they once knew and begin again, so could she.

Greg had rounded up all the personnel staying behind and took them for breakfast at a place called the Match Head. She'd almost bolted, and would have fled the sensory assault if Greg hadn't taken her aside and asked her if she wanted to leave. She'd wanted to, very badly, but set herself to go on to the next experience and entered the crowded room.

It took every effort of will to block out the surrounding world and concentrate on the few senses that mattered. Crammed into two large booths, Greg had been careful to leave her a spot on the end, a courtesy she appreciated more than he knew. New tastes and textures of food were exotic experiences. Things called scrambled eggs and pancakes served with various spices and sweet syrup. A version of milk was served with the meal, although she'd been uncertain if she liked it or not. Normally food was something to be wolfed down to quench an appetite, for she never knew when the next chance to eat would come. Humans enjoyed meals as both tasty nourishment and a social gathering, both alien concepts to her. Judging from the variety of scents in the room, eggs and pancakes were only a tiny part of the new realm of taste.

Sitting with her shoulder and thigh pressed against Greg's, she'd been reminded of another world to explore. It was both frightening and exciting, although she'd been relieved when he left the seat to chat with each person individually, as the sensory input started to push her into overload. It was too much all at once, and she needed more time to experience one thing at a time.

He'd given each of his former soldiers a credit card containing a substantial amount to begin their new lives. For some reason, two of them, a male and female who's names she didn't remember, refused to accept the donation for the fresh start. They were hiding something, she could sense that, but it wasn't malicious. They were happy, and secretly enjoying the frequent body contact the crowded booth forced on them. Greg had given their cards to others in the group. He'd advised everyone to come up with new names and identities, just in case the returning forces got the message back of the deserters. The only one there not happy or filled with a zeal for life was the other lieutenant. He brooded over a foul smelling beverage all by himself, and made comments from time to time that nobody seemed to take notice of. There was sorrow and rage burning the man up inside, and Natarsha found herself keeping track of him to make sure he intended no harm

The rest of the morning and early afternoon had been spent taking care of details she knew little about and accompanying Greg to talks with people she didn't know. None seemed to recognize her for what she was, although there was some suspicion felt around members of the mercenary company, First Strike. Later in the afternoon he'd called it a day and headed back to the R.V. She couldn't have been more grateful, her head full to overflowing with new experiences to process and new concepts to think over.

Her mind drifted back to the Coalition soldiers that had chosen to return to the lives they knew and homes far away. Some were filled with mindless aggression, but most were experiencing heartfelt longing for people they cared for back home. They knew the risks, and some even expected to die, but they were willing to endanger their lives for the love of something left behind and the embrace of lives they knew. There was a sadness at departing company with close friends, but a conviction in their loyalty and a flame of hope to carry them back to the ones they cared for so deeply.

Past impressions mingled with flashes of carnage and battle. This was different from the frequent sensory flashbacks that forced past memories to the present, a constant struggle since she'd freed herself of slavery to Varles. A touch, scent, or other sensory stimuli would trigger flashbacks to experiences she'd blocked out for her short life in order to remain sane. It had only been eight months since her birthing, but there had been a lifetime of atrocities committed her masters orders.

But the flashes of carnage she felt when thinking of the departed soldiers were different. It was as though the men and women she was remembering were amid a fight for their lives, with loud explosions, explosive shock waves, smells of burnt flesh, and searing energy beams all around. Was it a premonition or more depth to her earlier memories of them? She pushed the sensations and thoughts away and concentrated on more pleasant things.

Approaching sounds of speech drew her attention outside. Several individuals had stopped along the crooked muddy road and were working their way to the R.V. Natarsha sensed no immediate threat or ill will, but pulled Greg's MP-10 from its holster and tried to revive him from his slumber.

"Wake up." She tapped his arm. "Wake up." She tapped harder.

"Huh, uh, uh, what?" He sat up and banged his head on the fiberglass roof above the loft. "Ow. We really need a bigger place." He laid back down.

"People are coming."

"What time is it?" He looked at his wrist comp. "It's only been an hour. The sun is still out."

"Here."

Greg felt the cold handle of his sidearm pushed into his hand, the feel of it bringing his mind to fuzzy alertness.

A knock sounded on the warped fiberglass door and he could hear several voices talking outside.

"Go away. I'm sleeping."

"It's me, Anja."

"What the ...?" Greg groaned, swinging his feet off the loft and lowering himself to the uneven floor. He pulled the bent metal latch back and swung the door open. Anja and Sir Renfield led a compilation of people clad in body armor and geared up for battle. Behind them, a large D-Bee whose name Greg couldn't recall watched him with expectant eyes.

"Sorry to wake you, Lie-, Mr. Merrick, but we need your help." Sir Renfield began.

"Uh, okay." Greg's sleep-fogged brain wasn't awake yet.

"Can we come in and talk to you?" Anja asked, stepping up to the doorway.

"Sure, I guess, come on in." Greg waved them in, noticing too late that he was bidding them to enter with a handgun. He put it back in its holster and clipped the belt around his waist, all the while being forced farther and farther back in the tiny R.V. by the influx of visitors. He found himself pushed up against Natarsha where the rotted wood door to the restroom met the back of the dining area bench. The old R.V. creaked and shuddered. Sir Renfield pushed his way to the front, a loud pop and cracking sound making him a foot shorter than everyone else. Stepping gingerly out of the hole in the rotted floor paneling, he tried to distribute his weight over the reinforcement beams below.

"Sorry. I'll have someone fix that for you."

"Don't worry about it." Greg stared at the hole, his groggy brain trying to replace sleep with reality. "I was planning on moving anyway."

"Good to see you again, Natarsha." Anja smiled and got a barely perceptible return.

"I'm assuming this is important?" Greg looked around at the crowd and at the giant face trying to peak in one of the windows.

Targo accidentally brushed the R.V., nearly tipping it over and breaking the window.

"Sorry."

"There's a good reason you woke me, broke my window, and put a hole in my floor?"

"Sorry," Sir Renfield and Targo apologized in unison.

"There is, Greg." Anja wormed past the Cyber-Knight. "And we thought you might want to help."

"Several scouts have spotted Zenjori Suka's mercenaries moving to a ruins west of town," Sir Renfield reported.

"I wish I could tell you more, but you may want to hold off attacking the Army of the New Order for a few more days." Greg advised. "I believe First Strike may have plans for Zenjori Suka."

"We would, Greg, but your friends, the ones who left this morning, are in great danger." Anja's eyes emphasized her words.

"They knew the dangers when they left."

"But I've seen a vision of the future, like I did before the battle at Youngstown. It's Zenjori Suka and his army that will kill your friends unless we stop him."

"How do you know?"

"Sometimes I see things before they happen, how things will happen if nothing is changed. I've seen visions of cyborgs killing your friends, and I know Zenjori Suka is there. I could feel it."

"Okay." Greg sounded doubtful.

"I too believe they are in danger." Natarsha spoke up. Only two present knew who she really was.

"How?"

"I do not have the words to describe it, but I feel your men will die."

"Sir Renfield, have the scouts confirmed that Zenjori's army has moved within striking distance of the return route?" Greg searched for more concrete proof.

"That's what I've been told. I have it on the authority of some trustworthy sources."

"We're going, with or without you." Cyndiara spoke up from her place standing on the couch.

"Assuming you're correct, and Zenjori is going to ambush the convoy, how can we stop it? He still has borgs and robots, and we've no armor to throw against him."

"Van's working with Darren on fixing his power armor," Anja voiced.

"And we already spoke with your former tech officers. They're trying to get your SAMAS units ready to go," Sir Renfield added. "And I have my Samson power suit, and Targo is as good or better than any robot."

"How far out?" Greg's mind started working again, formulating battle strategies and tactics.

"How far could they have gone?"

"Farther than you might think, even with the APC slowing them down."

"You could warn them." Sir Renfield suggested.

"Now you're onto something." Greg punched a code on his wrist comp — the only thing left of his Coalition paraphernalia — and hoped old habits died hard for others too. "Brian. Brian, do you copy?"

"This is Brian. They found you, sir?" Brian's voice sounded tinny and distant over the small communicator.

"Yes. I need you to find Lisa and have her power up the Skull Walker's communications system."

"Already did, sir."

"You know about the possible risk to Sergeant Winters and the convoy?"

"Yes sir."

"Have Lisa send —"

"We already did, sir."

"Good thinking. What did he say?"

"We didn't get anything back. Lisa said the APC's comm system was replaced with an inferior one. It probably doesn't have the range to transmit back to us."

"Repeat the warning several times, I think Private Yoshi and Gerald are at the controls."

"Lisa's still trying."

"I sincerely hope you didn't tell Winters where the warning came from."

"C'mon, sir, I'm not stupid." Brian sounded offended. "We just left a few things out and stretched the truth a little. If Sergeant Winters got the message, he'll be ready."

"How are the SAM's doing?"

"Not good. Giz and I are trying to get one finished. The other two are in pretty bad shape. The one we haven't taken apart is in no shape to go out."

"Get them ready anyway. Where's Lieutenant Sorenson?"

"Looking for Sharp and the others. We couldn't find them."

"I'll be over there in a few minutes. Have a SAM warmed up and ready to go."

"Yes sir."

"Brian, don't call me sir." Greg clicked the communicator off.

"We can't keep up with your SAMAS," Sir Renfield cautioned.

"I know. Darren's SAM doesn't have wings, so he can go with your group. We need a squad to go ahead and give Winters armor support, and you might not get there in time. Sorenson and I will go ahead and find the return convoy, make sure they got the warning, then radio you their coordinates."

"What about Zenjori Suka?" Cyndiara asked. "I thought we were going after him."

"If Anja is right, we find our convoy, we'll find Zenjori Suka, correct?"

"Yes, I believe so." Anja looked at Cyndiara to give confirmation.

"But what if he's not there? He could get away again."

"We'll get the man sooner or later." Sir Renfield vowed.

"You've all failed before. How is this different?" Cyndiara's features hardened, hatred of Zenjori seeping into every word she spoke.

"I will find this man," Natarsha volunteered, feeling the intensity of the Burster's dedication. That was something she understood. "If all you want is to kill this man, I can do that."

"That's not enough." Cyndiara clenched her teeth together.

"How will you find him?" Greg asked.

"Give me his general location. I will hunt him."

"If you do find him, please tell us before you do anything," Sir Renfield admonished, not sure what to think of the blue haired woman. He didn't even know her name.

"I'll go with you." Mr. Kent volunteered. The scarred Wilderness Scout tried to get Natarsha to make eye contact, but without success. "I have an idea where Zenjori's base camp is. You've done this type of thing before?"

"Yes."

"You two keep in touch with us." Greg unbuckled his belt and moved aside so he could hand it to Natarsha.

"I have some extra radio sets. I'll see she gets one." Mr. Kent paused, then moved out through the small door.

Natarsha hesitated, then worked her way as quickly as possible through the maze of bodies making as little body contact as possible.

"That all you're taking?" Sir Renfield watched the woman grab a pair of soft soled boots in one hand and carry Greg's MP-10 caseless in the other.

"Yes." She hopped out the door.

"Who was —"

"Sir Renfield, you'll coordinate the ground attack force, okay?" Greg suggested, taking command of the operation without meaning to.

"That's acceptable. If you're flying in by SAMAS, it could be hours, many hours before we catch up and can offer support."

"Hopefully I'll get to Winters before Zenjori does, and we'll work with our scouts to keep track of Zenjori and his army. They won't get away." Greg looked into Cyndiara's green eyes. "When you all arrive we'll combine forces and finish this for good."

"One thing." Cyndiara's eyes flashed.

"What's that?"

"Zenjori's mine."

"Something's wrong," Drake mumbled, searching the road and distant hillside with telescopic vision for some sign of the Coalition convoy that should have reached the river crossing hours before.

"Patience, Drake," Zenjori soothed, perched in a man-made blind by the side of the rugged dirt road.

His army lay in ambush on both banks of the river, waiting for the convoy to arrive and begin crossing. They would strike when the Coalition forces were in the open and most vulnerable. Having lost their contact in First Strike, his army had to rely on their own scouts for intelligence. The last report from their spotters along the road indicated the Coalition convoy was a mere four miles away and only a few minutes from the river, despite the road conditions. They'd lost contact with their scout several hours previously.

"They've spotted us somehow and turned back." Drake stood.

"We'd have heard from Barm if they had. They may have gotten that ridiculous APC stuck again."

"Neriff should have reported in. Something is wrong. It's almost dark."

"Perhaps they made camp for the night. But you're right. Something peculiar is going on. Kruno!" Zenjori called on the radio, his Terrain Hopper power suit hopping down for a better view of the river and the Multi-bot's hiding place. Most of Carnivore squad was on the front-line, with Sledgehammer Squad scattered along the west bank to ensure nobody made it through.

"Yah! What's up, boss!?"

"Send a small squad up the road to find out what the Coalition is doing."

"They're probably takin' a leak. I'm sendin' Tabben, Pedro, and Meffis ta go check 'em."

"Fine. Send whoever you want." Zenjori snapped.

It was bad enough leaving base camp defended by a few of Kruno's new recruits, but having to put up with them on the battle line was testing Zenjori's patience. Two rat-like D-Bees with make-shift armor and battered weapons started lurking up the road, darting from tree to tree along the edge. A third, a human in patched plastic armor, sauntered along behind them as if he was simply on a leisure stroll. No question which of the three looked least suspicious.

"I assume you gave them radios?" Zenjori asked, having learned not to assume anything.

"I think Pedro has one."

"Check, please."

"You got it, boss." There was a pause. "Yep, Pedro's got ears on."

"How thoughtful of you to check before you sent them on recon."

"Whatcha want us ta do now?"

"Stay put."

"Those fools are going to blow our ambush," Drake observed.

"As you said, something is wrong. Our ambush may be lost. Send two, four man teams down the river and another two up it, just to make sure the Coalition isn't trying to sneak past us."

"We'd have heard their hover rovers crossing the river."

"But if they do get over the river, there's nothing stopping them from leaving the APC behind and going full speed with their hover craft."

"And we'd never catch them. I'll send the squads, Suka San." Drake started relaying orders to his borg units and remaining Headhunters.

Zenjori knelt back behind concealment and waited. He could hear the borgs crashing along the banks up and down stream, but it was Kruno's Multi-bot that kept drawing his attention.

Concealed in a clump of trees, it passed the time by crouching and then standing, crouching then standing again, each time knocking the poor hatch gunner in the head with oak branches.

"Kruno, please stop that. You'll give away your position."

The wait continued. Zenjori examined the east bank from across the river, looking to make sure his forces were out of sight from the road.

When Zenjori had reached the point where he didn't care which robot crew should be executed first, the call came in from the scouting party.

"Hey, boss, Pedro says the Dead Boys aren't on the road."

"That's fantastic, Kruno. Does Pedro say where they are at?"

"Ratlings is sneakin' up on the APC. It's off the road stuck in a ditch. Nobody 'round it. Wait. Pedro says Meffis just bought it. So did Tabben. Coalition crawler's got a crew. No rovers 'round it."

"That's strange. Tell Pedro to just watch and not do something stupid like the Ratlings."

"He's sittin' on a stump gnawin' a turnip."

"And that, means what to me?"

"He ain't drawin' fire, just like—"

"Shut up, Kruno. Stop acting like a fool and get Carnivore together for attack."

"No ambush?"

"What does it sound like? Assemble and move down the road and take out the APC."

"It's a hook squirmer."

"What?" Zenjori asked after a long pause and a failed attempt to make sense of Kruno's statement.

"They's just usin' it as bait."

"Then take out the APC cautiously. Just get rid of it and find out where the rest of the convoy went."

"Sledgehammer's gonna back us this time?"

"Do what I'm telling you!" Zenjori shouted, feeling the calm control he usually possessed slip away. "Find them and kill them!"

More curses followed the arc of the tool as it sailed across the garage. Greg and Mike exchanged looks, but let Brian do his job his own way.

"SAM 419 is hosed. I can't get that jet to work!" Brian kicked the replacement maneuver jet and it fell off the SAMAS to the concrete floor. "That's a stripped hover jet off a Sky King. It wasn't meant for a SAM."

"So my SAMAS won't have as much maneuverability," Mike conceded. "I got it back here like that, I can fly it like that."

"What about SAM 117B?" Greg knew the answer. The power suit lay in various stages of reassembly.

"Twenty-four hours, if I could work on it that long." Brian's bloodshot brown eyes pleaded for rest.

"How far did you get with armor repairs?" Mike inquired.

"Giz and I only figured on getting one SAM operational. SAM 312 is close to spec. Best I can do with 419 is spend an hour or two spot bonding armor patches and tell you not to get hit. At all."

"If that what it takes, do it." Mike looked over his SAMAS, realizing Brian's estimate of its combat effectiveness was optimistic.

"Take mine" Greg offered. "I'll fly 419."

"That almost sounded like you wanted me to take your SAM and you'd fly my hunk of garbage."

"Don't push it. Go on, take 312, before I change my mind."

"I can fly 419, I just won't be much good to you."

"Mike, let's cut the macho crap. We both know you're the better pilot. You were flying these things when I was still hoofing it with the grunts. Take SAM 312, I'll back you as best I can with 419."

Mike looked at his former military rival and wondered if it was some kind of trick. No, Greg was sincere. He could see it. True, he was the better pilot of the two, but he envied Greg's ability to command far more. Mike would have given up all his skills and military training just to do what Merrick could with a look.

"Okay. I'm on point then," Mike agreed. Greg smiled.

"No argument on that. Do what you can, Brian. Quickly." Greg patted the tech on the shoulder. "We'll be on our way as soon as you're done."

Private Yoshi swung the sensor turret a full 360 degrees, searching for another target. Several minutes had passed since she'd opened up on the two rat-like creatures trying to sneak up on the APC.

"Ben, you done with the booby traps yet?" she asked, feeling more and more like a trapped animal the longer they stayed in the immobile APC.

"Just a sec. I've still got to wire the other top hatches." Ben ran a cord to one of them and started rigging it into a charge set to blow on delay.

"Hurry up. You're leaving us a way out, right?" She left the pilot's seat and started climbing back into the rear compartment.

The APC shuddered, and Yoshi turned to get back on the guns. The pilot's compartment exploded inward, shrapnel reaching the rear compartment. Yoshi slumped through the inner compartment hatch, blood gushing everywhere.

"No!" Ben dropped the cord and rushed to her.

The APC rocked again, smoke and sparks coming from a hole in the side. Ben didn't have time to see how bad Private Yoshi was hurt, desperation cutting through fear and making him take action. He hit the switch and opened a side hatch, then dragged her to the door and dropped the three feet to the bottom of the ditch. More incoming fire shifted the APC's position. He didn't know where it was coming from, only that he had to get away and take Yoshi to safety. Bending down he pulled her out the hatch onto his shoulders and stumbled up the short embankment into the tree line, blood running down his black armor to the ground.

Explosive shock waves jerked the earth and forced Ben to his knees, but he kept his balance and pitched back into a clumsy run. The APC blew apart, shrapnel and components raining down in the trees around him. Laser fire passed him from somewhere behind, Ben not bothering to check where. He was almost there. He could make it.

Something hit his legs and the ground jumped up all around him. Dust cleared and he picked himself up from the blast crater. Spying Yoshi laying a few feet away, he crawled to her to resume the dash to safety. Muddy stumps of reddish material formed the ends of her legs. Dirt and dust settled on open, glazed eyes.

"Yoshi! Yoshi!" He shouted, knowing it was too late.

Pain registering across his back, Ben got up on wobbly legs and dashed frantically the last thirty feet to the trench.

Crossing the field and open trails behind him dozens of rebel troops opened fire.

Ben never made it to the trench.

Rows of weapons passed Drake's final inspection, but the last of his borgs had yet to return from checking the river. The Coalition convoy had been located.

"Hey boss! APC's crispified an' we got at least two Dead Boys." Kruno reported over the radio.

Zenjori paced the battle lines two miles away, waiting for Sledgehammer Squad to reach full strength before joining them himself in battle.

"Good, Kruno. Where are the rest?"

"Dug in on a hill 'bout a mile away. Got 'bout twenty of my boys pinned down in a trench at the base of the hill."

"Surround the Coalition position immediately and give me an estimate on numbers and firepower."

"Ya got it."

"Why didn't you have Kruno attack?" Drake asked.

"Contain, then eliminate. If the Coalition is dug in, a frontal charge is premature."

"Depends on who you send in first."

"Exactly." Zenjori rubbed the exoskeleton's hands together gleefully. "Off to a clumsy start, but all too easy."

"Watch yer fire," Winters ordered. "Just keep 'em pinned."

Dug into an extensive trench network on a defendable hill, Coalition troops laid down sporadic fire at the group of Headhunters and rebel recruits taking refuge from the elevated fire. A convenient trench at the base of the hill gave the rebels an excellent place to hide while waiting for cover fire to arrive.

"Now, Sarge?" Cody asked, fondling a remote detonator.

"Do it."

"Here's the Lieutenant Adams Special, Mark Two."

Cody thumbed the safety and pressed the fire trigger. Fusion blocks spaced evenly the length of the trench blew upwards in rapid sequence. It wouldn't have mattered if the rebels had been better armored, the effect would still have been the same. Unrecognizable body parts and gear fragments rained down amid the hovering dust cloud above the kill zone.

"Whoooh! Yeah, baby, come get some!" Cowboy shouted from a trench lower down the hill.

Cheers from the unit echoed on every side of the entrenched position. Sergeant Winters watched the settling dust cloud and smiled, forgetting for the moment what he thought of the deserters. The garbled warnings had been right.

"Wire the next one, Cody."

"You got it, Sarge!"

Zenjori paced faster, agitated but still in control. Losing a third of Carnivore before the assault even began wasn't part of the plan. Neither was the Coalition having a defendable position, with row after row of trenches to fall back on up the hill, and the ground they gave up too dangerous for Zenjori to risk taking.

He hated the Coalition. Before, it was never really hatred, more convenience, after all, one had to have an enemy to heap one's woes upon and use as the great evil for gathering an army. Now it was different Zenjori gave way to the emotion of blistering hatred. The battle was to go on until every Coalition soldier was dead.

"Kruno! Status!?"

"They got that hill. Even gots two rovers dug in up there with rail guns to boot. Must be fifty Dead Boys ringin' it. Lost seven more tryin' ta git in position. No way we can surround 'em." Kruno's report blared over Zenjori's helmet radio.

"They've dug their rovers in?"

"Yep. Right up past the jets."

"They aren't going anywhere. Pull Carnivore back to the north side and make a concentrated assault there."

"I'm punchin' them rail guns out with missiles first."

"Do not waste our medium range missiles on a pair of rovers with rail guns!"

"Whatever, yer the boss."

"Breach the northern defenses and Sledgehammer will use the hole to take the hill."

"Just explain it real good ta Drake first." Kruno broadcast over open channels.

Drake started for Carnivore's position, but Zenjori hopped his exoskeleton over him and came down in the borg's path.

"That's the last time. I'm not taking it anymore." Drake tried to step around his commander.

"Wait. Let him attack the hill. Then wait some more."

"What if he wins?"

"Then you can settle the offense. Either way, it's time to be rid of Carnivore Squad for good."

"How many mediums we got left?" Kruno asked his robot's gunner.

"Two. H.E.'s."

"What about the Forager?"

"Four. Two scorchers, a frag, and one smart A.P."

"Tell Britt to put the whomper on that rail gun to the east, and we'll use one of our H.E.'s on the west one."

"But, Zenjori said not to use our mediums," the Headhunter objected.

"We still got some mini-missiles," the pilot offered.

"No good. They've got the high ground. Any place we move to shoot they can drop steel on us. Take them rail guns out first."

"Goin' to manual targeting."

The gunner switched over so he could fire the missiles without a solid lock. The two robots stood on a rise partially concealed by trees a little over a mile away, the remainder of Carnivore Squad gathering at their feet. Missile trails left just seconds apart and crossed the gap on either side of the enemy position. In the thickening twilight two explosions left the hillside, one a bright flash and the other a slower detonation with trailers that reached down the hillside for several seconds. Kruno waited for the sonic concussions to pass before giving the order to advance.

Robbed of long range suppressive fire and another four men down, Sergeant Winters waited to see if the missile barrage would continue.

"Man, those were our rides." Cowboy looked at the mangled hovercraft and absent rail guns.

"Mark an' Kenny bought it on the east," Cody reported.

"Two of Pritchett's on the west. Althea and that tech, Martin," Robert added from his spot closest the west hillside.

"What are they waiting for?" Cowboy checked his scope, wishing it were either day or night, not that twilight that made his optics useless.

"Here they come!" A soldier in one of the lower trenches shouted as rebel troops broke into firing lanes radiating out from the hill.

"Fire at will!" Winters roared. "Lance, Willy! Git yer butts back on the north side!"

"Incoming!" Trenton shouted, sprinting for the lowest trench, narrowly being missed by a mini-missile from somewhere out in the twilight.

Weapons fire rained down from the hill and sporadic shots were returned from the rebel infantry assault. Rail gun and ion beams ripped into the hill from beyond visible line of sight. Blast craters cut away at trenches and kinetic steel drove through to slay the soldier next to Trenton.

"Where's that coming from!?" Nim shouted, dispatching a Headhunter at fifty yards with a crisp plasma blast.

Laser fire converged on his spot, but Nim ducked and crawled past it. The laser rifles from the next trench up cut down the rebel fire team before it could fire again. Ion beams cut the air in a gradual ascent up the hill, tearing through another trench then following with rail guns to rip through where Cowboy had last fired from.

"Trenton! Get that thing off us!" Cowboy shouted, popping up to fire at rebel squads trying to reach the base of the hill. The rebel squad took cover in the nearest trench.

"I can't find it!" Trenton shouted.

"Cody! Hit number three!" Nim ordered, not sure how many rebel troops had made it into the deadly cover.

Detonations threw up a dust and bone wall at the base of the hill, pausing the fire fight momentarily while both sides scrambled to reposition during the lapse in visual contact. Two ion beams continued staggered fire into the hill unabated.

"Shephard! Cover me!" Trenton ordered.

"On the way!" Shephard used the dust shield to sprint from trench to trench around the hill and join the fight on the north side.

As the dust began to clear, the Coalition threw hand grenades into the reorganized rebel squads forming for the next charge. What little formation was left in the rebel assault dissipated under withering fire, Headhunters and D-Bee warriors finding what cover they could to wait out Sledgehammer's charge. One by one they were found by invisible targeting beams and eliminated. Several tried to flee the failed assault only to make easier targets for the veteran troops on the hill.

"Watch yer ammo!" Winters ordered, knowing the Army of the New Order wasn't done yet. "Don't fire unless ya got a target!"

The ion cannon barrage continued, turning the north slope into a post marked landscape of smoking craters and secondary detonations from demolition placements.

"Where is that comin' from!?" Winters watched another troop sprint for cover in a smoking trench and get ripped apart by kinetic steel.

"They just got Silverston!" Cody cried.

"Trenton! You got the rail gun! Get rid of it!" Winters yelled.

Ion beams worked up the slope to the next trench.

"Shephard! Cover me!" Trenton shouted, running down to join Nim in a blast crater.

"Gotcha!" Shephard opened up full auto with his laser assault rifle set to the lowest power setting, trying to distract and suppress the heavy firepower coming from someplace out of sight.

Ion beams and rail gun fire paused. Shephard's head and part of his upper body disappeared in hues of orange and white, crackling air to ozone and body to atoms.

"We're gettin' pounded!" Cody ducked into a trench and finished wiring the charges laid down its length.

"I can't find 'em!" Trenton searched for a target.

The staggered ion barrage started walking along the trench above them. Nim turned his head to face Trenton as the air popped above them. Trenton's mechanical features couldn't show the sinking feeling they all felt. Out of visual range they were being pounded to death by one or more opponents they couldn't silence. It was only a matter of time. Nim nodded. Trenton knew without words.

Nim leapt up and started running the length of the hill, drawing the ion beams and rail gun away from the soldiers in the upper trenches. Trenton rolled out of the crater and sprinted for the smoking tree line, enemy eyes watching someplace else.

Dodging back, Nim's eyes fell on the empty blast crater he'd just left. He had to give Trenton more time. Bionic legs took him in an erratic pattern under constant fire. Armor smoking and legs leaking artificial blood, Nim took cover at the east end of the hillside. Precious seconds passed as determined cannon fire cut through earth to reach him. One more pass.

Legs buckled under the strain but Nim scrambled on, will power not allowing his mechanical body to fail him. Back on his feet, he staggered across the battlefield discharging his plasma cannon into the twilight until the barrel glowed and the cell was dead. Converging fire ended his heroic run.

Half a dozen rebel droops had fallen between the Coalition stronghold and the two robots. Trenton shifted course slightly to crush a hairless D-Bee's skull with a passing stroke of his spiked elbow. The two robots were now in sight.

Single-minded purpose drove the man and machine the last stretch, coming to the very feet of his targets before they realized he was there. The X-500's belly gun rotated down and aimed. Trenton opened up on the sensor cluster, putting four rail gun bursts into it as he slowed to a stop before the Multi-bot. Barely reaching the twenty-six foot tall robot's knees, Trenton dodged to the right of the slower unit and swung around behind it where its ion cannon couldn't reach. A startled hatch gunner tried to bring the mounted rail gun down on him but Trenton tore the mecenary's head off with a well-aimed burst.

The Multi-bot's entire body tried to turn on him, Trenton always staying to its back as he'd done in thousands of video games. Smaller and far quicker up close, the borg cut through the armor and mechanical workings of the robot's torso, each time the rail gun feeding metal to places where the robot had no defense. Blinded and unable to see the event, the X-500 could do nothing but listen to the shouts of dismay coming over the radio. Gears ground and bearing supports snapped, the weight of the upper body urging the Multi-bot down. It wobbled, then tipped back, missile launchers carrying it over backwards.

Something burst out the sides and the upper half lifted off the robot chassis before the dead body crashed to the ground. Hover jets fired the Multi-bot hovercraft off the humanoid machine. Trenton raised his left arm and armor plates slid back as he prepared to defeat the multi-stage monster. Three mini-missiles converged on the escaping craft and brought it crashing down into the forest with a sickening thud.

Two Headhunters fleeing the hillside battle reached the scene in time to be ripped to shreds by Trenton's rail gun.

The X-500 was now alone.

Trenton's targeting dot fell on the exposed and occupied missile tubes.

Fragments of armor and rail gun rounds flew in a random pattern at Trenton's feet. The next grenade damaged his forearm mini-missile launcher. He whirled to see a figure clad in patched armor and coonskin adorned helmet approach from the wreckage of the Multi-bot hover craft. Trenton swung the rail gun and fired, but the feed belt hung severed. Another grenade and more laser fire came at him. Trenton was mad.

Cycling another round in the oversized handgun, Kruno aimed higher and hit the heavy borg in the head, blowing off a metal eyebrow and shattering the right eye. The other eye lit more brightly.

"You sunnuva!" Kruno emptied the last round and tossed the empty weapon aside. He slid a high frequency blade from a back sheath. "Now I'm gonna hafta open up a whole can o' woop-ass on you, boy!"

"I got your woop right here," Trenton answered back, extending three high frequency claws from his right forearm.

They faced off, each waiting for the other to move. A stillness in the air signed the end of Carnivore squad. Kruno looked around and listened to the silence. He put his blade back in its sheath and placed his hands on his hips. Trenton relaxed his posture, saluting with the blades.

"Now what"

"We walk. I'm done." Kruno held up empty palms.

"Just like that?"

"Yep. You win. Git back on the hill before Zenjori Suka and Drake git here. Back me up."

"Go." Trenton waved.

"Here." Kruno took off his prized coonskin cap and tossed it to Trenton. "Souvenir."

Particle beams and plasma charges demolecularized Kruno's body what was left of his flesh and blood vanished in the pile of melted bionic parts.

Blades humming Trenton's only defense, the Coalition cyborg turned to find an old nemesis with four arms leading an array of Headhunters and cyborg troops. The rebel borgs fanned out around him, and on command, the crescent cut Trenton to the ground.

Uneasy calm descended on the Coalition stronghold, but hearts still pounded for the next attack. The heavy guns were silenced. Trenton hadn't returned.

The pause was a short one. Coming through the clinging smoke and haze, Sledgehammer Squad hit the hillside with everything it had.

Rail guns dropped two Coalition soldiers before anyone returned fire. The first trench fell as nothing more than a skirmish to the squads of borgs and mercenaries pouring up the hill. Bursts of Coalition weapons fire felled a borg as it reached the next set of trenches, but four more stepped over its burning body to fill the gap.

"Fall back!" Winters barked, dropping an empty e-cell in a trench and slotting his last full one in its place. "Fall back to the top!" He grabbed Robert by the shoulder plate and yanked him out of a trench, forcing the soldier to flee for the last stand stronghold at the top of the hill. Mini-missiles and heavy weapons fire came in waves, sweeping up the hill just in front of the charging bionic army. Cowboy left blazing holes in another then grabbed his teammate and scurried for the top. Only Cowboy made it.

Winters ducked a wave of fire and then jumped up to dodge the next. Cody was pinned down in a lower trench and not even the combined firepower of the dwindling Coalition force could free him. Robert topped the hill and plopped down in the trench to lay down cover fire for his friend. Plasma and steel threw Robert's lifeless body back in to its final resting place.

"Sarge!" Cody waved, cover rapidly dissipating and borgs no more than steps away. "Sarge!" He waved the detonator.

"Damn!" Winters cursed, another of his men shredded in an attempt to retrieve the detonator.

Cody stood and hurled the detonator. His body was torn apart before the device hit the ground.

Twenty feet away in some brush, the detonator waited for Winters to make the dash to retrieve it. The last of Pritchett's unit rolled into the trench beside him, most of the soldier's left leg gone and spurting blood everywhere.

"Go! Sergeant, go!"

Winters ran for the clump of shrubs, hearing a war cry from the trench he just left silenced by massive overkill. Device in hand, he sprinted the last few yards to the hilltop, weapon fire spitting at his heels.

Winters looked around the small trench in disbelief. He and Cowboy were the only ones at the top.

"Mark's still down there!" Cowboy shouted.

"Cover him!" Winters barked, crawling to an armored case set deep in the back side of the position. "Buy me time!" He yelled, frantically finishing the last codes of the detonator relay box.

"Mark's gone, Sarge! Borgs just got him!" Cowboy ducked low, the upward angle of the hill the only thing keeping the advancing borgs from blasting through the trench and killing them.

"Ten seconds!" Winters set the box to full detonation and rapidly attached the score of wires leading into the destructive nexus. "Buy me ten seconds!"

Cowboy held his gun over his head and emptied the canister.

"I'm out!"

"Here!" Winters shoved his plasma cannon over. "Eight seconds!"

Cowboy grabbed Robert's lifeless body and hurled it over the edge, using the distraction to empty Winters weapon at the enemy. Plasma and metal slugs tore apart the gun and took most of Cowboy's right hand. With his left hand, he slapped the ring of fusion blocks on his belt, each set to a five second delay.

Cowboy dove over the edge and rolled through the incoming fire right into the first rank of advancing borgs. He stood, pausing the advance long enough for them to turn his way.

"Yippi-ca-yay"

The explosion caused the ground to jump up beneath Winters' chest, knocking the detonator from his grasp. It fell in the trench on the far side of the earthen fort. He dove, slamming into the trench. Winters came up, detonator in hand, turning to greet the enemy with the last laugh.

Winters body jerked violently to the right, his arm and active detonator returning to earth. He stared at the shredded stump and drew the TX-5 pistol from his belt with his left. He jerked back around and pointed the barrel at the line of borgs topping the hill.

"Oh, now you D-Bee luvin' have gone and really pissed me off!"

Chapter 23

Two Coalition SAMAS circled slowly and descended on the smoking remains of a battle not long past. The mangled body on the hillside lay still, blast craters all around hot from the fighting. Not a living thing stirred when one of the flying exoskeletons landed at the last stand atop the hill and the pilot got out to view the dead with naked eyes.

Mike circled several more times and checked the surrounding area before joining Greg at the hilltop. The former Coalition officer sat on the ground toying with a device. Mike left his SAMAS running, replacement spotlight illuminating the carnage. As Mike got closer, he noticed with some apprehension what Greg had in his hand.

On and Off. On and Off. Greg flipped the safety hood on the transmitter, each time brushing the trigger with his thumb. The detonator nexus lay exposed a few feet away, wires leading into a series of small covered trenches radiating all the way down the hill. Mike looked briefly at the remains of the the body at the top, not recognizable except for its insignia. Just over the rim, what was left of Cody lay a few feet from the edge of a massive blast crater. What had probably been Sergeant Winters lay in a trench, still clutching a TX-5 with one round missing. The bodies in the trenches on the north side of the hill looked untouched, as the attacking army had simply retreated without so much as removing a weapon or prize of victory.

"There's nobody left, is there?" Greg asked, eyes not leaving the remote transmitter.

"Doesn't look like it. APC's burned out in a dry creek bed, and there are remains of a Multi-bot and two borgs half a mile from here, but nothing else." Mike looked around. "These were probably the last to go."

"There are mines all over, in the trenches, under bushes, in the trenches. Fusion blocks, grenades, everything. Jerry planned to take them with him." Greg still didn't look up, Mike watching the transmitter with trepidation.

"We didn't get here in time."

"Eight years. Eight years Jerry and I served together. We grew up in the burbs together, fought in the same gangs, joined the military at the same time," Greg went on, no emotion showing on his face. "I should have been here."

"You'd be laying there in a trench just like the rest of them."

"I know." Greg stopped flipping the safety. He felt numb, as though it wasn't all real. Sergeant Winters' marred helmet lay in the trench at his feet, but he hadn't wanted to lift the faceplate, knowing reality would force the tragedy to sink in. "I've been thinking about giving them a proper burial." Greg flipped the safety off.

Mike watched in heart-stopping horror as Greg pressed the trigger.

Nothing happened. Greg tossed the detonator transmitter to Mike.

"It's broken."

Mike breathed again. "Don't do that again, please. Do I want to know how you knew it was broken?"

"No."

"You could have told me first."

Greg stood and looked around in the light from the SAMAS spotlight, a grim expression on his face.

"I just wanted to see if you still cared."

"What's that supposed to mean?" Mike tossed the transmitter into the dirt.

Greg's gray eyes bored into Mike with an intensity that made him shudder. Mike knew for certain what the former officer meant to do.

"We're going to make them pay."

Metallic cheers and war cries filled the rebel camp. Partially protected by the ruins of a railroad station, the Army of the New Order celebrated its latest victory. Though the cost had been high, word of the triumph would spread to towns and villages for hundreds of miles, and the Army of the New Order would soon be an army again.

"Well done, Drake. You've proved yourself once again," Zenjori congratulated his second in command.

"Just promise me Kruno's replacement won't be some backyard-bred hillbilly."

"Have no worries," Zenjori beamed. "Sledgehammer will always be the core of our army, with you to command the mechanized, and my friend Colnae will assemble a whole squad dedicated to magic and the means to confuse and mislead our enemies. Whoever Kruno's replacement is doesn't really matter."

"Good job, Drake." Colnae extended his hand, but the borg didn't acknowledge it; his disdain for magic was no secret.

"Shame we couldn't retrieve that arsenal on the hill."

"You saw it." Drake defended his position. "The entire hill, on every side and in every trench, behind trees, and every place you could think of. Mines, explosives, and booby traps. We didn't know what was wired to what. One mistake and it could have chain-fired for all we knew."

"I'm not upset. It would be nice to examine the battlefield and retrieve anything of use," Zenjori consoled.

"In the morning. When it's light out. Not at night."

"Of course."

"The X-500 will have to wait until daylight too. We pulled it back to the river but the Coalition cyborg destroyed the optics. Too dangerous to try moving it at night."

"Relax, Drake, a fine victory." Zenjori was feeling himself again.

"I left a squad to watch it and guard the crew. I will need a new crew in the morning."

"Is that necessary?"

"They were Kruno's men. Loyal."

"I see. Replacing them is best. I agree."

"Then we're staying here the night?" Colnae asked.

"Absolutely."

"Good. I think I'll expend what's left in my 'human mine' now that I won't be needing her. She was far too easy, I'll need a much stronger subject next time."

"Maybe I'll join you."

"I'll take my time then." Colnae gave a sinister grin and then headed for the ruins of a warehouse where the screams echoed nicely.

"We should not let down our guard." Drake was still all business.

"Then I leave the camp in your capable hands. I have need of some diversion."

Passive night vision goggles gave Mr. Kent a view of the rebel sentry in the ruins, allowing him to approach the camp unnoticed. It was Natarsha that first alerted him to the sentry's location, though how she knew he couldn't tell. The rebel camp itself required no special vision enhancement as vehicle headlights and light bars illuminated the celebration well. Mr. Kent settled into a comfortable position in an overgrown boxcar and started looking for the rebel leader.

He'd left his exhausted horse in a grove a mile away, having ridden hard and switched over to the more dangerous railroad tracks for the final few miles. He was more mystified by his companion of the evening than intimidated, though he guessed she could have killed him at any time. The only thing she'd said the entire trip was her name, and that was only after several proddings on his part. Natarsha had refused to ride a horse, wear body armor, or even carry a rifle, instead securing a borrowed high frequency saber on her back and running alongside his horse the entire distance. The only times she stopped to rest were when Mr. Kent had paused to water his horse at creeks they passed. Though she was breathing heavy and obviously very weary, she never uttered a word or slowed down the pace. The only people Mr. Kent had ever seen keep up that kind of trek were augmented humans, Juicers, and Crazies. She showed no signs of artificial augmentation.

"Natarsha, do you copy?" Mr. Kent sub-vocalized over the radio. No response. "Natarsha. Natarsha, are you reading me?" Still no answer. She'd said something about checking the ruins north of the camp and vanished in the darkness. Now Mr. Kent wished he'd done a radio check first.

"The man you seek is in a large building to the north." Her voice spoke into his ear without the earphone.

Mr. Kent breathed deeply, trying to still the flash of adrenaline. Natarsha crouched just behind him and to the left.

"I gave you a radio." He responded, more irritated at being snuck up on than the miscommunications.

"I don't like that thing in my ear." She handed the radio back to him.

"Learn to like it." He grumbled. "Where's Zenjori?"

"He and another man are torturing a woman in an open building north of the camp."

"You saw him?"

"I know his voice."

"You're sure?"

"Yes."

"How many guards?"

"None. I can kill both men."

Mr. Kent was torn between reporting in and helping Natarsha finish the rebel leader. Too many times Zenjori had slipped through the fingers of pursuers. Finally, he handed the radio back to Natarsha.

"Put that back on. I showed you how it works. Go watch and make sure Zenjori doesn't get away. I'll tell the others we've found him."

"Merrick. Greg. Where are you?" Mike called on the radio from inside his SAM.

"Checking the detonation wires on the north slope."

"Mr. Kent just checked in. He's found Zenjori and the rebels. Roughly five or six miles from here."

"I'm on my way back up." Greg finished rewiring a chain of fusion blocks and carefully worked his way back up the hill using the multi-optics band to retrace the treads left by his own steps. Mike motioned with the exoskeleton's hand when Greg reached the top.

"Our scouts say there's no sign of any robots, just borgs, some Headhunters, and the rebel leaders."

"Zenjori?" Greg stepped in front of SAM 312.

"Tracking him right now. Mr. Kent doesn't think the rebels are planning on moving tonight, and they set up a very poor defensive position."

"They're not expecting an attack."

"Something else. Remember that intermittent radar we kept picking up on the way in? Well it's on now, active. If we go up we can probably triangulate and pin it down. It's close, within a few miles."

"I have a better way." Greg walked to his SAMAS, climbing up to the head unit and ordering the power suit to active on all sensor systems.

"What are you doing?!"

"Going loud."

"They'll know we're here."

"Exactly."

Drake knocked the drink away from his next in command, glaring about to end the festivities.

"What was that for?" The Partial Conversion borg looked mournfully at the splash of alcoholic liquid on the ground. Just because Drake couldn't enjoy it didn't mean everyone else should suffer.

"No more party. Arden is picking up two Coalition SAMAS on radar back at the hill. Get your gear." Drake ordered.

"I thought we got 'em all."

"X-500's radar is back up. Two SAM's. We go finish them now!"

"What about —"

"Zenjori is busy. I'm in command right now. I'm telling you to get your gear." Drake picked up his own mini-missile launcher and pointed it at the sky. "Now!"

Borgs and Headhunters scattered to re-arm and move out. No two SAMAS were going to spoil Drake's victory.

Steel bore down on the thirty foot robot, carving notches in the heavy armor and increasing the frequency of return fire from a squad of four cyborgs guarding it. Greg tempted fate again, following Mike's lead for another run on the stationary robot. If it wouldn't come to them, they'd take the fight to it.

Burning plasma struck the damaged leg of Greg's SAMAS, invoking curses of pain and surprise. The exoskeleton was handling like a brick and couldn't take much more. Every turn and movement twisted the weakened frame and rattled armor patches. Something fell off into the forest, but the power armor kept flying so Greg assumed the missing part wasn't important.

Random ion beams dispersed the air, failing to connect with the two airborne units.

"It won't go down!" Mike shouted, throwing another burst into the robot and closing the distance to target the defenders at close range.

Swinging below the tree line just above the river, Mike searched the forest with thermo-optics, registering heat from the cyborg's armament. Firing bursts through the trees, he watched the hot spots move erratically as supersonic steel passed through foliage to hit the unsuspecting rebels. Random fire zipped through the forest in return, the borgs adopting the heat of the SAMAS thrusters as their primary target.

"Draw their fire!" Greg shouted. "I've got the X-500!"

"Take it!"

Greg slowed and locked the pair of forearm mini-missiles on the stubborn robot. The instant the smoke trails left their housings a warning tone sounded in Greg's ears.

He spun the exoskeleton in time to get hit from the rear by a missile. Impact stunned his body, a strange sensation of detached weightlessness coming over him as he watched one of his rear engines pass him on the right and break the tree line below. Distant explosions sounded the impact of his mini-missiles, but the SAM was on its way down. Greg desperately tried to slow his wingless descent, keeping the legs ready to help absorb the impact. The collision jarred every bone in his body and made the world spin madly. Force of will made him stand, though every part of him didn't want to. Warning tones sounded damage reports. Greg tossed the useless rail gun away and looked to confirm the missing wings on the diagnostic. Whining protest, the legs stabilized and the exoskeleton remained active. Even the throbbing in his head couldn't stop him from smiling with elation. Down but not out.

He still had a score to settle, armed or not.

"Merrick?"

"What?" Greg was surprised the scratchy sound on the comm still worked.

"It didn't get you?"

"I'm not done yet." Greg forced the exoskeleton into a heavy march for the X-500 still a thousand feet away through the forest.

"One borg down. I'm still getting radar. Forager's still hot!" Mike banked SAM 312 above the river and headed back the same way for another pass. Plasma fires burned in patches across the power armor showing where his tactics were successfully returned. Borgs came through the tree line at the river's edge, pouring fire into him as he passed. Mike flew over the attackers, creating a blast of steam with the hover jets, he broke over the tree line for the Forage and it rotated to face him.

"Sayonara!" He hit the boosters and flew between two incoming missiles to pause a second above the robot. Aiming for the blazing craters left by Greg's rockets, Mike launched two mini-missiles through the fractured armor. White hot globs of metal ran down the sides and deep inside the robot's pilot compartment as the plasma warheads reached past the protective armor to melt the robot from within. Mike passed overhead not needing to confirm the X-500 Forager's end.

The missile warning didn't go away as one blip on radar closed fast from behind. As if reaching from beyond the grave, one of the the Forager's departing missiles finished what the robot would never witness. Wings, thrusters, and armor left in radiant starburst, silhouetting the falling SAMAS against the sky. Traveling a mere 35 miles per hour, the exoskeleton seemed to pause mid-air before crashing through the trees and bounced to a stop in a contorted heap.

Mike gasped, wind knocked from him and stunned; his body refuse the orders his impact-shocked brain was giving. He couldn't make the exoskeleton get off his broken arm, and a somewhat familiar warning tone preached of radiation leaking from a ruptured power pack.

Something tipped him over and wrenched the helmet off his head.

"I let you borrow my SAM and this is what you do with it."

In the blurry haze, another SAMAS pried the dead exoskeleton away from Mike's body, freeing him and not quite gently removing him from the useless encasement.

"Merrick?"

"Darren was right."

"Just leave me here so I don't have to listen to you." Mike tried to stand but his legs gave out.

"We got their attention. Mr. Kent says the whole rebel camp is empty except for a few sentries and Zenjori. The rest are headed here."

"Oh." Mike's head throbbed so bad it almost sounded like the deranged officer was happy about an army of borgs coming to kill them both.

"Your arm doesn't look right."

"It's broken." Mike snapped the bone back in place, not even feeling the pain.

"Can you run?"

"No. I don't have a weapon, either."

"Now I have to save your sorry hide again." Greg reached down and scooped up Mike in the power armor's arms.

Incoming fire struck a useless wing joint. Three damaged borgs burst through the blazing clearing around the downed X-500. Swinging clumsily around, Greg made the exoskeleton run for all it was worth, feeling the heat reach his back from burning remnants of the SAMAS propulsion pack. The borgs didn't let up, firing wildly as the damaged Coalition armor unit slowly put more space between them. Mile after mile, the cyborgs unrelented, finally stopping when the fugitive SAMAS reached the battle zone of hours previous. They fanned out, covering the sides of the hill. All they needed to do was make sure the enemy didn't escape. When Drake and the rest arrived it would be time to attack.

Cyndiara's hands shook when she grasped Van's arm and pulled him aside from the main group. He stopped and looked down at her, sensing a boiling point in her that was a simmering urgency in others. The militia was halted again to pull an ATV out of a ditch, Sir

Renfield doing his best to make good time with the assorted horse, vehicle, and civilian force he'd organized for the attack. By nightfall the convoy had been reduced to a crawl, horses and vehicles unable to keep up a safe pace over broken roads and uneven terrain. Twice the militia had been attacked by monsters, every passing minute increasing chances of another encounter with a different beast. Chances of reaching Zenjori in time were fading away. Now the reports over the radio were more grave, Greg and Mike surrounded by borgs waiting to attack them, and the militia too far away to assist in time. Surely if Zenjori knew of the approaching retribution he would flee before it could be administered.

"Please. Take me on your cycle," Cyndiara urged, pointing to the Sky Cycle Van had just arrived on.

"There's fifteen or more borgs, and Headhunters, Cyndiara. You and I can't win." Van grasped her armor clad hands and shook his head. "Maybe Darren and Targo will get there in time."

"Please, or we'll never get him."

"We can't take on that many borgs without help."

"I don't care about the borgs!" She ripped her hands away, removing her helmet and facing Van with fiery eyes.

"What, What are you getting at?"

"Zenjori Suka. You heard the scouts. He's there. Unprotected."

"Are you suggesting we ride double on the cycle into the middle of their camp and just attack on our own?"

"Yes. We have to."

"Without backup?"

"Yes! He'll get away if we don't!"

"There's got to be a better —"

"There isn't," she stated defiantly, grabbing his wrist and looking him dead in the eyes. "You know. You and Darren know. You're the only ones who do."

Van looked into her eyes, remembering the scenes of carnage at Youngstown, and the tortured body he and Darren had rescued from Zenjori's interrogation chamber. He knew. He knew the images in his mind were only a spark compared to the rage that burned the psychic Burster where fire never could. He knew.

"Okay. Don't tell Sir Renfield. You and I will finish this."

Van noticed a mournful stare from Anja as he and Cyndiara mounted the Sky Cycle. Nobody said a word as he hovered above the group and then sped away. It was no secret what had to be done.

Stride for stride, Targo covered much more ground than the wingless SAMAS running alongside him. Miles stretched ahead of the two as Darren and Targo made a dash to reach the battle before it ended in morose tragedy. Anger kept Darren going, knowing that most of his friends were already dead.

The Shemarrian rail gun in his right hand was now linked to the targeting HUD of his helmet, and the feed system hooked to an ammunition drum replacing the old C-40 magazine. Targo wielded his massive rail gun and kept up with uneven strides, his heavy 100 mm battle armor clanking loudly as the giant ran. If the borgs thought the battle was won, they had another thing coming.

A mist shrouded the hilltop, cooling blast craters and burnt trenches. Drake surveyed the hill with a caution his previous attack had lacked. This time he knew more than bodies ringed the hill and lay in the trenches. Sporadic plasma and laser fire from the hill left the exact number of defenders a mystery. He was more ticked that he might have missed killing the soldiers on the first attack than failing to destroy both SAMAS before they found cover somewhere above. Only one damaged armor unit was left. That was about to end.

"Cy! Karrigan! Take your fire squads up the east and west slopes. Cutter, watch the south side, but advance slowly. The rest of you, with me!"

Borg squads broke off to assume positions, leaving Drake with the most heavily armed cyborg units and Headhunters at his side.

"Spread out and advance slowly." Drake waved, then clicked on the amplifier to hurl metallic laughter at the hill. "Here we come! Ready or dead!"

Engine noise got the sentry's attention. Not sure where it was coming from, the headhunter walked out onto the railroad tracks for a better view. Something was flying closer.

"Groder to —"

A laser beam from the Sky Cycle cut through battered armor and ended the warning. Noise from the Sky Cycle racing into the unoccupied rebel camp did what the dead sentry could not. Another defender leapt out from a vehicle. Van rotated the cycle in mid-air to let loose a rocket for the kill.

"Let me off! Cyndiara shouted, grabbing her rifle from the back and leaping the six feet to the ground.

Rolling in the thruster wash, she came up, her TX-16 rifle at the ready, searching for something to kill.

Weapon fire erupted from a boxcar several hundred feet away, dropping a sentry crouched behind a crumbled stack of pre-Rift's freight.

"He's in the warehouse north of you!" Mr. Kent shouted over the radio.

"On it!" Van shouted, lifting higher.

Something crashed into the Sky Cycle and sent it ten feet back down to the ground on its nose, throwing Van from the controls to the gravel. Stunned, Van rolled over and looked up to see a shimmering wall that hadn't been there before.

"What in the —"

"Look out!" Mr Kent warned.

Cyndiara was flattened by a grenade from the one sentry nobody had seen. Rushing from near the warehouse, the Headhunter fired repeatedly, raining grenades on the box cars, intruders, and his own camp with the Coalition make C-14 rifle.

Van rolled for cover behind the grounded Sky Cycle. He was about to engage magic barriers on his armor when unexplainable pain racked his body, forcing him to his knees. He rolled and rolled, unable to free himself of the torture that came from nowhere. He could hear Cyndiara enduring the same a few feet away, neither able to focus on the source of the pain.

A slumped figure missing his left arm hobbled out from one of the vehicles and approached his two victims. Notec Depi smiled, letting the insanity finally take him. He turned the high frequency blade on and off in his good hand, gleefully anticipating the deaths of his new visitors. He waved at the Headhunter happily. The smile faded.

Like a mirage, the figure slipped up behind the Headhunter and drove a H.F. saber through the flexible neck joints from behind, calmly waiting for the body to fall. The figure yanked the blade free and rolled the body off its rifle before striding boldly onward without fear.

Danger tingled in Notec's crazed brain, and he whirled to find another intruder leaping into the fray. With a thought Notec made the man collapse. Mr. Kent still fought to free himself of the psionic paralysis, almost getting the rifle up to Notec's level. Notec increased the effect and sent the man down in psionic induced agony.

Notec limped around the Sky Cycle to face the last standing adversary. A woman. All the better, Notec cackled and assaulted her mind with psionic pain. She never broke stride. He tried again, fear starting to reach his insane thoughts. She came on.

"Stop!" he shouted, encasing her in a telekinetic force field.

He smiled again, but the mirth left as she dropped the barrier with the sentry's rifle and closed the gap at a frightening speed.

Notec's terrified wail ended in a harsh gurgle, his head leaving his body with a flawless arc of her blade. Freed of the flesh, the psychic spirit languished momentarily above the body, unbelieving its own demise. Then it was gone.

"This way." Natarsha turned, unceremoniously leading the way for the others to follow.

Relieved of virtual suffering, Van and Cyndiara fell in behind.

Finding a few charges left in weapons on the hill, Mike and Greg held off the army of borgs and headhunters one trench at a time. Mike painfully replaced a clip, using his broken arm to steady the C-12 rifle. Misplaced fire walked up the hill, forcing him to sprint for the next cover. Without armor there was no room for mistakes.

Greg laid down cover fire and moved, trying to create the illusion of many defenders. The borgs were cautious but unwavering in their resolve.

From below, Drake's mini-missile found its mark, hitting the SAMAS in the left shoulder. The armor plating fractured above the occupant's living equivalent, spinning the exoskeleton and sending shrapnel through the left side of the helmet. The SAMAS kept walking up the hill only to get hit again from behind. This time it never got up.

Blood flooded the helmet. Greg was losing contact with the real world. He couldn't hear or see. A gurgling sound opened the smoking pilot's compartment and, in a haze he struggled out of the dead power suit trailing blood from multiple wounds.

They were so close, Drake could taste the victory. He could make out the fallen SAMAS through the smoke and mist. He put one more mini-missile in it for good measure and then reloaded. The lack of return fire left the corridor open for attack.

Shouts of dismay from the east side brought his squad to a halt. Two borgs were down and a third was under fire. Someone was attacking their flank. A quick order sent the remaining perimeter borgs around to take care of the interference. Unfamiliar rail gun concussions sounded the end of the last east flank warrior.

From out in the darkness, an answer to Drake's metallic death cry came back.

"Payback's hell."

Glowing tendrils left from Colnae's hand and wrapped Cyndiara fast. Natarsha leapt clear of a similar fate, not even registering the magic illusion that gave Van pause to fire. Four identical mages blocked the way and acted as one. Natarsha sensed only one, hosing the real mage with the last energy charges to no effect. She tossed the C-14 to the concrete, drawing Greg's MP-10 for the first time and discharging three rounds at Colnae's magic barriers. The battle pressed inside the ruined enclosure.

On the far end of the warehouse, Van and Cyndiara could see Zenjori Suka finish suiting up in his Terrain Hopper exoskeleton. The rebel leader engaged the jet thrusters to escape, and the pack went through the roof on its own without him. Natarsha smiled. Zenjori would never know the real reason his means of escape had been sabotaged. Colnae reacted to buy the rebel leader more time.

"No!" Cyndiara struggled, watching Zenjori cut down a bleeding hostage she recognized from Youngstown and use the tortured woman as a shield as he retreated from the enclosure.

"Die!" Colnae hurled a fire bolt at the nimble figure, torching a wall where she'd been.

Van lined up his shot, sure which was the real mage. Someone tackled him from behind, slashing at him with a Vibro-Blade. Van threw the attacker off him and paused before the kill. Kent Tristan glared at them with hateful eyes.

"Hey, now wait a —"

The boy lunged. Kent's brains splattered Van's armor. Natarsha lowered the smoking weapon, never breaking stride as she moved toward the rebel magic user.

She came at him in a flash, drawing the saber and striking him before he could weave another spell. He leapt back, along with the three illusionary versions spread out in the warehouse. She slashed again, but the magic net caught first. The tendrils wrapped the warrior woman tight, her blade slowly working its way to free her of the bonds.

"Greetings." Van shook off the shock and distress, then blew Colnae several meters back with a telekinetic blast from his modified weapon. Van touched the bonds wrapping Cyndiara and they fell away to free her. Without a word, she leapt to her feet and sprinted across the warehouse past the prone illusionary mages to where Zenjori had fled.

After Van knelt to free Natarsha, he noticed the mage was getting up, not a mark on his fine clothes or features. Colnae smiled wickedly and struck the ground with his fist, a wave of energy crossing the concrete and adhering Van's knees and right hand to the ground. Colnae stood and started weaving a complex protective spell.

"Bad move." Van advised, waving his free hand for Colnae to see. The hand with the gun.

Telekinetic bolts splattered the mage and his illusions across the dusty warehouse floor.

Leaning on the shaft of a melted C-27, Greg wired the last cross-over to the detonator nexus. Mike watched him from behind a few feet away, randomly firing over the trench sides with different weapons to confuse the borgs on the hillside below. They were close now.

"Checth ith!" Greg shouted, rolling away from the wires.

Mike gaped, unaware of the extensive injuries the other officer had endured. He'd seen the burnt pant legs and crimson stained shirt. There was barely any face to recognize, a bloody mass where once there were features he remembered. Merrick's right eye was smeared with blood, but clear, speaking words the shredded lips could hardly utter. Mike tossed aside an empty C-18 and crawled beneath the overhead fire to see what Greg had done. The wires converged on a single gap, the space between them connecting the circuit of death.

"We don't both have to be here!" Mike shouted above the roar of rail gun slugs passing inches above their heads.

"Go."

"I'll stay. You can make it down the east side!" Mike pointed.

Greg's eye focused on Mike's steel blues.

"No. You haveth thhe besth chance." He spat blood. "Go!"

Mike looked at the detonator nexus and then back at Greg.

"Go!" Warm blood splattered Mike's face.

Mike sighed and picked up Winters' TX-5. He pushed it into Greg's hand and wrapped bloody fingers around it.

"No. No. I don't have anyone to back to."

Greg stared back, the words cutting through the bloody haze to clutch his heart.

Mike smiled gravely.

Greg nodded.

Stumbling over bushes and through the trenches, Greg ran down the hill.

Zenjori crossed the tracks and dragged his human shield up the embankment on the other side, by the barbed wire binding her body. When he looked up from his struggle he saw he wasn't alone. Fear gripped his black heart and panic took over. Ripping his laser sidearm from its holster, he emptied it on the short figure in plate and chain armor. Weapon empty he watched in horror as the figure stalked closer, fire burning through the cracks and holes in the armor, igniting the shell and bursting forth a fiery being from within. Cyndiara's eyes blazed like white hot coals, her body shedding the external covering to accept the flame's embrace.

Zenjori held the blond hostage closer, jarring the unconscious woman awake. Oozing burns covered her feet and lower legs, and hundreds of small cuts leaked blood across her body.

"You know what will happen to your friend, don't you?" Zenjori searched for a reason to prolong his existence. "Are you willing to take the innocent life of your friend just for petty revenge?"

Cyndiara stepped closer, flames increasing.

Panic searched for a way to survive. Zenjori whipped out the last thing he could bargain with. He held the disk up for Cyndiara to see.

"You know what this is? If you kill me it will all be for nothing."

"No, it won't."

A voice from the tracks below spoke out. Zenjori dared to look. The disk left his hand and flew to the outstretched palm of a man in Explorer armor. The palm circuitry glowed less and Van's hand closed on the disk.

Zenjori turned back to see the flames heat go white hot.

Topping the rise, Drake and his borgs surrounded the hilltop. A lone figure lay exposed in a trench, a wire in each hand.

Mike rolled over and smiled.

"Welcome to armageddon."

A distant flash of light reflected in Zenjori's helmet visor, the ascending funeral pyre miles away rising up behind Cyndiara's blazing form. The woman expiring in Zenjori's arms looked to Cyndiara with pleading eyes and mouthed only two words on blood caked lips. A single tear left Cyndiara's left eye and turned to steam on her cheek.

Fire leapt up at Zenjori's feet and rose in a pillar to engulf both man and dying shield. The scream came not from her, but Zenjori. He flung himself from the pillar of fire.

Cyndiara passed through the pillar of flame where her friend had been. Zenjori lay a few feet away, staring at the melted stumps that had once been hands, his armor smoking. Through damaged visors, he watched the angel of vengeance descend upon him.

Chapter 24

Muffled sounds penetrated the fog hanging over Greg's consciousness first. He opened his eye to focus on the overhead light of some vehicle's interior. He could make out garbled conversation and sounds of activities going on around the vehicle, but was unable to determined specifics. In fact memory failed to place him in the vehicle altogether. Pain registered as discomfort and the sensations his body felt were surreal. Something warm was holding him still from behind. A soft, accented voice spoke in his good ear.

"You are awake."

"I guess," he mumbled, feeling something tugging at his face.

"Be still. You are badly injured."

"Natarsha?"

"Yes."

"Where ammm I?"

"Do not speak. The battle is over. Your enemy is dead."

"Good. Guess I'mmm not mmmuch to look at anymmmmore."

"It does not matter. I am blind."

Greg's mind grasped the disclosure and accepted it. Maybe it was the injuries, but maybe it didn't matter after all. A familiar face appeared in his fixed line of vision.

"Hi, sir, I mean, Greg." Brian squinted and fiddled around with something Greg couldn't see. "We bandaged you up and stopped the bleeding, but you're not well off. I gave you an IRMSS injection, but I'm sure you have internal injuries that require a doctor."

"I'mmm alivve."

"Yeah. Barely. Good thing I rode along, too. Otherwise one of those magic users might have gotten hold of you."

Greg couldn't tell if Brian was serious.

"Did —"

"Quit talking. You're bleeding through your bandages. Sir Renfield and some of the others are chasing a pair of borgs that got away, but Zenjori's dead, and I've got some more good news."

Van's face appeared next to Brian's. A disk with a Coalition logo waved in Greg's face.

"Thought you might want this." Van handed the disk to Brian, then looked down for a closer look at Greg. "Jeez, you weren't kidding. His eye?"

Brian shook his head.

"Jeez. I can't fix that. The rest of the obvious injuries are bad, but his face is real bad. I can heal it, but there might be some scarring."

"Bbrian —"

"I'm not hearing any of this." Brian looked serious. "Kind of different when it's you, huh? I'm going outside for about fifteen minutes to work on some salvage, and when I come back, I'll check you again and see if my diagnosis was premature." Brian smiled.

Greg chuckled hoarsely as Brian exited the vehicle.

It wasn't until evening that Greg regained consciousness. Alone in the hotel room, he showered and donned the black eye patch he found on top of his clothes. In the mirror he could see a series of hairline scars covering much of the left side of his face, but it was still him in the mirror.

The large queen-sized bed still called him from the bedroom, but he had no idea how long he'd been asleep and only guessed he was back in Liberty. The door opened before he reached it, and he found Natarsha waiting for him in the hall.

"Come. Your friends have a surprise." She waited for him to join her and then followed him down the hallway.

Darren and Cyndiara were in the lobby when he descended the stairs, as were Joel Peterson and a short haired brunette in the other corner. All looked rested and wore clean civilian clothes.

"Sir! Sorry, uh, Greg?" Joel asked hesitantly.

"I'm not that deformed."

"Dude, you're up. Cool." Darren jumped up from the couch and came over to inspect the eye patch. "Bummer face grind. Nothin' a Cyber-Doc can't fix, though."

"If I cared."

"All right, dude, ya gotta come with us outside."

"Please." Cyndiara stepped forward and led Greg outside with a bit more tact and grace.

Parked across the street taking up several parking places was a sleek black, large van-sized hovercraft. Brian and Lisa were playing with one of the fan skirts, stopping when they noticed the group crossing the street.

"Surprise!" Lisa waved her arms and strutted in front of the hover craft.

"What's this?"

"It's yours, dude."

Greg looked around at the happy nods and faces of other former troops piling out the back of the craft.

"This is. . ."

"We all pitched in some and got it for you with the money you gave us," Sharp announced, looking happier than Greg ever remembered seeing the soldier.

"Yeah, but something like this . . ."

"We bought it from First Strike. Their shipment came in today, and this was one of the transport vehicles." Brian looked at the hover craft proudly. "Some import, I don't know from where. Narumi, or something like that. Anyway, since Giz and Lisa and I are cleaning house salvaging robot and vehicle parts, we pitched in a little extra. First Strike must be hard up for cash, plus when they found out we were buying it for you they sold it to us real cheap."

"That more or less makes it theirs again." Greg smiled, wondering what the next year was going to be like serving in a mercenary company. "I really don't know what to say."

"It's new, or well, almost new." Lisa examined some scratches on the fan skirts. "Had a long trip to get here."

"Electric engine, full charge on the cells, and it runs like a charm." Brian beamed.

"Thank you. Thank you all. I'm not sure what to say." Greg grinned at Natarsha and walked over to examine tits aerodynamic design.

"We've been hangin' out here like all afternoon," Darren said. "Okay, some of us have. How about you drive us all to the Match Head for some serious grubbage and we'll call it even."

"Deal. Pile in."

Greg worked out some stiff muscles before getting the access code from Brian and opening the pilot's compartment hatch. He allowed Natarsha to hesitantly climb the short ladder then followed her in.

Through Liberty and many random detours, the sleek hover craft the party. Greg was impressed by the handling — minus a mail box or two he considered too close to the street — and performance, landing behind the Match Head where cleared piles of rubble opened up a field for First Strike's new arsenal.

Piling out, the group drooled at the stylized robots, hover craft, power armor, and aircraft being examined by happy mercenaries. The aura of excitement was carried inside, a buzz of conversation occupying the customers within. First Strike was leaving the next day and the small civilian militia was taking their place defending the town. With Zenjori's army gone, Liberty was free to exercise its own laws and defense.

"Took you long enough!" Dave shouted from the corner, starting to remove the pile of chairs reserving two large adjoining booths.

"I'll take yer orders in a sec." Freya escorted the group back and bustled off to the kitchen, apron tails flying behind her.

Darren ushered Greg and Natarsha in first, and reluctantly she complied. Others crammed in around the tables.

"Woah! Check it out." Darren pointed to the bar. "Hey Gibs!"

"How's it going, Darren." Gibs raised a beer and waved.

Darren did a double-take to make sure his eyes weren't fooling him. Sitting next to Gibs was Delwin Moonbeam.

"Hey, Darren, isn't that —"

"Sure is, Dave. When did Delwin meet Gibs?"

Cyndiara reached for the back of Darren's head and brought his face around for a long kiss.

"You can drink with your buddies later," she ordered with false sincerity.

"We're not late, are we?" Anja came to stand by the table, Sir Renfield and Van standing head and shoulders behind her.

"Nah, we ain't even grubbed yet." Darren rearranged the seating pattern to accommodate the newcomers.

"So, tell me." Greg leaned on his elbows and looked around with his good eye. "Who planned all this?"

"Me an' Brian mostly," Darren answered. "But everyone had good ideas and helped out with something."

"I went and talked to the Cyber-Doc." Corrinne self-consciously traced the scars on her own face. "He said he could fix any nerve damage and reconstruct without scars, if you want. He said it might take time before he can get a bio-systems eye to match yours, but he could get a multi-optic implant if you want it."

"I'm leaving with First Strike in the morning, next stop Kingsdale. I can do without an eye for a few days." He nudged Natarsha under the table. "Thanks for checking. What are you planning on doing?"

"Well, we've all been approached by the sheriff and the town militia and asked to join, those of us that are staying here. The sheriff wants us to help train the militia. Sharp, Jameson, some others, and myself. We plan to join up. We'll find something to keep us busy."

"And I've already got a job as a deputy." Dave flashed a badge Greg hadn't noticed before.

"Wow. Deputy Dave. Congratulations." Greg reached across the table to shake hands.

"Thanks!" Dave beamed, thrusting his chest and badge out prominently.

"So what are your plans, Brian, Lisa?" Greg watched the response carefully, still curious what his two former tech officers were up to. They were always up to something.

"Lisa and I are working at Gizmo's."

"We're going to be part owners." Lisa smiled excitedly, blue eyes dancing.

"Really?"

"Yeah, uh, we're buying into the shop and are going to expand it." Brian threw Lisa a "be quiet" look.

"That's impressive. Got some extra cash from salvaging rebel bots, I take it?" Greg raised an eyebrow, the only one he could.

"Something like that. One of those detail losing things."

"I see." Greg leaned back and smiled.

"Except we have to change the name, Brian," Lisa advised. "Gizmo's garage just doesn't sound right."

"We talked about this already. Everyone knows Gizmo."

"Sure, but think how much better it would sound as the 'Mechanical Superstore', or something like that. Gizmo's garage sounds so, so backwoods."

"Compared to Chi-Town, everything is backwoods."

"Whatever you decide, you might want to find a better place for the Skull Walker by the time more Coalition forces arrive."

Greg's comment sobered the mood. Lisa brightened.

"Oh, si-Greg, I almost forgot." She squirmed free a wad of paper from her back pocket.

"That's right! The disk!" Brian got excited.

"You downloaded it?" Greg leaned on the table anxiously.

"1.44 terrabytes worth. Wasn't even frosted.

Lisa started unfolding the wad of paper.

"I hope it has something to make it worth the price."

"I don't know," Lisa answered hesitantly, a pang of remorse striking a memory of Mike. "There's some interesting stuff on it, and I haven't finished looking at it. Do you want me to, ya know, talk about it, here?"

"Classified?"

"Yeah."

"I'm not wearing a uniform, are you?" Greg looked around.

"Okay, here's the basic scoop, some of this we already knew."

Everyone leaned in closer expectantly except Sir Renfield, who, naturally, was above such things.

"Colonel Lyboc hires Zenjori Suka and the Army of the New Order to attack and occupy towns and villages between Chi-Town and Tolkeen, making the lives of the inhabitants so bad that they'd welcome the Coalition coming in to drive the 'rebel army' out. It looks good for publicity, and the C.S. commanders making the advance don't know they're getting a set-up for easy kills and victory. Zenjori somehow finds out ahead of time about the coming attacks and pulls out, leaving behind token defenses to take the fall. Somewhere along the way, Colonel Lyboc tries to cash in on some prototype robot program, and sends a Glitter Boy to the Dubuque outpost to be captured by the so-called rebels. He gets justification to approve these automated skelebots and kick-backs from the manufacturing branches, while the Army of the New Order gets one of the most powerful man-made power suits ever constructed.

"This much we had figured out before the disk." Lisa paused, all eyes on her. "We'd found out about this so-called disk that had a list of fifth column members on it, and we just figured that was the secret cover story for what Lyboc was up to. Well it turns out the whole village-occupying thing and skelebot program were only a superficial part of the plan. There really is a fifth column in the Coalition, a loosely organized group of commanders and leaders who want to overthrow Emperor Prosek and give the power back to the people. They've been helping scientists and scholars escape Coalition internment centers and have been working with secessionists in Free Quebec to gather support."

"The fifth column is real." Greg leaned back and pondered the possibilities relating to his recent career change.

"Well, this fifth column thinks Zenjori and his Army of the New Order are actually real rebels, and they're the ones who started warning him about attacks, contacting the mercenary group to get support, and that's exactly what Colonel Lyboc wanted all along. The fifth column helps route goods and armament to the rebels, hoping to delay the Tolkeen invasion. It's ingenious, really. Not only is Lyboc tricking the fifth column into actually helping the invasion, but tricks them into exposing a vital link in their operation. The Dubuque outpost. When Lyboc finds that out, that's when he has the Glitter Boy accidentally shipped there, knowing the fifth column will move it to the rebels and help expose their operation even more.

"This is where things started to go wrong. Zenjori and his rebels are contacted by the fifth column and are supposed to stage a fake raid on Dubuque, the fifth column's idea as far they knew, including the capture of the Glitter Boy. Other equipment is supposed to fall into rebel hands, that way Duboque can request more supplies and personnel, helping them bring in their own people to reinforce and strengthen their position. Only Zenjori double-crosses the fifth column and actually does raid the outpost for real, killing quite a few of them, and getting into their database and interrogating the leaders. He gets a list of fifth column operatives working in Chi-Town and most of the information the fifth column was planning on using to gain popular support of the people. There's a whole list of stuff the fifth column was going to use to combat Emperor Prosek's propaganda machine.

"Zenjori pulls out with the captured equipment, and the disk, and is going to deliver it to Colonel Lyboc for a substantial sum. That's when a total accident happens that messes everything up. The rebels accidentally run into a patrol and waste a unit under General Ross Underhill. It's an accident, but before Lyboc gets the disk, General Underhill launches a surprise attack on the Army of the New Order just north of old Chicago. Underhill pretty much cleans up, taking out some 500 rebel troops and armor units, except a few stragglers make it to the Chicago ruins."

"That's where we came in." Brian nodded, remembering the fiasco of the first encounter.

"Right. Zenjori thinks Lyboc has double-crossed him, so he decides to use what inside contacts and information he has to get clear of the invasion zone and escape with the disk as his shield against future attack."

"Yeah, but Lyboc still sends us after the disk." Darren's brow furrowed.

"But we didn't recover it the first time. Questions were being asked about how the rebels kept escaping Coalition attacks, and Lyboc's head was being put in the noose, so he tried to shift the blame by making Mike Sorenson look like the traitor, that way the heat comes off himself and leaves the fifth column to continue exposing themselves. Except they found out because Emperor Prosek ordered everyone executed at Dubuque. The fifth column finds out about the disk, so I'm guessing they were after it too."

Several faces looked at Greg.

"Don't look at me." Greg waved his hands.

"Don't worry, you're not on the list." Lisa unfolded the paper and handed it to Greg.

"Fifth column?" He asked, gingerly taking the papers.

"Part of it. Most of it."

"What are these notes?" He pointed to the corner.

"File names. The disk also has ways to prove that Emperor Prosek is having the water and food in Chi-Town treated with drugs to make people more susceptible to suggestion, that's one of the reasons all the scientists that weren't part of the military were rounded up as troublemakers and imprisoned, so nobody would find out. There's also files on hypnotic suggestion, brain wave patterns, genetic engineering, population control, the PRP, secret magic safeguards in Chi-Town, and civilian tracking systems. I've only read a little, and it is scary stuff."

"And we've been away from all that out here," Greg concluded, running down the list of names. "No wonder they try and keep deep field ops on a rotation once every few months."

"Right," Brian added. "I can't believe they would do that to us. They. We don't even know who 'they' is!"

"You read the same files I did." Lisa looked at him.

"I know. I just don't like thinking I was being suckered all my life."

"What about all the people that don't know?"

"That's right! Who's going to spill the beans?" Darren asked.

"Not the fifth column. Not anymore." Greg flipped to the next page.

"You know those people?" We only recognized a few names." Brian exchanged a look with Lisa.

"A few. I'm remembering most of them because the ranks shifted when they disappeared during the month before we left."

"How did Lyboc find out? Zenjori still had the disk."

"You see this name? Major Fowler?"

"Yeah. We didn't know if you knew." Brian sighed. "That's the CIS guy, Karren Fowler's father."

"Would have been Mike's father-in-law." Lisa saddened. "Do you think . . ."

"He's probably dead. As part of Coalition Internal Security, he was probably covering up all the fifth column operations. The fifth column exposed themselves trying to get that disk back. If Lyboc got Fowler, he probably got anyone else he knew." Greg read on.

"Did you see the one at the top of the third or fourth page?" Lisa asked.

Greg raised his eyebrow at the paper.

"General Ridgewell?"

"I didn't believe it either." Brian shook his head.

"Isn't your old C.O., Colonel McFarland in tight with him?" Lisa asked.

"Yes, but I doubt the Colonel has anything to do with a fifth column.

"I didn't see his name on the list."

"You saw this one, right?" Greg turned the paper and pointed to a name.

"Major Ratello. Yeah. We know." Brian smiled.

"That isn't necessarily a good thing, Brian." Greg handed the paper back to Lisa. "I'll take a copy of the disk when you get the chance."

"Sure thing."

"Yeah, but if Major Ratello is fifth column, he's not going to mess with us, right?" Brian asked.

"He and a full company will be here in a few days. Do you want to ask him if he's here for the disk or just doing what Lyboc told him to? Either Lyboc knows Ratello is fifth column and plans to kill him once he recovers the disk, or Major Ratello is unknown and is out here to protect the fifth column on his own. You pick. Keep in mind we're deserters, and fifth column doesn't mean disloyal."

"Oh. Oh yeah." Brian deflated.

"You two had better disguise yourselves just in case, in fact that goes for all of you. Officially, we're all dead, so there won't be any bounty hunters or search parties coming to hunt us down. Don't slip up and give it away," Greg advised.

"You could dye your hair, Brian!" Lisa rustled his red hair playfully.

"I will if you will."

"I've always wondered how I'd look as a brunette." Lisa examined a length of her blond hair.

The clatter of a heavy plate being placed on the table made Natarsha jerk. The huge platter of french fries attracted eager hands with its aroma.

"There ya go." Freya wiped her hands on her apron and reached back to retrieve a large pitcher and mugs from another table. "Ya can't drink ale on an empty stomach. That'll hold ya until I get yer steaks and greens." She was off to the kitchen.

Natarsha smelled the liquid Greg poured for her. The bitter aroma suggested something unsatisfying. From her limited experience, if it smelled bad, it tasted bad. Everyone else seemed content downing mass quantities of it, so she braced herself and took her first sip of alcohol.

"If any of you would like, you can accompany me on my quest." Sir Renfield spoke up, he and Anja the only ones refraining from spirits.

"Oh, that'll be the day," Van quipped sarcastically.

"Hey, if that Sploogie thing came from Atlantis, that's one place I plan not to go." Darren voiced a common agreement.

Natarsha was silent. The determination she sensed in the Cyber-Knight would not be swayed. He would be captured or killed. This she knew for certain.

"I wasn't asking you, Van." Sir Renfield responded irritably. "I know what your opinion is. Targo is accompanying me, as are some other brave souls seeking adventure and the opportunity to fight the evil that comes from that place."

"Yeah yeah yeah. . ."

"So you don't want to come, Darren?" Sir Renfield pressed the recruitment, pulling Darren away from a very close verbal conversation with Cyndiara.

"No. Not just no. No! Me an' Van are gonna try to swipe some more of those guns from those cybernetic robo-chicks."

"And after that?"

"Who knows. Maybe I'll go join up with First Strike." Darren looked at Greg and smiled.

"Me too." Peterson grinned.

"Great." Greg looked over the top of his mug.

"I would ask you, Anja, but I know your place is with Van." Sir Renfield looked sad.

"We'll be staying around here awhile longer." She patted his hand. "Don't leave without saying good-bye."

"I'll come, man." Delwin squeezed into the booth next to Sir Renfield, practically sitting on the knight's lap.

"No, no, uh, Delwin, it's too dangerous," Sir Renfield protested.

"I am sensing some very positive waves from you all tonight." Delwin looked around with a stupid grin.

"Hi Delwin." Anja giggled.

"So, Gibs can come too, man, like all of us." Delwin said, motioning for Gibs to pull up another chair at the table.

"Can I come?" The dragon in disguise asked. Kro-Mar had forgotten all about the "scare humanoids" game.

"Well, that isn't really what I had in mind..." Sir Renfield felt his willpower and irritation fading away as he looked around to the amused grins and smiles around the table.

Forgotten for the moment were the problems and dangers that awaited the treacherous days to come. For once, human, Crazy, D-Bee, dragon, psychic, and practitioner of magic sat at the same table without fear or prejudice. For many, their lives were just beginning.